DEDICATION

To my mother
Catherine McKeown
and my father
Edward Francis Xavier McKeown

AGAINST THAT TIME

By
Edward McKeown

AN IMPRINT OF COPPER DOG PUBLISHING, LLC

The Maauro Chronicles: Against That Time

Moondream Press
An Imprint of Copper Dog Publishing LLC
537 Leader Circle
Louisville, CO 80027
www.copperdogpublishing.com

Ordering Information:
Special discounts are available on quantity purchases by corporations, associations, and others. For details, contact the publisher at the address above.
Printed in the United States of America

Credits:
Author: Edward F. McKeown
Managing Editor: Michael H. Hanson
Creative Director: Helen H. Harrison
Proofreader: Julie Harrison Saunders
Cover Art: Pat Ventura

ISBN: 978-1-943690-06-0 (Paperback)
        978-1-943690-08-4 (Kindle)

Library of Congress Control Number: 2016943936

Fiction: Science Fiction

Against that time, if ever that time come,

When I shall see thee frown on my defects,

When as thy love hath cast his utmost sum,

Called to that audit by advis'd respects;

Against that time when thou shalt strangely pass,

And scarcely greet me with that sun, thine eye,

When love, converted from the thing it was,

Shall reasons find of settled gravity;

Against that time do I ensconce me here,

Within the knowledge of mine own desert,

And this my hand, against my self uprear,

To guard the lawful reasons on thy part:

To leave poor me thou hast the strength of laws,

Since why to love I can allege no cause.

—William Shakespeare

CONTENTS

CHAPTER ONE

To All Guild Operative Staff-Classified-

From Thieves Guild Central Advisory Committee

Subject: Artificial Intelligence Entity calling itself Maauro; first encountered in Kandalor system, present location unknown. This being is thought to be a self-aware AI created by an unknown and possibly extinct species. It has the appearance of a human teenage female, details below. All Guild operatives who have encountered this entity have been killed, wounded or disappeared. Several bases and vessels have been lost as well. Avoid all contact with Maauro. If attacked, alert Confederate or other government military authorities to her existence and the threat this ancient war machine poses....

Advertisement: Lost Planet Expeditions: Survey, Security, Trade Missions.

Exno-archeology a specialty

Contact Wrik Trigardt, Master of SV "Stardust" at First Landing Spaceport, Star Central.

"We find the lost."

"I LIKE IT," JAELLE SAID, SMILING AT ME AS SHE LOOKED over my shoulder at the holo-screen. The smile was not for the faint of heart. Nekoans were humanoid; but with her fangs, yellow slit-eyes and mane of rough, blond hair; she had a leonine look.

I smiled back. "Maauro vetoed my original suggestion: *"We're the people who find your previous expedition."*

"She's a very sensible, ancient killing-machine."

I coughed. "Ah, she prefers android."

Jaelle gave me the enigmatic look she reserved for discussions of Maauro. The rivalry between them for my attention was usually good-humored. Unlike Jaelle, Maauro had no sexual interest in me, but in some respects my relationship with Maauro was the closer. I'd found Maauro, abandoned for 50,000 years on an asteroid base of what we called the Old Empire. I'd saved her then and she'd returned the favor with interest since. Truth was, Maauro was my first real friend since I'd fled my home-world in disgrace.

"The question is," came an unwelcome, gravelly voice, "will it bring in any business before we starve?"

I turned from the screen and threw Dusko a sour look as the Dua-Denlenn strolled in and casually draped his lean form over a cheap lounge chair. He looked like a woodland elf gone bad: tall, with salt and pepper hair through which pointed ears poked. I could never get used to the pupilless eyes; blue from lid-to-lid.

"No reason it shouldn't," Jaelle said, leaning back in her own chair, complete with a cutout for her tail. "After all, Wrik is known for finding that Old Empire Base before the government grabbed it up."

"No need to remind me," Dusko said. "His other find on that rock cost me everything but my life."

"Pity about that last," I muttered.

"Wrik," Jaelle reproved. "I thought you two buried the hatchet when we escaped from the Infester Artifact."

"We are, perhaps, too much prisoners of the past to escape it so easily," Maauro's high, gentle voice injected. As usual, and despite weighing more than any of us, she'd silently padded up on the group.

We all turned as she slipped into the room. The slender android brushed back an errant lock of her long, black, hair-like filaments, which, bound with a yellow bow, cascaded down her back and framed her pale, delicate face with its impossibly large aquamarine eyes. She wore a midnight blue and dark red jump suit, which was simply her outer casing textured to resemble fabric. Maauro had patterned herself on a game simulation she'd hacked out of my ship's computer; not realizing the image was an animation. Her ability to morph into different shapes had failed her soon after, or so she claimed. I suspected she'd come to identify with her new appearance and simply preferred it.

"Where have you been?" I asked.

"Wandering about the city, observing the diversity and functions of biological life. I have no need to rest and curiosity consumes me."

"You know what they say about curiosity and the cat," I replied, then looked at Jaelle. "Whoops, sorry."

"I am not a cat. Your poor little monkey brain just looks for familiar patterns to hang labels on."

"In any event," Maauro said, "you need not worry for me. I believe I have persuaded the Guild that conflict with me is unrewarding."

"Too true," Dusko replied.

She eyed the Dua-Denlenn. "Do you still identify with the Guild? They cast you out."

He yawned. "Old habits die hard. I suppose. No, I have thrown my lot with all of you. The Guild is no friend to me now."

"Good," she said. "The past should not concern us anymore— only the future. Speaking of the future, Jaelle, how did your arrangements go?"

"Well it took some doing to get us back in the good graces of Tenevan considering it's been five years since we last did any shipping for her. But I believe I can talk her into letting us ship sunstones for her since we're the only carrier that will go express to Star Central. We'll barely break even on the first few loads in terms of shipping, but by taking a percentage of what the stones will go for locally and acting as her agent, we'll clean up. We were incredibly fortunate to find her here on this world heading back to Frosteer."

"So you are off to see her tonight?" Dusko asked.

She nodded.

"Sure you don't want company?" I said.

"Too much chance of letting something slip if we are both there," she replied. "We have too much to hide. Besides, you weren't enthusiastic about the Nekoan baths."

"Not at that heat! That's not relaxing, it's cooking."

"Well, if I am going to make it," Jaelle said, "I'd better get going. My bag's back in my office."

Jaelle kissed me. I was a little shy of doing that in front of the others, especially Maauro, who was watching with considerable interest, but shyness was not part of Jaelle's character. She waved at Dusko then patted Maauro on the shoulder. Just short of the door, Jaelle exploded into a backflip and leapt with a yowl. Maauro casually, but quickly, changed position and snagged Jaelle out of the air.

"Why," Maauro asked, holding Jaelle upside down, "do you persistently try to pounce on me? This has not worked once."

Dusko shook his head. I grinned ruefully.

Jaelle smiled. "It keeps you on your toes, Kit-sister. One of these days I may get lucky."

"Even if you did," Maauro said, "your teeth and claws would never make any impression on me."

"Nor should they," Jaelle said, offended. "We are just playing, Kit-sister."

Maauro upended Jaelle and set her on her feet. "Have fun on the southern continent."

"I will. Keep the boys out of trouble." She reached over and tousled Maauro's hair before leaving.

"Your girlfriend," Maauro said to me, "is an amalgam of unusual behaviors."

"Hey, at least she likes you. That's more than any of my exes would have managed under the circumstances." Behind us, I heard Dusko give a Dua-Denlenn version of a sigh as he turned back to his screen.

We closed up the office on a successful day, our treasury full of credits for the first time since we'd arrived. Dusko vanished to pursue whatever occupied his spare time. Maauro forbade any genuinely criminal activity on the former crime-lord's part, but we knew he kept his hand in on the local doings. As usual, we did not say good night.

I had no particular plans for the evening with Jaelle gone on a trading mission. When she wasn't around, I sometimes hopped bars to kill time. I never came back to the apartment drunk, she wouldn't put up with that unless we were both doing it, but Jaelle was used to males being gone for extended periods. It was part of her culture and she was independent even for a Nekoan female. Sometimes this left me with more time to kill than I was comfortable with.

I stood, suddenly restless. "Well good night, Maauro. I'm going to go hunt up some food and maybe a few belts afterward."

Maauro turned to regard me. "So soon?"

I looked back in mild surprise. "We've been here twelve hours; it's already nine. Not much left to do today anyway."

"Oh."

"Are you going up to the rooftop to visit the stars?" I teased.

"I suppose so," she said distantly. "I have not had the opportunity to make new friends since we arrived. Any friend I do make constitutes a threat to our security. My pretense of being a mutated human is difficult to sustain on close exposure."

"Yeah, I suppose so." On our second voyage after fleeing Kandalor, Maauro had tried to pass as a teen girl with a pack of kids she'd fallen in with on Stauver, only to find out later that they had almost immediately realized her artificial origin.

"My friendship can be an unsafe thing," she continued. "I fear that my nature and the occupation we have chosen to pursue would cause ordinary friends to be targeted as vulnerable parts of my network."

She turned back to the window and the vast and bejeweled city glowing beyond the spaceport. Her shoulders were slightly hunched and her hands twisted together and pressed to her chest.

How could I be so stupid, so thoughtless? Maauro spent her nights here, usually on the roof, or wandering by herself in the city. Why didn't it occur to me that a thinking being with emotions would fall prey to loneliness? I walked over and put my hands around her shoulders; contact she would not permit with anyone else. She half-turned, but did not look up at me.

"God, I'm an idiot. I don't know why you put up with me. How about you come out to dinner with me, and then home? The apartment isn't big, but you travel with less stuff than any other female I've ever known."

"Jaelle will not mind?"

"Of course not, she'd probably rather I hung out with you than wandered around in bars. That was a pretty stupid waste of an evening anyway."

She gently bumped her head against my chin. "Thank you, Wrik."

We walk to the elevator bank with Wrik chatting amiably in his self-appointed mission to cheer me up. Meanwhile, I struggle with being ashamed of myself. The gestures I used, the duck of the head, the bent shoulders, the anxious twisting of the hands, are all artifice that I have picked up from various video entertainments. They had the desired effect, triggering Wrik's strongly protective impulses, a fundamental structure of his personality. I have long noticed that the more I act like "a girl" the more Wrik treats me as one. Even as I have this thought, he is opening a door for me. A door I could as easily rip from the wall and crumple into a small ball. Intellectually he knows I am a genderless combat android, but on an emotional level, I am something else to him.

It bothers me to be dishonest, to be so rankly manipulative. For while I do prefer the stimulation of company, I do not fear solitudes as Wrik does, else I would have perished during my 50,000 year sojourn on the asteroid where he found me. But I do know that my other arguments against his plans for dangerous locations and altering his consciousness with unhealthy chemicals might fall on deaf ears. I fear that when he has too much time on his hands, he returns to old, self-destructive behaviors, taking foolish chances, brooding on old failures.

He will perhaps realize this at some point and I will tell him that I am a changed being since we met. With the part of my consciousness not occupied with light banter with Wrik, I wonder if this is not, in fact, true. My plan for this evening was to maneuver myself close to Wrik to guard against his reckless impulses. But I cannot deny something that is also true as I contemplate the evening before us. I am, in my own way... very happy.

CHAPTER TWO

MAAURO AND I SPENT THE EVENING AS PLANNED, DIN-
ner, then a lot of quiet conversation at my place. We watched
old and bad video entertainments for hours as I made fun of
them to her evident enjoyment. Just before I drifted off to sleep in the
early morning hours it occurred to me to wonder how it could be so easy
and so comfortable to be with an ancient machine that somebody made
somewhere. All I knew was that it was true and that whoever built her
had my undying gratitude. Maauro was the easiest being to spend time
with that I'd ever known. She slipped off as I went to bed, for a bit of
stargazing, with a promise to see me at work.

I walked into the office the next morning to find her there, true to
her word. Maauro sat perched on my desk, beside her two cappuccinos
sat steaming. She didn't need to drink of course but liked to keep me
company.

"Ah," I said, reaching for the blue stone cup that was mine. I'd never
been a morning person.

"Please do not be alarmed," she said as I took a long appreciative
sip, "but we are surrounded by Confederate Security Forces."

I spat the cappuccino across the desk.

"Was it bad?" she asked, looking at the messy desk. "I made it the
same as usual."

"Confed?" I managed, looking around and out the window. "What do
we do?"

"At present, you should finish your drink, which I spent time and
energy to make for you and regain your composure."

"I was thinking something more along the lines of grabbing guns
and fleeing."

"And where would we flee to on such a well-ordered and policed
world as Star Central? Doubtless our ship is already locked down. No,
we do not have sufficient intel to decide on a course of action. I do not
believe we are to be assaulted without warning. Their tactical disposition
and equipment suggest that they are more concerned with protecting
themselves than with an immediate attack. I also doubt that Candace
Deveraux has come all this way to watch someone fire a plasma rocket
into our office."

"Candace!" I said. "Well, well, it's a small galaxy after all."

"Not really," Maauro replied. "The Milky Way is—"

"Never mind," I said. "Should I get a weapon? Warn the others?"

"No to both. A powerful jammer is operating over our building. I
could break it in a few minutes. However that cuts both ways. I am

blocking their scanners. If it comes to weapons, stay flat on the floor. You know what I am capable of."

I nodded.

She cocked her head. "I will observe from behind the frosted glass partition. Take your place, Wrik. Candace is approaching the door."

I quickly wiped up the desktop with some tissue and slid behind the desk. Maauro disappeared behind the frosted glass. The door chimed. I hit the switch and the doors slid back revealing a tall, full-bodied black woman in an expensive suit.

"Hello, Wrik." Candace Deveraux of Confed intelligence said as she flashed me a warm smile that did not reach her dark-brown eyes. Candace had hired me to take a group of treasure-hunters to the asteroid where I found Maauro, before revealing she was a Confed agent. She'd gotten the base. I'd gotten Maauro but only because she hadn't known about the android.

"Good to see you," I lied.

"You too, Wrik. My, my, but it's been almost nine years since Kandalor and you haven't changed a bit."

"Yeah, well you know how hyperdrive travel is."

"Yes, Wrik, I know precisely how hyperdrive travel is, which is why that is just another of those insoluble things about you. You don't have a past. You don't seem to age. You're just full of surprises."

"You threw me a few curves too."

"Well," she chuckled. "I have those to spare."

"You're far from Kandalor," she continued, looking around the office.

"It wasn't that much fun after you left."

She snorted a laugh. "You seem to be doing well in business too with Jaelle Tekala as a partner," she gave him a speculative look. "You didn't strike me as a cat person."

"I wouldn't say that around Jaelle if I were you," I replied.

"It's Dusko that I can't fathom," Candace said, seating herself across the desk, "once a deadly enemy, now, your office manager?"

"Yeah, I wonder about that one myself. However, times do change."

"So they do. When I met you, you were a no-account local spacer with a bad reputation for bugging out on people."

"People change too," I said tightly.

"You surely did. You came back to Kandalor an enemy of Dusko and the Guild. Yet six months later you're still around on Kandalor and the life expectancy of Guild on that world starts getting measured in days. So much so that they start bringing in outside talent that ends up just as dead as the locals. Then Dusko disappears along with a ship; word is that he betrayed the Guild.

"Soon after we hear of death and disruption throughout Guild operations and start decoding warnings to avoid a ship carrying a human, a

Nekoan, a traitorous Dua-Denlenn and the prettiest little slip of a girl. And now, here you are on Star Central."

I shifted. "I'm afraid I don't know what you're talking about."

"Oh, please, Wrik. You found something on that dead asteroid base that has made you very formidable. Or should I say that it found you? Very naughty of you not to share that information with me."

We stared at each other.

"Sweetie you're thinking dangerous thoughts there. I didn't come alone. Outside this door are six humanform combat robots and a SWAT team. If I yell, or should my heartbeat suddenly cease, it would be very unfortunate. I don't think even your new friend could handle all of that."

"Your assumption is invalid." Maauro appeared from behind the frosted glass divider. She nodded pleasantly at Candace who moved only her eyes as Maauro walked over and sat next to me, gently putting one of her hands on mine.

"Is this wise?" I managed.

"We always knew Confed would eventually learn of my existence. It did happen sooner than I expected. Further subterfuge will avail us nothing."

She turned back to Candace. "Let us establish some guidelines for our discussions."

"We will," Candace said. "You'll be coming with me."

The door to our office opened and in walked six HCR robots, slender machines not dissimilar in shape to Maauro, all with long hair that doubled as antenna and cooling. They wore uniforms with colored sashes, their faces held rudimentary features.

I started to move but Maauro held my hand in place with a gentle pressure. Then I noticed worry and surprise on Candace's face. The machines lined up next to her. Then to my complete shock, they performed a delicate ballet pirouette, bowed and walked out the door single file.

We sat in stunned silence.

"I could," Maauro said, "as easily had them kill you and your SWAT team. I am quite a good killer, literally made for it. I no longer extinguish biological life casually, unless it threatens me or my friends. Then I do so without mercy. Are you threatening me and my friends?"

Candace moistened her lips. "Let's say for now that I am not."

"You have come to me because I represent both a threat and an opportunity. Let me respond on both. I do not threaten the Confederacy unless it threatens me. As the Guild has found out with the loss of operatives, ships, stations and command staff, I am a formidable opponent. You will likely overwhelm me with sheer numbers if you need to, but I'll make it expensive.

"I am willing to work with the Confederacy as an operative, occasionally, but I am a free and sentient being, not a machine like your dancing robots. I live. I will destroy myself before I allow myself to be captured. That is an imperative placed in me by extinct Creators and I agree with it."

Candace looked at me.

"Doubtless you are thinking that so long as Wrik is here, he'll be useful as a control on me. Within reason, you're correct. But I guarantee you disastrous retaliation on yourself and Confed interests if he, or anyone else I befriend, are harmed or imprisoned."

"Or you can have what is behind door #2," I managed.

Maauro looked at me. "Are we doing commerce again?"

I nodded.

"Then perhaps I should leave that to you?"

"That would be best," I said.

"What do you want, Candace?" I said turning to Candace who could not take her eyes off Maauro.

"Well what I wanted was to turn your—"

"Her name is Maauro."

"— Maauro, over to our scientists so we could build a million more and then I might set myself up as the first galactic empress."

"Assume that won't happen because we'll all die if you put that plan in motion. You first, Maauro last. And no one will profit."

Candace looked at Maauro and shook her head smiling. "I think I believe you. Honey, were you on that asteroid for all that time?"

Maauro looked at me again, "Honey?"

"It's a figure of speech; she's trying to be nice."

"I was on the asteroid for 50,109 years before you arrived there. In case you are curious it was I who saved your life initially by refilling your tanks with oxygen."

"Initially?"

"Wrik later saved both of us when we were attacked by Dusko. After 50,109 years I was not in optimal combat readiness. That has been remedied."

"Thank you, Wrik." Candace said. "I didn't think you had it in you."

"Wrik's courage has been demonstrated on many occasions since. You will make no further disparaging remarks about that. Nor will you again refer to him as a, "No-account spacer with a reputation for bugging out on people."

"Maauro. It's ok."

"I say that it is not ok."

"My God, she is alive," Candace said, "and off hand I'd say she was in love with you. I wonder what Jaelle makes of that?"

I wondered myself sometimes. Aloud I said, "You won't learn anything about Maauro's creators from her, another programming inhibition. Other than that, we are open to doing some work for the Confederacy, for pay of course."

"Of course. For an asset like your little team I'll make it worthwhile."

Inspiration hit, "And for one other thing."

"Yes?"

"Confed citizenship and recognition as a sentient being for Maauro."

Candace started to laugh, then immediately stopped. "Hell…"

"Yep, full protection under the charter. I think she qualifies in any event. Confed's extended that right to every sentient we've met."

"Other than the Conchirri," Candace said, putting her chin in her hands and staring at Maauro.

"They were trying to eat us."

"And the Evolvers."

"Those were AIs, but no one ever proved they were self-aware; merely machines left carrying out instructions from ages ago."

"There'll be a condition on it," Candace said.

"What?" I replied in dread.

"You'll both accept reserve commissions in the Confed military. You want citizenship, Maauro? That comes with responsibility."

"Reserve?" I demanded.

"Oh you won't be on active duty; there will be occasional lucrative work for me. But I want to know that if something big and bad springs at us from beyond and I need a superbot and her sidekick—"

Maauro shifted.

The humor snapped off Candace's face, "—if I need the services of Maauro and her valued friend, they will be there."

Maauro turned to me. "Commerce?"

"It's the best deal we're likely to get."

"Very well. We accept. But I will tell you what I told Madame Ferlan of the Guild before she incurred my enmity and disappeared. If you harm my friends, I will not forgive you. Know now that I mean what I say, exactly as I say it. I will kill you and lay waste to all you value. I will neither tire of this mission, nor feel pity, nor mercy. I am M-7, the supreme accomplishment of my Creator's science: deathless, unyielding and created for destruction."

Candace's face was cold and remote as she stared back, but I could see sweat trickling down her neck. "And that will be the last time you threaten me, Little Miss Metal, now of the Confed Space Service."

"It will certainly be the last time," Maauro agreed.

There was a long moment of silence before Candace began again. "I'll have the papers drawn up. This will have to be done in secret of course. I don't want to announce to the galaxy at large that there is such a… strong-willed artificial life form running about. However the acknowledgements for your existence will be in the judiciary, executive branches and you'll be on the military rolls. You'll have the legal protection you want."

CHAPTER TWO

"Now, to my business" Candace continued. "You'll have a visitor soon, a boy named Telberd. He'll be looking to hire you for a mission involving a company called Udexco. He's heard enough about you folks through his own criminal connections to approach you. We monitored him checking your advertisement through the net then he started searching for any information that exists on you. We made that easy for him. It serves our purpose if it appears that he hired you and not us, thin cover, but useful in diplomatic circles.

"Udexco," I muttered. The Combine was one of the largest human run corporations in space, formed by independent spacers it had always had a tempestuous relationship with Confed, frequently preceding the government in exploring and relations with aliens. Some people considered it almost a government in itself.

"Yeah, them. Udexco sent a team into Ribisan space two years ago in one of the first joint ventures with the hydrogen-breathers. We don't know much about the venture; it was done in extreme secrecy, even though we have almost as many spies in Udexco as the Thieves Guild does. We do know it was a biotechnology experiment."

"What actions is the company taking to recover the mission?" Maauro asked.

"None. Udexco has money and operatives, but none in Ribisan space. They have some small warships, but nothing bigger than a destroyer escort. They've pressed the Ribisans as far as they can."

"They came to you?" I asked.

"Never. Udexco would turn to the Conchirri before the government. They've written the matter and the people off. We're not content to let it quite ride. First we want to know why the Ribisans had such a desperate need for weapons level human bio-technology and why they wouldn't approach Confed about it. That's where you come in."

"We're not a warship," I said. "You're not hiring Captain Fenaday and the *Sidhe*. Our ship is a courier-freighter."

"I'd have no interest in someone like Fenaday with his propensity for setting large parts of the galaxy on fire. God knows he gave my grandfather enough trouble—"

My eyes widened. "You're grandfather was Avery Deveraux?"

"You're being a bit thick, Wrik. I'm Confed Intelligence and the name isn't that common. Yes, Grandfather ran Captains Fenaday and Rainhell; well to the extent anyone ever controlled either of those lunatics. Of course after meeting you and Maauro, I now feel a lot more sympathy for him.

"This mission is to be discrete. In the event of...significant armed opposition we would prefer you withdraw— if you don't think you can handle it."

"That would be legalese for, if you get captured or killed don't call us," I said to Maauro.

Candace smiled.

"We'll set you up with false identities as being from Udexco, Confed or anything else you need. We can loan you additional ships and weapons as needed, even cover your commercial obligations with Tenevan and her sunstones. Your mission will be to find out what was going on, make a determination if it needs to be stopped immediately, or if there is some value to Confed Intelligence, more specifically me, in allowing it to continue. Otherwise you'll be expected to protect Confed life, law and the other usual bullshit, without starting a war with the Ribisans."

"Is that all?" I asked.

"Until you get back to me with a plan," she said, sliding a data crystal across the table to us. "There's all that's known and a list of available equipment for you."

"As to pay," I began.

The haggling lasted a considerable period before I was satisfied that I'd pushed Candace as far as she was willing to go. Maauro sat silent and motionless next to me, watching the Confed agent. I think that's why she gave in on the last 50,000-credit concession, just to get away from Maauro's wide, pacific-green eyes. To me they were always big and gentle. Candace evidently saw something else. But when the Confed agent's ample backside went out the door, I had a deal we could be happy with.

"The legal recognition," Maauro said, "was inspired thinking. Even without it being public there will be too many places for the data to be for them to risk reneging."

"I'll insist on some hard copies as well," I said. "You can spread them around in locations only known to you. They would be hard-pressed to find them all. Make one place one of the biggest law firms on the planet. Spies hate lawyers, for all they have a lot in common."

I watch Candace leave. Then, while leaving part of my attention on Wrik, I switch another part to the lead machine of the sextet of HCR I seized control of. This one is a command model and linked intimately to the human controller. The machine is a primitive device, not even the equivalent of a Creator M-1 series in its programming and cybernetics. I have already partitioned its CPU with commands that write and erase themselves so fast that they cannot be detected by the human controller or his electronics, yet they always exist. The HCR and its team are subject to my control anytime I choose to exert it.

The human woman controller is visibly shaken as she faces Candace. "I don't understand. All six of my units went autistic, then marched into the office and came back."

"I damn near opened up on them," grumbled the SWAT Commander, a powerfully built human male.

"*Which would have only gotten you killed,*" Candace returned. *She is staring at the unit I am using, as if trying to divine something. It is with some difficulty that I restrain myself from making it wink at her.*

"*Someone in there seized control of them,*" Candace says.

"*Who?*" demands the Controller. "*That's supposed to be impossible; HCR secure nets are the best we have.*"

"*Never mind. That's classified over your level. I'm just wondering if we should scrap this entire team.*"

"*Scrap them! Are you out of your... this team costs more than a light cruiser, not to mention how long it takes to get a team like this functional? This is a third of the HCRs available for the defense of this planet!*"

"*You've checked them?*" Candace says, *looking at the machine I am in with narrowed eyes.*

"*Yes, they're nominal. We'll run them through every cleaner we have back at the base. There will be no contamination.*"

Candace sighed. "*ASAT command would blow a gasket if I ordered them slagged. I have a feeling that I'm going to regret not doing it anyway.*"

Only if you attempt to use a Confed cybernetic system against me, I think with a touch of smugness. *I have traded programming blows with the Infester Artifact itself and defeated it. You will neither stop my infiltration programs nor even detect them. My abilities are as far above your computer skills as a laser is above a stone ax. Any cyber system you attempt to use against me will either defect to my control or explode. As Wrik is fond of saying, it is always nice to have an ace in the hole.*

CHAPTER THREE

AS SOON AS WE COULD RAISE JAELLE, WE TOLD HER about Candace. Against my vote, we also told Dusko, who took it in his usual fashion. He blamed me until Maauro told him to be silent. Jaelle wrapped her business up with Tenevan and returned quickly; the sunstone shipment would be moved for her for free, care of the Confed military. We then huddled up with the information Candace brought and tried to sort our next move.

Maauro absorbed the data crystal instantly, parsing out extracts of information for the rest of us. We studied what was known of the Ribisans and their expedition. It seemed shockingly little. The Ribisans were the least well known of the species of the loose Confederacy, secretive and too different for the oxygen-breathers to deal with easily. Politically, they were associate members, with minimal contacts. A thousand years ago the Nekoan, Ribisans, Vanians and Skurlocks had their own trade empire before the Conchirri and the Evolvers, struck them two centuries ago. The Vanians went extinct under attack from the Conchirri. The Evolvers nearly extinguished the Skurlocks and the Nekoans were knocked out of space by both. Most of the recorded history of their dealings with the Ribisans vanished in those wars. What was known came through the Nekoans, who handled trade relations for the Ribisans after the Confederacy destroyed the Evolvers.

But of Ribisan culture and life, little was known and less understood. Ribisans traded engineered goods and technology with the other members of the Confederacy. Often they occupied worlds in systems held by the other species that had no use for the gas giants that they savored.

"It is obvious," Maauro said, as we sat around the conference table, "reviewing the history of this species that the Ribisans have systematically controlled what the other Confederate members have learned of them. They have embassies and legations on Confederate worlds, yet there is little contact beyond the basics of trade and rudimentary military coordination."

"I heard a Ribisan symphony once," Dusko offered. "It sounded like small animals being ritually strangled."

"I am surprised that the other Confederate species put up with this situation," Maauro added. "The Ribisans seem to have gotten into the Confederacy by the adoption of the original Concord they were in with the Nekoans, Vanians and Skurlocks. None of whom had living memory of their dealings with them."

Dusko shrugged. "They do not generally compete with oxygen-breathing species for territory or resources. While they are members, few of us would ever see or communicate with one. We Dua-Denlenn call them the "ghosts at the party."

"So what now?" Jaelle asked

"We await the individual Candace said would come to hire us," Maauro said

The next day, opportunity, of sorts, came knocking at our door when the monitor on Dusko's screen lit up.

"I take back my doubts about your advertising skills," Dusko said. "A prospect has appeared. Perhaps this is Telberd?" "

"As if on cue, more cloak-and-dagger stuff," I said.

Jaelle looked a question at Maauro.

"He is full of incomprehensible sayings," Maauro responded, "but I believe he feels our visitor is here surreptitiously."

Great, two women telling me I'm full of it, I thought.

"I'll bring him in," Dusko said.

"Let's meet him in the conference room," Jaelle suggested, looking around our shop with its detritus of machinery and equipment. We followed her into the one respectable room we had, with its oblong table and frosted glass partitions, where we'd faced Candace. The window showed the field beyond, where a small, yellow ship was lifting off in the distance. We slipped into the comfortably padded chairs.

Dusko returned with a short, slim young man dressed in fashionable form-fitting dark clothes. The newcomer followed the current fashion craze for skin dyes in the inner worlds and his skin was a glossy midnight black under a shock of yellow hair. He looked narrow-eyed at all of us as Dusko returned to the conference table.

"This is Doman Telberd," Dusko said, his face revealing nothing, before he joined us on our side of the table.

Telberd's eyes flicked to me. "Before I discuss anything with you people, I first want to know if you have had any dealings with Udexco?"

"That would be a private matter," Dusko replied.

"What do you care who we work for?" I said

Telberd's lips thinned in anger and he stepped forward.

"Do not approach closer," Maauro said. She stared evenly at the slim man, yet something in that regard brought him up short.

"Look, I didn't come here for trouble," he said. "But I have to know if you're employed by Udexco. It bears on my own commission."

Maauro considered. "We have not been approached by them. Beyond that we will say nothing."

"Good," Telberd, said, visibly relieved.

"Why don't you sit down and tell us what you want?" I said.

Telberd pulled up the furthest chair. He was staring at Maauro, as if trying to figure out what she was. The crazes for dye jobs and cosmetic surgery had rendered Maauro's claims of being a mutated human more plausible, but she was still unusual by any standard.

"I'm interested in hiring you to find my older sister," he began.

"Who is involved with Udexco," Maauro added.

"Clearly," Telberd replied. "I wonder if you are all I've heard rumored."

"What have you heard?" Maauro asked.

"That you look like a girl but aren't. That you breathe, but it's for show. That few people cross you and are ever seen again."

"He's Guild," Dusko said.

"Nope," Telberd retorted. "Not even as much as you were, Dusko, and yes, I know who each of you are. I'm an independent. Mostly a gambler and courier but I do know Guild. That's where I heard some fantastic rumors about a…girl…named Maauro."

"Rumors," I repeated, deadpan, "can't put much stock in those."

Telberd gave me a wolf-like grin. "Yeah. Whatever. Look, I have an older sister, named Diralia Shon. We lost our parents at an early age and she did her level best to raise me. But I wasn't brainy like her. Didn't like school and didn't care much for being a corp-rat. She got the education and the good job. I got in trouble.

"We both kind of cut legal corners; me in the streets, and her in a variety of companies that researched things the Confed government might not like.

"Three years ago she took a job like that with Udexco. She was going out-system into Ribisan space to work on some project she couldn't tell me about. It was big though, I could tell by how excited she was about it. She promised to stargram me regularly and left."

I stood and poured some glasses of spiced, iced tea, sliding one to Telberd and another to Jaelle. "So no stargrams?"

"No, they came steadily. Sometimes they were batched, as ships to that area weren't that frequent." He raised the iced-tea to his lips. I noticed his hand trembled slightly and he suddenly looked more like a frightened kid then the hard case he pretended to be.

"Then something changed," Maauro prompted.

"Yeah, there was a lot less visual data, then even the audio dropped off and I got mostly text. After a while I realized that whoever was sending them wasn't my sister. There were little things, expressions she used. Also, none of my grams to her were addressed in her return correspondence in any but the vaguest of terms.

"She's overdue to return. Udexco tells me the contract was extended but my sister and I have some codes between us so that we always know if the other one is okay. She'd have used one in a stargram or sent a message to me somehow. I think either they won't let her return…or she's dead.

"I want you people to find out and, if possible, get Diralia out of whatever jam she's in. I have the system coordinates for the planet that she's on." He leaned back, pushing away the tea and rubbing a hand over his face.

"An expensive proposition," Dusko said, "interstellar travel, enemies of unknown power and intent. How do you propose to pay for such an expedition?'

Telberd nodded. "You're right. I don't have the credits for it. I'll give you what I have: 80,000 credits. Diralia's the only family I have. I may have other things that could be of value."

"It would be useful," Maauro said, "if you were to serve as a source of intel for me on any Guild operations that concern us. Guild has learned to avoid me after many casualties and disastrous outcomes, but such lessons sometimes need to be re-taught. Our friend Dusko is no longer in good standing and our local contacts are few."

I sighed. One of these days I was going to bang proper negotiating into her armored skull.

He licked his lips. "A high price indeed, Guild would nail my privates to your office door if they knew I was spying for you."

"That would be unfortunate for both you and the door," she replied. "However, if you wish to help your sister, you will agree."

"Yeah, I know. It's a deal."

"Think carefully on that," Maauro said. "While I no longer destroy sentient life casually, if you were to deceive, or fail me when you could have helped, I will pursue, overtake and destroy you."

"Everything she chases," I added, "dies. It doesn't matter how formidable, how fast or how connected."

Telberd swallowed and suddenly looked even younger. "Okay, no need to get tough. I knew you were serious people. I don't need it proved."

I felt a brief stab of shame over menacing someone little more than a child.

I consider the proposal, along with the high probability that, despite what Candace said, this could be an elaborate Guild trap. Telberd is not the sort of client that I envisioned for our agency, any more than Confederate Intelligence is, yet the expedition promises benefits.

Beyond this is my concern for Wrik. Since Candace's reappearance, Wrik has been moody and distracted. She is a witness on a past he would prefer not remember. Keeping him busy may be the best hope of warding off the cycle of depression he brings on himself.

Truth be told, I too am restless. I have enjoyed many quiet nights watching the stars, sat near the fountain downstairs and listened to its water dance. I have sampled music and art in this young but cultured place. All my indulgences were enjoyed thoroughly, but I feel as if I should somehow be doing more— be using more of my abilities than I am.

CHAPTER THREE

Wrik is aware that I am studying him and gives me a quizzical smile. It pleases me to see him smile and that tips the equation into finality.

"Putting a family back together," I say, "is a worthy goal."

The smile vanishes. Too late I make the correlation that I have reminded him of his severance from his own family. I am stupid, how could I have failed to realize that?

He looks away, then back at Telberd. "Yes, it is. Whatever family you have is precious to you. Even," he turns to regard me, "if it is not the original one that you had."

Relief floods through me. "Yes."

Dusko cannot roll his eyes as do humans but he makes the Dua-Denlenn equivalent of the gesture, as he often does when he feels Wrik and I are being overly sentimental. If he repeats it, I will pound his head on the table.

"We'll take the job," Wrik says.

CHAPTER FOUR

JAELLE STOOD, LIMNED BY THE MOONLIGHT COMING through the window. I felt a slight shiver as I contemplated her silhouette. Her tail drifted high and her large bat-like ears were up; one was twitching. Most disconcerting was how her eyes would catch and reflect the light. Somewhere deep in my hindbrain a primitive ancestor was chittering abuse at me for sleeping with a lioness.

Might be some reason for that, I thought drowsily. Jaelle had been known to bite and scratch a bit in the middle of having a good time.

"Wrik," she called softly.

"Yes?"

"Do you ever miss human females?"

Uh-oh. Red Alert.

I rolled up onto one elbow and looked at her. Her eyes flared in the moonlight as she turned back to me.

"No," I said after a moment.

She gave me a skeptical look. "We fit together well, sexually, for beings from two different species. Certainly better than any other two I can think of. But it is different; there are things that we do not do for each other. Do you never desire a woman of your own kind?"

I wondered where this was going, but I had painfully learned that as alien as we were to each other it was always best to take the questions literally and answer as honestly as I could bear.

"Human males are monogamous by culture, not by nature. If you're talking about mere sexual interest, then yes. If you're talking about putting that into action, or about an emotional attachment, no."

"I see."

"But obviously you feel that something is missing."

"Not as you mean that, in terms of sexual satisfaction. Despite some physiological differences, you satisfy me as well or better than my own kind. Sex with Nekoan males can be rough and one-sided. That is just our biology and our sociology hasn't quite overcome that."

"But...well, Wrik, this is a funny question, but how old are you?"

I laughed. "God. Can it be that we've never discussed this? No, I don't know how old you are either. I guess looking at you, I always assumed you were young and around my own age.

"Even so, it's hard to answer. Between cold sleep, time displacement in hyperdrive and the gravity and time distortion of our battle in the Artifact, I'm about thirty-two years from the time of my birth, but I've only lived about twenty-five of them."

"Ah," she said, a little surprised. "You are a little younger than I expected. We both gained five years time when we were in the Artifact, but my true age is closer to thirty-two years."

"A sexy older female," I said. "Lucky me."

"Our species are similarly lived, which is good," she continued, evidently determined to be serious. "But there are some things about my kind that we should discuss."

I sat up.

"Have you ever considered children?" she asked.

I looked at the window and realized there was no escape there; we were too far off the ground. I sighed. "No. I never have."

"Really, so important an issue and you have never given it any thought?"

Now it was my turn to frown. "You may recall that I haven't done so well in family matters. That's not something I want to inflict on a child."

"Perhaps you should consider some of the good things that you might give to a child, like kindness. You always doubt your courage, Wrik. Yet look at all that you have survived."

I looked away. I'd never discussed the details of my disgrace over Retief with her though she'd pieced together the basic fact that I had fled a battle over my homeworld, deserting my friends. I'd fled to Kandalor afterwards, the furthest place I could reach.

After a few seconds she walked over and sat on the bed next to me. "Nekoan females tend to have children in their twenties and thirties. Our fertility is not long and complications are common in later pregnancies. I've been giving some thought to having children. I too have had my issues with family, but that won't stop me from trying it. I always intended to have kits."

"Not something I can do for you," I said, my mouth going dry.

"Nor could I for you, which is why, if you wanted to have a human woman, or a child with her, I would understand. I would want our relationship to continue, but there would have to be room for these others.

"I know that bonding is different for our kinds. The children remain with the mother, though they are part of the father's clan. I did not have children before, as I had no intention of giving them up to another clan, nor of staying contracted to a male I do not love. You might say that I have been around humans too long. I want something different."

"And what is that?"

"Kits of my own, that I'll raise with your help. I want you to be my consort."

I lay a bit stunned. Consortship was something done between species. It left the partners able to marry within their own kind, but created a legal bond throughout Confed territory.

"You'd still be free to marry in your own species," she said. "I'd want her to be someone I like, of course."

"Wait, wait a minute," I said, feeling things slip utterly and perhaps irrevocably out of my control. "Consorts? I guess I hadn't thought that far ahead."

"Do you ever?" she said with some exasperation. "Wrik I have never known anyone who spent less time thinking about the future than you. You live in survival mode, only worried about getting through the next few hours."

Probably true, I thought. Aloud I said, "Maybe I think more in some ways and less in others. Less in that I hadn't really considered it, but more in that it never entered my mind that I'd need more than you to be happy. I don't feel the need for a human female in my life."

"Now," she said. "But I find it hard to believe, unless humans are so unlike Nekoans, that this won't be an issue in the future. On my side, what male I choose will be a temporary feature, to give me kits. Beyond that, males are not much involved in the raising of children and marriages among my kind are contract affairs usually only for a few years."

"Why do we need other people?" I began. "I truly had given no thought to kids. I mean, I suppose we could adopt some?"

"Nekoan children are rarely available to be adopted unless a clan is wiped out in some fashion. We don't have such arrangements."

"How about artificial insem—"

Jaelle shot to her feet.

We stared at each other for a few seconds before she sat down.

"Sorry," she said. "I guess there is no way ... no way that you would know that such a thing is not done among my kind. Not even discussed. It's for the lowest of low, rejects and outcasts."

Like us, I thought.

"So, no. Impossible. I may be alienated from my father, a far lesser matter than being rejected by my maternal line, but my clan is a proud one. That cannot even be considered."

She smiled at me. "But don't worry, Wrik, this will merely be about sex and children, not love."

My head was spinning like a gas giant's rings. "So you're going to go and get pregnant by some Nekoan—"

"Well, not tonight."

"Good."

"Likely not from this world either. When that's over, I would like to leave him behind. I want to raise my kits my way, not following all these archaic traditions. There's a progressive colony world about six weeks voyage from here where my clan has a substantial position. It would be a good place to find a forward-looking male who'll do what I want and then let go of me. Likely I'd be gone less than a year. You could use the time to experiment with some human females.

"That so?" I said from a place out beyond dazed.

"Provided," she said, her tail sliding across my back in a playful slap, "you don't get too involved. I may need to share you with a killer android, but I do not intend to play second place to any real female, male-of-mine."

"Right," I dropped back on the bed.

"Good. I am so glad that we were able to have this talk, though as usual I had to get you naked and exhausted in order to have a serious discussion of anything. Well, it will make for a long and fun consortship. Just think, your human children and my kits playing on the rug. Holidays surrounded by our own consort group. A lot to look forward to."

Satisfied with having arranged the future to her satisfaction, Jaelle lay down and placed her head in its accustomed place on my shoulder. As usual, she slipped into sleep quickly, her breathing and the weight of her head telling me she was well into dreamland.

I lay watching the moonbeams strike through the virtual slats of the window for an hour. Sleep eventually overtook me and the nightmares returned. I'd been free of them for so long I thought they'd gone. But Candace's visit had invoked the old Wrik. She'd known the coward, skulking in Kandalor's corners, eking out a living, betraying some customers to Dusko, to robbery and yes, death.

Beyond that Wrik lay the original, the one who fell out of his life in the brilliant blue sky over Retief. Firmly and inexorably, my old nemesis dragged me back to face it.

I'm twisting and jinking in the skies over the jungle farms of my homeworld as my squadron battled the first wave of the Confed Pacification forces. We're being slaughtered in a hopeless battle. Our obsolescent Wirriways are no match for the latest model Spacefires.

We are a ritual sacrifice by the graybeards who rule our colony and keep our separatist history; the last of the Boertrekkers. Retief will fall and change will come as it did in Africa centuries ago. The new inevitably forces its way in. But we will die first.

We, the young, either know no better, or as with many of us, we don't believe the teachings. But we've been sent into battle by our fathers and grandfathers, shoulder-to-shoulder with our brothers and sisters. How can a man hang back? How can he say no?

The squadron is already half gone. I am climbing with my wingman toward the descending roof of Confed landing barges and fighters. There's a flash and she is gone. Now it's just me. The others are far below, fighting. I am alone.

The moment comes and there is no way to change it. No way to redeem it. I wingover and dive, gathering speed, ignoring the outraged calls in my headset.

I am diving away. If only I had known then that I could never dive far and fast enough, I'd have taken my chances with my squadron. They became the honored dead, or the champions of the lost cause. Some even worked for the Confederacy, ushering in the new changes, their battle scars giving them legitimacy to call the whole corrupt history to account.

I lost my name, my world: the whole person that I'd wanted to be before that day, replaced by the broken, fearful, Wrik Trigardt of Kandalor.

Jaelle and Maauro both knew something had happened, that I had run out on my comrades. Maauro even knew my real name, something I'd told her when I thought I was dying. But she was sworn to secrecy and nothing would prise that from her synthetic lips. Still, I'd never told either of them the full story. It hadn't been a squadron I'd fled. Retief was a small colony and the militias and wings were all local. I'd run out on my childhood friends, my relatives. There could be no more complete betrayal.

Since then I'd found a measure of courage and self-respect again. Yet the wound would not close, no certainty returned to me. My courage was always held onto by my fingertips.

Now Jaelle wanted to talk children— not only hers, but eventually human ones for me? I could not face that, could not imagine telling a child about Retief, could not imagine a life with such a lie, even of omission, underlying it.

Morning finally came. Jaelle had an appointment at a shipper's for some equipment for *Stardust,* so breakfast was quick. I was used to covering my lapses in mood and Jaelle, perceptive as she was, was still an alien and didn't pick up on it. She kissed me and ran out to the aircar.

I killed some time reviewing the material Candace left us, then working on some bureaucratic junk for maintaining my pilot license. Without Jaelle there, cooking lunch lacked any appeal so I hit a nearby diner. After that it was back to work, checking *Stardust's* maintenance records. The ship was primarily my responsibility, but I could not focus. After a few hours I finally slammed a fist on the desktop and realized that I had to get out of our apartment, which now had a prison feel to it.

In something like the panic of an escaping prisoner, I changed into a tracksuit before the irony of my trying to outrun my depression struck me. The run helped anyway. Star City was a beautiful backdrop for it. Overhead, ships and aircraft slugged it out with gravity. It lifted my spirits some. Spaceports always seemed like places of possibility to me. I jogged on past floods of commuters and office workers from every species of the Confederacy. But they too were backdrop, mere faceless strangers. The guard at the side gate knew me and waved as I jogged through the scanners, but quickly returned to his screen when I didn't stop to shoot the breeze.

I could see *Stardust's* dark-green and gold hull and next to it the combination office tower and hanger that was our new home. My footfalls sounded softly on the material of the field as I dodged around carts and port vehicles scurrying on their endless errands.

I wanted to see Maauro. Just being around her eased most of the trouble in me. I slowed as I neared the tower and considered the why of it. Why was I running to Maauro? Why hadn't I talked to Jaelle about the nightmares, about my doubts of the future? About my doubts of having other lovers in our consortship? Was it just because Maauro was so strong that I turned to her? I couldn't fail Maauro because in a very real sense she didn't need me. Was that it?

When are you going to stand on your own two feet, Wrik? When are you going to be a contributing partner to all this?

The door AI recognized me and let me in. Instead of Maauro, I found Dusko, frowning at a screen. Pungent fragments of his lunch were scattered on plates nearby.

We usually exchanged grunts when we took notice of each other at all, but today he waved me over. "What do you make of this?" He gestured at the screen. On it glowed a message, but one devoid of audio, visual or any of the usual originating data.

Come to Dock 139 Section A. Look for a Morok wearing a sub-service uniform in blue and black. Information you need about humans on a Ribisan world for a reasonable price. Use code access 43718 Ceta.

"Interesting," I said. "Maybe Telberd put the word around?"

"Possibly. It would be stupid, but our young hoodlum is not as clever as he believes he is."

"I should check it out." The message seemed like a godsend to me, an excuse to flee my doubts and fears and **do** something.

Dusko stared at me as if I was a dull child. "It would be better to wait for Maauro."

"I can handle myself," I said brusquely. "I survived for years on my own."

"Hardly well," he replied, rising from the chair.

"Thanks to you," I snapped, "and others like you." I shouldered past him and slapped my hand on the arms cabinet. The door slid open and I pulled out a short-barreled stunner and two recharges.

"At least call Jaelle," Dusko demanded. I noticed that he did not offer to back me up.

"She went to Felistown on that trade job. She's five hours south of here by now. And what would I tell her? Some submarine jockey calls in with a tale about seeing humans on a Ribisan station? Where would a submariner learn that? It doesn't mean much. Odds are good all I'll end up doing is paying a few credits to hear a tale repeated from an old spacer who got drunk at the docks."

"Why would they know we have an interest in Ribisans?" Dusko demanded, crossing his multi-jointed arms over his chest.

"Like I said, probably from Telberd, hunting for information on his sister. We weren't the only, or the first people he contacted."

"I still think you should wait for Maauro or Jaelle."

"I can't go scampering to Jaelle or Maauro for every damn thing. I'm a partner in this agency, not a ward."

Dusko stared at me in incomprehension then shook his head. "Odd that Maauro is out of contact for so long."

I shrugged. "It's happened before. There are a lot of dead spots with all the embassies, corporate HQs and security offices causing dropouts in communications. I'm not going to use the emergency channel for something like this. I'll call in if there's trouble."

As I headed for the door, I heard Dusko mutter something in his native tongue. I doubted it was complimentary.

I hopped a robocab at the front of the building. It dropped me off at the docks an hour later as the sun drifted westward. The air was turning crisp as fall approached. Around me the dock area was slipping into evening mode. The docks never quite shut down; they just switched to a slower pace. Ships lay by the piers, from huge bulk-carriers to cargo subs bound for the underwater colonies, to local skimmers. A passenger ship, lit like a holiday tree, glittered in the distance, ready to take those who loved the sea out into its embrace. The smell of the ocean came in with the breeze. I took in deep lungfuls, my mood lifting some. I strolled up past departing workers of various species heading for the guard station.

"May I help you?" came the well-modulated voice of the AI station.

"Code access 43718 Ceta."

"Admitted," the speaker replied. The gate slid open. Beyond lay a series of long modern warehouses. A security bot passed me without pausing; the main AI would have registered me with all systems in the complex. Star Central was too wealthy and sophisticated a world to have too many living workers in something as basic as warehousing.

I wandered about, checking some signs and found my way to the warehouse my contact specified. It was almost all the way down to the dock, an older building of gray, stressed-concrete with a roll-back roof to allow the massive dockside cranes to drop containers in.

I looked around for the Morok I was supposed to meet, but saw no sign, so I went into the building. The security scanner bleeped at me as I passed it. Inside the warehouse was full of shipping containers, ten-high in places. I walked around, my hand inside my jacket, resting on the butt of the stunner. The only movement I saw was some cleaning robots slowly working on the rough flooring. I looked up. One panel of the rollback roof was back, admitting slanting yellow beams of light into the dim interior.

I sighed. This was turning into a wild goose chase. The wisdom of my solo mission was also looking more and more questionable. Truth was I was feeling inadequate. Maauro really didn't need me. Jaelle had been a successful merchant before she met us. All I brought to Lost Planet was my piloting. Even Dusko with his criminal connections was more useful than I was. But I wasn't going to be carried in the group like some useless appendage. I needed to contribute. I needed to provide something. My footfalls echoed off the walls as I hunted the Morok.

I return to the office late in day. I've been conducting some surveillance of the Ribisan legation then refueling myself from a concealed powertap I have created near a local fusion plant. I like to stay in top shape.

Dusko greets me at the door. "Where have you been?" This is unusual; he is normally circumspect with me. Something is wrong.

"I have been engaged in diagnostics and self-maintenance."

"I've been messaging you for hours!"

I frown in incomprehension. "I received no messages."

Dusko slams a first into his palm. "I was right. We've been hacked. Our communications interrupted."

Now I am surprised, I'd set the program safeguards myself. I thought them proof against anything the Confederacy could do. But why would Candace want to interfere with our communications?

"Listen," Dusko added. "There was a message sent here today for you and Wrik, offering us information about this new commission we've accepted. It promised a meeting down at the docks." His hands fly over the message board and I read the data in an instant.

"A trap," I say, "given that we have been hacked." While Dusko has been retrieving the message, I extended my senses into our computer net. I detect an infiltrating virus of immense complexity and subtlety. It reacts to me as soon as I touch it and it self-erases. I am alarmed and puzzled. This wasn't Infester or Creator tech. Nor did I believe it Confederate work.

"Wrik decided not to wait for you. I told him not to go but the damn fool—"

Dusko is talking to empty space. I accelerate to my best ground speed. The door will open too slowly so I simply dive through it. I am messaging Wrik as I go, but the hack must be affecting his com. I cannot reach him. I leap into an aircar, hacking into the traffic control system in a preprepared intrusion that allows me use the police altitudes. I should be mistaken for an unmarked police car if anyone considers me at all. I have prepared for all eventualities other than Wrik's sudden attack of stupidity. Why would he go on a possibly dangerous venture without me? This smacks of his occasional self-destructiveness back on Kandalor. What have I missed?

CHAPTER FOUR

I press the aircar to its max and lament its deficiencies in speed and agility. Even with the best I can do with the traffic control, I can only move so fast without creating situations impossible to control.

Wrik, you and I are going to have a long conversation when this is over. Assuming we both survive.

CHAPTER FIVE

I FROWNED AS I CAME AROUND YET ANOTHER STACK OF containers. No Morok submariner. This was beginning to smell bad and it wasn't anything rotting by the piers. The instincts that had kept me alive on Kandalor were now jangling furiously. Truth was they'd been doing it since I arrived and I, having grown too used to being backed up by Maauro, had been ignoring them. I jumped for the edge of one container and pulled myself off the floor.

Something slammed the container below me and I nearly fell off. Another heave got me up and I scrambled forward, got to my feet and ran bent double. A laser crisped the air over me. I could feel the heat through my jacket despite the armored panels Maauro had made for it. I went down in a roll, came back up and cut in the other direction, leaping up a series of stacked containers until I was ten meters off the ground. Only then did I have leisure to draw my stunner. I lay panting as I searched the dim quarters of the warehouse.

Not the only thing around here that's dim, I thought. I came here alone, ignored all the warning signs and now I'm cut off in a warehouse with a heavily armed enemy. I moved back from the edge, trying to get higher still and pulled out my com. As I expected, there was no signal. Jammed. Our enemy had planned well.

I heard a sound below me, not the tread of feet, though it had that rhythm, but something more mechanical. I pocketed the com, dialed the stunner up to max, then leapt to another container stack. Not a second too soon. The stack I'd left tipped forward with a tremendous crash to lean against an outer wall. What the hell was after me? I scrambled upward, trying to put vertical distance between us at least.

Through a gap revealed by the toppling containers I saw something. A large figure in an armored suit, over two meters tall—not a military job— more like a loader adapted for weapons. The occupant stomped forward with a whine of servos, evidently searching for a crushed me among the containers.

I looked for a way out. We were in the back of the warehouse, far from the front entrance or the open roof. I'd have to get past my steel nemesis. I fired the stunner. It buzzed in my hand but I might have hummed at my assailant for all the good it did. The suit leaned back, looking up. Both arms came up and I rolled backward away from the ledge as a storm of laser and accelerated metal ate up the edge of the container. I ran further back, hearing the machine thirty meters below stomping after me. At least speed and agility were on my side.

CHAPTER FIVE

I saw the gap ahead of me almost too late. With a last burst of speed I jumped the gap, but lost my stunner as I frantically clawed for a grip to keep from sliding off the canted container top. The weapon tumbled out of sight and I ran on.

With a little lead, I opted to change directions and slow down. My armored friend didn't seem interested in coming up after me. I wondered what he was. From the size I thought he might be one of the ursine Okaran, but one of them would have come up after me, disdaining hiding in something so clumsy. Either my opponent was short on nerve, or perhaps some disability kept him running around like a tank chasing an enemy soldier through a village.

I moved as silently as I could manage. The thing probably had audio sensors and infrared. Positioned below me, he could not use his infrared through the containers. I had to hope the vast echoing space of the warehouse made audio problematic.

I spotted a metal buckle on a bit of strapping a worker had left behind. I whirled it over my head and flung it as far away as I could. It landed with a clatter on a container. Instantly a laser slashed up at that container and then the tower of them rocked as the powered suit tried to shake its imagined prey off.

I ran the other way, desperate to circle around my misdirected enemy. Luck wasn't with me. The container stacks were shorter and as I leapt down on one, a slug hit me in the side. I screamed and fell, unable to breathe for a few seconds. One of the armored panels stopped penetration, but I felt like I'd been hit with an aircar. I got to my feet and retreated into the shadows. More shots came up singly, puncturing or occasionally bouncing off the containers around me.

Bastard can't see me, I realized.*He's trying to get me with a ricochet.* I reached into a sealed inner pocket, pulled a trauma tab and pressed it inside my shirt against the ribs. I didn't know if they were fractured or not, but I had to stop the pain and immobilize the ribs or I couldn't run. With a hiss, the tab fired, injecting painkiller and anti-inflammatory into me. Sensing no open wound, it slid a spider-web-like worknet over the ribs; not quite as good as wrapping, but it helped.

A wash of yellow flame came over the edge of the container. My enemy had new tricks. I yelped and backed away. He'd shake the containers next.

But I'd underestimated him. These containers were on moveable pallets. I heard servos start and saw the various container stacks moving. He was taking away my hideaway over his head. I looked longingly at the other stacks, particularly the high ones in the back, but not knowing where he was below me, I didn't dare risk leaping the widening gaps.

Sweat trickled down my side.*Well, you wanted to be independent, I thought, and here you are by yourself with blanked-out communication, no weapons and an armored alien hunting you. If he doesn't kill you, Jaelle and Maauro will draw lots.*

I looked for something I could dump down on my enemy, crushing him, but while the containers varied some in size and shape, the smallest was the size of an aircar. There was no way to drop them on him using only muscle. I looked at my useless com. Quickly I flipped it open. There was a strobe and alarm setting for emergencies. I set it to drain the whole battery, then crawled to the edge just as the alien struck the tower of containers. His tipping it gave away his position. I leaned over and spotted him. His armored hands were bending the metal of the containers. He looked up but I could see no face through the glass. He jerked in surprise.

"Fire in the hole," I yelled and dropped the com toward him. It instantly flashed and emitted an ear-splitting whoop that I hoped would overload his sensors. Either thinking it was a bomb, or dazzled by the light and sound, my enemy stumbled back, crashed into a low rail and toppled over.

I raced to the other side and over, half-falling, half-climbing down. Then I hung by my hands for a second and dropped. Rolling lessened the impact but brought a white flash of agony from my ribs. I scrambled to my feet as the container pile heaved and tumbled toward me. Fortunately the upper containers missed me, standing so close to the lower ones. I ran, clutching my side, praying there was a fire exit or something on this side.

There wasn't. I heard the pounding of the machine's feet behind me as it rounded into the lane I was in, up against the back wall of the warehouse. Now it had a straight shot at me and there was nowhere to hide. I was dead.

The wall next to me exploded inward and Maauro appeared, standing between it and me. "To the floor," she shouted, her artificial voice so loud that I obeyed instantly.

She turned toward my enemy and raced at him head on. A torrent of laser, flame and gunfire embraced her.

I see my enemy. More importantly, he is diverted from targeting Wrik to face me. My tactics are limited to a frontal assault by Wrik's foolish creation of this scenario. I am very cross with him. The flames licking out at me are irrelevant, far too cool to be of any concern. Automatic weapon fire smashes into my body but is deflected. He is firing too high at me to get the prone Wrik. The laser is the concern. It's a commercial model, not military. I exploit this by cyber attack, creating a feedback loop that will short-circuit the laser. Still, I have no desire to endure even a millisecond more of the powerful beam. I perform a high-speed forward shoulder roll, coming out of it in a vertical leap. Against anything like myself, all this time hanging about in the air would be ill advised. But the slowness of my enemy's reaction time tells me this is a biological life form and he will have extreme difficulty targeting me as I move in three axes.

This proves true as I slide out of target lock well over his head, his fire trailing me considerably then sputtering as my cyber attack disables his weapon. I unleash a torrent of flechettes but his armor is proof against them. I do not have time to prime and activate my plasma torch as I drop toward my enemy. I elect for brute force as we crash together.

This time I am surprised as I grapple with my enemy, tearing at his suit. The unit is immensely powerful, generating almost as much force as I do. It seizes my arms and attempts to rip them out, but I am made of malleable ceramic and collapsed metals. My arms have more give and, as he tries to pull me apart by holding me in front of him like a child's toy, I lash out with my feet in a series of strikes that destroy the arms holding me and a substantial portion of his midsection. I detect methane, silicon and a number of highly unusual organic chemicals as I tear free of my shattered enemy. This identifies it as a Ribisan. No other being would use that atmosphere.

I am unsure if he is totally destroyed, so I smash his midsection again, pick up the entire unit and fling it some ten meters into a wall. Dust and metal fly up and I am briefly concerned that I may have overdone it and brought down the wall. But only the interior concrete is damaged and the enemy lies in a pile of rubble.

Wrik runs up to me. "Are you alright?"

"No," I reply. "I have a very stupid friend who takes unforgiveable risks with his life for insufficient reasons."

"I'm sorry. God, I really am. Maauro, you're damaged."

"I understand that a traditional method of dealing with misbehavior of your children is to beat their posteriors. I am giving serious consideration to how yours will withstand my armored hand even if I leave the palm blades retracted.

"Honestly, Wrik, how could you be so stupid? How could you fail to see the probability of a trap? Why would you explore this tac-intel without me? You're fortunate beyond reasonable odds that I was able to detect the weapon fire and home in on your location."

He hung his head. "I really have no excuse."

"I do not seek excuses," I said, moderating my tone, I realized that my fear for his safety had made me sound and appear harsh. I also detect the scent of a trauma tab and, ignoring his protestations, pull open his jacket and quickly scan his interior. His appallingly fragile body has taken soft tissue injury but no structural damage. I note that his jacket armor is dented by a round that would clearly have been fatal if it had hit an unprotected spot. I must fight again to control my anger.

"Excuses," I repeat, "do not interest me. But there are reasons for this behavior that you and I will deal with later when time permits. I have not forgiven this. Not yet."

The suit lay where Maauro had flung it.

"Are you sure you're alright?" I demanded of her.

"Its grip was formidable," she replied, even as the scratches and cuts on her body disappeared. "Had it been able to root itself more securely, it would have torn me to pieces. I have some minor stress fractures that my damage control can deal with."

"Who the hell is it in there?"

"Its individual identity is unclear but that it is a Ribisan is beyond doubt. This has serious implications for the mission we have just undertaken."

We walked over to the prone Ribisan.

"Wrik, please stay behind me. It may still be dangerous."

Wisps of gas escaped from the powered suit, but the being inside was still alive. I'd never seen a Ribisan in the flesh, or even paid that much attention to them on Vids. Staring at this one told me little though. At this range, I could see better into the helmet. I couldn't even find something like a face to regard. Its head, if that's what it was, looked more like a cluster of grapes. The body, from what I could see, was a central stalk of ropy muscles that seemed to branch out below, like the arms of a squid. The bipedal shape of the power suit was evidently just a device to allow it to use Confed facilities with greater ease. The Ribisan seemed to be a cross of starfish, jellyfish and squid. Yet it was a powerful sentient and had crossed great gulfs of space to try and kill us.

A light played on its chest. "The lost must be returned to the holy," a mechanical voice intoned from a speaker somewhere in the suit.

"We do not understand," Maauro said. "Nor do we know why you attacked us. I know little of your species, but enough to know that this atmosphere is poisonous to you. We cannot repair your suit or transport you to safety quickly enough. You will be dead soon, from that, if not from the injuries I dealt you."

"Do you have any final wishes to make known to us?" I added. "Anyone to notify?"

"NNNnnooooooo. Dieeeee..." The alien quivered violently and went still. Lights on its chest plate shifted in color intensity.

"Is it dead?" I asked.

Maauro stared intently for a second. "Yes. It attempted to detonate a small charge of plastic explosive in its power pack. I interrupted the signal. It was quite determined to kill us."

I gulped.

"My scans of its electronic systems lead me to believe that this assassin did not expect to return. Virtually all data and programs beyond the minimum necessary to run the suit are wiped. Beyond the fact that this is a member of a species rare on this world, we can learn little from the body."

"Surely someone from the legation will know who it is?"

"If it was sent with government sanction they will deny it, though it seems unlikely that it could have arrived here without such help. Also, if we report this death, whoever sent it will know that his mission miscarried and possibly make additional efforts."

"This isn't Kandalor, Maauro. We can't just go around killing people. The authorities are going to ask questions."

"I will dispose of the body."

"How?"

She looked up at me.

"Scratch that, I'll be happier not knowing."

"Yes, return to the office. Make no mention of this beyond warning the others that enemy agents may be tracking us."

"What else is new?" I muttered.

Wrik leaves and I lift the alien carcass. It is heavier than me, so I must balance carefully. We were fortunate that the attack occurred in the evening near the docks. The area was left mostly to automatics and lesser AIs, which I can easily blind. As I close in on the waterfront with my awkward burden there are occasional biological workers. I wait for activity in the area to lessen, then sprint to the end of the nearest dock and tumble us both into the water. I surface and scan the area. We are unobserved.

I return to the bottom and seize the corpse, then set up an ECM barrier so I do not register on any of the various traffic or police sensors of this busy port. Reshaping my feet into paddles, I vibrate my legs at sufficient speed to move myself and my awkward burden at 50 kmh. Greater speeds will have to wait until I am in deeper water and further from port instruments. An hour sees me out of the danger zone and I accelerate to 300 kmph for two hours, heading for the deepest abyss within practical distance.

An hour into the journey we are stalked by a large predator, doubtless attracted by some leakage from the Ribisan's suit, a simple misfortune that the predator finds these exotic fluids attracting. I fire a barrage of high-speed pellets though its brain. It begins to sink, trailing a ribbon of its own lifeblood, doubtless to attract others of its kind.

I swim on, dragging my dead enemy until I reach and descend into the abyss. At bottom I examine the environmental suit. While it is of Confed standard, its power cells and some other equipment are far in advance of Confederate tech. The Ribisans are renowned as master engineers and I can see why. I absorb the power cells, which are sufficient to bring me up to full reserve power. I then scavenge some rare and exotic metals that are useful to me.

Secure from observation I disassemble the suit, tearing it into small and difficult to identify fragments, which I distribute over a wide area. The Ribisan's body looks natural in the fluid environment and I wonder if this depth might have been more like its home. I dissect the creature to learn as much as possible. After extracting all the intelligence I can, I extend my hand, fingers wide and rotate them at 5,000 rpm. In a minute the body is reduced to tiny fragments that will surely dissolve or be devoured.

No trace is left of the sentient who wagered his life against Wrik and me only hours ago. I wonder about this being, who has come so far into an environment that must have been strange and frightening to it, compelled by … by what? A sense of duty? Payment? Threats? What is said at the end about "the holy" hinted at a religious fervor.

I dismiss the question; there isn't enough data. However I cannot help but wonder about my enemy, now gone as if it had never existed. It must have had a network, must have been important to someone, who would now never know its fate.

I remember the day when Wrik lay near death, after having been shot by the Guild gunwoman, Lostra. He asked me never to delete my memories of him. I note in my memory the GPS location of this place and unlike with some I have killed, I will not delete this memory. The Ribisan fought well and was an adversary to be respected, dedicated to whatever causes that brought him against us.

I know that many biologicals have beliefs about some invisible part of themselves that survives death; for all that there has been no verification of this belief in the history of sapience. It is not a question that I have pondered much till now, alone in the great deep, in a cloud of microscopic fragments of my enemy. To me this belief in an immortal part is a delusion born of an inability to face truth. I have no ability to so delude myself. While I am sentient, as I suppose my steel sisters may have been, I was made. My own existence is not so limited by time as biological life; 50,131 years have passed for me already. Yet eventually I must cease, either destroyed or overtaken by eventual entropy of my systems. I too will pass from the world of the living. And I do not have the comfort of any such delusion to embrace.

I have spent enough time alone in this dark depth. Unburdened, I accelerate to my best speed. I am anxious to return to Wrik and my network. I find myself suddenly weary of cold, silence and solitude.

CHAPTER SIX

I RETURNED TO OUR OFFICE, NOT WANTING TO FACE ANYONE
until after I'd seen Maauro. I retreated to her favorite spot, the rooftop.
I should have stopped for a heavier coat, or a drink, or some medical
attention, but it just seemed to be prolonging the coming confrontation.
Truth was I felt the need for forgiveness from my friend, whose existence
I had so thoughtlessly endangered by endangering my own. I'd be lucky
if she was talking to me at all.

The door behind me opened and Maauro stood there, her facial
expression gentle as ever, her eyes their usual pacific green, empty of
any sign of anger. But she did not speak and walked past me to lean
against the railing, looking up at the stars.

I took my place beside her, hoping the silent treatment would not
last long. I'd have been happier if she was hopping mad. We stood that
way for some time, a time I am sure could not have been as long as it
felt. Beside me Maauro gazed up at the stars as if the firmament was her
private jewel box. I shivered from a combination of the cool night air
and the effects of stress. With a sigh, I contemplated Star City, a glowing
kaleidoscope of office towers, bridges and other buildings attended by
swarms of aircars.

"So," I managed. "Do you plan to throw me off?"

Maauro glanced reprovingly at me. "Wrik, have I not demonstrated
repeatedly that you are the most important and irreplaceable part of my
network?"

"God knows why," I said.

"Why," Maauro, said, "do you allow the events over Retief to define
you? We have repaired this deficiency many times. Yet in some way I do
not understand, you remain broken."

I sighed. "Maauro…"

"I am entitled to an answer."

Which was the truth, "You heard what Candace called me: a no-account spacer with a reputation of running out on his friends."

"You did not believe in the cause your homeworld was fighting for."

"Oh, Maauro, I don't think many of us did. But we were from Retief.
It was our home and we didn't fancy Confed moving in and remaking
it. Despite all that politicians and others tell you, soldiers fight mostly
for the person to the left and the right of them. The worst crime a man
can commit is to run out on his teammates, only more so when they're
people from your own hometown. I did that. No one else in my wing
did. That's something that really can't be bought back. To the people

who I ran out on, I'll always be that; the guy who left them. What's worse, I'll always be that guy to me, too."

Maauro stared at me pensively.

"Do you know why I feel I can be your friend?" I blurted out.

"Tell me."

"Because you're so strong, so damn near indestructible. You can take all that I manage to give you, but you won't be harmed if I can't hold up my end of it."

"That is frankly stupid. My strength and durability are finite for all that they are greater than yours. Yet time and time again you have made the difference between my continued survival and my destruction. Yes, I am not as vulnerable as you or Jaelle, but no, I do not depend on you any less."

I looked at her, my heart suddenly hammering.

"You and I have both failed in our previous lives. I have the advantage in that before meeting you, I simply erased those failures and they did not mark me. But since the day that Lostra shot you and you made me promise never to delete any memory of you, I have not deleted any memory at all. I have learned to tolerate my errors and learn from them. You, who taught me this skill, remain tormented and this I do not understand.

"You have shown no reluctance to risk your life for Jaelle, or for me. Or do you imagine that I have forgotten your reckless charge across the asteroid, in an unarmored suit, when I malfunctioned before the Thieves Guild?"

"No," I said, warmed by pride. "That was the day I started to live again. It was preceded by many failures."

"You make too much of math. Plusses and minuses added together and the result is coward or hero? The universe is not so simple. I know you better than you perhaps know yourself. I do not harbor these doubts. But there is more to this latest misadventure. Something else has changed to bring this on."

I told her about my midnight conversation with Jaelle.

"Are you sure that the fact Jaelle must have her children with a male of her own species is not the central factor?"

I winced. "For someone who didn't know anything about biological lifeforms, other than how to kill them two years ago, you're getting goddamn perceptive."

"A consort arrangement is not exclusive, by definition; it binds two beings of different species."

"My girlfriend may have cat-ears and a tail, but the idea that she is getting pregnant by someone else is hard to take."

"Did this never occur to you before?"

I sighed again. "No. I didn't realize how important it was for Jaelle to have children while she was young."

"She promised to return. Do you not trust her word?"

And there it was. "I don't know. Once she's back among other Nekoans and with children of her own, the idea of living with a disgraced pilot and an ancient android may not seem so appealing. The thought of her leaving me…"

Maauro looked away and we stood silent for a few minutes. I realized as time dragged on that I had upset her, though no trace showed on the youthful face.

"Maauro?"

She ignored me.

"What is it? Please talk to me."

"I respect your pain. I know you fear losing Jaelle and that she is networked with you in a way I cannot be." She turned toward me and now I could see hurt in her eyes. "But I am still here. Am I nothing? Does my presence have no value? Do I offer you no comfort? Am I not reason enough not to risk your life in these stupid—"

I reached both my arms around her and hugged her hard. Perhaps not a smart move with a deadly android but, she did not object. We stood like this for minutes, silently.

"I'm sorry," I said, my voice, husky. "I took you for granted, didn't I?"

Maauro nodded, her hair soft against my neck.

"Whatever happens to, or with me, never doubt what I said to you back on the Artifact. I do love you, Maauro."

"Then we will remain networked whether Jaelle returns or not?"

"We will remain networked while I live, though it may be another reason for Jaelle not to return."

"I do not understand. She and I are networked too. There is no reason for her to feel sexual jealousy toward me. Appearance aside, I am essentially neuter."

I grinned at her. "From the conversation of the last few minutes I would say you were pretty female. Jealously need not be sexual; I think she's unsure of which one of you I have stronger feelings for."

Mauro tipped her head up. "Which one—"

"Nope," I said raising a hand quickly. "The Confederate charter on sapient rights states that I need not testify against myself." *Besides,* I thought, *what if I don't know?*

She raised an eyebrow. "As you have returned to speaking nonsense, I assume the serious part of our conversation is over."

"Yes. It's late. I'm cold and tired."

"Very well, but we will discuss these matters again."

"Maauro, you really are female."

The chewing out I received from Jaelle on her return quickly eclipsed the one I'd received earlier from Maauro and at points looked like it was going to involve actual teeth. Maauro showed neither discretion nor mercy in relaying the details of my unfortunate encounter with the Ribisan to both Jaelle and Dusko on the grounds they needed "intel" on our new enemy. I really couldn't contest the wisdom of that, especially given my current low stock level with the rest of the team.

I learned that while Nekoans yowl in frustration, which happened repeatedly before Jaelle advised that she needed to take a walk to cool off and would see me at home later to continue "the discussion." I had a feeling that there would be little talking by me during that conversation.

Surprisingly, it was Dusko who found a few kind words for me, just after Maauro left to do some checking on her various spy taps around the city.

"Good thinking about using your com to simulate a bomb," he said, as he rose, heading for the door. "I wouldn't have come up with that."

"You would be entitled to add," I said, "that you wouldn't have been stupid enough to have walked straight into a trap like that and that you told me so."

He shrugged. "You're young yet. The young make mistakes. The lucky young live to learn from them. I'm the one who kept attacking Maauro despite her annihilating team after team of Guild until I ended up as her captive." He turned to the door then hesitated. "I don't suppose that I ever thanked you for dumping me into that ejection pod the day Maauro decided to kill me."

I looked back. "Not necessary. To be brutally honest, and I think you're entitled to that from me, I did it to save her from the sin of murder."

Dusko nodded. "Understood. Still, for what it is worth…"

I grimaced. "Maybe next time I should listen to your advice."

"Maybe next time you will." He slipped out

In the morning life had returned to something like normal. Jaelle and I had quickly shelved the trauma of the day before after she extracted a heartfelt promise never to do anything that stupid again and further, to take Maauro with me on anything that smacked of danger. Her own rivalry with the android quickly disappeared when matters of our security surfaced.

When we returned to the office, Maauro and Dusko were already there, winding down our other business operations or subcontracting them out. Since money was not an issue, through the Confederacy's largesse, we were able to keep customers and business partners happy with liberal doses of government cash.

CHAPTER SIX

The desk com chimed for our attention, interrupting our planning session. The screen lit with the message. "Incoming encrypted call – no video."

Maauro looked at Jaelle. "Please answer."

She keyed the com but kept the screen off on our side as well. "Lost Planet Expeditions, Jaelle Tekala speaking."

"Hello Jaelle. This is Candace Deveraux, doubtless Wrik and Maauro mentioned me to you."

"Doubtless."

"I hope to make your acquaintance in person, before you all leave."

"What can I do for you, Agent Deveraux?"

"You can call me Candace if you like. I don't stand on ceremony. Are Wrik and Mauro there?"

She looked at me and I shook my head. "Not at the moment."

A derisive laugh came from the screen. "Honey I never ask a question I don't already know the answer to. Anyway tell them, when you, ahem, see them, that I received some interesting information from the PBI."

My stomach did a flip. The Planetary Bureau of Investigation handled interspecies cases.

"Seems the Ribisan legation just reported a missing person, a merchant with an unpronounceable name. He arrived about a month ago and was supposed to exit according to his visa three days ago. He's disappeared.

"Why tell us?" Jaelle asked.

"Don't play with me, Catgirl. I'm not stupid and neither are you. PBI knows that he was last seen down at the docks in one of the powered exoskeletons that he was here marketing. Seems there was some sort of to-do there. Huge amount of property damage, small fires, oddly enough none of the security systems detected or recorded a damn thing."

"How unfortunate," Jaelle said. "Perhaps his exoskeleton went out of control."

"Hmmn, good one. Then maybe it marched him into the depths of the ocean where he will be found millions of years from now by very confused archeologists. Say hi to Wrik and Maauro for me."

"Will do," Jaelle said as the line clicked off.

"Interesting," Maauro said, "and perhaps helpful."

I looked at her. "How do you mean?"

"The attack on you was not random. It indicated an awareness of our operation and personnel. Presumably the Ribisans had become aware of us and launched countermeasures."

"How has that changed?" Jaelle said, as she crawled up the table and curled her legs and tail under her.

"If the Ribisan government had sent a mission against us, they would not have contacted the police and called attention to their missing operative. This seems to indicate that there are factions among the Ribisans and that the government is not the faction determined to kill us. Some other party is moving, but it is unlikely they can project power this far. This relatively clumsy attempt, with only one operative, indicates this. Likely we will not be attacked again until we arrive at their system."

"Good," Dusko said. "I'd hate to be killed close to home when there is a chance to die a miserable death on a gas giant."

"It does mean that it would be worthwhile to adopt protective camouflage when we travel. Not all of our enemies may know or recognize us," Maauro added.

Dusko stretched out in a chair, resting his feet on a low table. The sun slanted into the room, but the light just reflected off his pupilless blue eyes without bothering him. I had to narrow my eyes against the glare. Maauro noticed and sent some computerized command to the windows, which polarized. I smiled at her.

"So," Dusko said, "we have a client who thinks we are working for him, the Confederacy who thinks we are working for them, and, of course, we are all dancing to Maauro's tune."

Maauro threw him a cool glance but I noticed that she didn't correct him. "We need to come up with a plan to obtain access to the site of the expedition. Candace's data crystal places the location of the Ribisan joint venture in the fifth planet of the Cimbar system. It is over 500 light-years from Star-Central."

I whistled.

Maauro looked at me in fascination. "That was wonderful, Wrik. Do it again."

Jaelle smothered a laugh as Dusko sighed. I obligingly whistled again.

"Five hundred lights is a long hop," I added.

"Yes," Maauro replied, then she whistled. It was a perfect reproduction, only longer. "Interesting. Why do you this?"

"It called whistling. It can indicate surprise or be used to signal for attention."

"Thank you, Wrik." Maauro smiled at me. "It pleases me to learn from you."

For some reason I was suddenly too choked up to speak and simply nodded and looked away, hoping no one noticed.

Her new skill mastered, Maauro returned to the business at hand. "There is a route that involves three small star jumps from Central to an express route that takes us out of the Confederacy proper and into Ribisan territory. Cimer is one of the border worlds, doubtless why it was selected."

"So do we warm up *Stardust* and set out?" Jaelle asked, showing more enthusiasm than usual for one of Maauro's ventures. Her ears were even twitching.

"I believe we need covers and to use more than one vessel," Maauro said. "The Ribisans have blocked or simply ignored Confed inquiries, which have not been hard pressed. They would not find it difficult to believe that Confed might redirect a courier or scoutship to look into the matter, under guise of taking in some diplomatic or trade communications, perhaps even an inspection of the human habitation sections. Candace can probably provide us with genuine diplomatic documents."

"With what crew?" I asked, not liking the idea of splitting up.

"Only you and me," Maauro said. "I trust Confed Intelligence no more than you do. Couriers have small crews anyway, but we can simulate some additional crewmembers easily so long as we are not boarded, something the Ribisans would not dare with a Confed warship, even a small one. Once in orbit, Wrik should be able to get access to the Ribisan installation."

"To what purpose? They'll be watching every step I make once I land," I asked.

"You would come down first. I would drop in a modified escape capsule and join you surreptitiously. I have not met a computer system in this time that I could not back-hack and conceal myself from."

"What do you have in mind for us?" Jaelle asked.

"You would arrive after us, as a Guild runner seeking contacts in Ribisan space."

A frown spread over Dusko's face. "Unwise. While I was not well known beyond Kandalor before I met you, your hijinks have made me quite a black reputation in the Guild. That, combined with the disappearance of Madam Ferlan and her ship, has elevated my profile. My continued survival is testimony to the fact that I am in Maauro's shadow, where none care to seek for me."

"True," Maauro conceded, "but yours will not be the face they'll see. Rather it will be a new and more attractive one."

"Ah, that would be me," Jaelle said

Dusko looked at her. "I think Jaelle is likely the smartest of our biological team, but apt as she is, I do not see her as passing for Guild on sustained exposure. I can try training her up."

"Risky in the time we have," I said.

"And unnecessary," Mauro added. "While we will train to the limit possible, Jaelle's safety requires that she carry Dusko's brain with her."

"Oh, and how do you propose we do that?" Dusko said with asperity.

"I thought I could remove it, trim the unnecessary parts and implant it in Jaelle."

We stared at her.

"Was my attempt at humor unsuccessful?" she said finally.

We all released a whoosh of pent-up breath and nervous laughter. Maauro gave me a wink.

"Very funny," Dusko said.

"Since you would clearly prefer another method," Maauro continued, "I have labored to produce a device which will allow for mental communication over distance. Not telepathy, but the devices can pick up mental emanations, condense and transmit them, head to head. The communicator chips have limited range and power. If I made them stronger, they would be detectable and the emanations might be injurious to your health. The effective range of these in normal atmosphere is thousands of kilometers. In a gas giant, it could be far less and highly variable. Do not count on them."

Maauro opened a panel in her chest and pulled out a container from which she extracted three small gelatin pills. These she placed on the desktop. Jaelle walked over to the dispenser and drew three cold soft drinks.

"Will I be able to talk to Wrik?" she asked, placing drinks in front of us.

"Not directly, yours is paired with Dusko, as you are operating separately, as Wrik must be to mine. I can speak to all three of you as a central nexus."

"Why can't we all communicate?" Dusko said, looking narrowly at her.

"Again, the devices need to be small and low-powered and, in part, forgive me, it is due to the limitations of your biological brains."

"Oh," he said.

"You can only process data from the device as fast as you can think and talk. A multiple channel would require a more powerful implant and if two of you spoke at once it would likely scramble your brain, possibly resulting in personality confusion. With my quantum logic brain, I can handle all four channels simultaneously and operate."

Jaelle sighed. "Kit-sister in the middle again."

"Sorry," Maauro said, but Jaelle waved it away with a smile.

We looked at the pills, then downed them with the soft drinks. Maauro said the capsules would dissolve quickly and the organic net would travel imperceptibly through our blood streams to our brains. I wasn't sure I believed the imperceptible part.

"Guess, I'd better start on the liftoff arrangements," Dusko said, turning back to his computer screen.

"What do you say to lunch?" I asked Jaelle.

She smiled her lazy smile. "What I usually say: yum."

Jaelle, who lived very in the moment, had let go of her anger at my idiotic encounter with the Ribisan. I'd been busily engaged in giving her reasons to forget about it. Maauro, as if sensing I needed more time and space with Jaelle, had made herself scarce, so I did not have to check with her about lunch. She could also handle all the logistics for our upcoming voyage far faster without our "help."

CHAPTER SIX

Jaelle and I visited the Sundowner, our favorite café, in a tower overlooking the river. When we returned to the shop it was to find the hallways filled with crates and containers. Maauro had been busy.

Jaelle's ears wiggled again. "Well I have affairs of my own and our cover business to resolve, and that means using the people I put on standby to run our operations for an exorbitant bill."

"I'll just add it to Candace's tab," I said.

"That woman frightens me."

"I think that's a very sensible reaction. She probably frightens the Guild as well. But she's a factor in our lives from now on."

"Because of Maauro," Jaelle said.

"Jaelle," I said gently. "With the exception of Dusko, we'd all be long dead without Maauro."

"Yes, I know. Maybe it's selfish, but it may simply be that I'm not cut out for this life we are leading with her."

"Didn't I find you on an expedition into the deepest darkest part of Kandalor, searching for an ancient race and pursued by the Guild?"

"I am beginning to reconsider my reckless youth," she said. "I won't deny that life with Maauro is lively, but I would like to live through it. Right now, though, I am worried for you. You two will be going down first. If this op blows up it will catch you both on the surface. We, at least, will have a chance to abort."

"I have my worries too," I kissed Jaelle on the lips. "I'm still not comfortable with you relying on Dusko."

She glanced over her shoulder at the Dua-Denlenn at the back of the office, who was arguing with the port inspector over something on a com screen. "He'll be all right. If I have to pass as a Guild agent, I'm going to need him whispering in my head to get me through. I can't say I'm all that happy about Kit-sister putting these coms directly into our brains. She knows too much of what goes on with us as it is."

"She says they'll dissolve in about five months."

"And do you always believe everything she tells you?" Jaelle said, pulling on my ear. I couldn't quite tell if the exasperation was all fake, all real or a mix. "You do recall she was created to annihilate the universe fifty millennia ago."

I sighed. "She was created to protect her makers. And other than staring possessively at the stars, she has shown no signs of embarking on a mission of galactic domination."

"Hmmnn. I think she has made some conquests closer to home."

"Jaelle."

"Mostly kidding, Honey. I like Kit-sister too and I am glad she is on our side. I'm also glad," she flicked her tail around my upper thigh, "that there are some things I do that she doesn't, yet anyway."

"What would those be?" I asked playfully.

I had my arms full of warm catgirl for a few moments as she demonstrated.

"Well," she said finally. "I will see you later. Love you, male-of-mine."

"Love you too. Watch Dusko."

She grinned at me. "Have to say good bye to Kit-sister first."

"That's never going to work."

"I could get lucky."

Before I could say anything else, Jaelle bounded away, she could run faster over a short distance and jump higher than anyone else I'd ever met. She leapt atop some nearby packing crates and then plunged down the other side.

A moment later Maauro emerged from the other side with Jaelle tucked under one arm, her tail swishing in frustration.

I could not help but laugh, and smothered it as best I could. Maauro gently put her down. Jaelle spoke to her briefly, then exchanged hugs with the android and walked off toward Dusko and the waiting ship.

Maauro came over.

"Not even close?" I asked.

"Please Wrik, in addition to the noise generated by her running, leaping and breathing; she was in the air for a full .3234 seconds. I was able to catch her easily, minimize the impact to avoid any injury to her and secure her under my arm. It did take some effort not to pull her tail in revenge however."

"Easy on the tail," I said, "that's sensitive and mildly kinky in her culture."

"And you know this why?" she said as we started walking toward our own ship.

"You're too young. Come back in a few years."

"I am over 50,000 years old."

"The five in artifact space don't count and all but the first seven and last four years were spent contemplating your navel on an asteroid."

"Wrik, I do not have a navel, even now, and certainly not then."

"I think you still have growing up to do."

"I will not increase in size. In fact I am 40% smaller than I was when first activated."

I stopped. "What?"

"I was blown up in the original asteroid attack. Two legs and an arm severed off. I reconstituted myself from spare material I contained inside my chassis."

"How come you didn't do that when your arm was blown off on Kandalor?"

"I had used up most of my spare material in the initial repairs. I have enough for minor impacts but not for a full arm." She flexed the arm she'd salvaged from the Infester machine found at the bottom of the Tar

Sea on Kandalor. "This has served well with the improvements I have made in it. In raw strength, it's nearly equal to my right arm, but it will never have the feedback sensitivity or malleability of my original equipment."

"No chance of making more of your chassis material?"

"I continue to work toward it but the ceramo-alloy of my true body was the supreme accomplishment of my Creators. I have not as yet come close to the flexibility and strength of my OEM. I must avoid major material loss until I do. "

"That would be good. I think I'll follow the same plan."

"As fragile as you are, you should avoid even minor material loss."

"True enough."

"In fact if I were as fragile as you, I would seldom go outside."

"Thanks, Maauro. I got it."

We spent the next day scrambling about our tasks, readying for the mission. Candace called me to the spaceport in the afternoon. I thought an in-person meeting with the spymaster unnecessary, but she insisted. Maauro declined to come along. "If she has some ulterior motive in approaching you," she reasoned, "better to obtain the intelligence quickly. I suspect however that she is still trying to get a sense of you."

"A sense of me? What for?"

"You are the closest of our unit to her, a male of the same species. Jaelle is a Nekoan and daughter of a Guild agent, Dusko is a professional liar, and I am the most mysterious to her. If she hopes to gain a greater insight and control of us, it will be through you. We should encourage this information pipeline. It will bring in more than it drains out I think."

So I ventured out alone to the military section of the spaceport, albeit in a little-used corner for storage and salvage. The guards expected me and after a cursory review of my ID, let me in, directing me to Bay 17.

That bay held a Confed scoutship, towering a hundred meters into the sky and painted a dark grey with a red flash insignia on the tail. The ground around the ship was puddled from the recent rainstorm. Clouds scudded behind the needle shape of the four-being ship. It was an older model, a *Constellation* but well maintained. Under her hull number was the name, *Pisces*.

"Congratulations," Candace said from behind me. "Lost Planet Expeditions is now the proud owners of the *CSS Pisces*, surplused yesterday and sold to you for 10,000 credits."

"Which I assume you will add to the money you are paying us," I said automatically, "and that there is a warranty."

"You're kind of tight with the credits aren't you?"

"Habits of an uncertain lifetime," I replied. A sudden gust of wet, cool wind made me seal my jacket. "Poverty marks you for life."

"Yes," she said, a rare note of sympathy in her voice. "I suppose it does."

"That sale of course allows you to say should we be caught or killed—"

"That we knew nothing about it and you were a bunch of scammers up to something with a surplus ship and some fake uniforms. Did you expect something else?"

"I try to keep my expectations of the universe modest. It limits my disappointments."

"So can you fly her?" Candace asked.

I didn't turn but merely continued leaning on a railing looking up at the ship. "Flight characteristics are similar to *Stardust's*, just a lot more discretionary power. Room for fifteen in a pinch, that's nice. Maauro and I have been working on a simulator she set up right after she picked the model."

"She picked the model," Candace came up and joined me against the railing. "How much does she run you?"

"Divide and conquer, Candace? You wanted to see me on my own. What's next: bribes, threats, and appeals to my loyalty to the Confederacy? I'd expect more out of a granddaughter of Avery Deveraux."

"No offense," she said. "It's an honest question. I see three living beings, yet clearly the AI is in charge."

"If it pleases you to think of it that way."

"Is there another way to view it?"

"Maauro is smarter than I am, certainly. She's already survived over 50,000 years despite a lot of people's efforts to make sure she didn't. So in some things she leads. But she doesn't force anyone to follow her, not even Dusko anymore. For other things, well, I've taken her by the hand on quite a few."

"Taken *her* by the hand?" Candace's eyebrow's rose. "That's a lot of anthropomorphizing going on there. It's a machine, an incredibly complicated, undoubtedly dangerous machine."

I looked up at the clouds. "I don't really understand what Maauro is, but she's much more than a machine or even an AI. Somehow, somewhere, somewhen, the divine spark started racing over her circuits. Maybe it did for others of her kind. Maybe not, or why haven't we run into more like her?"

Candace shrugged. "Maybe they fled this area of space? Maybe they slaughtered their masters and don't want to serve any others? You can't know about her."

"No I can't," I said. "No more than I can know about you, maybe even less as you're so adept at deceptions. In the end, the one thing I know about Maauro is that she is the first true friend I found in my life as Wrik Trigardt."

"So sure?" she murmured as if surprised.

"I'll bet my life, which I still have only because of her: any day, any place, on any odds you care to wager."

"I hope for all your sakes I never have to take you up on that offer," she said.

"The offer stands as long I do," I said straightening. "Now if you'll excuse me I'd like to spend some time on the ship. Maauro wants to pick out some new curtains."

Candace laughed. "Ok, Wrik. You and your little android go play house."

CHAPTER SEVEN

WE ROSE FROM STAR CENTRAL WITH THE SUN. OUR ships launched simultaneously but from different locations. I took *Starfire* up from our launch pad near the office, accompanied by Dusko and Jaelle. Maauro lifted off in the *Pisces*, although what the launch commander of the military base thought of an apparent teenager taking off in a scoutship, I had no idea. Still, that had been Candace's problem and she'd evidently handled it as Maauro joined us in orbit. We synced up with boarding tubes and the grapples *Pisces* came equipped with.

From there, we refueled with a military tanker Candace arranged for, then shaped a course for the accelerator, where she'd also arranged a free transit. The accelerator would boost us to .75C without the need to burn fuel.

We quickly settled down to the regularity of shipboard life. Dusko had his hydroponic gardens both on *Starfire* and on *Pisces*. Jaelle, ever mindful of the possibilities of trade, took up her jewel crafting. For me, I had started a model of Fenaday's famous starship, the *Sidhe*. Finding out that we were "being run" by the daughter of Avery Deveraux, the Confederacy's wartime spymaster had piqued my interest in the grim Irishman who searched the stars for his lost wife, and in Shasti Rainhell, the genetically engineered warrior who'd been his lover and later commanded the *Sidhe*. The model was nearly a meter long. With Maauro's help, I'd progressed well. She made whatever parts or paints I needed inside her body and even created a tiny reactor to power the model's lights, which was the only actual construction that I left for her. It was, after all, a reactor. Jaelle admired the work, even as she wrinkled her delicate nose at the solvents and cements I used.

We came upon the accelerator on the third day out and decoupled the ships to pass though its rings. The maw of the giant accelerator was large enough for a battleship, but it wasn't safe to fly our ships through while connected. Once the massive accelerator spat us out, we reconnected for the trip to the outer solar system where the hyperdrive, unencumbered by the gravity well of the star, would function. When next we separated, it would be for the star jump and we would proceed on our differing missions.

Jaelle and I spent all our time together, as if to make up for the impending separation. Maauro discretely made herself scarce. Dusko, ever solitary, we saw only occasionally.

On the last night before jump, we lay on Jaelle's custom-made bed, a luxury we'd had installed for us and vastly more comfortable than a bunk. Jaelle lay on her stomach, face to one side as I kneaded the long, strong muscles of her back, feeling the inhumanly flexible spine below them. She purred, an affectation she'd picked up after I told her about Terran cats. I looked down at her, the small, sharp, alien features that suggested a woman's face, but really didn't look that much like one. "Jaelle?"

"Yes," she said, a drowsy tone in her voice.

"When we get back, let's have a proper consortship ceremony and register it."

She rolled over. "Truly? This will make you happy as well?"

"I won't pretend that your having children with someone else won't take some getting used to, or that at times it won't be hard being from two different species, but I do love you. I know that you won't be happy without children of your own, so this is how that has to be. I want the things that are best for you."

She gazed up at me with big golden eyes. "You know that if you ever wish the same, I will accept it too."

"I won't, but thanks. No, from my side all you'll have to live with is Maauro. It will be a complicated road for us, but we will travel it together."

She laughed and patted my chest. I could feel the sheathed claws in them. "Yes, you, me, Kit-sister and actual kits, a complicated orbit to be sure, even if you continue to foreswear human females, something I do not expect—"

"Jaelle."

"No matter," she shrugged. "I do not care about occasional females unless you should want a child with one. There I must be consulted."

"As I said, it's not going to come up."

"And Kit-sister, do you think she will always travel this road with us?"

I nodded "I'm pretty sure, at least as far as I can see the future. You're alright with that?"

"I care for Maauro," she said, "but not as you do. Sometimes I am jealous of your closeness with her, and do not try to reassure me that she is merely a machine."

"I'd never say that about her in any event. She's not just a machine, but as for gender, she assumed that only after I found her. Her original appearance was humanoid, but frighteningly corpse-like."

"Maauro," Jaelle said archly, "is thoroughly and completely female now and I suspect always was."

I laughed. "Maybe so."

Jaelle laughed too. "Well, we will not resolve every issue at the start of our journey. It is enough that we will travel together and that you want this too."

Our lips came together, followed by our bodies.

Afterwards, I turned to her. "So when do we tell people?"

"That depends a little on how you think Maauro will take the news?"

"Huh? She'll be happy for us, of course."

"You sure?"

"Yes," I said slowly, "as sure as I am about anything."

She shifted, rolling up on one shoulder to look at me. "You really feel you know her well enough to say?" There was no edge to her voice; the question seemed an honest one.

"Yes. But even after all we have been through, you still have doubts."

Jaelle considered. "Yes, small ones, but still doubts. I'm fond of her, as you know, but I can't forget the times when her M-7 programming ruled her and she dragged us all into hell. Even you, Wrik, who she loves as much as her synthetic little heart is capable of, how much did she miss you by when she reverted to being M-7 aboard the Infester Artifact?"

"But she did miss," I replied, "and she never does. In the end, Maauro was the stronger personality and it was our friendship that made the difference."

"Then M-7 was gone and we have Kit-sister, a good trade no doubt. I certainly don't miss M-7. Maybe it's just hard for me to believe it's entirely gone and she can't turn on us again."

I fought back a surge of bitter memory. Being born into the universe, instead of made, was no guarantee against betrayal and failure. I was living proof of that myself. I pushed the thoughts back into their locked box.

"But back to your question," Jaelle said, a drowsy note creeping into her voice. "I want to hold off until we are safely back on Star Central. That is assuming we can keep this a secret from Kit-sister. She is linked to us mentally."

"It's not telepathy. Maauro said that she only hears us when we push thoughts at her. It's like speaking but without a voice. That's one reason it's so fatiguing and uses so much energy when we practice."

"No wonder we're both so hungry lately. Anyway, I'll be very cross if she learns of this and ruins the surprise."

I put a hand on my bare chest. "Trust me, if there is anything I can do, it's keep secrets."

"Good, then when we get back, we'll take Maauro, Dusko—"
Dusko?"

"He's part of the Lost Planet Expeditions now for all that he started as our prisoner, part of our team. He's content to leave the past—"

"When he was trying to kill us!"

"And we were trying to kill him, too. And we came closer. Besides, didn't Maauro ask you to put all the past in the past?"

"He doesn't think of us as friends."

He's Dua-Denlenn. The word means something else to him but we are probably the closest things he has to such. Friendship is a learned response for his kind."

I sighed. It seemed I was alone in being a prisoner of the past and now both Maauro and Jaelle had chided me for it. "OK so we take Maauro and Dusko…"

"And Bizel, Rana and Latome from my trading company, to a fancy dinner at the best restaurant in Star Central, maybe the Terra Nova or the Ether?"

"Yikes. You're not only planning on surviving, you're planning on hitting it big."

"You negotiated quite a good deal with Candace, and I know you, you will find a way to extract more. Then there will be my own little trading efforts with the Guild on Cimer. It would look bad if I didn't make us some money there."

I kissed her on the forehead. "Sometimes, darling, you are too practical."

"I just want our consort party to be special."

"Yes. Anything you want. Anything. I want you to be happy,"

She pressed her cheek against my neck. The delicate down of pale fur tickled some. "Then fall asleep with me," she said slowly, "now, and on all the nights of the future."

"That's the best deal I've been offered in a long time," I said, my own eyes feeling heavy as a gentle lassitude gripped me. It was only mildly shaken by the recollection that I had said nearly the same words to Maauro after our first adventure on the asteroid, when she'd offered to join forces, so we could protect each other and remain free. But the recollection was a pleasant one and I continued my drift to sleep, thinking that all of time and space could slow as far as I was concerned and we could happily remain in this moment forever.

I woke early, as I always did when something special was in the offing. Jaelle rose and stretched in ways that would have crippled me. We showered and made our way to the galley, me toting a duffle bag as I was bound for *Pisces* after breakfast. Maauro and Dusko were already there. Maauro must have been monitoring our cabin door, as she slid hot coffee and chai in front of us, immediately followed by fluffy eggs and all manner of breakfast goodies.

We reviewed the plans for the last time, calling each other by our codenames and feeling a little like children sneaking off on an adventure, or at least, Jaelle and I did. Dusko had a sour look as if we actually were misbehaving kids. Maauro's true thoughts were hidden behind her calm, gentle face.

"I'm leaving you the dishes," I said to Dusko as we rose. To my surprise, the Dua-Denlenn barked a short laugh. Maauro reached down and lifted my heavy duffle as if it was a napkin.

"My gear is aboard," she said. "It's time to go."

CHAPTER SEVEN

We walked down to the airlock together. Jaelle stepped forward and put her mouth to my ear, whispering. "Remember all we said to each other."

"I will," I promised and kissed her.

She turned to Maauro and embraced the smaller android. "No pouncing today, Kit-sister. You take care of yourself and be sure to return my male with all parts intact."

Maauro gazed up at her. "I will protect Wrik with my existence. His safety exceeds all other mission parameters."

"Good," Jaelle kissed her on the cheek and stepped back.

Dusko looked us over. "Don't get killed. It would annoy me."

This time it was I who snorted a laugh. "Watch out for Jaelle and stay out of the ship's safe."

We turned and walked onto *Pisces*. At the last second, I turned back for a look at Jaelle. She smiled and winked at me as the door closed. Maauro waited for me at the other side of the airlock, sealing the door after I entered.

"Well," I said. "It's just you and me again."

"I will miss the others," she replied, "but I am always happy to be with you."

I put an arm around her shoulders. "Let's get up to the bridge. Time to kick free and head for the jump point."

I lined the *Pisces* up on the entrance to the warp-point. Maauro, more precise than any supercomputer in the Confederacy, handled the course set-up. With her calculations, we would shave weeks off the real-time absence from the universe that a starship normally experienced. In an additional advantage, we'd arrive weeks before any enemy would expect our arrival. But there was a certain intuition in approaching a warp-point: a touch, a sense for choosing the exact moment to initiate the jump. In that sense, star travel remained as much an art as a science and Maauro left those brushstrokes to me.

The warp-point looked like every other section of space, except on our instruments, which showed the fracture lines in space-time and the bending caused by the singularity in our stardrive. I braced myself. Time didn't pass for biological entities in stardrive. Everything had to be set at the entry and exit point; otherwise it was like riding on a bullet. The transition to hyperdrive was rarely pleasant, though by the time you really experienced it, you were out the other side and back in space-time.

I looked at Maauro. "Well, here we go."

"See you on the other side," she replied.

I engaged the stardrive.

Discontinuity, dreams, discordant blasts of light, sound and smell.

Our entry into hyperspace is excellent. While I am the more precise, somehow Wrik, with his instincts about space-time and spacecraft, remains my superior in this. It should not be, but is.

Time is distorted in hyperspace. Unlike Wrik, I am aware. But it feels as though it takes hours to turn my eyes to look at my friend. He is motionless, his biological system in a form of suspended animation, not imposed by science, but by the very nature of the universe we now travel in. His kind is not meant to be here. In a very real sense he does not exist here, being merely a potential Wrik who will again act and think upon emergence. Though I can operate here, my systems do suffer disorientation: colors are off. I do not experience smell as Wrik does, but readings for certain things are clearly incorrect.

I continue to study my friend. His eyes are open but unaware. His expression is almost eager, excited. Wrik is at his happiest in space, at the controls of a ship. I know this is where he feels he contributes the most to our group, another reason I leave almost all ship functions to him wherever possible. It is pleasant to study his face for the time of the trip, though even that is wrong, as there is no time where we are. Yet I am conscious from second to second, though my chronometers and my elapsed experience do not and will not tally, in one of the great mysteries of hyperspace. I sit, thinking idle thoughts and log the experience.

"Emergence," the ship's computer, which was now merely an extension of Maauro and spoke in her voice, sounded in my ear. I groaned. This was a particularly foul emergence and my stomach threatened to rebel.

"Here," Maauro said. She had the vial of restorative fluid and anti-nauseants. I gratefully gulped them down while wondering how she managed to get them so quickly. I scanned my instruments. "Nothing on short-scan. Good, I'd hate to hit even some dust at this percent of light speed."

"That would void even *my* warranty," Maauro agreed.

I grinned at her and she returned it.

"On course insystem," I added. "This feels a little odd. Usually I do airbraking on a gas giant to slow down for entry to the inner worlds of a system. Today, it's our destination." I finished the restorative. "I hope Jaelle has an easier emergence."

"They should. Their angle of entry puts them days behind us, and should stress their biology less."

I nodded. "Time to announce our presence?"

"Yes."

I took a deep breath then keyed the mike. The message would outpace our speed by a day.

CHAPTER SEVEN

"This is Lt. Jedaya Fels, *CSS Pisces* to Tir-a-Mar Space Control, Planet Cimer, Cimbar System. We have entered your systems and will be assuming standard orbit over your floating city after air-braking. Please prepare to receive standard star mail and Confed diplomatic correspondence. We will be conducting inspections of habitations of all oxygen-breathing species on Cimer and accounting for all Confed personnel aboard. Please make ready to receive a pinnace from our ship. Acknowledge upon receipt."

I kicked on the ship's thrusters, determined to lose some speed to lessen the strain of air-braking on the gas giant's atmosphere. "Well the fat's in the fire now."

"And that is a bad thing, I gather."

I grinned. "Yeah, I guess so. I don't know much about cooking."

Pisces sped into the system. A terse acknowledgement came back from Tir-a-Mar, along with approach coordinates. Maauro checked these thoroughly. It wouldn't do to brake at too severe an angle and disappear into the cobalt-blue skies of Cimer. Later, a more civil response came as the authorities sorted themselves out in reaction to our unexpected arrival.

We used Maauro's simulated crewmen, mere projections in the computer, to handle most of the routine communications. As commander, I was invited to a reception aboard the floating city.

Five hours later, we completed airbraking in the outer edge of Cimer's atmosphere, drawing a hellish blaze across their sky as if we were some harbinger of doom. Perhaps we were.

Maauro prepared her escape pod for her separate descent. I pre-flighted the pinnace, then returned to my cabin to change into uniform. Twenty minutes later, I grimaced in the mirror at the Confed dress uniform I now wore. The jacket was an elegant dark-blue over medium-blue pants with a gold stripe. The crossed, shooting stars of the Confed navy decorated one raised collar, the bar and comet of a Senior Lieutenant the other. Maauro had felt I was too young to pass for a Lieutenant Commander in a small scoutship in a peacetime navy. The collar chafed, but perhaps it was simply being back in uniform that ailed me. The associations were unpleasant.

"You look very handsome, Wrik."

I looked at Maauro with a surprised laugh. "So androids feel the same way about a man in uniform that human females do?"

She cocked her head at me in the characteristic way she had when I'd said something puzzling. I wondered if she was aware of it, or if it was a signal to me. A smile stole over her face. "Yes, we do. I will have to beat all the M1s through M6s away from you."

"Android humor," I said ruefully. "What next?"

But she had seen something in my face. Maauro walked over and put a hand on my shoulder. It was warm and light. Always it was in the little things that Maauro amazed me.

"No more dwelling in the past," she said, giving me the slightest shake with a hand capable of shearing armor. "Whatever you once were, you are now Wrik Trigardt and you have proved yourself many times."

I put my hand over hers and had to resist an urge to kiss her. My feelings for Maauro were getting more complicated and heading in directions that I hadn't imagined before. Sometimes I could no longer clearly describe them to myself. It caused an unsettling mix of guilt and confusion.

I realized that I was staring at her and felt myself blushing like a fool. "Well not only Wrik Trigardt. Now I am Lt Jedaya Fels, CSS *Pisces*."

"And I," Maauro snapped off a perfect salute, "am your trusty crew of three. I've programmed the ship's AI with three additional artificial personalities, including visual images, that will respond to any messages with military precision and reticence.

"None of them look like me, of course. It's best to assume that we have some enemies down there and they may recognize us. I am especially distinct."

"Whereas I am merely one of billions of brown-haired humans undistinguished for beauty or ugliness," I returned.

"Just so," she agreed.

"Pity that malleability skill you showed when we first met is gone. It would be useful if you could change appearance."

"Perhaps. I can still alter many details of my Maauro matrix; my outer casing was optimized for that. I have slowly and carefully made minute adjustments to look a little older, but an overall change, such as when I first switched to Maauro-appearance, is very disruptive, even if it is quick. I believe that fast change I made when we first met may have been responsible for my malfunctions on the asteroid and on Kandalor. That ability was new to my model and had not been used much. Even if I could do so, I would be loath to try any permanent change again without a Creator tech team in support. My M-7 matrix is gone. If I disrupt my Maauro appearance there is no telling what could follow."

I sighed. "Might was well wish for a battleship to back us up while we are wishing."

Again came the smile. "Might as well."

"Time to go?"

"Yes, I will walk with you to the pinnace."

I picked up my duffel and we walked through the scoutship's narrow central corridor to the compact bay that held the pinnace, a slender atmospheric craft with folding wings that filled the bay amidships near the AG drive/reactor core. It was hard to believe a crew of four could get into it, but it and the escape pod were all the auxiliaries we had.

I stowed my gear and did my customary preflight. Maauro had attended to such details, but I'd have no use for a pilot who wouldn't inspect his own ship before launching. I dogged the hatch, slipped into the pilot's chair, and looked at Maauro through the canopy. She smiled and waved. I waited. She looked at me.

"Wrik," her voice came over the speaker. "Go ahead. I promise not to die from explosive decompression."

"Right," I said, swatting myself on the head. I triggered the control that sucked the oxygen out of the bay, and opened the doors. Maauro stood there and gave me a thumbs-up. The pinnace slowly dropped away from the scoutship. I looked up at the small, gentle face that watched me go and wished I wasn't leaving. The bay doors closed and I lined up for entry.

The pinnace quickly heated from reentry and it bucked as I hit thicker atmosphere, glad for all the hours I'd spent in the simulators. Cimer was a pilot's nightmare. It was closer to the main sequence star of Cimbar than was Sol's Neptune, which it otherwise resembled, so there was far more ambient light, but the extra energy also stirred Cimer's atmosphere, fueling tremendous storms. As I dove into the clouds, the light quickly faded to twilight.

Meanwhile, the drag of gravity continued to build. The pinnace had no AG field, although the pilot's seat was designed to be used in high-G, with all controls reachable from fully supported positions. The god-awful flying conditions for my small craft kept my mind off the high-G.

I concentrated on the controls on my screen, keeping the cross-hairs centered. The ship's automatics did the rest, but I was too much of a fighter pilot to trust entirely to automatics. Down I went through canyons of blue clouds, past flashes of lightning of mind-boggling strength.

A speck appeared on my instruments and shortly later I had it on visual. The Ribisan floating city was a sight for sore and amazed eyes. It sat on a boundary layer, a mass of dark-green metal, dozens of kilometers in length and width, larger than any space station or ship. Only the Infester Artifact, a planetoid-sized ark made by Maauro's ancient enemies exceeded the city in size. And this was far from the largest of such installations the Ribisans could build. This was, after all, a frontier world. The station's dark-green metal was lit by a riot of colors. I was grateful for the contrast with the grim and violent world around it.

"This is Lt Jedaya Fels, *CSS Pisces* on final approach."

"This is Tir-a-Mar landing control. Welcome, Lieutenant. We have you on instruments. Prepare for ALS landing."

"ALS landing, aye." Another pilot might have relaxed, leaving the automatic landing system to bring them in, but we had enemies and maybe some were on the floating city. I kept my hands poised over the instruments, but there was no need. Giant doors opened on a landing field. Light spilled out as my pinnace lowered itself into the bay within. The oppressive embrace of the planet eased as I entered the AG field inside of the vast floating city. I sighed in relief as the pinnace settled on its landing jacks inside the hanger.

Outside, Ribisans moved easily in the poisonous murk of Cimer's atmosphere. The green-tinged light was low by Confed standards, but they saw by other organs. I switched to night-vision to get a look at them. Even that was difficult. Immobile in armored suits in 02 environments, here they darted about the hanger, skittering on their multiple legs, trunked to a central core. They reminded me of a bizarre cross of a squid and a child's top. These wore vests and belts festooned with tools. The heads were the strangest of all, appearing like large clusters of grapes. In the low-light scan, the grapes glowed with some form of bioluminescence.

They moved about my ship, chocking the landing gear and hooking up power cables so I could shut down my reactor. Overhead the great doors began to shut. The Ribisans scattered to my right, heading for large airlock doors that presumably led to their section of the city.

Bright white light replaced the dim green. Blowers swirled out the native atmosphere and my instruments showed a standard oxygen-nitrogen mix replacing it. The hanger went from being a fantastic stage for the bizarre, to Confed gray and blue. Other small ships dotted the deck, a mix of standard Confed and Ribisan models.

At the far end of the hanger a door slid back and a variety of Confed humanoids marched in, the welcoming committee.

"Maauro!" I sent mentally, suddenly feeling the need for contact with my deadly companion.

"I'm with you," her mental voice sounded in my mind: calm, quiet and reassuring. "I will only speak when necessary so as to not divide your concentration, but we are always connected."

"Yeah, good," I said, trying to keep relief out of my voice. Silly, she knew how scared I was from monitoring the adrenalin levels in my body. I rose and slipped on my cap, squared my shoulders and got ready to make contact.

CHAPTER EIGHT

I OPENED THE SIDE HATCH AND SLIPPED THROUGH THE small opening down to the metal deck. The welcoming committee moved forward en masse. I studied them as they approached. Candace's briefing material had covered many of the senior staff, but it wasn't recent information so I was uncertain of who was greeting me. The five were a common mix of Confederate species. A stocky human woman led them. Her steel-gray hair matched her air of practical efficiency. Behind her followed a male Dua-Denlenn, a Morok, a human male and a hulking Okaran in a police uniform. The Ursinoid Okaran was far smaller than Dusko's old bodyguard, Truff, so I guessed it was female.

"Welcome to Tir-a-Mar, Lieutenant Fels," said the woman. "I'm Dorothea Fenster, assistant city administrator." She turned to her staff, pointing at the Morok: "Arzat Akeel, Public Relations, Jon McCaffer, and Ruskan." She didn't introduce the guard, whose brown, animal-like eyes gazed into the middle distance with no sign of interest in me.

"Thank you," I returned crisply. "My orders." I handed her a printout in an ornate binder. A formality, as all this had been handled via download long before, but the ceremony was as old as spacing.

"We are happy to have your visit," Fenster said, "but as I informed you before, most of the personnel on that list you sent are no longer here. By and large, they moved on to other projects and locations."

"Odd that none of those involved returning to their points of origin or communicating in any verifiable fashion with family and friends they left behind," I stated. "My orders require me to make a full investigation of these personnel matters. I'll also need to review and renew the habitation certificate for Tir-a-Mar for oxygen-breathers—"

"Ah," said the Dua-Denlenn, Akeel. "The station has been certified by the Ribisan authorities—"

"All stations supporting Confed life must be subject to annual review by Confed authorities if they support member species other than the original builders. I'm looking at four Confed species right here. The Ribisans built this place and their membership in the Confederacy is only associate level. They do not have the authority to certify the habitability of space stations used by full members."

"This is a Ribisan floating city, not a space station," the Morok administrator objected.

"Negative. It's not built on a planetary surface. Per Confed law this is a station in low orbit of a gas giant's core."

"Lieutenant, I think you are exceeding your authority," Fenster said, raising an eyebrow. "We may have to take this up with your superiors."

CHAPTER EIGHT

"I can do that for you. There's a Confed flotilla with a heavy cruiser, under a Commodore due to transit through a nearby warp-point four galactic-adjusted weeks from now. I can have the Commodore reroute the fleet and conduct his exercises here. Of course, you'll be under a suspension and trade moratorium until I return. It should only be a few months—"

"Perhaps, we are all being hasty," she said, raising her hands. "Really, you need to talk to the chief city administrator. We are also being totally remiss in our hospitality by conducting business on a hanger deck like Free Traders. Our staff will secure your luggage and bring it to your hotel."

After searching it thoroughly, I thought. A sense of amusement ghosted through my consciousness, I felt as if Maauro was laughing somewhere. The thought that she was with me, even as only a silent presence, cheered me.

"Please follow us," Fenster said. "We'll take you to the main office for refreshments and a meeting. I imagine that even if it's only to a floating city, you're relieved to be out of your small ship."

I allowed a tight smile. "Well, I guess about now I know every nook and cranny of *Pisces*, so yes, getting into some new and open space is a relief."

Fenster smiled in a fashion that showed me why she had been successful at running for office. "Please follow me."

I noticed the Okaran Guard fell in behind us as we moved. Force of habit, or warning that I was on their turf? I wished Maauro was already down on the station.

My escorts took me to a railcar, which whisked us off to the administrative section of Cimer. As we rolled on, I saw the floating city was just that. We passed neighborhoods, shops, and factories in the human section. Confed citizens of various species wandered about – all oxygen breathers. I knew that for all the sections I could see, it represented only about fifteen percent of the structure. Beyond the well-lit halls and walls of Cimer's O2 section, the Ribisans lived their lives, with religions, politics, entertainments and even a biology that was barely understood.

"What's the primary industry here?" I asked of my hosts, playing the part of a not-too-interested officer saddled with an unwelcome administrative task.

"As is usually the case with Ribisan trade outposts," Akeel the Morok said, with an air of you-should-know-this, "exotic chemicals and metals, but we have a brisk trade in intellectual property."

"Such as?"

"Well they are the premier chemical and physical engineers in high gravity and high pressure. We, of course, have the advantage in low pressure and oxygen work."

I frowned. "I seem to recall that this station was set up for biogenetic research from my briefing materials."

"Oh that," Fenster laughed dismissively. "Yes it was, still is in a small way. We brought in some biologists and genetic engineers. It never really amounted to much. Ribisan biology is too different."

"Still," I said. "I should check into that. A Dr. Malich was with that team. He never returned to his homeworld. His family was particularly concerned about his disappearance."

"I hear most of them continued into Ribisan space or moved on to other company business," Fenster added with an almost elaborate lack of concern.

We pulled up into a carpeted lobby with a scattering of abstract statuary and a beautiful fountain. My escorts conducted me past desks and staffers to a large office with glass walls and potted plants. On the other side was a broad conference table filled with administrators, scientists and probably some lawyers.

A tall, lean, older, man rose. "Greeting, Lieutenant. Welcome to Tri-a-mar. I'm chief city administrator, Arn Mysol."

"Greetings, Mr. Mysol. I have already tendered my credentials to your staff."

"Yes. I hope your descent wasn't too difficult."

"No, but I certainly won't be shuttling up to the ship. I packed a few extra uniforms."

A perfunctory chuckle sounded around the table.

"Then you plan an extended stay?" Mysol asked. His face indicated only mild interest.

"My mission here is twofold. My orders are to check into the status of certain Confed citizens who have not been accounted for in over one solar year and to update the Confed habitability certificate for this floating city which is five years out of date."

"Please, Lieutenant," Mysol said, "a habitability certificate? Does anyone actually pay attention to those? I mean—"

"They are as much to make sure that no one is setting up a pocket tyranny as to ensure habitability," I interrupted. "My charge is to ensure the safety of Confed citizens on the frontier. It may sound old-fashioned, but I take my duty seriously. I have a lot of inspecting to do. If there's nothing to find, then I will be out of your hair sooner. I do want to interview all section heads and then, frankly, I am going to wander about unescorted and unsupervised to talk to the being in the street. I'll know if I am being watched or interfered with. As to the missing staff, well, I will want to talk to anyone who knew them or the other personnel in their disciplines."

"No need for melodrama. We have no interest in obstructing Confed officers. However we also have no interest in being subject to overzealous inspections by a junior officer. Our staff counsel will want to be consulted on your activities. I do advise you to be quite careful in remaining within your regulations," Mysol said, his face calm and even. "If you do, you'll find my staff more than accommodating to your needs.

"As for the personnel you are asking about, only a few are still here. Likely, most of these missing staffers went on to other business opportunities. Space is vast."

"Leaving no word and making no further contacts?" I said.

"We are far out on the frontier of the Confederacy. Your couriers and scoutships are the fastest means of communication out here. When was the last time you put it at your original command base?"

I grimaced. "The time I got these crappy orders. I suspect some politicos on Malich's homeworld kicked up a fuss and HQ decided to mollify them by sending *Pisces* here. However, orders are orders and if I'm going to get this inspection done..."

"We will give you all the assistance you are legally entitled to," Mysol replied.

I nodded stiffly. "It appears we do understand each other."

"I'll set up a series of meetings. It's 1800 hours local time. Could they wait till planetary morning?"

I yawned. "Yes. The flight down was quite taxing. If you could arrange for the original files and data I requested to be sent to my accommodations, I'll get some work done before hitting the rack."

"Oh, I was going to arrange for a few of our executives to take you to a late dinner," Mysol said.

"Perhaps we could save that for later. I'm beat and I have a huge amount of reading to do. I must update my ship reports as well."

Did I see a flicker of relief across Mysol's face? Briefly, I wondered if I should reconsider, but decided the people that they'd throw at me would either be too well coached, or would know nothing. Their purpose would be to run out my clock. I also knew that during my first night down here their ad hoc security arrangements would be easiest to elude. By tomorrow morning, Maauro would be down and I would feel better about everything.

I was escorted to a nearby hotel, the Star and Comet, and installed in a suite. I suspected some of the hotel staff were security, assigned to watch me. But no one interfered when I made some unexpected forays out of my suite, talking to a few random citizens and grabbing some local food. Any attempt to contain me would clearly backfire, so my job was to push the envelope as far as I could, without making killing me a preferable course of action. However bold or connected my enemies were, there was still a Confed warship hanging in their sky. More formidable for what it represented than for its own powers.

I discovered all the hidden cameras in the suite using the small robot that Maauro had made for me. The spider-like machine had ridden down in my flight bag and ran about the room, webbing everything under its own control. I was as secure as possible.

"Maauro," I sent, fighting fatigue. "So far so good. Should I try and get out and find out anything else?"

"No," her voice came back as a whisper with static making my head hurt. "We have pushed far enough for tonight. Have the spider prepare option B-2 in case we need it. Rest. I will be down in the morning. We will operate together thereafter. Sleep well, Wrik. I shall see you soon."

I open the window and the palm-size robospider scuttled out it and down the sheer side of the building with no apparent difficulty. It had been programmed by Maauro to find something near the hotel that it could rig to cause an explosion with a small capsule of HE that it carried. I hoped I wouldn't need it, but I had to be free of observation to get Maauro inside Tir-a-Mar.

CHAPTER NINE

I BOARD MY SMALL CAPSULE AND IT KICKS FREE OF THE PISCES. IN *moments I orient myself and begin to drop toward the massive gas giant below. Pisces will continue to orbit and I have programmed the ship's computer to simulate two additional crewmen while we are away. They will give terse replies to any incoming radio traffic.*

The immense blue world stretches below me like an infinite ocean, rolling and tumbling its layers of gasses and titanic towering clouds. Lightning bolts of fantastic power rip across the cloud gaps, promising a stormy descent. I am grateful for my armored body; at least Wrik has the comfort of a stout shuttle for his descent. I am using a modified escape pod. It will be disposed of after I land, disappearing into the vastness of the gas giant.

I right my capsule and dive. The nose quickly begins to glow as the pod hits atmosphere and slows for proper reentry. I am cybernetically and electronically cloaked, but can do nothing about visual detection. Still it is unlikely that anyone is looking up at me from beneath the titanic layers of cloud.

My pod begins to heat as it slows and sinks. I am 55 minutes from a stealth landing on the floating city below. All is unfolding per plan.

I access my internal link to Wrik; fortunately it is working despite interference from the gas giant's fierce electromagnetic field. I must tune it to full gain though I know it will cause Wrik discomfort.

"Ouch!" Wrik answers.

"Sorry, Wrik. The atmospheric interference is even worse than expected. What is your status?"

"I'm in the hotel with a very bored minder sitting down the hallway. I'm looking at reams of data that I do not understand. They've decided to drown me with cooperation in the form of meaningless operational data."

"Can you slip away when I land to let me in?"

"I have that little robot you gave me to fool their security sensors and I used it to arranged for a small explosion and fire near my quarters. Hopefully that will let me get away."

"Good. I will call you when I am closing in."

"I'll see if I can slip away. If not, well I have the little boom to fall back on."

I reach the outer layers of the cloud deck and continue braking and sinking from orbital speed. It's ironic to think of this as a stealthy approach when I create a thunder in the heavens and a glow across the sky.

CHAPTER NINE

My senses pick up metallic objects below, rising on an intercept course. I refine and enhance the images quickly, alarmed by this unexpected encounter. The images resolve into three ships. The types are unfamiliar. Ribisans do not use standard Confed equipment, but their shape tells me that they are aerospace fighters. I have been intercepted. I cannot fathom how this has occurred. Even Wrik did not know the path of my orbital entry. In the atmosphere of a gas giant it should have been impossible for scanners to find me. The odds of simple visual detection through the many layers of varying gas and clouds were similarly astronomical. Yet the interception is here and the fighters will destroy me in forty-five seconds. Already I detect their scanners trying to lock on my capsule. I disrupt these signals. They will have to get much closer for a firing lock.

The fighters go to emergency thrust, seeking to close the range. Unusual, it is as if they are wary or afraid of my small, unarmed craft. This time I cannot prevent a partial lock. Missiles jump from rails. The fighters follow, struggling in the turbulent sky. All I can do is fling cybernetic attacks at them, but their systems are well protected, far above Confed standard and I cannot penetrate them in any useful time frame. I turn to the missiles winding their way through the chlorine sky toward me. These are simpler and I cause them to explode or lose tracking, but not even my best efforts can turn one back on its fighter, or explode one still on the rail.

The fighters continue to close, seeking to use their direct-fire weapons. I employ electronic counter-measures but that will simply cause them to come closer before firing. I am totally on the defensive and the situation is hopeless. Escape and evasion are my only alternatives.

Decision made, I program the pod into a climbing turn as if I was seeking the safety of space. Then I seize a parasail, eject the hatch and fling myself into the freezing blue sky, curled into a ball. Gravity seizes me and I hurtle down. Yet for all my speed I have a vast distance to fall and much time to consider my course of action. I aim myself in the same trajectory the pod was traveling.

I roll on my back to see if my ruse has worked. I am rewarded by the sight of my pod disappearing into the clouds above, pursued by the fighters. I do not see the pod's destruction but it is assured. The immediate danger from the fighters is past. While I could do nothing more to conceal the pod's entry, my own fall should be undetectable unless I was to hit one of the fighters. Yet the odds of the fighters finding my pod in the first place were nearly as great, I must take nothing for granted.

I turn back to face the world below, spreading my arms to stabilize myself. I slow slightly but I am afraid to open the parasail for fear it will fail instantly. I thin the material of my arms and legs, spreading it out to generate more atmospheric resistance. This involves some delicate balancing, as my Infester-made replacement arm is not malleable like my original limbs. I slow and judge it safe to pop the parasail. It jerks me upright. I check the canopy of the thin but tough metallic-plastic. It appears to be holding. The painful intersection between high gravity and high atmospheric pressure is balanced for now.

I steer for the floating city's coordinates. I must be precise as I fly my parasail, since I have no way to climb. My only chance is to come down on the city. I need more speed. The parasail cannot last long in this crushing night.

I open a hollow place in my chest, using the material from my chest to form the elements of a crude jet engine. The plasma torch in my right hand migrates through the interior of my body until it is in the right position. The newly formed engine whines to life as its ramjet sucks in atmosphere and thrusts it out between my shoulder blades. I acquire forward speed and directional control. The power drain is significant. I am already operating at full military power but for once waste heat is useful to me. It is keeping my body from freezing.

A lightning bolt of immense power flashes through the sky. If it hit me, I would be vaporized.

I carefully open my internal link to Wrik, hoping the feedback will not cause him too much pain.

"Ouch, yes, I'm here. How is it going?"

"Not ideal. Listen and do not interrupt. My pod was intercepted by fighters and destroyed. I had to bail out. I am floating down in a powered parasail—"

"WHAT!"

"Quiet please. I will land on the floating city in 45 minutes and 33 seconds if my sail holds out. But I am exposed to the elements and using power at prodigious rates. You must evade attention and reach an airlock to bring me in. I will signal again just before landing. I will have little operational time after I arrive.

"By your location signal, you are in the admin section. I believe the safest place to try would be the central core in the industrial power section."

"I'll get there if I have to kill someone. I'll use the robot-spider to defeat surveillance scanners. How did they find you-?"

"No questions now, please, I must conserve my power."

"Yes, Maauro."

I sense fear in him. Fear for me, for what his life will be if I am lost. "I intend to arrive safely. But if chance is against me … it has been an honor and a privilege to share existence with you."

"And with you," he managed. "Concentrate on staying alive. I'll see you in 44 minutes."

My hands shook as I fought a rising dread. Maauro was in trouble. How she'd survived the initial attack seemed incredible to me, yet she was still on her way. But without the pod for her to shelter in, I have to get her inside quickly. I cracked the door to my suite. Down the hallway I saw the bored minder, leaning back in an uncomfortable, cheap chair. I moved to the window, looking at the drop below. No way I could manage that, not without equipment I didn't have.

I switched out of my uniform jacket and hat, throwing them in a carryall with my laser. I pulled out a light windbreaker that would cover my uniform shirt. Thin disguise, but it was more to avoid notice than for any other purpose.

I turned to the robot spider that Maauro sent with me. It sat on the bed in its own little valley. The weight of it hinted that it was made of very dense matter, possibly some of Maauro's own chassis material, which she was usually loath to risk.

"Unit," I address it. "Option A for the guard."

The spider blinks a green light at me. Order understood. I open the door and the spider scuttles down the hallway in a series of short rushes until it reaches the guard. I see a slight wisp of gas escape from the spider. After a few moments the guard stopped leaning the chair backwards and planted it on all four legs. He settled in a bit more comfortably, then the slow-acting sleep gas put him under and his hands fell at his sides.

I ran out, scooped up the heavy robospider and hit the elevator button, though it risked running into someone, since I was nine floors up. I resisted the urge to hammer uselessly at the button even though it seems to take an eternity for the damn thing to come.

Mercifully it arrives empty. I slipped in and hit lobby, then opened the pouch at my belt for the robospider to slip into it into it. "Activate B-2 as soon as we hit the lobby floor," I ordered.

The green light winks conspiratorially at me.

As the doors to the elevator slid open a dull boom shook the floor. The lobby was full of people, all of whom shot to their feet, alarmed by the detonation. Perfect. No one was paying any attention to me. People began to run toward the entrance as an alarm sounded.

I cut left; the hotel had several entrances and the left-most one opened directly on an escalator running into the nearby mall area. People ran past me into the building, but none addressed me or took any notice. In seconds I was out and down the escalator.

I pulled my com from its pocket. It would be too risky to call Maauro now, but the small screen displayed her path down toward Tir-a-Mar, beamed from her to the spider, to my comp. She was still on course for the central industrial area. Good. I cursed not being able to rent a robocab, but that meant using credits and would be like firing a flare saying, "*Here I am!*" So I jogged at my best pace, hopping slidewalks and annoying other pedestrians.

CHAPTER NINE

The journey began to assume that nightmare quality where you cannot seem to get to your destination no matter what you do. Life in space didn't make for a good runner and it had been weeks since I'd legged it any distance. My chest began to hurt and my legs began to burn. I pushed on.

The com began to point upward. I was below Maauro. An elevator shot me many levels into the industrial sector, to the top of Tir-a-Mar. But the signal was starting to flicker on comp. I cursed savagely and this time couldn't hold back from slamming the elevator button. If the doors opened on the way up I was going to shoot whoever slowed me.

Inspiration hit. I opened my pouch. "Unit," I demanded, "block out any signal on this elevator other than mine. Make it go express."

Green light from the little spider that could.

The doors opened and by the flickering com I went right. Maauro should be minutes above me.

The com locater signal went dead. I tore open the pouch. The robot winked a green light at me. It was still operating. Maybe that meant something about Maauro. I raced down the corridor to the only airlock in the area, according to my com.

"Okay little fellow," I said, pulling it out and placing it on the airlock control panel, "one last job to do for our lady."

I sail through the glowing blue sky, gradually sinking through the canyons of clouds to the layer where the floating city awaits me. I have no sense of scale. There is only the endless sky around and above, the gradually thickening layers below and my tiny parasail. I could be alone in all creation, outside of time and space. Indeed time itself seems to have lost any meaning for me.

Shock. My wandering thoughts are a sign of degradation as the temperatures and pressures of Cimer take their toll on me. I focus and concentrate on inspecting my sail. Just in time, it is showing severe signs of wear. I activate a small factory inside of me that can produce a durable plastic. I force this up into one of my finger flechette tubes and spray it on the underside, reinforcing the structure and closing small holes before then can become tears.

Alarm. The factory has failed, as my system redirects power to my Infester-made left arm, which is beginning to seize up. Additional power heats it back to mobility, but I am now in a race with entropy. I shut down all non-essential systems to scavenge power.

A dot appears below me. I focus on it with some difficulty. It is the floating city. I check my descent and correct my approach. I am coming in steeper then I would prefer, but the parasail is unreliable and I must get down as soon as I can.

"Wrik," I send, "I am 79 seconds from set down. Status?"

CHAPTER NINE

"Maauro, thank God! I'm in the industrial section at the airlock. I have installed the anti-surveillance intruder program you gave me so I can fool the surveillance systems. I am backing through an airlock. There should be environment suits inside."

"Good, I am homing in on your signal and will land as close as I can."

I detect cracking in the parasail and steepen my descent angle. I must get down but my chassis is beginning to freeze. If I land too hard, I may shatter.

I am over the city perimeter, heading between the pylons and towers, descending toward the industrial center and the power core. I will come down short of Wrik's location, yet I must reach him quickly. The city has been designed to be secure in the terrible gravity and pressure. Its hull is several meters thick, consisting of molecularly linked metal-ceramics. The airlocks are reinforced both mechanically and cybernetically, so I will not be able to force one in my remaining time. I must rely on Wrik to open it.

Disaster. The parasail evaporates. I plunge down over a hundred meters in the savage gravity. I direct all damage control and remaining power to my legs. It barely suffices. I land hard, shock rattling through my systems. Slowly, I stand as damage control does its best to preserve me, but I have drained most of my resources to survive the landing. I turn toward the central core. I have retained my fix on Wrik, but due to damage I cannot raise him. I stagger forward. It is cold and dark. Ammonia snow is sleeting down on me. I am freezing as I crawl across the surface of the drift station. System after system cascades into failure as my damage control programs try to save me, hoarding power to my most critical systems.

The maintenance hatch stands like an unreachable tower on my horizon and I know that I lack the power to open it, even if I last that long. The cold equations of entropy stare me in the face, yet I am too much of a living being to simply give up.

My left arm fails first. I struggle forward with it frozen in front of me. My mind seems to drift free of my present struggle. I am conscious of the terrible beauty of this place, with its titanic lightning, vast clouds of blue chlorine and mountains of methane ice. Still I wish I could see the stars again, but the vast roof of the sky seals them off from me.

I reach the airlock, but it is useless. I cannot extend the finger filaments to directly infiltrate the systems and the system's cyber-defenses are too powerful for me to penetrate in the time I have left. I raise my head to look up at the lock and it is my final movement. The cold penetrates and my systems go into final save mode. I retreat to the innermost redoubt of my body, connected to the outside by only a single subroutine, as it was for me in the 50 millennia I spent on the asteroid.

CHAPTER NINE

My self-awareness fades. Help me, Wrik. I'm dying.

The spider robot cut off the airlock controls using a barrier loop program. With luck it would loop the video signal continuously so no one would spot me slipping out. I slid into one of the armored pressure suits lining the airlock. Even in the reduced gravity of the station, the suit was bulky and difficult to don by myself. I sweated, cursed and struggled with the seals in gloves that were even thicker than the usual spacesuit gloves.

I'd gotten too complacent– not keeping up my EVA training, always leaving the outside work to Maauro. Now that complacency might end us both.

Finally I had the suit sealed and ready. I punched in the code and the airlock began to cycle, scrubbing potentially explosive oxygen.

"Open, God damn it," I swore.

The lights from my helmet lanced out into the maelstrom of blue sky outside and fell on Maauro. She lay frozen, only meters away, one arm outstretched in desperation toward the airlock. Her beautiful eyes were mere panels of onyx ... dead.

"No," I screamed and ran toward her, violating the first law of high gravity; never take an unbalanced step.

Cimer's inexorable 1.8Gs waited for me on the other side of the door beyond the floating city's AG field. The universe blurred and I fell across the city surface until I slammed into an antenna stand, disoriented by the speed of my fall.

I don't know how long I lay there, stunned, but when I regained consciousness it was to the flat taste of blood in my mouth and strange smells in my suit. Awareness crashed back, strange smells in suits meant system malfunction and death. I struggled to focus my blurred vision on my helmet readouts, which showed a chilling amount of red lights. Servos whined as I struggled to my knees, the smells grew worse.

Where was Maauro? I realized that I'd fallen more than five meters across the gentle slope of the drift station. Had it been more of a slope I'd surely be dead. I began to crawl, my armored gloves grasped any projection and I set each limb before I moved. There was no way the suit would survive another mistake. Slowly I struggled upwards as the howling wind of the gas giant sounded in my ears. Lightning flashed in impossible blues among the chlorine clouds. But the universe narrowed for me until it was only the pitted surface of Tir-a-Mar. Every atom of my body protested its extra weight and my face felt like it was pulling free of my skull. Time lost meaning for me. I was Sisyphus sentenced to push a boulder uphill for all eternity.

I bumped into something. With an effort that strained my neck muscles, I brought up my head to see Maauro and beyond her, the hatch to the station, with its blessed lower gravity.

I tapped on her carefully, placing my helmet against her, hoping that conduction would carry my voice to her. She didn't respond.

"No," I said, gritting my teeth, "not after 50,000 years. Not after Kandalor. Not after the Artifact. You are not going to die here!"

Think, dammit. She's frozen to the deck, means she's not generating any power. I've got to cut her free. I triggered the cutting torch in the suit arm and prayed to the God I wasn't sure I believed in, that I wasn't hurting her. The torch cut through the methane ice quickly. I got to my knees and tried to move her. She barely shifted. I groaned; I'd forgotten how much heavier Maauro was then she appeared to be. Lifting her was impossible in 1.8Gs.

I put my shoulder to her and pushed carefully. If she toppled down the slope…

We gained a foot. Servos whined and I caught the whiff of burning electrical systems. More lights on my helmet panel went yellow or red.

Push, recover, push, scream when the pain became too great. Cough as the air in my suit became toxic as leakage defeated the scrubbers. My suit was failing. If we didn't make the hatch soon, we would refreeze here, perhaps to be found by some maintenance crew, or perhaps to be swept off in an endless fall.

Would Jaelle ever learn how we had died? Would she think of us? Would she think of me? I coughed and tasted more blood, then shoved again. With a thunk we struck the edge of the airlock.

I looked at the edge of the airlock in despair; the lip of metal was only three inches high but it seemed a wall. I knew I couldn't rest, couldn't regather my strength. God only knew how much longer my suit would hold death at bay.

"Don't shatter," I demanded. With a final effort, I toppled Maauro over the lip and into the airlock. My suit pinged and snapped as servos blew, but she went in. With my last rags of strength, I crawled in after her.

The horrible smothering weight vanished as we crossed the gradient back into artificial gravity. Relief gave me the will to hit "close" on the hatch before I fell into blackness.

CHAPTER TEN

HEAT IS CARESSING MY LOWER LIMBS. IT MUST HAVE BEEN DOING SO *for some time as I am so far gone that the rudimentary functions still operating did not permit me self-awareness. But as the heat-energy supplements my own systems I reacquire sentience. I cannot see or hear, but subsystems report light blows on my chassis and a low heat level far below any temperature that could damage me. I dare to risk a little more energy to sense the outside world but to no avail. All I gain is the sense that I am being moved in a series of shoves. I wait through an eternity of seconds but the heat source is gone and I begin to refreeze.*

Another blow and I am being upset. Am I plunging into the abyss of the gas giant, beyond any hope of recovery?

No. I am saved. I immediately record a drop in gravity to Confed standard; temperature and pressure are within normal limits. I know my own form of joy.

Relieved of the utter hostility of Cimer's gravity and cold, I reroute power and repair systems. All this is done with an agonizing slowness I can barely tolerate- perhaps thirty seconds pass before essential systems are restored. Sight and hearing, both distorted and granular, return in the same instant.

An armored body lies next to me. At first I think it is a Confed robot, then I recognize it as a powered space suit. I know who my savior must be.

I shelve all other system repairs to concentrate on movement. I reach Wrik and my few working sensors show me severe damage to the suit. It could not have been airtight. I tear it open with my original arm. I must get him out. I fling off the chest plate to reveal Wrik, pallid and still. Traces of Cimer's poisonous atmosphere still waft from the suit's interior.

He is not breathing. His heart is still.

Immediately I compress his chest with my sensitive right hand, simultaneously sending an electrical shock through it. My chemical factories kick into overdrive. I produce a needle in my left hand, glad that I took the time to upgrade this Infester-made arm. Epinephrine and other chemicals to counteract the poisons are injected. I manufacture a small IV and implant the needle.

I must do more. He remains unresponsive. I place my mouth on Wrik's and, with continuous pressure, send pure oxygen into his lungs, scrubbing any toxins with the reverse suction. All the while I continue cardiac massage.

I must dare another shock or all is lost. Wrik's' body spasms as the maximum voltage I can risk courses through him. Not for the first time do I wish that I could cry.

CHAPTER TEN

But it is not tears of grief, but of joy that I now envy. His heart restarts. The sinus rhythms steadies, pulse and blood pressure head for where they belong. A deep indrawn breath makes him shudder. I switch to a more normal mix of air but continue to push air into his lungs until I am sure of their function. His eyes flutter.

There's a tunnel above me, gray around the edges, with lights swimming in the center. I must be getting closer as the lights brightened. Awareness began to seep back in. I grew conscious of my body lying on a deck. Something was pressed against my face: soft, warm, with the scent of ginger cookies. Thick, silky hair rested against me.

Is she kissing me? I wonder, still dazed.

Maauro raised her head, her huge eyes, once again aquamarine, deep and aware, met mine. "Wrik, I am so glad you have awakened. You stopped breathing for a few seconds before I could get oxygen into your lungs. I have removed as many toxins as I could from you while unconscious."

"If you wanted to kiss me, you didn't have to go to this extreme."

"I know that," she said.

I wanted to laugh but feared it might send me into a painful coughing jag.

Maauro gently helped me into a sitting position and I noticed that the pressure suit had been ripped open, along with my shirt. A very small IV bottle was attached to my chest along with a few injector tabs. Maauro must have manufactured them in her body.

"Your vital signs are now stable."

"Thank you." I placed a hand on her face, amazed as always at how warm and soft she managed to make her exterior. "Are you all right? When I saw you all frozen...your eyes were black."

She touched my hand with her right one. "All is well. My damage control has repaired all vital systems. Most were simply frozen, which does not affect me as it does your delicate tissue. Sometimes I marvel at the courage of you biologicals. So delicate and yet you risked yourself once again to save me."

"Perhaps we won't tell Jaelle about waking up with your lips on mine," I said, embarrassed and trying to change the subject.

"I do not believe she would object, and Wrik, I am never ashamed for anyone to know that I love you."

This time I put both arms around her. "I love you too."

"Good. Now we must turn our efforts to regaining the station's interior. I need to replenish myself."

"We're in the industrial section," I said, struggling to my feet with her help. The soreness in my ribs and rawness in my throat were receding thanks to whatever medicine Maauro had injected me with. I looked back at the wrecked environmental suit and marveled at my own survival, but for now I needed to focus on getting us back into the station and doing something for Maauro.

It took Maauro a few minutes of study to breach the inner door, during which I watched the spider bug that I'd used to hack in the loop on the surveillance camera. It still glowed green, showing that it had power and that no security program had targeted it. Soon Maauro leaned back in satisfaction and the door gaped open. I leaned in to see the corridor empty in both directions. We entered quickly, Maauro lugging the remains of envirosuit, which she ditched it in a utility locker. The spider robot leapt from the wall onto Maauro's shoulder. She pressed it against her body and it disappeared into her.

I followed Maauro as she moved purposefully down the hall, grabbing up my duffel bag as we went.

"I accessed a general schematic of the station when breaking into the station airlock," she said. "This station was designed to be operated by both oxygen-breathers and Ribisans, so there is access to the power plant. Both sides have such different needs that it required separate industrial sections. I should find at least some of what I need here."

We walked down a hallway, then down two levels on a circular staircase. I was surprised that other than a general soreness and rawness in my throat, I was none the worse for my exposure to Cimer's atmosphere. Chalk up doctor as another of Maauro's skills.

We spotted two Ribisans in power suits on some errand and ducked into a side hall until they disappeared down the companionway. A group of human technicians in green uniforms made us backtrack and take a passage on the level below.

Finally we entered a control room by an elevated walkway. On the floor below, some human technicians and a Morok were engaged in a heated debate about something. We couldn't hear them, but there was a lot of arm waving going on. We passed through the room into a section of heavy machinery, power conduits and an industrial conveyor.

Maauro set to work on one conduit, prying off an access panel. She stuck her original right arm in and a brief arc flared before she made the connection. She settled on her haunches with what I could have sworn was a sigh of contentment.

After a few moments she looked up. "I needed to find a power source large enough to replenish me and not show a measurable loss that would attract attention. This will buy me some time and enough power for a disguise."

"Is it enough?"

"Yes, if we are not interrupted for fifteen minutes." As she spoke, her normal skintight gray-and-red jumpsuit morphed into the looser-fitting, green overalls the Tir-a-Mar crew wore. "Watch the door."

I nodded and moved to keep watch as the minutes dragged slowly by, but luck seemed to have returned to us as no one entered the control or process rooms. Thank God for automation. Eventually I heard the sound of Maauro reattaching the access panel. We slipped out of the area and back into the main hallway.

"I accessed a subroutine of a maintenance AI," Maauro said. "I have to be far more careful than usual as the computers and cyber systems on this floating city are far above standard. Still, I was able to locate a cache of rare metals and exotic radioactives two levels down in the central core area. It is guarded. I must admit I have no plan for getting past the guard. While I can easily overcome him, it will cause an alert."

I considered. "I'm here on a surprise inspection. We can cover my recent disappearance with the ruse that I decided to slip out to conduct inspections without oversight. What could be more natural then inspecting the most dangerous materials aboard?"

"With me as your unwilling and drafted local guide? Yes, very sensible. Let me see what repairs I can make to your uniform while you wash up in the bathroom across the corridor."

I gave her my shirt, which was truly worse for the wear, and ducked into the room she indicated. I gulped cold water for my abused throat and washed the last of Cimer's atmosphere off me. I still looked rough, but not like I'd spent part of the day mostly dead. When I got back Maauro had repaired my shirt and was extruding the laundered material from her midsection. "Is there anything you can't do?"

"Open an airlock door when I am frozen solid," she replied. "Perhaps now you will accept that I rely on you as much as you rely on me. For all the difference in our strength, again, it was you who saved me."

I smiled at her. "Perhaps." I changed back into my uniform jacket, disposing of my civvy one in a nearby recycler along with the duffle bag. I sat the Confed military cap squarely on my head and belted on my laser.

We ceased skulking and walked down the corridors and slidewalks as if we belonged there. We attracted some attention from passing crew, but not more than Maauro, with her big eyes, normally did on when we were out and about at home. My uniform seemed to attract a mixture of looks: some merely curious, some seemed afraid, others hostile. But no one stopped us.

We rounded the curve to face a guard station.

"I don't care about authorizations," I said loudly to Maauro. "All the authorization I need is on my collar. We're inspecting this area. Now."

"Yes, sir," she replied meekly.

The guard stood, eyeing me warily. He was a human mutation of a type I was unfamiliar with. His brown skin was either tattooed or naturally striped. Like Maauro, his eyes were larger than a standard humans' below prominent brow ridges.

"This area is off limits," he rumbled.

"Not to a Confed officer on a snap inspection," I stated, walking forward with an assurance I didn't feel.

"I'll accompany the officer," Maauro said. "It's my job, I guess. Not sure how I got so lucky. I mean I was just standing downstairs and he points and says, "Hey you—"

"I'll have to call it in," the guard interrupted what he clearly felt was going to be a long story.

"Go ahead, but make it quick, or you're going on my report as obstructing a Confed officer," I added.

The guard relayed my demand to someone. I could dimly hear someone replying over his com. "So that's where he went off to!" said the voice. "All right, let him in, but can you keep an eye on him?"

I shook my head.

"There's one of our techs with him, sir," the visibly relieved guard said. "I was going to leave it to her."

"All right," the voice, which sounded like Fenster, also sounded reluctant. "Report afterward."

The guard sat back down and gestured for us to proceed.

We went in through a series of thick, powered doors that Maauro opened as if she did it every day, dropping them behind us. Inside lay a storage room filled with waldoes, their mechanical arms hanging from the ceilings, armored glass panels and storage bins.

Maauro looked back at the door we'd come through; which held a small glass panel. "Be sure the guard doesn't peek in on us. I have blinded the sensors in here."

She moved quickly to examine the bins and then began working some waldoes. "Excellent, these are high quality radioactives and exotic metals," she reached into the containers and pulled out bars of refined metal, placing them against her chest to be promptly absorbed. Life with Maauro was always something of a scavenger hunt.

"Wrik," Maauro called, excitement in her voice. "There are materials here that I have not seen since I was last maintained by a Creator team. I can process some of these into replacement material for my body. Not enough for an entirely new arm, but I will be much more sound then I have been in 50,000 years."

"Maauro, that's excellent."

"One can see why the Ribisans are so prized as chemical and metallurgical engineers. They are not the equals of the Creators, but they show great promise."

"Pity they are trying to kill us."

"It will be dangerous for you to be present when I open some of these containers."

"I'll step out and wait at the guard post." I hit the panel on the door and waited as it rolled back. The guard looked up as I walked back to his station.

"Everything in order?"

"Yeah. The tech is finishing up before we continue my tour. I'm glad I found her. She's pretty easy-going."

He grunted. "Cute, isn't she? Looks a bit young though."

"You have to like a big-eyed girl," I said opting for congeniality.

The guard grinned. "I prefer them with big breasts. Maybe she has an older sister?"

"I'll ask."

"Has she been here long? Can't say I've seen her around."

I twitched slightly. "Don't know. I just got here. These floating cities are pretty big." Over our private link I sent, "*Maauro, the guard is getting curious about you.*"

"Acknowledged, I have uploaded a false history to his screen."

"Check your comp," I suggested to the guard.

He idly flicked up a query on his screen. "Yeah, Estrella Lostly, human mutant like me. Came in on the last trading vessel. God, that must have sucked, traveling on a Ribisan ship."

"This is a Ribisan station," I said.

"Yeah, but this was built as a trade station for 02 breathers. Ribisan ships have some small accommodations for our kind, but not much."

"Still," he said, stretching, "the gasbags have it best here. Sometimes they freefall off the station to the deeps, where they have their other facilities. A shuttle brings them back up here."

"No other cities below?"

"So they say, but you could drop sixty Earth-type planets in Cimer before filling it up. Who can say what's in the deep below? This is a relatively new colony for the Ribisans, only about fifty years old."

Maauro returned from the radioactive bunker to rescue me from the garrulous guard. Perhaps it was just my overwrought imagination, but she seemed to have a pink glow of health. On her chest a nametag now read, "*Lostly.*"

"He wants to know if you have an older sister," I said, slightly giddy at our success so far.

Maauro looked at the guard. "They would be very much older than I am and, to be frank, rather large and—"

The guard smiled. "I get the picture."

"Shall we continue with your inspection, Lieutenant?" Maauro said, turning to me.

"By all means," I replied.

CHAPTER ELEVEN

MAAURO AND I FINISHED MY "INSPECTION" OF THE power plant as soon as we could and returned to the street level.

"What do we do now?" I asked, looking around wearily at the streets and buildings that made up the interior of the floating city.

"We must return you to your hotel," Maauro said. "In the morning we must conspire to find a way to attach Estrella Lostly to Lt. Fels for the duration."

"Let's get to the hotel first, but I think I can handle that one. I've already made it clear that I'm not going to be handled or minded while I am here. What would be more natural then that I select my own guide?"

I looked at the street and approached a panel set in a crosswalk, dialing for a cab. "No more sneaking about for now. I'm damn near out on my feet."

"I agree."

The ride back to the Star and Comet was long, reminding me of how huge the floating city was. But the cab delivered us back to the street of the hotel. The city was in early morning mode; only a few people were wandering about, though there were robocleaners and other automatics working. We exited the cab and moved to the tower of glass and metal. Automatics opened the doors and we slipped in.

But we were expected. McCaffer, the PR guy, stood in the lobby, looking worse for wear due to the early hour.

"Let me handle this." I said.

"Lt. Fels," he began, his facial expression belied the friendly tone.

"Mr. McCaffer. You've had some excitement tonight."

"Yes, there was an explosion. It seems a maintenance conduit had a power overload. Then, of course, there was the matter of your disappearing."

"I believe I explained that my investigations would be conducted at times and place of my choosing and without surveillance or handlers."

"Yes, but surely some notice of your excursions is warranted. How can we account for your safety?"

"I'm pretty good at watching out for myself." I said, then quickly mindsent to Maauro. *"Complain about how you were just minding your business when I grabbed you."*

Aloud I said. "I'm on a fact-finding mission. Facts show up at the damndest times."

"Yes," Maauro piped in, "but did they have to show up at the end of my shift? I was minding my own business—"

"Now, Lostly," I said, with my best smile, "didn't I offer to make it up to you with the finest dinner to be had on Tir-a-Mar?"

"You did," she replied. "I intend to hold you to it, considering the trouble you've landed me in."

"If you need a guide," McCaffer said exasperated, "we have many highly-trained people—"

"Thanks, I prefer to pick my own guide. She knows the station but she wasn't here when Dr. Malich and his staff were, so she has no reason to be less the forthcoming around me."

"Lieutenant," McCaffer said, "no one here has any reason to be less than forthcoming with you."

"Then there should be no objection to her."

He sighed theatrically. "I take it that you don't mind if we talk to our employee?"

"I'll be in the bar," I said.

McCaffer comes over to me. The professional affability that he showed with Wrik has snapped off. He has a portacomp in his hand and its holoscreen unfolds to a foot square. On it I see Estrella Lostly's file.

"Estrella Lostly," he reads aloud, "age twenty standards, unmarried, general services electrical and mechanical tech. You came aboard with the last freighter."

"Yes, sir," I reply feigning meekness. "Sir, this isn't my fault. I was just repairing a flux damper on an AG subassembly when the Confed officer walks up to me and showed me his credentials—"

"Why didn't you call in?"

"He said not to," I said, raising my hands. "I didn't want to be arrested." I judge it a good time to raise the pitch of my voice and twist my face slightly. My analysis indicates that the typical reaction of an older male to an upset young female will be to back off.

"Now, now," McCaffer said, raising a hand to my shoulder. "It's ok. I understand."

"And we did see the security guard by the radioactive center." I add.

"Yes, yes. Quite correct. You did the best you could. Now calm down. You're not in trouble. In fact, this may work out for the best."

"Sir?" I question.

"Do you like the Lieutenant?"

"Sure," I reply with what I hope appears to be girlish enthusiasm. "He's kind of good-looking and the captain of his own starship. He did promise me a fine dinner out."

"Hmmn," McCaffer said. "Well, watch your step. I think he has his heart set more on breakfast. But you say he's been nice to you?"

"Yes, very."

McCaffer looked a little disquieted. "Okay. Stay here, please."

He walked out of earshot for a normal human. I could have hacked his com but my hearing was more than sufficient to allow me to listen to his conversation.

"Ms. Fenster. Yes, McCaffer here. I've found the Lieutenant. He seems to have settled on a young tech he met by chance as a guide. You know he's refused everyone else we've proposed.

"No, she's recent. Wasn't here. Yes, she's young and cute. I suspect he's more interested in her than in anything she knows. It might be a good distraction. She doesn't know anyone or anything."

"OK, I'll arrange it."

I quickly relay the conversation to Wrik.

"Refuse at first," he answers. "Make them order you to be my guide. Don't worry, they will. They'll offer money, promotion, other benefits."

"Commerce?"

"Yes, Maauro, commerce."

McCaffer returned to me. "I've spoken to the mayor. He would like you to serve as the lieutenant's guide while he is here. Take him where wants to go, to whom he wants to see."

"Sir, I mean I like him and all, but my section chief—"

"Don't worry about any of that. I'll send an order though channels transferring you to my staff for the duration of his visit."

"Well, I was really just interested in a dinner date."

"Whatever you do or don't do with him is up to you, but we need a guide and to be frank, a set of eyes on him. You'll be paid time and a half."

"Ask for double time," Wrik whispers in my mind, "and since it's a twenty-four a day job to be paid that way."

I relay this to McCaffer, who grimaces. "Yes. Provided I get regular reports from you on his activities."

"They really want you with me," Wrik says.

"I'll try," I say to McCaffer, "but he's so suspicious of everyone. He keeps looking over his shoulder and checking with some portacomp he carries for bugs surveillance devices, intruder software—"

"Does he? Good to know"

He taps his portacomp. "Give me your portable and I will load my private code on it.

Because I am a computer, it did not occur to me that I would need such a ridiculously limited device. I realize my mistake too late for my internal factories to make one. I still have my spiderbot in my body. I rearrange its limbs in a tight package around its core, in a square shape and extrude it into the pocket of coverall, then pull it out of my pocket.

McCaffer looks at it. "Odd-looking model."

"I made it myself. They were all the rage back in my colony." *I place it against his unit and affect the transfer of his confidential code. Another coup for our side.*

"Ok," he peers at me. "Are you sure you're twenty?"

"Twenty-one in three months," I reply. "It's one of the features of the genetic drift on my colony under a red star: large eyes, pale skin, and we are small and slim."

It occurs to me that I may need to use some artifices to appear older. Altering my basic Maauro matrix could be dangerous and I will not attempt it now, but there are cosmetic methods. Not for the first time I note the disadvantage of having been patterned on a game simulation with huge eyes and an almost impossibly slender figure. Still, I had lost forty-percent of my mass in my last combat on the asteroid, 50,000 years ago, so I could not be much larger without creating hollow places inside myself that would not be combat-effective. Beyond that, I have grown accustomed to my own face and have no more desire to alter it than any other living being.

"Well," McCaffer continues. "I'd say your colony did well in the genetic lottery. Ok, keep an eye on Fels; call in if there are any issues." Again he reaches out and pats me awkwardly on the shoulder. "Word of advice, watch yourself with Fels. He strikes me as the sort to love a girl and leave her."

I decide that defending Wrik's' fidelity is not indicated and merely nod as McCaffer walks off.

I enter the bar to look for Wrik to find him in a quiet booth in back, asleep while sitting up. His body is doubtless taxed despite all the repairs I have made to it. I slide silently into the booth, forestalling the approaching waitress with a hand. She fades back to the other few occupied booths. Despite the late hour there are some other people scattered about, but none near us.

It will appear odd if I sit motionless and silent, yet I do not want to wake Wrik. I set my body to go through a series of motions for the next fifteen minutes so I will appear to be conversing with Wrik. He is far into the booth and with his back to the restaurant. My mouth moves, my hands stir and I change facial expressions, but all without sound or enough motion to disturb him. Meanwhile I monitor Wrik's vitals. He shows considerable stress and is in need of food and rest.

Eventually, his eyes open and I immediately cease my meaningless motions.

"Oh, hi? Guess I must have drifted off for a catnap."

"An odd expression for a brief sleep considering that animal spends eighty percent of its life asleep."

"Right now I envy it. How did it go with McCaffer?"

"Not only has he accepted me as a chance encounter, but as a suitable minder for you. I have his private access code to report your movements and activities to him."

Wrik gives a weary nod. "Yeah, I made a fuss about free access and not being followed. They'll be glad to get one of their own close to me."

"He warned me to expect attempts on my virtue by you."

Wrik grinned. *"Sound advice for a young lady and I second it, nothing more untrustworthy than a spacer on leave. A respectable girl like you should be more careful of the company she keeps."*

"My onboard weaponry should suffice to protect my reputation."

"Yeah, from anything short of an ASAT Team."

"Now," I say, leaning forward and waving to the waitress, who approaches, professional smile firmly in place. *"You need to refuel with an expensive meal to support our cover."*

"Great. I am starving. Given McCaffer's suspicions of me I don't think anyone will be surprised if you spend the rest of the night with me and we rise late. Once my head hits a pillow, I am going to be down for a while."

"Agreed. Champagne?"

"Finest kind."

I woke hours later to find Maauro on the bed watching me. I rolled up to sitting, feeling refreshed and surprisingly healthy. I suspected that Maauro had continued her ministrations while I slept.

"How do you feel?" she asked.

"Ready to get on with the mission and get the hell off this crushing, stinking planet."

"I have sent for your favorite breakfast."

"Thanks." About then I focused on the fact that Maauro was wearing one of my shirts and appeared to be wearing nothing else. Other than the fact that the high-end bed under her was crushed by her weight, she looked like a young lady who'd enjoyed a good night. "Is that your chassis?"

"No, it was easier to simply don one of your shirts."

"Looks good on you."

She smiled. "Are you flirting with me, Wrik?"

"Not with my girlfriend due on the same planet."

"Would you be more comfortable if I donned the coveralls I was wearing?"

"It might be best."

Maauro rose and, to my surprise, simply unbuttoned the shirt and slipped out of it. For a second she stood there, her pale body shining. I looked on, startled. Her body was slender and perfect, but the mounds of her breasts lacked nipples, her flat stomach held no belly button and she was entirely hairless and sexless. Her form shimmered, and a moment later, the loose and flowing green coverall appeared on her.

The sight of her body unsettled me. I wasn't sure if it was because it was so close to real, or by the omissions that kept it from being so. I also wasn't sure if it meant anything that she had showed me herself this way.

The door chimed.

"Breakfast," she said.

An hour later, shaved and showered, I accompanied Maauro to a series of meetings with Mysol's staff, and interviewed the few people on my list of the original biogenetic staff. The three of them were minor functionaries, lab techs and a security guard, none of the doctors or scientists. Maauro waited outside during my interrogations, seeing and hearing through my eyes. It was she who pointed out the rehearsed quality of the responses.

"This indicates a single source of briefing for these people," Maauro whispered in my mind. "These people may have remained here for the reasons we have been given; a marriage, a better job – but they are hiding something."

"What do I do?"

"Continue the interrogations. Have lunch with the section heads. Ask the questions I have listed for you. If you forget, ask me."

CHAPTER TWELVE

WE RETURN TO THE STAR AND COMET AFTER OUR FIRST FULL DAY OF *poking and prodding to no avail. Wrik had gone through the motions of his investigations and certifications, checking employment and housing records on the missing science team.*

As Estrella Lostly, I filed my false reports on Wrik's activities with McCaffer's office. Fenster had me transferred to McCaffer's staff for "the duration" as she put it. I was to keep the public relations man informed of all of Wrik's activities. This came with a salary increase and an increased degree of security for me. No one would miss the nonexistent Lostly in her old section, the ubiquitous and numerous Department of General Services, and no one on Fenster's or McCaffer's staffs would have known her before. I could not have engineered a more elegant use of bureaucracy had I planned it.

So while Wrik manipulated the physical world of witnesses and documents, I mined troves of data, both what the City authorities willingly gave him and what I could hack my way into without betraying my presence. I was truly impressed by the depth and nature both of the city central AI's security and the thoroughness of the data-scrubbing efforts in the less secure secondary systems. All I could tell is that these personnel left the city on a series of Ribisan ships for interim destinations where they were to proceed further with their journeys. The fact that no final destinations were listed for the freighters and transports and their next ports-of-call were all Ribisan, made it impossible to crosscheck against Confed records. So seamless a story had to be a cover.

Unfortunately, it was an excellent one. All trails led to the Ribisan side of the equation where the Confederacy had already made inquiries, which drowned in red tape before we were assigned. It was quite likely that the ships were real and had even run on the dates indicated. Whether the scientists had been on board was another matter.

I further discovered that vast amounts of money were being funneled through Tir-a-Mar's treasury, sums that would be a significant percentage of a planetary GNP. With that came equipment and orders that could have supplied computers for a dozen Tir-a-Mars.

Wrik sighs with relief as the door to our suite closes. He looks at the small monitor bot that we left; he calls it a spider. It blinks a cheerful green, indicating that no one has attempted to enter or penetrate our security.

We walk directly to the bedroom. Wrik throws his jacket over a chair, kicks off his shoe, and falls full length on the bed with a groan. I draw the curtains so we will not be spied on.

"Another corporate dinner with the notables," he says. "How long did this one go on? Damn it's 12:30 a.m.."

"Was the food not excellent?" I ask.

"Yes, as was the wine, but who could relax and enjoy it? Every question is a chance to blow my cover with a lot of very sharp people. God, this is the third night of this. I am not even sure what lies I have told. Maauro, I don't know how much longer I can keep this up."

"You worry overmuch. I have monitored your stories and prompted you when continuity errors surface. Beyond that most of these people are just making conversation with a far-traveler, much more in accord with what you have informed me your customs are. They likely do not remember the details and any variance will be chalked up to the human tendency to tell "tall tales.""

"I'd still feel better if you were next to me."

"No one would expect Estrella Lostly to be there. Further my cover is far thinner than yours. It doubtless raises some eyebrows that I am spending nights with you. Hopefully they put it down to your sexual prowess and my desire for advancement. "

He laughed. "Hopefully."

"Remember, you are only the commander of a minor vessel. You need not know the answers to many of the questions asked. On anything significant plead that you cannot respond due to security or that you need to defer to higher authority. As tightly as Mysol and Fenster run Tir-a-Mar, it should resonate with them.

"Rest now. More awaits us tomorrow. We must do as much as we can before Jaelle and Dusko arrive. The additional players will accelerate the pace of the game."

After a brief morning coffee with a number of people who really didn't want to talk with me, I started making calls on people with knowledge of Malich or the biogenetics work his team had done. One of these was a Morok professor named Dok. We entered the glass-walled turbovator. McCaffer led, flanked by his two young aides: Lesley, a colonist favoring a dark-blue body dye that reminded me of Telberd, and an earnest and somewhat high-strung intern named Dothea, from an old colony. She had the look of an albino, an adaption to her native orange star. She wore dark lenses in her eyes that gave her an eerie look, but was otherwise the more talkative of the pair. She was about Maauro's size and apparent age and kept trying to involve her in discussions of clothes and fashion.

Lesley had a father in the Confed Navy, so he was relatively friendly. McCaffer was professionally well mannered and only barely gave the impression of being on a fool's errand.

"I've confirmed with Professor Dok that he's available for our meeting," McCaffer said, "though he seemed reluctant to waste your time having nothing to add to his earlier statement about not knowing Dr Malich's plans."

I smiled without warmth. "He may know more than he realizes. Some comment Malich made about his family, his interests, finances, relationships, and studies. For the completeness of my investigation, I must interview all witnesses myself."

"Yes, yes," McCaffer said with a dismissive air as one of the aides pressed a control on the elevator's virtual panel.

"In any event," Dothea said, clearly trying to defuse tensions, "we will see Professor Dok shortly and find out."

The elevator started forward down the well-lit tubeway that mixed clear plaststeel and other metals, giving one the feeling of standing in a slow-moving groundcar. We passed over a street, then into another building for the vertical trip from the upper section of Tir-a-Mar to the lowest, where Dok worked. I took hold of the pole and raised my eyebrows at Maauro. With her blindingly fast reflexes she was able to counter the elevators movements and was the only person not holding a pole or railing. She caught my gaze and reached for a railing.

The turbovator started down. Levels passed by us and we could see citizens and machinery moving about their daily chores.

"It's twelve kilometers to the spectrography lab," Lesley added, to break the silence. "Since they study Cimer itself, it's the logical place for it."

"Of course," I replied.

The elevator jolted, then slowed. McCaffer frowned then leaned forward and pressed our destination button again.

With a further lurch the elevator dropped.

"Free-fall!" I shouted. Dothea screamed as she floated off the floor.

"Don't worry," McCaffer yelled, wrapping both hands around a railing. "There are full safeties. We'll stop in a second."

"Wrik," Mauro mind-spoke to me, "we will not stop. The safeties have been locked out."

"Sabotage," I hissed back mentally. "Can you do anything?"

"Not electronically. You must distract McCaffer and the others so I can stop the elevator by force."

"We're not stopping," Dothea cried.

My mind raced. "The panel must be locked up. All of you on the floor! Face down and cover your eyes." I pulled my laser from its holster, dialed it to low power while trying to keep on my feet in the plummeting elevator. Only a trained spacer could have managed it.

"What are you going to do?" McCaffer demanded, eyes wide.

CHAPTER TWELVE

"Do what you're told," I ordered. "Face down, eyes covered. There could be fragments." The three complied. I aimed at the panel. *"Ready?"* I sent to Maauro.

"Yes."

I fired over the heads of the three on the floor. The panel shorted and sparked. Dothea screamed. At the same instant, Maauro's right hand emitted a glow and a wash of heat she slammed it through the plassteel walls of the elevator and into the wall beyond. Immediately a long trail of sparks lit up the outside. Her grip on the railing kept her wedged on the floor as she exerted her strength. The elevator slowed jarringly. The three on the floor raised their heads.

"Down," I shouted, firing again.

My hand, fingers flattened into a wedge, rips through the elevator wall. At the same instant I trigger my plasma torch. The plasma around my hand protects it as it cuts into the wall, otherwise I would have to accept material loss from my chassis due to abrasion with the wall. The metals that compose me are far harder than the material of the elevator, or wall, but the forces involved are great. I am grateful for the protection my weapon gives me. Drag created by the plasma and my arm slows the plummeting turbovator. But the g-load is too much for the railing I have hold of with my Infester arm. A flaw in the metal yields a stress fracture that multiplies immediately, causing the railing to rip free.

No matter. I spread the fingers of my plasma-protected hand to create greater drag as Wrik fires again over the three humans on the floor, covering my actions. Dothea is screaming and crying in panic, which aids our plans. I snatch at one of the vertical take-holds that are better made to distribute the load and put a crushing grip on it to make my handhold more secure. We jolt and slow, the pole degrades but bears the stress. Excellent, my only other choice would have been to brace myself against the ceiling and that would have been harder to hide.

The elevator slows and I bring it to stop almost even with a floor. I do not want it to appear as if this was a controlled stop. Before the others can raise their heads I rip a slab of wall metal, cut with my plasma torch so that it tips into the elevator car and jams against the ceiling. To the humans it will appear as if this stopped us. I extinguish my torch and nod at Wrik. I then step away from the others as far as I can and begin emergency cool down procedures, exchanging those surface parts I can, with deeper parts so that I do not burn anyone who touches me. I redirect heat into the soles of my feet to radiate into the elevator hoping no one realizes I am the source.

The others are on their hands and knees now as Wrik holsters his weapon.

"Thank God," Lesley says. He turns to comfort Dothea. The thin girl is shaking and incoherent.

"Told you, told you," McCaffer stammers. "Full safeties."

"There's your full safety," Wrik says pointing up at the ceiling. "We must have snagged something in the shaftway when we were bouncing around. It bent in and jammed us."

"Out, out," Dothea pleads. In the distance, alarms shrill.

"Are you all right, Lostly?" Wrik calls to me across the elevator.

"Yes, yes. I think so." I imitate the higher-pitched speech and stammer of the humans.

"Really?" he mindsends.

"I am undamaged. Thank you. But I will need to refuel soon."

He nods.

McCaffer and the male aide move carefully to the doors and try to force them open. After a second, Wrik joins them. As the smallest and weakest-appearing member of the crew, I must kneel beside the terrified Dothea and pat her shoulder while they struggle with a door I could simply run straight though if I needed to. It is rather annoying, as is this whole assassination attempt on us.

The elevator rocks as they pull and Dothea squeaks in fear.

"Do not worry," I send to Wrik. "The metal supporting the elevator is nowhere near fatigue point. While I would rather not break cover, I will not let the elevator drop again even if I need hold it up by force."

"Good to know," he grunts.

McCaffer looks at him. "What?"

"Wrik that was aloud," I caution.

"Nothing," he says. The doors slide open. Exclamations of relief ring out around me.

Wrik stands to one side. "Women, children and civilians first."

Dothea is first out. Wrik gestures to me, but I push Lesley and McCaffer out first, and then go, turning immediately. At the first hit of slippage I will wrench the doors off and hold the elevator up if need be. But Wrik is on my heels and out of danger in a second.

Emergency personnel appear from around the bend of the long corridor we are in, racing past curious onlookers who are peering out of rooms and adjacent hallways. The medics take charge of the unnerved Dothea and her companions. Wrik and I wave them off.

Seconds later, city police in blue arrive, rolling up on the individual scooters or debouching from other elevators and slidewalks. A muscular blonde woman, five-feet seven inches tall, whose elaborate hair almost covers one of her eyes, strides forward. She is dressed in loose-fitting blue trousers trimmed in gray. She wears a double-breasted jacket with badges and decorations. On one hip hangs a saber-hilted baton, as if it was that bladed weapon. I detect a stunner in a shoulder holster under her jacket. It is not necessary to see the captain's bars on her collar to tell she is in charge. I check my database: this is Olivia Croyzer, Human Colonist, 32, Chief of Police, former Confed Marine. She exudes command presence and walks past everyone, unconsciously assuming they will get out of her way. She spares assessing glances at all of us, and then leans into the elevator. Waving her hand at the smoke, she spared Wrik a somewhat contemptuous glance.

"That panel," she says in a deeper than usual voice, "would have been of interest to me, if some trigger-happy star-jockey hadn't blown it to hell." She turns, hands on her hips and glares up at Wrik. Although she is five inches shorter than him, Wrik looks taken aback. His face flushes slightly.

"If I hadn't blown it to hell," he shoots back. "You'd likely have been inspecting it among the fragments of what was left of us after a twelve kilometer fall at terminal velocity."

McCaffer stood shakily. "Now Olivia, I'm sure the Lieutenant just did what he thought was necessary—"

"That's Captain Croyzer to you," she said barely glancing at him and keeping her eyes focused on Wrik. "Perhaps I should relieve the Lieutenant of that sidearm he's so fond of firing off in my city—"

"Perhaps," Wrik interrupted in a deadly tone that surprised both Croyzer and me, "you should get hold of yourself. You're a captain here, which means precisely not a goddamn thing to me. I'm the senior Confed officer on this station. If I decide its necessary, I can federalize you and place you under my direct command, or for that matter, declare martial damn law and have you arrested for interfering with me."

The police in the area looked on in astonishment: apparently someone talking to Croyzer in such a fashion was highly unusual. Several of them shift to where they can cover Wrik. They do not notice that I am positioned where I can hit all of them. If one moves, I will kill everyone in this corridor before their weapons can clear holsters. Something about me causes Croyzer to flick her eyes to me momentarily. I remain very still.

She cocked her head and looked at Wrik as if studying an interesting bug. "You're pretty cocky for a scoutship commander. I'm the duly appointed law on this world."

"As I pointed out to your boss, I'm the tip of a very large spear. If you want to see a pissed-off commodore and a flotilla, you just keep on. Confed deals with at least one or two pocket dictators a year."

I am surprised. I have never seen Wrik quite this way. He is rarely stirred to anger but is almost face-to-face with Croyzer.

To everyone's evident surprise and relief, Croyzer grins at Wrik. "Ok, you don't scare easy. That's good. I scare lots of people professionally. It's tiresome if there's no challenge. Ok, Starjockey, what do you think happened?"

"Someone tried to kill me and incidentally these other people."

CHAPTER TWELVE

"You think you're that important?" she said.

"Someone does. You've doubtless been informed of why I am here."

"Yeah," she replied, "mystery of the missing scientists. We sent you all we had on those folks. They left. No forwarding address."

"And that makes sense to you?"

She grimaced. "The more you do police work, the less anything people do surprises you." She glanced sidelong at a nearby officer. "Sgt Sendis."

"Yes, Captain."

"Continue the investigation. Take statements from McCaffer and the others. Get some of the engineering crew down here to investigate why the hell the safeties didn't kick in."

"The Lieutenant is going to come with me." She stares up at Wrik as if daring him to disagree. For a moment I think he is going to, simply because he objects to her commanding him. Then he nods.

"Come on," he says to me before I can mindspeak and warn him not to.

Croyzer did a double-take. "What are you two, joined at the hip?"

"Wrik," I began to say mentally.

"I've got it," he returns. His mental tone is forceful.

Aloud he says. "I like Lostly. She's been a good native guide. I find her perspective useful." His expression is defiant and his breath comes quickly.

Croyzer looks at me narrowly as if seeing me for the first time. This is not good. Wrik has focused her attention on me. I am puzzled by his actions. He is responding in an unusual manner to the woman. Further, he has not disregarded my advice in such a cavalier fashion before.

"Where are you from, Lostly? I don't recall running into you before. You're unusual-looking. I'd remember."

Wrik, I think I am going to be very cross with you. "Lacaille 8760," I say. "One of the early lost colonies, around a red dwarf. We were cut off during the First Sector War and had a lot of genetic drift, mutation to the third degree."

"How about we return to finding who was trying to kill us," Wrik says. "Lostly's family history can wait."

She looked around. "Take a ride with me."

We followed Croyzer back to her aircar. Her driver, who had impressive musculature for a human, opened the doors and we slide in. The car slides smoothly from the curb and into a tunnel. Croyzer reclines on the other side of the car. She tosses her head, throwing the long, thick locks of hair out of her face. I thought it odd that she would affect such a hairstyle, given how it seems to interfere with her vision, then detect that the eye under the thick bang is artificial, optimized for infrared and UV.

Wrik watches her narrowly. He seems to have a fascination with her. This bears further consideration.

CHAPTER THIRTEEN

"**T**HIS WAS A QUIET LITTLE OUTPOST BEFORE YOU arrived, Fels," Croyzer said, leaning back in her seat in a confident pose. "Twenty-four hours after you arrive, we have one explosion and a sabotage attempt on an elevator."

"So you do believe it was an attempt on my life."

She nodded. "There are too many safeties for such a thing to happen by accident. So, yes, someone wanted to kill someone on that elevator. Probably you, but even that can't be taken for granted. McCaffer, the aides, even Lostly here, might have enemies. What do you say, Lostly? Any ex-lovers with a hankering to do you in?"

Maauro regarded her coolly with, I realized, too much assurance for someone her age and position with a Chief of Police. "Sorry, no. Lt. Fels has been my first diversion since I arrived."

"Back to you then, Fels. You *are* the new factor."

"Was that explosion near the hotel," Maauro asked unexpectedly, "also aimed at Lt. Fels?"

Croyzer gave her appraising look. "Hard to say. But as an explosives expert myself, I can tell you whoever did it went to extraordinary lengths to ensure minimal damage, with maximum smoke and no chance of collateral damage. It was perfect as a diversion for someone who, say, wanted to be unobserved for a while." Her chilly eyes locked on mine but I gazed blandly back.

"Tell me about your mission here," she continued.

"Surely you were briefed," I responded.

"Surely I was. Tell me anyway."

"*CPSS Pisces* was ordered to Cimer to ascertain why a party of UDEXCO employees with strategic-level skills in biogenetic engineering, haven't returned. Nor have they made any *verifiable* contacts with friends, loved ones or colleagues. That investigation naturally raises the issue of why people with such a high-level, indeed military level sets of skills were assembled and sent here in the first place. The Confederacy hasn't forgotten the Eugenics Rebellion on Olympia. Beyond that, any time Confed citizens disappear in the wayback, it raises the prospect that somebody may be setting up their own little empire. So in the course of my investigations here, I am to determine the health and safety of Confed citizens working in a very hostile and dangerous environment. That means renewing the habitability certificate for this city for non-native life forms."

Croyzer leaned back in her seat, stretching. "Colony worlds have gone bad before, no denying that. But we're not Olympia. In any event, space is vast and communications slow. For all you know, these people showed up at their homes, only days after you, or whoever communicated your orders to you, left. How would you know?"

I shrugged. "I have to assume Command took that into account before they diverted a starship, even a small, old one like mine, here."

"I believe that's the modern version of 'Fuck, I got my orders.'"

Despite myself, a grin shot across my face. "I guess so. Some things don't change."

"So do you think we have a pocket dictatorship going here?"

"Hard to say yet. I haven't gotten around to meeting that many regular folks beyond Lostly here. Everyone does seem to be toeing the line around here and frightened to talk with me unless McCaffer or his people are nearby. Normally a spacer far from home, the only link to Confed, is sought after, invited to homes, presented with petitions for grievances, loaded with toys, trinkets to take back and tell people 'Hey we're out here.' I seem to be persona non grata."

"Maybe you're dislikeable."

"I'm pretty charming actually. Isn't that so, Ms. Lostly?"

"Quite charming when you work at it," she replied, "which you should start doing again after this ride."

"Careful," I mindsent to her. "Dial down the self-confidence."

"You two are so cute together," Croyzer said, "it's about to make me sick."

"Of course," I added. "If this was a pocket dictatorship with something to hide, that would make you the enforcer here. If anyone was to make an attempt on my life, logically, it would be you."

"Well, that's ridiculous."

"Really?"

"Oh yes, because if I wanted you dead, rest assured you'd be dead. I wouldn't have stooped to anything as random and unreliable as an elevator fall. Not to mention how obvious an assassination attempt it was. No, if I wanted you dead it would be quick neat and quite plausible as an accident. That is … if I wanted you dead." She gave a wolfish smile.

"Police manuals must have changed recently."

"I started with the Confed Marine manual. Semper Fidelis. Don't tell me you weren't smart enough to check up on me."

Actually I hadn't been, leaving that to Maauro in another of those times that I'd clearly become too dependent on her, complacent even. Though Maauro thought many times faster than I did, it was no excuse for my not thinking at all. "I spotted the close combat badge on your jacket. How long have you been out?"

"Three years," she bit off, her expression suddenly cold and remote. Croyzer didn't want to discuss her separation from the Marines, yet she still wore her service ribbons and badges on her police uniform. *Useful information to have, but not to press for now,* I thought.

"Where are we going?" Maauro asked.

Croyzer didn't look at her, her eyes continued to bore into me. "Where do you want to go, Lt Fels?"

"We were on our way to see Professor Dok. Perhaps someone didn't want me to meet him. So that really piques my curiosity. However, I neither need nor want a police escort."

"I can't be held responsible for your safety if you won't accept my protection."

"Anything happens to me and my ship heads out and comes back with a flotilla. Whoever tried this had better realize what stakes they are playing for."

Croyzer hit a panel by her right hand. "Jefel?"

"Yes, captain," came the voice of the unseen driver.

"Professor Dok's office."

"Yes, sir."

She hit the switch again.

"You're right about that," she continued. "Whoever would try to kill you is either an idiot, Confed takes care of its own, or they're big and playing for stakes that maybe we can't even see on the table yet."

"Guild?" I ventured.

She shook her head, the thick, glossy, blonde hair shimmered. "No, not unless you have some issue with the Guild of your own or they took a contract. I doubt the latter as they wouldn't take such a contract here. Guild on Tir-a-Mar is a small operation, well, at least on the 02-breathers side. God alone knows what goes on in the Ribisan areas. We know most of the local Guild operatives: small stuff, petty crime and vice."

"Interesting," Maauro said, evidently unable to restrain herself. "Then why don't you wipe them out?"

Croyzer laughed, evidently mistaking Maauro's question for naiveté, not strategy. "What, and have this place be like a Unity Church? Then I would be up to my neck in murders. People need a place to blow off steam. Besides, if I wipe out the crew I know, they will simply be replaced by ones I don't. Still, we are rounding up the usual suspects. I am going to take as many Guilders out of operation as I can while you're here. Reduces X-factors in case I am wrong about them being after you."

"That leaves the Ribisans, or parties in the pocket dictatorship."

"About the first, I can tell you nothing. About the second, you likely wouldn't believe me as you would suppose I am on their side."

"Would you, in my place?"

"Hell no. For what it's worth, I do get the impression something went on here about two years ago. A lot of personnel turned over, a lot of money moved around, offices were moved, some were closed, along with their projects. I was new. Most of it meant nothing to me, as it wasn't cop business. I was also told to keep my attention on street crime and domestics. Understand, Fels, I'm a company cop in a company town. Tir-a-Mar is an investment, not a political entity."

"It sounds like you're trying to warn me."

The full lips curved into a smile again. "You sure you don't want police protection?"

"Sure."

"What about Ms. Lostly here? Or do you care if she catches some mail addressed to you?"

"Thanks. I can take care of myself," Maauro said.

"What happened to dial down the self-confidence?" I sent. Nothing came back.

"I'm being paid daily more than I make in week," she continued, perhaps finally paying attention to my prompts. "Who knows, I may be able to hit them up for triple time after this."

Croyzer sighed. "Yeah, when I was your age I thought I couldn't die either." She glowered at me. "Don't get her killed. She's just a kid. If she had a mother on station I'd send her home to her."

"I'll do my best. But I also think you'll find that your people want her keeping an eye on me."

"Hey, I'm not—" Maauro began.

"Of course you are," I interrupted. "I just hope you're not telling them *everything*."

Maauro picked up the cue and crossed her arms, directing her attention out the window at the spiraling levels of the roadway we were on.

A light glowed on the com on Croyzer's belt. She picked up an earpiece and listened. "My detectives say the elevator was sabotaged mechanically, with the software looped out of the diagnostics. Very sophisticated. They must have had some idea of your movements and routed this particular model to your location.

She looked at me narrowly. "You got any Ribisan enemies, Fels?"

A frisson of fear shot through me. "Not that I know of. Why?"

"This elevator was last serviced shortly after you arrived on the Ribisan side of the station."

"Is that unusual?" I asked.

To my surprise she turned to Maauro. "Lostly, care to answer that?"

"It is unusual," Maauro replied smoothly. "O2 equipment is normally maintained on our side. The Ribisans maintain the station proper, their equipment and most of the dual-use equipment. But that does include some transports that run between the O2 and methane sections, so it is not without precedent. I've worked with Ribisan techs occasionally."

Croyzer looked almost disappointed at the answer.

"That is because she suspects I am more than I seem," Maauro mind-sent, "possibly because you have done everything possible to expose me to her at short-range and for sustained periods beyond asking me to disrobe."

CHAPTER THIRTEEN

Oh-oh, I thought, *pissed-off killer android at twelve o'clock high.*

"That makes it harder," Croyzer mused. "It's difficult to get information on criminal or social matters out of the Ribisans and impossible to verify any of it. I have a feeling my investigation will hit a stone wall soon."

We pulled to the curb. Around us, students and academics walked or rode small transports. A fountain glimmered in the distance under bright artificial daylight. A sign on one of the builders said Cimer University.

"We're here," Croyzer said. "Professor Dok's building is 32-1A. His office is on the second floor science lab, there's a receptionist."

"Thanks for the lift," I said. "We'll take it from here."

Croyzer nodded.

"Let me know if the investigation makes any progress," I added.

Nod. Cool, one-eyed stare.

The door opened. Jefel, the large officer, looked down impassively at us. Maauro slipped out of the car with commendable speed. I slid across the seat to follow her.

"Fels,"

I looked over at her.

"There's more going on here. With you, with the little princess there, and with the Ribisans and it involves my city. You're Confed, I know there's not a lot I can do to stop you, but you might find yourself in need of an ally soon."

Taking a page from her book, I nodded.

A vexed look crossed her face then, as if she realized what I had done, she grinned briefly.

I got out of the car.

Maauro and I made our way into the building and past the students.

"You know," I said. "I just realized that I smell of smoke and fire and you don't."

Maauro paused. "Yes, I was sanitizing myself and just realized that could have been a mistake. I wonder if Croyzer noticed?"

"She's sharp, that one." I pointed at a bathroom and ducked in. After a few minutes washing up I judged I was ready for company.

But we were to be disappointed. Dok evidently had a lecture and as we were an hour late, he'd moved on. We took advantage of the situation. I demanded to inspect the school's fusion reactor lab. After ordering everyone out, I gave Maauro the chance to plug in and recharge to her heart's content. I sat outside to avoid radiation poisoning. In twenty minutes she appeared at the doorway and waved.

"Well, I am refueled. There is a school cafeteria. We can get something for you."

"Great," I said without enthusiasm. Then I spotted a sign: *Rathskellar.* "Ah, good to see that some things about colleges never change. This will be better than a cafeteria. Follow me." We walked down to a sublevel of noise and young people, many in full-body dyes and some not wearing a great deal beyond that.

Funny, I thought of them as young people though I was barely seven years older than most of them. Yet those years had tacked almost infinite miles between myself and these carefree students. No one had tried to kill them today.

Some people smiled at us. One group actually waved us over, but we declined with smiles. I asked the waitress for a quiet place in the back.

"No quiet place around here," she grinned. She had dark-skin and eyes, golden earrings bounced and flickered on her earlobes. "But there's a make-out corner that's not being used. Hey, you aren't supposed to be kissing on duty are you?"

I winked. "We'll control ourselves. Beers and pizza, please."

"Sure," she showed us to a booth in a dark corner. We slid into it. The noise level was low enough for normal conversation and while we still caught looks from the crowd, there was no one close by.

The waitress slid tall, frosty beers in front of us. "Pizzas just come out. How many slices?"

"Four for starters," I replied.

I lifted the beer and held it before Maauro's eyes. "Cheers."

She duplicated my gesture and we both put a good dent in the contents. I sat back with a sigh. "Go ahead." I said. "Let me have it."

"Wrik can you explain your reaction to Captain Croyzer?" I asked, lowering the stein.

He hesitates, then his jaw firms. "You know your life changes. You think you are past certain things. Past being treated a certain way. Then you meet someone who brings it all back."

"I'm afraid I do not understand."

Now his face takes on an embarrassed cast. "I guess that I'm no longer used to being treated like that anymore. Like I used to be when I was nobody and nothing in the offport of Kandalor. The local cops treated me like I was something stuck to their shoes. That's the way she looked at me. I guess that got my back up."

Further conversation is delayed as the waitress returns and slides plates of pizza in front of us. Wrik orders refills on the beer. I wonder if this is wise, then consider that he has had a narrow escape from death, the second in days. Perhaps it would be as well to allow him some rest and relaxation. So we enjoy the pizza and beer for a few minutes. Wrik orders another slice and then leans back in apparent contentment.

I cocked my head at him. "Captain Croyzer is an attractive human female, isn't she?"

His face was a mix of surprise and a touch of guilt? "I suppose if you like the type."

"What type would that be? She appears to be somewhat older—"

"Yeah, she doesn't look like it though," Wrik said with an air of distraction.

"Her hair seems odd, the way it hung in her face, even though it covers an artificial eye. There was little need for concealment; it is a quality prosthetic."

"She pays serious attention to the way she looks."

"Were her features what would be considered pleasant?"

"Yeah, in a severe sort of way. She had very full lips ... Maauro."

"Yes."

"Why are you asking these questions?"

"Because I think your somewhat extreme reactions are the result of an attraction to her."

"What!?!"

"It is hardly surprising. She is by your own comments: attractive, intelligent and powerful – qualities one looks for in a mate."

"I'm not looking for a mate, or have you forgotten Jaelle?"

"I forget nothing. I don't even delete anymore."

"Sorry, figure of speech. But God no, I don't need any additional complications."

"Wrik, I did not accuse you of intending anything toward Croyzer, but you are a young human male and she is an extraordinary female. Your having an attraction to her is probably not something you can completely control."

He grimaced, which told me that I was correct.

"She," he hesitated, "she reminds me of the girls from homeworld. I guess I wasn't prepared for it."

"It is not entirely one-sided."

"What?"

"Attraction in the female of your species is marked by a dilation of the eyes and flush to the skin, as well as a fuller redness to the lips. These signs were all there."

"Umm, I think those are the same signs for suppressed rage. A state I believe she spends a lot of time in."

"My point, Wrik, is that Jaelle, with her wish for children, has upset the balance of our network. By doing so, she has also caused you to reassess your relations with females of your species."

"Now really does not seem to be a good time to be worrying about this."

"That is true," I conceded, "I only wish you to be aware of the attraction between you. It may be either useful or dangerous to us. Perhaps both."

"Ok. I'll watch it. Though I can't imagine why a woman like that would be interested in me."

"You are not unattractive."

"Thanks." He raised his beer in salute and drank.

"You command a ship, which gives you status. Beyond that, you are not from here and neither a superior nor subordinate of hers. That makes you an acceptable choice to her, at least as an item of interest. If it turns out to be a mistake, it is a self-limiting one, as you will not remain long."

"You mean she just wants to use me for sex?" He gives his lop-sided smile. *"I feel so cheap and tawdry."*

I judge the last comments to be humor based on context and his expression. I decide that I've conveyed as much warning as he is capable of dealing with for the present. I reach for the last slice of pizza.

CHAPTER FOURTEEN

HOURS LATER WE RETURN TO THE HOTEL THAT WRIK IS STAYING AT. THE *Star and Comet building is light and airy with many levels. Only the sleeping quarters are entirely inside as there is no fear of bad weather inside the floating city.*

When we enter the lobby, a slender and attractive red-haired female in a tight dress that reveals much of the body beneath, catches my eye and motions me over. I slip away from Wrik, who is checking for messages and picking up some items from the front desk. I send him a brief message not to look for me and to take his time.

The woman takes my arm and leads me into an alcove behind some plants. "I'm Baracia. They sent me over to entertain Lieutenant Fels. Can you introduce me?"

I am tempted to introduce her into a long fall into the planet's interior. "Plans have changed. The Lieutenant and I have visited some of the same worlds. I will be handling the entertaining."

"You?" she said. "Aren't you a bit young—"

"I am older than I look," I reply. I scan her portacomp, cracking its pitiful security instantly. I see she is promised a thousand credits for a night of sex with Wrik. I message a false order to her portacomp canceling her appointment and reroute a thousand credits from Wrik's account to hers, laundering it through several transactions. This takes .023 seconds. "In any event, you've been paid for your time."

She gives me a dubious look, checks her portacomp to find the message and check her credit balance. She brightens visibly. "Well, that gives me an evening all to myself. Pity though," she casts a calculating eye at Wrik. "He's not bad-looking and it's always fun to meet someone new. These spacers aren't usually much work after months in transit. They go off like rockets themselves." She gave a knowing laugh.

I smile in response, as something seems required.

"Have fun," she says over her shoulder as she steps back into the street.

We gain the security of Wrik's apartment. The robospider I sent with Wrik is no longer needed and I have reabsorbed it. I check our security myself. They have no cameras in the bedroom so I need not invent a loop of video for our unseen watchers there. I guide Wrik into the bedroom and close the door. Ambient music will cover our conversation. A proper scanner could isolate speech, but my software defenses will prevent that. It might raise suspicion, but less so than being eavesdropped on.

We order room service and a live waiter brings up the food. I again don one of Wrik's uniform shirts and the server's intrigued expression tells me that I am successful in planting the desired implication.

Doubtless someone will interrogate him about his observations. Between my intrusions into their computers and the natural tendency of bureaucratic organizations not to questions orders, I am comfortable no one will figure out how I assigned myself to Wrik. They wanted him entertained by a female; the details will not concern them.

We enjoy our meal, discussing but gaining no clues as to how I could possibly have been intercepted high in the sky. I devour my dessert with enthusiasm, savoring the complicated chemical combinations. Wrik gives me a tired smile, as he always does when I show my affections for sweets. He likes it when I seem more like a real girl.

I notice however that Wrik's face is drawn with fatigue. I quickly clear the dishes. "You must rest. The toll on your body has been severe over these two days."

He shakes his head. "We have so much to do—"

"Must I use my stunner?"

He smiles again, but his eyes are closing. I push him gently to the bedroom. He tries to say something but exhaustion claims him and he is asleep almost immediately after he stretches out. I monitor his vital signs attentively, but it is only deep sleep. I remain on the bed, nearby, motionless, watchful.

A channel clicks open in my head. It is Jaelle, she and Dusko must be in orbit.

"Jaelle to Maauro, God this is weird sending a message with my brain."

"Jaelle, I hear you. Are you and Dusko well?"

"I got her!" she says aloud to Dusko. I fine-tune the signal and now can see out of her eyes. I could do so with Dusko as well if I wanted to but there is no need. I will hear what he says through her. I also know the suspicious Dua-Denlenn will be happier if I am not actively in his mind. I observe them sitting in the small bridge of the Stardust, Dusko in Wrik's place at the controls, which would make Wrik unhappy if he saw it.

"Are you and Wrik all right?" she continues speaking aloud for Dusko's benefit.

"We are now," I send using each one's channel so they hear me directly.

I give her a sitrep on our infiltration to date and my assurance that Wrik is well.

"Zazal's claws," she explodes. "It's a wonder you're both alive!"

"What is your status?" I replied to divert her concern.

"We are in orbit, keeping out of sight of the Pisces as would be expected if any Guilders are looking at us. Now tell me about Wrik."

"Wrik is asleep. The days have been strenuous but we are both in good health. What is of greatest concern is how I could be intercepted by fighters on my entry to Cimer. This is either an incredible stroke of

bad fortune, or our unseen enemies have intelligence on our movements from a source I cannot fathom."

"Shall we break off and return to Star Central?" Dusko asks. "If our covers are worthless..."

"I do not believe that is the case. Our cover story here has held up. I think that, as before, some faction among the Ribisans is moving against us. Cleary they have more assets here but they too do not want to break cover. Such surreptitious action tells me that they fear discovery and interference from other factions. If the human city authorities did not believe Wrik to be Confed military, we would have been detained by now."

"So we go ahead with contacting the Guild?" Jaelle asks

"Yes."

"No time like the present," Dusko says with a grimace.

Jaelle nods and switches on the radio. "I've got the Guild encryption on. Pity it's so out of date."

Dusko shrugs. "Given the distances out here the normal communication channels don't change much – too much time lag."

"SV Longshot to Cimer base," Jaelle says. A minute passes and she repeats the encoded call several times.

Finally. "Cimer base to SV Longshot, acknowledged. What do you want?" the voice was gravely with an accent I associate with Moroks.

"Oh the usual," Jaelle says, "easy wealth, no taxes, to avoid Confed Patrols and to live to a ripe retirement."

"Your code is an old one, Longshot," the voice replies dryly.

"I've been out of circulation, securing a very valuable cargo."

"That is of interest, who am I speaking with?"

"Fyvia Minogue, ship's master. I am last out of Manadar in allegiance to House Ferlan. Who am I speaking with?"

"For now, simply Cimer Guild Control."

"You're very cautious CGC, I approve. I have not lived this long by neglecting caution either. What is the weather forecast over Cimer presently?"

"Presently stormy and uncertain."

"Damn, what type of storms?"

"A small plague of comets," the Morok replies

"Slang for Confed Navy," Dusko sends mentally.

"Unfortunate," Jaelle replies, "I do not wish to linger in this area as other opportunities beckon."

"The weather might be better on another voyage."

"This one would have to demonstrate profit before I would consider a return. As I indicated I have valuables to trade and am looking to establish a connection here. "Can you get me down?'

"Whole ship or cargo shuttle?"

"Shuttle for now."

There was such delay in responding that I began to wonder if we had lost our contact. Several times Jaelle made as if to speak, each time Dusko forestalled her with a hand gesture.

"*Longshot, this is ground base. I am uploading code and coordinates. We have an automatic shuttle due in from one of the lunar mining operations. They come in by ALS in a section of the city used only by automatics. We can substitute you in at 27.60 local time. Synchronize your chronometers with Cimer's normal landing beacon. We'll give you a parking orbit free of comets and let you know if they move.*

"*You will be met on landing. Be prepared to prove your status. There will be a 5,000 credit addition to the customary fees for covering your landing. Up to you if it is worth it.*"

"*It will be. Longshot has received the download.*"

"*There will be no further communication until you land. Ground base out.*"

"*Charming rascal,*" *Jaelle says.*

"*The first test passed,*" *I add.*

"*I'm suspicious that they just happened to have a shuttle coming in six hours from now,*" *Jaelle says.*

"*They don't,*" *Dusko replies.* "*I used to keep an automatic lander in near orbit back on Kandalor. I could always use it on short notice to cover any Guild connection or landing I needed to make. My bet is he does the same. The fact that he's agreeing to land a Guild ship he doesn't know, with an obsolete code, tells me he is hungry, looking for profit and willing to take risks. It'll also make him dangerous.*"

"*Agreed,*" *I send.* "*It was wise to offer to land only the shuttle, it preserves our options and he will be less concerned about a shuttle. Getting Stardust down unnoted would likely be impossible.*"

"*I'm not thrilled about it in any event,*" *Jaelle says.* "*Candace gave us a bunch of nasty stuff, drugs, illegal medicines and software, not to mention the weapons. If we get pulled by real station authorities, we could be in the gas mines for the rest of our short lives.* "

"*Only such items can command enough money to make shipping them interstellar pay,*" *Dusko replied. He stands.* "*I'll get started loading the shuttle. Glad I am not going with you.*"

"*You will follow Jaelle down as needed,*" *I remind him.* "*For now continue to simulate a larger crew, make sure your orbit does not allow for Wrik's ship to detect you. That would raise suspicion.*"

"*I am not addled,*" *Dusko snaps.* "*I am quite aware of that.*"

"*Don't mind him,*" *Jaelle says laughing.* "*He's been grumpy since we came out of hyperdrive. Must be getting old.*"

"*And hoping to get older, unlikely as it seems in this crew,*" *he retorts.*

"*Any chance I could talk to Wrik?*" *Jaelle asks, after Dusko leaves.*

"*You know that direct linking more than one of you is dangerous,*" *I say.*

"Yes, but you can tell him what I say."

"Truly it would be best to let him rest. I will relay your greetings when he awakes."

"Kit-sister this is far from satisfactory."

"I am sorry."

"It also makes me suspect that things are worse than you're telling me."

"The situation is presently nominal. Hazards have been overcome."

"I'm sure. I will want to hear more about those in due course. Are you taking care of Wrik?"

"With every skill I have."

"Good, Kit-sister. Continue."

"Jaelle, please be careful. There is some power moving against us that I do not understand. It seems erratic but it occasionally seems to know things that it cannot possibly have found out."

"Dusko?" she sends, whispering, for all that I keep their mental channels discreet from each other.

"No. I would have detected malfeasance on his part long before. Nor do I think he would risk my enmity, having seen the fate of others who have done so. I also believe him to be as trustworthy as one of his kind can be. He is too invested in our network and his survival without my protection is unlikely. No, it is something else. Guard yourself. Wrik would never forgive me if something happened to you on this mission."

"It seems we are very tied together, Kit-sister. It's a good thing I like you so much."

"I am honored by it and return your affection in full measure."

"Give Wrik my love when he wakes."

"I shall. I will monitor you and Dusko both through a subroutine. You will not generally be aware of me and absent severe planetary storms the link should be stable. Anything unusual will bring my full attention on you."

"OK. I'll see you both sometime after I'm down."

I remain silent for hours guarding my sleeping friend. Again I administer restorative and medications to heal the body he has been using too hard lately. Six hours later I make arrangements for breakfast. Again a live server brings up the meal. It is someone from the TAMPD operating undercover, but I have hacked enough of the payroll files to identify him.

I hear the sounds of Wrik stirring and walk into the room bearing a tray with coffee and juice. Wrik is not a morning person. He opens his eyes at the smell and sits up, the blanket falling to his lap. He must have wakened and undressed in the night as his clothes are on the floor.

I hand him the coffee. "Jaelle and Dusko have arrived. They are safely in orbit. Jaelle sends her love to you. She misses you and looks forward to being reunited."

"I wish I could talk to her."

"I can relay anything you want to say to her."

"That would be kind of awkward."

"She said much the same thing."

"Tell her I am well, and I miss her."

"I have. She says that her response would be too naughty for me."

He laughed. *"That's my girl."*

Wrik finishes the coffee. *"I'll hit the shower."*

I nod and sample the juice; complex molecules appeal to my palette. Wrik continues to look at me.

"Yes?"

"Um, I'm not wearing anything?"

"Don't you customarily sleep naked?"

"Yes, I don't customarily prance naked around the room in front of you though."

"Were you planning on actually prancing? That might be amusing to watch."

He sighed.

"I take it," I added, *"that you are concerned by one of your societal taboos."*

He nods.

"I shall protect my virtue by closing my eyes and not peeking," I say

"Good," he replies.

I close my eyes and Wrik scampers off to the shower. Through a variety of other sensors I can detect every detail of his body.

With Wrik occupied I switch my attention back to Jaelle. I have monitored her through a subroutine, as she transferred to the Guild lander. She has arrived in the cargo section of the city reserved for automatics. The area is pressurized and sealed. Through her eyes I see server-robos scurry about unloading the cargo, which would not have survived the pressure and corrosive atmosphere of Cimer. A small boarding tube snakes out to her ship. Guild work, as it brings a viable atmosphere to Jaelle and an exit from her ship.

"Maauro," she sends.

"I am with you."

"Would that you were in body too."

"A sentiment I share."

"I'm armed and ready."

"Dusko?" I send.

"I am linked to you and to Jaelle, but you were right communicating with both of you is difficult. I find myself confused—"

"Retain your link with Jaelle and concentrate on advising her. I will maintain the link between us three but I will not speak to you save at great need."

"Agreed," Dusko says, pain in his voice

CHAPTER FOURTEEN

A series of clanks means that the boarding tube has reached the shuttle's passenger compartment.

I feel Jaelle steady herself; feel her senses sharpen and focus in a way that I had not experienced in my link with Wrik. While he is descended from apes that stood upright, she evolved from an omnivorous cat-like hunter. There is something appealing in her warrior-like focus that reminds me of myself as M-7.

The door cycles open into a white hallway. Jaelle rises, settles her weapon on her leather-clad hip and strides into the corridor. The boarding tube takes her into a hallway. Two Guilders await her in the hall, a human male and a female Dua-Denlenn with a scarred face. Neither is obviously armed but I suspect concealed weapons.

"Minogue?" says the female.

Jaelle nods, careful to keep her hands clear of her weapon.

"Say nothing," Dusko advises over the link. "Make no small talk. This is not trade and you will convey weakness and an unhealthy curiosity if you do."

"We'll take you to the Guildmaster. You'll leave the hardware at the door or you do not see him.

"Understood," Jaelle replies, "I am familiar with the ways of Guildmasters. My own is no different."

They move through an industrial area, unobserved by the robots and the few biologicals in the area. With the machines, I believed it was electronic-blinding such as I myself did. With the biologicals, the blindness was affected most probably with bribes or intimidation. Once at a main junction they slip into a railcar and speed into the city proper. The section they eventually stop in is in the lower part of the floating city, a factory area with low-income residences and many inexpensive restaurants and entertainment sections.

"We appear to have found the red-light district," Jaelle sends.

"The natural environment of the Guild," I agree.

They enter a building over a narrow street. It appears to be the sort of hock and pawn common to spaceports and stations where people can trade items for credits.

At the front desk an unassuming human greets Jaelle's two escorts. The Dua-Denlenn extends a hand for Jaelle's weapon. With a sigh, she hands it over.

"Follow her," the bald storekeeper says. "When you get out, come back to me for your weapon. We've had your gear moved to the Spacer's Rest. It's inexpensive and discrete."

"Be alert," Dusko says. "The Guildmaster will be the next person you see."

Jaelle follows the other female. They go through a series of doors and pressure doors to a well-appointed room of luxurious furniture and fine art treasures, though these latter are of the eye-hurting Morok style.

CHAPTER FOURTEEN

Jaelle scents a Morok in the room beyond. Her bat-like ears detect the door closing behind her and footsteps in the corridor.

The back door swishes open and a heavy-set Morok enters. He looks at her through red-eyes, then pulls back a chair to an ornate desk made of actual wood and gestures at a chair well away from him. The Dua-Denlenn female takes up station between them and against the wall, immobile but alert.

Jaelle approaches the Guild rep. The mental link between us gives me a sense of her body as well as what she is thinking. Her walk is confident, belying the anxiety that I read in her body chemistry. I am aware of her in a fashion that Dusko is not- he will only receive the direct thought communications that she pushes at him. I am a quantum computer at heart and my system can process vastly more data than he can. I realize with a shock how young, alive and vital she is. I feel the muscles of her lithe body move as she stalks forward.

This is unsettling. Jaelle is Wrik's lover, am I spying on her sensuality? Yet I find I am reluctant to reduce my awareness of her, yet with a fleeting sense of embarrassment I do so. I must concentrate on the Guild Rep.

"I am Guild Rep Hartain," the Morok begins. His ape-like body overspills the chair as he leans back to look up at Jaelle.

"Fyvia Minogue from Manadar," Jaelle says, *"from the House of Madame Ferlan."*

This is the central facet of our plan with the Guild. Ferlan had captured Wrik when I was on the trail of what turned out to be the Infester Artifact Planetoid. We knew more about her then anyone who was not true Guild, because of the bizarre friendship that had developed between Wrik and the elderly Guildmaster. With her disappearance and presumed death there was little chance of our being exposed.

"The Collector is well-know to us," Hartain says, *"a fine lady and a great asset of the Guild. How is the good Madame? One trusts that her many ventures prosper and that her enemies fail in their attempts on her life."*

"I regret to say that my mistress has been lost on an expedition into uncharted space, along with most of her inner staff. Their vessel's life support span having been exceeded and with no word of them, she has been officially declared dead."

"You bring dire and unpleasant news, young Minogue," Hartain says, blinking rapidly, *"tell me what your relationship is...was to Ferlan?"*

"A member of her house, I fulfilled a number of duties, aide-de-camp, and bodyguard. My background in deep space trade was often of use to her."

"And now you seek to freelance?"

"Well, I do have my connections and Madame Ferlan's estate is... unsettled. I have no desire to be involved in any resulting territorial

adjustments. Truth be told I share much of my late mistresses' wanderlust and love of ancient secrets. She often found great profit in them."

The Morok gave a guttural laugh. *"It did not end so well for her, this love."*

I feel Jaelle shrug. *"She reached an advanced age for one so high in the Guild and in great luxury. In the end the claws of night close in on us all."*

"Too true," Hartain said. *"So what can the local Guild chapter do for you?"*

"I have cargo to move; small arms, recreational drugs and such."

"The usual Guild cut of course."

"Of course. I can also pick up any communications you need taken back toward the inner systems. Perhaps you have cargoes that you need moved or special projects that require assistance?"

Dusko's voice whispered in Jaelle's mind. *"Do not overplay. He knows all this. The hook is baited. If you try to go too far too fast he will become suspicious. Complain about the Confed warship. Then wrap it up."*

I must resist the desire to add my exhortation to his. The additional channel to her mind could be disorienting.

"Damn bad luck to find a Confed warship here," Jaelle says aloud. *"Or is that common?"*

Hartain grimaces, his pronounced canines very much in evidence. *"No, thank the Gods. Some officious snot of a lieutenant is grandstanding all over the station inspecting its habitability and operations. We have decreased operations while he is here. Some fool, I cannot find out who yet, actually tried to kill him. As a result the TAMPD under Croyzer, a name you will learn to detest the longer you stay here, is busting our collective reproductive organs.*

"Still the Confed won't get anywhere near us. He may cause grave irritation to the Ribisan interests. He commands only an older scoutship with a small crew."

"Good," Jaelle says, *"then I should have little concern about remaining hidden. A cruiser would be throwing out fighter or shuttle patrols if only for practice."*

The Morok gazed at her. *"You seem to have played this game before."*

"As I said, deep space trade was my profession. What trader hasn't ducked customs or navy patrols?"

"Well said. I will consider what you told me. Perhaps there will be some cargo for you. We are a small operation. It may be that we can benefit each other."

Jaelle nods. *"Call on me when you decide. Your people know where to find me."* She made a Guild salute, the Morok returned the gesture and Jaelle backed away. Whether the Morok thought that odd, or merely sensible, he did not comment. Jaelle walked quickly through the door.

CHAPTER FOURTEEN

"*Slow down,*" Dusko sent to her. "*You must look like you are in friendly territory.*"

Jaelle obliged and I felt her breathing slow. A lightness came to her body that made me feel slightly dizzy.

"*Looks like I pulled it off, Kit-sister. What now?*"

"*Proceed to the Spacer's Rest. Await contact. Dusko, any thoughts?*"

"*I do not like this head-to-head chatter. I prefer my thoughts kept private.*"

"*Any more useful thoughts,*" I send with some asperity. This evidently amuses Jaelle who gives a brief laugh.

"*You will be contacted by low level staff to relieve you of your cargo,*" Dusko continued. "*Bargain, but not too hard. Hartain will expect a good deal as you wish to ingratiate yourself with him, yet he will look to make sure you are not a fool. The balance is a delicate one. He will not wish to overplay his hand, as ships to his location are few. You might consider kicking him an additional 5% if he gives a guild pledge of a return cargo. He would not risk reneging on that, even with Ferlan's House in disorder.*"

"*Why?*" Jaelle asks.

"*Because whoever inherits the house, inherits the grudges, debts and obligations and might be looking to make an example of someone unimportant as a warning to those more so.*"

"*You live in a scary world, Dusko,*" Jaelle sent.

"*It is the same one you inhabit. I just see it with fewer illusions than you or your boyfriend.*"

"*Enough of that,*" both Jaelle and I send at the same moment.

Now it is our turn to feel amusement from the Dua-Denlenn.

"*Attend to your duties about the ship,*" I order Dusko. He fades out of my mind.

"*I suppose I have to let you go too,*" Jaelle says, but I feel a touch of fear from her. With the link closed she will be alone. While I can spare power to monitor her, the link is two-way and she cannot maintain it constantly with a biological body.

"*Yes,*" I say. "*Eat a large meal; the unit draws power from your body. You will find yourself—*"

"*Starving, yes, already the case.*"

"*Call Dusko when the Guild traders come. Call me if you are endangered or even if you are just afraid. There is no power drain on my side.*"

"*Thanks, Kit-sister. It's surprisingly comforting carrying you around in my head. But I wish your armored body was right here with me. Still you watch over Wrik, that's what I want most. And remember.*"

"*Remember what?*"

"*No kissing my boyfriend.*"

CHAPTER FOURTEEN

I consider. I do not think she had the mouth-to-mouth resuscitation in mind. "Order understood."

"Ok, Kit-sister. I'll check in later or if I get any bad vibes. Over and out."

CHAPTER FIFTEEN

AFTER ANOTHER DAY OF WORKING OUR COVERS ON CIMER, WRIK AND *Jaelle bedded down in their respective hotels but not until they complained to me about being so close and still so far apart. I sympathized but there is no present help for the situation. I am as glad that Wrik will be resting and continuing to recover from his two close brushes with death rather than seeking vigorous comfort in the arms of his Nekoan lover.*

Jaelle too could use a rest from the readings I am getting off her body after her first day of infiltration. Maintaining the mental link with me is far more draining for Jaelle than it is for Dusko. The Dua-Denlenn finds it painful mentally and curiously physically. Wrik is untroubled by our link but does not transmit much beyond those surface thoughts that he pushes at me. I am surprised that the difference in their species has made so much variance in how my biological friends interact with what is essentially an identical neural net in their brains. However I must more carefully ration the contact with Jaelle as it renders her fatigued and if she became any hungrier I might be concerned for lone pedestrians crossing her path.

I must also confess that I find it somewhat unsettling how much of her personality comes across the link between us. I am flooded with unfamiliar sensations when linked to her that I do not experience with the others.

I stand guard in Wrik's room, while maintaining a light and periodic contact with Jaelle, enough to tell that she too is asleep and uninjured. Above, Dusko continues his solitary watch on the skies, monitoring any traffic, looking for signs of other vessels. He is in direct contact with Pisces on a secured channel, monitoring the AI and fake crewmembers and their occasional interactions with ground base.

"Maauro," he calls in the early morning hours.

"Yes."

"Guild shuttle approaching. They're here for the cargo."

"Understood. Are you prepared to deal with this?"

"I would be happier if you unlocked the arms locker and I could pick out a laser."

"Very well." I send the unlock code.

"Ah," he says apparently pleased and surprised that I have allowed him access to weapons. He quickly takes advantage, picking out body armor, a shock baton, stunner and a laser.

"They will not know you are alone," I remind him in the midst of his warlike preparations.

"It does not do to underestimate Guild."

I remember one of Dusko's operatives, Lostra, who planted a cyber-boobytrap that blinded and crippled me, almost leading to my destruction. *"You are correct."*

Dusko, armed and suspicious, greets his fellow Guilders in the shuttle bay after they establish a soft dock, their shuttle being too large for Stardust's bay. Three Guilders come aboard along with a loading robot. Conversations are short as Dusko leads them to the bay and supervises their unloading of our illicit cargo of drugs, weapons and other materials I wish we did not need to inject into Cimer's life. However, the biological imperative to violence and self-destructive impulses is a fact of life, just like gravity and pressure.

We only relax our guard when the Guilders detach to make their way back in a surreptitious approach to the floating city below.

"Return the laser to the arms room," I direct. *"You may retain the rest of the material if it comforts you."*

"It does," Dusko replies. *"It surely does. As does being up here and well away from the insanity of this mission."*

"Duly noted. Hope that it remains that way. Call me at need." Contact ceases instantly. It is a measure of how concerned Dusko was that he opened the channel at all. The solitary Dua-Denlenn never seems concerned by a lack of company.

In the morning we breakfast on the terrace of our room. Above us the roof of the city is projected in the rusty orange of the Okaran sun, the day is warm and Wrik is clad in a light robe as we both look over the city inside the dome below us. The buildings are of light construction, as they did not need to fear the elements. The wind is never above a breeze, rain rarely more than a mist, snow is reserved for certain winter holidays and then usually only for a few hours. Everything is built for "indoor" use from the rail cars and robocabs to the slidewalks.

"Do you have any ideas for how to press our investigation?" I ask. *"I am frankly at a loss unless Croyzer turns up some investigative avenue."*

"If she does," he says, running his hand through hair not yet dry from the shower, *"we'd have to wonder if she would share it. We have to do something to change the situation. The longer we stay here the easier it is to contain us, or the more likely some part of our cover gets broken. We have to press the pace, we can't lay back."*

"Again, how? A clever enemy would ignore us, leaving us to run out our clock. You cannot pretend to investigate the stations habitability for much longer and all avenues we have looked at in regard to the project or the personnel have dead-ended about as quickly as we anticipated they would."

"We have seen signs our enemy is not so clever," Wrik says, *"or rather trying to be too clever for their own good. The elevator sabotage was an overthought plan. Since it would be detected that the elevator was*

interfered with anyway, why not go with a bomb? Much more likely to get the job done. There's something amateur about our opposition."

"Yes," I reply. "They are not hardened trained espionage agents like us."

He looks at me, startled for a second, then bursts out laughing. "Yeah, I suppose."

"I did not intend humor at your expense. I myself was designed as a direct combat unit. While I have skills at infiltration, it was usually merely a prelude to a direct assault."

"On Kandalor," Wrik says, "you lived either like a hunter or the hunted. I was on the hunted side. When you live like that it gives you insight into spies, you see what others don't, learn to see traps before they spring because you won't be strong enough to get out of them after. You see the patterns that go with Guild, with spies, with those who are trying to avoid lawful oversight. What I perceive is a force here, as back on Star Central, that wants to attack us, but is having difficulty reaching us. Either they are simply not that good at it, or they are being blocked and forestalled by some other party and hence these half-assed attempts."

"Half-assed? How would—"

"A colloquial expression for ineptitude," he laughed.

I wonder is full-assed was better or worse and then decided to simply drop it.

Wrik suddenly put down his juice glass. "Croyzer did say that the elevator had been serviced on the Ribisan side of the city?"

"Yes."

"Perhaps it is time for Lieutenant Fels to pay a courtesy call on the Ribisan authorities."

I frown. "Is this wise? While they may use, or be in alliance with oxygen-breathers, there is no doubt that our enemies are Ribisans. We would be walking into an environment hostile to both of us and where my capabilities are markedly degraded."

Wrik grins picking up the glass again. "Getting cautious in your old age?"

"No," I retort, "merely trying to insure that you have an old age."

He laughs again but there is a bitter undertone. "My instincts tell me the sooner we get out of this tin can in a gas ball, the more likely an old age is for both of us. You've done your usual incredible job of hacking into systems and databases, but even you can't invent friends and co-workers who know Lostly. Your interactions as a human mutant have improved immensely since those kids picked you out on Stauffer but the longer people are around you the more likely they are realize that you are not human, mutant or otherwise. Too many little clues and cues accumulate and bang, realization."

The bold tactic appeals to me, who was designed for direct combat. Yet I must balance my enthusiasm with the realization of how fragile my network members are in the corrosive gas and pressures of Cimer and of my own vulnerability.

"Very well," I say after considering the pros and cons. "I am persuaded. We shall attempt the Ribisan side. But how to go about it?"

"What have you uncovered about it?" he asks.

Beyond the fact that it is eighty-percent of the floating city and the basic schematics of the structures and major utilities, only what we both saw on the way down. Their systems are far more secure then Confed ones and I have not judged it safe to probe them. There is an interface zone between the O2 breather section and the Hydrogen section where the gravity is 1.2 gs and where the airlocks, cargo interchanges and changing stations for environmental suits sit. Think of it as a thin membrane covering our section, we are after all encapsulated in their city save toward the top where the power, and some of the industrial and landing sections are dual-use.

"Where is the nearest interface entrance?"

I stand and point to the far wall. "We are in the heart of the O2 commerce and residential section; the airlock is as far away as it can be and still be on this level. The entrance at Radial 13 is used for much of the diplomatic and light commercial traffic."

"Excellent. I say we get dressed and make our way there this afternoon."

"As you wish. But why wait?"

"Because it will give you time to demonstrate your value to Mysol and Fenster. Call in. Tell them what I am planning and how scared you are. I'll bet serious credit that when we get to the gate we find McCaffer waiting for us offering to take us to meet the Ribisan dignitaries."

"Won't that eliminate the element of surprise?"

"With our mobility and communications being so restricted and with no contacts among the Ribisans, I doubt it will matter. Our purpose is more to stir and unsettle things than to actually detect anything. I'll admit it's all a longshot but you can't hit anything until you pull a trigger."

"An apt analogy," I reply.

We finish our breakfast. Wrik suggests that I make my call from the lobby on the pretext of buying something in the gift shop. "Lostly would be too frightened to make a call from the room for fear I would walk in on her or overhear something."

After breakfast I slip out of the room and run down the hallway, which is monitored. This time I do not blind the sensors. I take the elevator to the lobby then find a darkened corner to make my call on McCaffer private line. He is excited to hear from me and reassures me that this is very important information, worthy of a bonus.

"Go along with whatever he wants. Do you know what time he plans to go across and where?"

CHAPTER FIFTEEN

I advise McCaffer that we will cross at the diplomatic door C-13 at noon.

"I'll be there. Don't worry about anything and keep up the good work." He clicks off.

I buy a random item in the gift shop and return to the room.

"We're on," I say to Wrik as I close the door behind me

We made our way to the oval of the interface entrance, where the familiar and unloved visage of John McCaffer greeted us. He was too much of a professional to sport a smug smile, but he couldn't completely conceal how pleased he was that the cat had made it to the mouse hole first.

"Good afternoon, Lt. Fels, Ms. Lostly. How are you?"

I gave Maauro a sour look for effect and she managed an abashed expression. "Apparently I'm predictable, Mr. McCaffer."

"Lieutenant, I believe you will find my presence a boon. I handle many of our negotiations and interactions with the Ribisans, who can be extremely difficult to understand. I can't imagine that you planned to wander about in a -100C methane-hydrogen atmosphere accosting random Ribisans from inside of an environmental unit about whether they sabotaged our elevator."

"See," Maauro said with an exasperated gesture. "I told you it didn't make any sense!"

This time it was my turn to act chagrinned. "As I said, I do not intend to be monitored."

"Of course, of course," McCaffer said, "I can say as much or as little as you deem necessary, but I think you would find even locating things on the other side of the airlock rather more confusing than you can imagine. How would you even find the office of the Commandant or obtain an audience with the Pillar?"

"The Pillar?" I replied.

"They don't use the terms mayor or manager. The actual position would best be translated as, "The supporting pillar of God's own community." The position is both religious leader and head of the civil bureaucracy."

"Very interesting," I said with a sigh of defeat. "Well, as you are here it would seem foolish of me not to make use of your services. As the senior Confed officer of a visiting starship, I should make a courtesy call on the local military and civil leaders. You do not have the former and I have already met the latter. So now it falls on me to pay that courtesy to the Ribisans and while doing so investigate the disappearances, whatever they were working on and the attempt on our lives."

"We have raised those issues with the Ribisans already, some as a result of your requests and in our own investigations."

"Nonetheless."

"I assumed that would be the case. I took the liberty of arranging a meeting for you with the head of the Naval Landing Forces, who provide our planetary security. We can also have a brief audience with the Pillar, though I have to tell you that neither was pleased by the shortness of the notice."

He turned to Maauro. "There's no need for you to go Ms. Lostly. I can look after the Lieutenant from here."

"Oh no," I said with a nasty tone. "I wouldn't dream of leaving Ms. Lostly out of this little picnic." It hadn't occurred to me that McCaffer would try to separate us. Of course he regarded her as merely a star-struck local girl, who'd attached herself to me. Hopefully he would write off my reaction as a petty revenge to her having informed him of my movements.

Maauro stuck her tongue out at me. "You probably couldn't find your way back without me."

Probably couldn't, I thought.

McCaffer gave a rueful smile, shook his head, and turned to lead us to the entry panel. Our palms confirmed our identities biometrically. I assumed Maauro hacked hers so that it did not register her as a machine. I'd so come to believe in her almost magical power over lesser computers and AIs that it hadn't even occurred to me to worry.

There were smaller personnel entrances set in the main pressure door. A group of Ribisans in environmental suits trooped out of one of them. I eyed them with renewed dread as they towered over us, for all that their suits were weaponless and without military armor. The Ribisans, despite their squid-like appearance, had little difficulty standing in our low G, though a suit breach would quickly be fatal due to the pressure and atmosphere difference. Their suits lacked the bulk of ours, as they did not need the servos and actuators that allowed us to move in Cimer's 1.8 gravities.

We entered the interface, staggering slightly with the 1.2 gravities of the interface area, which served as an intermediary step into the true high gravity waiting for us. We walked down a white hallway to a changing room for e-suits. An older man, heavy with muscle, served as the suit chief, he greeted us at the rack of powered exoskeletons.

"No need to worry about you in suit, L-tee," the chief said with a grin. I guessed him for old Confed Navy man. He looked on a screen then at McCaffer. "I see your suit certification is also up to date."

"Now to you," he said turning to Maauro. "Ah good, I see you had suit experience on the Ribisan ship you came out here on."

Maauro shrugged. "There wasn't much else to do, Chief. I got interested after the first day's lifeboat drill. I figured with the drill they'd showed me just enough to get myself killed and I better get some real training."

The chief laughed. "You're smarter than most young people I meet. You just saved everybody a two-hour wait while I certified you. All we need to do is go over the servos and weight supports, which won't take more than twenty-minutes."

I assumed Maauro had uploaded a certification to the city database while we were talking with the chief. I listened to her lie about her weight to the chief as he set the actuators but that too was not an issue. Maauro could carry the suit's extra weight without any trouble.

The chief chatted amiably with Maauro as he showed her the mechanics of the unit she could have manufactured herself, if needed. She managed to charm the old vet as he fitted her. In many respects, posing as the naive Lostly had honed her human interaction skills.

We were quickly suited up. McCaffer wore a white suit with a standard space helmet. I opted for orange and a bubble helmet similar to the ones the Ribisans used. I wouldn't have used it out in space where a star might be slowly roasting the back of my head, but in the murk of Cimer it could give me a better view of what was going on.

"Might as well check the sidearm, L-tee," the chief said. "A Mark-Niner might last twenty-minutes out there but that's about all. You'd need weapons kitted out for high-p and super cold to pack out there."

Reluctantly I handed over my weapon. He was right of course and in any event Maauro was my only real protection.

Maauro too wore a bubble helmet. I suppressed a groan when I saw she had chosen a pink suit. She was beginning to get lost in her part I thought. The Chief checked our displays and seals and gave us the traditional helmet slap before exiting the chamber.

I watched my pressure gauge as the O2 was sucked out. The 1.2 g wasn't bad as I rose, the suits powered actuators doing most of the work. The light then changed from the warm yellow-white to the wan blue of a Cimmerian afternoon. Our suit displays outlined objects, and supplemented with UV and infrared, but we couldn't use headlamps. The brilliant white light would be blinding, even dangerous to a Ribisan. I found that realization cheering.

The door opposite us slid open and we walked out into the nightmare landscape of the vast Ribisan side of Tir-a-Mar. I stood gaping at the odd angles of the interior of their city. Blue, green and red sodium lights glowed against the dark-green metal that was the shell of the floating city. Slabs of metal covered in lights seemed to jut at random angles. Vehicles, from teardrop-shaped air transports, to open hover cars, moved through the thick murk. Squat robo-loaders, full of crates and goods, rolled in all directions from the Interface Zone to unguessed destinations. The effect was of movement in all axes.

Ribisans themselves twirled in their tripodial balancing act on the long tentacle-like limbs. Here they seemed vastly different, more fluid and alive. Their grape cluster heads glowed with phosphorescence. It seemed for a second as if these had vastly more limbs than I had seen before, and then I realized that the creatures were wearing clothes that seemed composed of streamers of…something. At these temperatures and pressures some things that were liquid or gaseous, in our environment, were metal here. For all I knew they could be ceramic, or the skins of some impossible animal. Bits of some metal or ceramic reflected sparkles of light and it seemed some wore colored lights on their clothes as well. What any of it signified was beyond me.

I was surprised by sounds, transmitted both by speakers and by conduction in my suit: hooting, trilling, dull booms. Some of it came from Cimer itself, for while we were well down in the bowels of the city, the structure was open to the sky – just like any human city. Above us, I could see many levels, but in the distance, lightening flashed across openings to the outside world. Despite the fantastic blast of lightning, thunder was muted, either pressure or some science of the Ribisans.

Then there was the weight. We were unprotected save by our suits, which, carry our weight as they did, could not prevent every cell from feeling the pull of nearly double their natural load. The suits would massage our muscles and bodies just like an old G-suit trying to keep the blood from pooling in our lower limbs. It would work, for a while.

I felt disoriented, disassociated – as if I was locked in a childhood dream.

"Are you all right Wrik?" Maauro's mental voice sounded in my head. It was like a breath of fresh air. Suddenly I wasn't in a madhouse populated with monsters. I focused on her only a few feet away. She was facing partly away from me but I knew that was for appearance. *"I am concerned about your vital signs,"* she continued.

I consciously slowed my breathing. "I'm ok," I sent. "Just felt overwhelmed for a second."

"I am with you," she offered.

I wish she were facing me so she could see me smile. "Glad you are here. Stay close."

McCaffer had passed us and hadn't noticed my stopping. "Sorry, I forget how this affects folks the first time. No matter how many new worlds most people have seen this is usually the strangest. It will get more bizarre from here. Let's move. The sooner we do this the sooner we are out of this hell."

"Agreed," I said, my mouth dry, wondering why I had ever thought this a good idea.

McCaffer gestured. "There's our ride."

Ahead, next to a blinking pole, sat an open aircar. The vehicle was roofless and looked like a ground-effect cushion with a raised deck surrounded by a railing that reminded me of nothing so much as the frosting on a cake. Vertical poles and benches were provided for the passengers.

"Touch as little as you can on this side of the airlock," McCaffer said. "By Ribisan standard our suits are the equivalent of live flame. An unsuited Ribisan won't come anywhere near the brightness and heat as they perceive it. This car is for diplomatic and commercial use and is made with neutral materials safe for us." With a sigh, he sat on one of the benches, near an ornate panel of blinking lights that reminded me of a holiday tree. I sat further back. Maauro simply stood, holding on to a pole.

"Don't overdue the resilience of youth," I sent to her. "Later, at least try to look tired."

"Ribisan Central Military HQ," McCaffer said to the panel.

"Acknowledged," came a soft and surprisingly feminine voice. "Commandant Rallicallie is expecting your visit."

The frosting aircar lifted smoothly and slid silently on. Ribisans and their vehicles seemed to recognize the vehicle and give it a wide berth. I watched the life of the city as we slid through it; the disassociated feeling hovered at the edge of my mind. I saw much and comprehended little. Some of what I saw looked ordinary as a terrestrial street, other things refused to resolve into any pattern, merely being shapes and lights.

To my surprise I saw Ribisans floating out of buildings, rather than taking stairs, elevators or long poles. In the great pressure of the atmosphere and despite the gravity, they seemed able to float downward by spreading their limbs, revealing webbing between.

Gradually as my eyes became more accustomed, things began to make more sense. I recognized office towers and shopping complexes. If I didn't look too hard they could almost be normal. Maybe the beings flocking around, drifting up and down in the buildings, were just people, going to and from work, visiting friends. In some sense weren't people all the same and yet couldn't a man and woman of the same species be the ultimate strangers? I shook off the beginnings of another fugue… concentrating on the here and now.

About ten minutes later a tower, with a grim and guarded military look to it, bulked in front of us. The frosted aircar wound its way toward it. A guard post stood in the outer wall. Ribisans in armor and what looked like uniforms with sidearms examined the car and passed us through. When we slid to a halt, a solitary soldier stood waiting for us. As we exited the car, it spoke in a modulated artificial voice, "Greetings. You are expected. Commandant Rallicallie awaits you in his office." With that he turned and we perforce followed. We passed through rooms of comscreens and past Ribisan military personnel. Everyone drew back from our armored suits save for our guide. We passed through some sort of scanner before reaching an elevator bank. I held my breath as Maauro went through, but either it did not penetrate her suit or she had hacked it.

We walked onto a wall-less elevator and it rose through the multiple levels of the tower. The increased gravity from the elevators rise added to our misery briefly. Inside, it was even darker then the streets and I longed for the yellow clearness of my headlamps, but had to be content with the suit's displays.

"We'll be met in a conference room equipped to deal with both our kinds," McCaffer huffed. "Again, touch nothing you don't have to." The elevator slid to a stop and we followed our silent guide down a tall hallway. The conference room he led us to was brightly lit by Ribisan standards. Our escort walked in and stood against a far wall, gesturing at some square cubes set in the floor. We settled on them with relief. This time Maauro joined us.

A door whooshed open, admitting a large Ribisan, with clothing more ornate than any other I had seen; lights and metal twinkled on it.

"I am Commandant Rallicallie," the newcomer said.

"Greetings, Commandant," McCaffer said. "It was kind of you to see us on such short notice."

"The notice was short," Rallicallie agreed. "However the matter of an assault on a Confederate officer is a serious matter, deserving of our attention."

"Yes," he said, "the officer is with me here, Lt. Jedaya Fels of the Confederate vessel, *Pisces*.

Evidently Maauro was not going to rate an introduction or notice, which suited us fine. I stood and offered a regulation salute. The Ribisan evidently recognized the gesture and replied with something roughly similar.

"On behalf of the Confederate Navy, Military District 2030, Department 30, greeting from *CSS Pisces*," I said formally. "Our vessel has already off-loaded all diplomatic dispatches but we would be happy to transport any messages to Confed authorities that you, or your civilian government, wish to entrust to us."

"Thank you, Lieutenant, there are no matters currently that we need to entrust to you, but when you file your departure papers we will check again with the Pillar's office to make sure nothing has recently arisen."

"I would meanwhile like to turn to the other matters that have brought me to you. I assume Mr. McCaffer forwarded a précis of my orders?"

"Yes, we received them from your civilian authorities shortly after you landed."

"I have been conducting a series of investigations in the 02 section of Tir-a-Mar. A number of Confed civilian personnel who were stationed at Tir-a-Mar seem to have left, but not returned to the Confederacy. As these people possessed military-level biogenetic skills, Confed is concerned about their whereabouts."

"Those territories are under the jurisdiction of Mr. Mysol's administration. Why would that lead you into our territory?" The Ribisan did not shift. Other than electronic voice that sounded in my ears, it might have been a mere piece of bizarre statuary. It simply stood on the other side of what seemed a desk. The grape like cluster that was its head at least gave me something to rest my eyes on it, but it was not a face. There were no eyes to read anything in.

Play dumb if you like, I thought. "Shortly after I arrived an elevator I and others were on was sabotaged."

"Yes. Just before you arrived my investigative personnel sent me a preliminary report on the matter. I suffer distress in telling you that our efforts have led to little. It appears that the small firm that did the work on that elevator was a front. The facility has closed and the personnel have dispersed, as yet we have not succeeded in locating or identifying any of them."

"That is most unfortunate," I replied. "And rather surprising. You seem to have a large and efficient military organization here. How is it that people can disappear in even so large a city as this?"

"Lieutenant Fels, Tir-a-Mar is not a closed environment as is the 02 section, we are a very different form of life from your own. The city itself is large, 85% of it is in our hydrogen section, but beyond that many of our people live off of the city. There are many small installations or floating islands. We are not as vulnerable in our environments as you are in yours. It is not unusual for our people to live alone and in what you would consider wilderness. We derive much of our nourishment directly from the atmosphere and we are solitary beings in ways I do not think you could appreciate.

"Meaning," McCaffer added, "that it would be easy for the people who worked on the elevator to simply slip out of Tir-a-Ma—"

"—Almost literally with the wind," Rallicallie finished with an unexpectedly poetic turn of phrase.

"What then do you make of all this?" I asked, largely for lack of anything better. My channel to Maauro remained quiet. Either she was happy with my approach or simply had no better idea.

"You have criminals among the oxygen-breathers, the most efficient of which have created their own shadow empire."

"The Guild," I nodded, and then realized the gesture might mean nothing to Rallicallie.

"Just so. We are no more immune to criminality than any other species and the equivalent exists among us. As like clings to like, these organizations have reached tentacles to each other and cooperate now. We believe that this operation is one such.

"Do you have enemies, Lieutenant? Enemies among the Guild, or who would have the resources to employ them?"

"The Guild are more the traditional enemies of the System Patrol than the Navy," I said, "although we destroy their raiders, along with any other pirates we encounter. However, I'm not important enough to rate any enmity by Guild or anyone who would use them."

"Nonetheless," the Commandant insisted, "it seems that reasons for this attack most likely arose out of the O2 section of Tir-a-Mar, where even now Captain Croyzer is pursuing the Guild most diligently. The attack took place in the 02 section, where all the possible targets were beings like you. While the mechanism of the attack came from here, you should seek the motivations on your own side of the airlock. What reason would any Ribisan have to become involved in this matter save for being paid?"

"I believe," I said slowly, "that matters are more complicated than that. I believe the attack was directed at my mission of ascertaining what happened to the science personnel who were here and what it is they were working on in your joint venture with UDEXCO."

"I understand that Mr. Mysol's office has already advised you that these 02-breathers you seek left Tir-a-Mar over a year ago on matters of their own."

Was it significant that he said Tir-a-Mar and not Cimer? I decided to press further. "It would be of use to know the details of the nature of the project that they were involved in."

"I cannot divulge such information. It is classified far above the level of a junior officer."

"I am the senior Confed officer on—"

"I know what you are and what you are not," Rallicallie interrupted. "We are an associate member of the Confederacy but our military is not integrated with yours, though we recognize each other's ranks as a courtesy; a courtesy which you are abusing by questioning an officer so senior to yourself."

Impasse. Legally he was right and no reason or need to answer to me. My questioning could lead to a diplomatic incident. I wondered what Candace Deveraux would make of that.

"You are within your rights, Commandant," I said. Then I opted for a shot in the dark. "But it won't end here. We both know that something terribly dangerous is going on here. Something has set your people, or some faction of them, against the O2-breathers and perhaps your own authority. It began two years ago when a fantastic amount of money and influence was used to start some project that did something unprecedented, bring our type of beings into one of your worlds, and it hasn't stopped despite the information I have been fed."

The Ribisan shifted. Annoyance? Alarm? Who could tell with a being so different?

"If your suggestion of factional…issues on our side of the airlock is correct, it was most unwise of you to expose yourself to such elements by venturing into our city."

"Threats, Commandant?"

McCaffer stirred next to me. "Certainly not! The Commandant—"

"Has no trouble with his voice," I cut in. He subsided when I glared at him.

"As you point out, I am a junior officer with a small scoutship, but I am not wandering the dark alone. I am attached to Commodore Moko's 34th independent flotilla operating in this sector of the frontier. I do not have to return to my home base for orders. I can rendezvous with the flotilla and return with the Commodore, who is senior enough to treat equally with you, if you prefer."

"It would be ill-timed," Rallicallie said, "for a flotilla to visit Cimer just now. We too have our naval exercises and one is underway now. It would be inconvenient, possibly hazardous, for so many warships to be in close orbit of Cimer."

"Are you," I pressed recklessly, "as the senior military member of a planetary constabulary of an associate member of the Confederacy, advising the Confederation Navy that a visit of state would be unwelcome?"

"Not unwelcome, merely inconsiderate of our own arrangements."

"My crew did not report any Ribisan naval contacts," I said. *Other than the ones that blew Maauro's capsule out of the air*, I thought.

"Nor would you. My people have fought from inside of gas giant worlds for well over a thousand years. Rely on it that there are significant elements of the Ribisan navy as well as other planetary assets present. No matter, it is our desire to cooperate with Confed, even if their demands seem both excessive and undiplomatic. You seek information from us that you should have sought from UDEXCO. To the extent that they are unable or unwilling to enlighten you I can do no further. If you wish, I will post a memo to our Pillar that you are dissatisfied with this and lodge a protest. He will take it up with your diplomatic authorities through the proper channels. I regret that in that matter I can help you no further.

"Meanwhile we have not abandoned our attempts to hunt down the saboteurs who endangered you. I hope you will accept my assurance as the base commandant I consider that a serious matter to be pursued rigorously lest it damage our good relations with Confed.

"Please also accept that my concern for your continued safety is also genuine. As Ribisans have been undeniably involved, I wish you safely back in your own section as soon as possible and will make every effort to assure your safety within the areas of my authority."

"Wrik," Maauro finally sent. "I judge it prudent to end the interview. My belief is that the Commandant, while no friend, believes it is in his government's, or his faction's, interests, that you remain alive and that there be no incident that he can be blamed for. Let us diplomatically withdraw. We still have a call to pay on the Pillar."

"I hear your words, Commandant," I said, "and I am grateful for them. It does seem that my investigations on this side of the airlock will either be fruitless or better left in your hands."

CHAPTER FIFTEEN

There was no recognizable sign of relief save perhaps in the quickness of the response. "Wisely spoken. I shall see to all matters personally."

"Excellent. Confed thanks you."

"Do you still wish to see the Pillar?" Rallicallie asked.

"Yes, perhaps particularly now it seems important that all the necessary courtesies be observed, given that there has been strain, necessary but regretted, in dealing with some matters. He is the planetary head of state and it could be interpreted that I have been remiss in my duties by not appearing there earlier."

"If you believe you must, then clearly you will. You are a most determined young being." There was clear lack of enthusiasm coming across. "I will assign my adjutant and a detail to escort you to the Pillar and then back to the 02 section. I can only imagine the anticipation with which you look forward to the vastly lower gravity of your own section."

Low blow, I thought to myself as I carefully rose. The Ribisan and I exchanged salutes and this time I was conscious of the drag of gravity on my arm despite the servos. McCaffer exchanged a few goodbyes with the Commandant then the adjutant led us from the room. Outside two armed and armored Ribisans fell in with us, our escort. The adjutant took us to our frosted aircar and to my surprise joined us as well. He took the controls while the other guards moved as far to the back of the spacious air car. Their armor protected them from accidental contact with us, but it seemed they wanted as much room as they could get.

We rolled toward an ornate tower of green metal and glass, which lacked the grimness of the naval tower. We passed many more transports colorfully festooned with streamers and lights much as their occupants were. Our party seemed drabber by the minute. When we pulled to a stop this time, one guard secured our vehicle and the adjutant and the other led us in. McCaffer and I breathed heavily despite the servos in our suits. Gravity is a harsh mistress.

"This is the office of the Pillar," the Adjutant said. "Your visit will be a short one and if you would be guided by my advice; show more respect and caution here then you did with our Commandant, who was remarkably restrained in his dealings with you."

"Understood," I replied.

Mobs of Ribisans in the brighter colors, streamers and fashions of Civvy Street, noted our arrival mostly by fading away. Again we passed through security, a process expedited by our escort, no scanners this time. At the foot of a powered circular ramp, we were met by four guards wearing uniforms of far lighter color, than our guards.

"Please remain here," the Adjutant said. We waited with one guard as the adjutant moved forward, rather slowly I thought. Perhaps it was my imagination, but it seemed that the guards present were positioned so that they could cover us and each other.

CHAPTER FIFTEEN

I could hear nothing of the exchange between the adjutant and the leader of this new party. Their limbs did not stir and they could all have been frozen in a tableau. This went on for what seemed a long time until finally the adjutant turned and made a beckoning gesture with one of his upper tentacles.

We walked forward, although I immediately noted that our last naval guard remained where he was. Once on the spiral staircase, we found ourselves surrounded by the new detail with just our adjutant for company. The material of the spiral held our feet firmly as we rode it upward, something of a cross between a magic carpet and a slidewalk and fortunate, as with so many heights in the Ribisan section, it was not railed.

"I've never been here before," McCaffer said. The older man's face was haggard as the high-G sapped his strength, "nor met the Pillar directly. This is an honor we've not received before. I hope it was wise to incur it."

"Me too," slipped out of my mouth before I could stop it. But my evident caution seemed to please the older man.

Thirty seconds more took us to an ornate landing of columns that looked like frozen waterfalls and contained mobile floating lights, a relief to the eyes, but inadequate for natural vision. There was something that was either statuary or exploded metal, I couldn't tell. I was sure the walls were festooned with art and the whole place was a Xeno-anthropologist's dream, but to me it was mostly dim, filled with strange shapes.

We walked toward large metal and glass doors that opened onto the largest room we had yet seen. The room was created to impress and did. In its center, surrounded by Ribisans was a raised dais with two Ribisans on it. Screens of various sorts flickered about the room and it was clearly a communications hub. The tallest Ribisan was entangled in something that looked like a golden web. Since Ribisans did not sit, I assumed this was the equivalent of a throne or other ornate chair.

"I must remain here," the adjutant said. "Human McCaffer, I believe you know enough of our customs to conduct the introductions."

"Yes, I have been in most of the city negotiations. I will do my best."

"It is essential that you do. I will not be able to assist you."

Two guards stayed with the adjutant and two more came with us as we approached the Pillar.

McCaffer hailed the Pillar and began both a series of gestures with his hands and a short introduction of who we were.

"Maauro," I sent, "I get a feeling from all these actions that neither we nor our naval escort are welcome here. We may have found the first of the faction lines we have been searching for."

"Yes," she replied, "it is difficult for me to sense intent in biological entities, still more ones as different as these, yet there has been wariness among the guards. They seemed as much concerned about each other as about us. The fact that the adjutant is not welcome to approach closer is indicative of something."

McCaffer was continuing, describing the courtesy to his office intended by my visit. He turned to me. "I'm on our private channel, at least I hope it's private, but I wouldn't bet my life on it. We will not be speaking directly to the Pillar. I'm not sure why or what it means, but the smaller Ribisan up there is his, I don't know, call him the Major Domo, he will speak to us on behalf of the Pillar. I am getting a bad feeling from how we are being greeted. The sooner we are done here, the better."

Finally the smaller Ribisan moved forward slightly. An indicator on my helmet's heads-up display told me it was speaking, or I would not have known which one of the group to focus on.

"The Pillar has heard of your mission and your courtesies. Both could have been delivered electronically, without the need for you to so struggle in our environment."

"It is kind of the Pillar to express concern for our health," I replied. "My orders as a Confederate officer and the courtesies due a planetary head-of-state do not take personal comfort into account.

"I have also come on other duties that have doubtless been brought to your attention. The disappearance of a number of scientists—"

"The Pillar has already responded through proper channels on this matter and has nothing more to add."

Curt, I thought – *and undiplomatic to cut me off.* "Then there is the matter of the attempt on my life."

"Regrettable," the Major Domo said. "The Pillar leaves all such matters in the tentacles of the Commandant, who you have already had an interview with. The Pillar has nothing to add to that interview."

"Fels," McCaffer whispered urgently. "The Pillar seems to be very busy toda—"

"And scant of courtesy toward the Confederacy," I replied, watching as he blanched in his helmet.

Despite the pounding in my chest, I switched back to the main frequency. "The matter is not a small one to the Confederacy. In fact, neither matter is a small one. Confed headquarters is very interested in what project brought the disappeared so far from home."

There was a long silence during which no being moved. I began to wonder if I had pushed our collective luck too far.

Finally, to my surprise, the Pillar itself stirred in its golden webbing. The indicator told me that the Pillar itself was speaking. "If you have inquiries as to the business of UDEXCO, inquire of UDEXCO, a legal entity of your Confederacy. Ribisan internal matters are not within your purview."

The indicator flicked to the Major Domo. "The Pillar is considering a complaint to your superiors about your intrusive and perhaps illegal actions."

"Maauro," I sent.

"Agreed, we withdraw."

Aloud, I said. "I apologize to the Pillar if in my zeal, I have given inadvertent offense. I wished to express my personal appreciation that the Commandant has assured me that we will receive all possible consideration in the matter of the assault on my person.

"In regards to… the other matter, I have my orders, but I understand the limits of my jurisdiction. It appears it would be as well for my party to return to our section of the city and leave matters here in the hands of your authorities."

"Indeed," the Major Domo said. "This interview is terminated. Please withdraw. It is time for one of our religious observances that are not to be conducted before unbelievers."

"Of course," McCaffer said, hastily. He again made the complicated hand gesture and began offering ceremonial words of departure. I slowly added a Confederation salute, not wanting to alarm the guards, and let it drop, not waiting to see if it would be returned. Then we backed away from the dais. Deep down I wanted to run, but that would have been suicidal in this gravity and maybe for other reasons. Maauro brought up the rear as we went, backing all the way even after McCaffer and I turned to avoid falling over our feet in high-G.

We regained the side of the Adjutant. "Let us move with haste," he said leading us out.

Again the guards and the spiral staircase, this time the trip down seemed to last forever. We picked up our other guard and his entourage and made our way back to the frosted cake aircar. Everyone clambered in despite the high-Gs. We weren't even seated before the Adjutant took off, making McCaffer and I grab for poles.

"Apologies," he said. "Again, haste serves."

"That could have gone better," McCaffer said, his voice hollow with exhaustion.

"Perhaps," Maauro said, "it would be best to remain silent until we regain our side of the station."

"Careful," I sent, "you sound like Maauro, not Lostly."

But McCaffer nodded and we spent the trip back to Interface airlock in silence.

The Adjutant drove us right up to the airlock door and practically leapt out of the vehicle to open it. The two guards took up flanking positions, their weapons held upward pointing at the heights around us. "In, in," the Adjutant urged.

It took no further persuading and with no goodbye to our escort we walked into the airlock. It closed, blocking off the view of the nightmare city. I fought an instant's dizziness as the gravity gradient went from 1.8 to 1.2. What blessed relief. We walked down the corridor to the entrances to our section, then another airlock, now even more relief, one gravity, yellow light and air.

We quickly undid our helmets, not even waiting for the suit chief, who'd entered as soon as the atmosphere was safe. He went straight to McCaffer, the oldest of our party and helped him out of the heavy, servoed suit. McCaffer looked like hell. I suspected that I looked scarcely better. Only after I got out of the suit did I realize how rank with sweat I was, shaking with every limb.

The suit chief pushed a drink on me. "Anti-inflammatories and restoratives. You'll feel like shit tomorrow. You were out there a damn long time. You buying real estate, L-tee?"

I just gave him a tired grin.

He looked over at Maauro. "They must breed them tough where you're from, Miss. You look fresh as when you went out."

Damn. One of those little cues we hadn't realized. But if the Chief was frankly surprised, McCaffer looked too exhausted to notice. Maauro gratefully clutched at the drink and complained of aches and pains in an unpersuasive manner.

"Let's take this up tomorrow," I said, so drained and strained that it was hard to climb to my feet even in one-G. "Chief, get Mr. McCaffer into a cab. We'll look after ourselves. Thanks for everything."

"Sure L-tee. Come on Mr. Mac, you're not on overtime like the help. Time to get you home."

McCaffer just grunted at us as the chief led him off.

I looked at Maauro. "Sometimes your adorable perkiness can be quite annoying."

"Sorry," she replied, slipping under my arm and putting one of hers around my waist. "I would carry you, but it would be remarked on."

"It's not that bad," I said moving slowly and wondering if in fact it was. "But my plan for the evening is a bath, food and a long nap."

We return to the hotel and follow Wrik's itinerary. He lingers in the showers soaking out the soreness of our expedition into high-G. I attend to the details of the meal. Despite what I judge to be a selection of his favorite foods, he eats mechanically and talks little, even begging off finishing the meal to lie down. Once stretched out on the bed he is instantly asleep.

I take advantage of this to do a medical scan. The results upset me. Wrik has taken a battering since we arrived, including a few seconds of technical death. Over all this has been the strain of living under the eyes of our enemies and today, hours in high gravity. His body shows damage in many levels, his metabolism is highly stressed.

This is unacceptable. I immediately begin production of anti-inflammatories and other medicines far superior to what is available save at the best Confed medical facilities. I inject these with either air pressure or needles of great fineness. In addition I send in a detachment of micromachines to repair overloaded blood vessels and strained and sprained muscles. I add minerals and vitamins as I deem necessary.

Wrik is not resting comfortably. He has fallen asleep on his face and I know he normally sleeps on his back. Gently, I turn him over, undress him and arrange him properly for sleep. It is a measure of his exhaustion that he does not stir.

I remain concerned at the level of injury and damage. Exhaustion is cumulative in biological life and Wrik has been subjected to far too much in far too short a period. Tomorrow, I decide will be spent entirely in rest and healing. I administer a light tranquilizer that will ensure his sleep will last a full twenty-four hours. There will be no more sojourns into high-G unless mission failure is at stake. Even then I will weigh if it exceeds my primary mission parameter of Wrik's survival.

As I sit by the unconscious Wrik, I consider if the accumulated threats to my network have reached that point. We are targeted, albeit erratically, by an unseen adversary but have found no target to counterattack. The tactical situation is not desirable. Further, we have not succeeded at locating any information or the personnel we were seeking. There is no immediate prospect that we will do better and the longer we are here the greater the risk of discovery.

Yet I know that if I decide to withdraw, I will face resistance from Wrik, who will believe, correctly, it is being done for him. As he has said, he must be a contributing member of our team, so he will not accept this. The equations remain balanced in my mind, the mission will continue for now. However I promise myself that if the balance changes, I will extract my network, by main force if necessary.

I place orders for more food to be delivered when Wrik awakes. He will be ravenous, both from the healing and the elapsed time between meals. I will continue my monitoring and intervene with more medications and restoratives as soon as his body is capable of processing them.

While part of my mind remains present with my deeply sleeping partner, the rest ranges through Tir-a-Mar, checking data reports on Wrik and me from Mysol's various spies, avoiding cyber traps, maintaining my fictitious virtual identity. I avoid the Ribisan dataports, although I am tempted to crash through and see what the Pillar and the Commandant are doing and what reports they have created on us. But it is too dangerous; their superior defenses are too powerful to attack without triggering all manner of alarms. Yet it is the dual nature of the cyber world of Tir-a-Mar that has facilitated my efforts. Ribisan and Confed systems are vastly different, almost as much as the lifeforms themselves. Perforce there must be translation programs and intermediaries. These different code languages create a "no man's land" between the systems where I easily conceal myself.

Hours pass in this way before the channel in my mind opens

"Maauro?"

"Yes, Jaelle. Are you in danger?"

"No."

There is a brief silence in my mind. "Are we alone?"

I am confused by the question then I realize she means, "Can we be overheard?"

"Dusko can only hear you when you push a thought at him or are excited and alarmed. However, if you like, I can suspend the connection. He will not be aware of it. If he calls you I will restore it."

"Do so."

"Done.

But only more silence follows. I sense confusion, even some pain across the link and again wonder why it is that so much more travels across the link between Jaelle and I. Is it that she is Nekoan or female? I wish I had data with which to consider the point.

"Are you all right?" I prompt.

"Mostly, I suppose."

"It is the early morning when you should be asleep. Clearly something is upsetting or concerning you."

"Oh, so many things, Kit-sister."

"Am I one of those things, Jaelle?"

Confusion, tinged with guilt and a touch of anger comes back. "You're not a thing to me, Kit-sister."

"I am a complication to your life, to your relationship with Wrik."

"Yes, Wrik, who I gather is lying asleep next to you and not next to me."

"Yes, we ventured into the Ribisan section today. I am concerned that he has exhausted himself over the dangers of the past few days. I have administered a tranquilizer to keep him down for twenty-four hours."

"Damn it. I should be there watching over him."

"Mission necessities, Jaelle. But he is your lover, not mine."

"Yet you do love him."

"I do. You know this. It is not a physical love."

"Oh, is it something higher, and purer, above all the physical groping and lust?" she snaps.

"I mean that it is different, only that."

"Do you love me, Maauro?"

My quantum brain, so adept at hacking, at managing of ships, systems and weapons fails me. I am at a loss for how to respond for 1.8723 seconds. "You are a very important part of my network, original and irreplaceable."

"That would be a no, then."

Hesitation. "My feelings for you are not the same as my feelings for Wrik; I am unable to tell you why or quite how. I lack the life experience to formulate answers, or even perhaps to fully understand what you are asking me and why. I care for you, value you, seek your company and guidance, but I do not love you."

"That's ok, I don't love you either. You're my friend. I think of you that way; for all that I seldom understand all of what is going on in that ceramo-alloy skull of yours, not even when we are connected in this intimate way. "

"We are friends," I say cautiously. "We value each other. Yet there is a friction between us that plays out in those mock combats and this verbal sparring. That cannot be denied."

"I have hopes, Maauro, and dreams. Some involve a life free of danger, free of violence, with a beautiful house on a hill, kits tumbling over each other on a lawn. Do you have dreams like that?"

"I do not dream, Jaelle. My mental state is always self-conscious in varying degrees unless I am damaged or power-drained. I have a maintenance mode I slip into when nothing more complicated is required of me."

"That's not what I mean, Kit-sister. You know that."

"Then no, I do not have dreams. It sounds pleasant, to create, whether consciously or not, to create scenarios of a happy and secure future. I could do so, but it would not fulfill any need for me."

"So there is only the now for you and the past."

"Yes, the now. And the past, though I used to delete those parts of my past when they troubled me, or when I felt that they did not help me."

"Such as?"

I do not wish to respond but I also fear shutting down this communication between us that seems so much more open and honest than most of our interactions. "My actions during the Infester war, there are periods there that I have deleted. I have kept all of my memories since my resurrection on the asteroid where Wrik found me."

"Why the change?"

"A promise I made to Wrik. I would rather not explain further."

"And so we come back to Wrik again. It bothers me that you know him better in some ways than I do."

"I do not know how to respond, Jaelle. I intended none of this. My relationship with Wrik is something…difficult for me to understand or explain. He was the first being to see me as a…

"Go ahead and say it, Maauro… as a living person."

"I feared you might deny that I am alive. You did so once before."

"Don't ever fear that, Kit-sister. Even if I am mad at you, I know you are alive – a real person."

"Are you angry with me?"

"I owe you my life, Kit-sister. I'd never have made it out of that Kandalorian jungle without you."

"Evasion."

"You save Wrik's life too—"

"And endangered both your lives as much as I ever protected them. You continue to evade. Are you angry with me?"

"Yes. You. Wrik. The universe generally, and myself for being this way."

We were silent for what seemed like a long while to me.

"Maauro."

"Yes."

"It's good to have another female to talk to sometimes."

"I am glad to fulfill that function…glad you see me that way."

"Good night, Maauro."

"Sleep well, Jaelle."

"Watch over Wrik for me."

"With my life if need be." I feel her slip away from me into sleep, exhausted by so much use of the link. She will wake ravenous. I wonder if I could deepen the rapport and follow her into her dreams. But I fear to do harm both to her brain and our part of the network, which endures strains that do not occur anywhere else. I also suspect that there is no place for me in her dreams.

I continue to sit, staring out the window. I do not need rest as such, but find it a little discomforting that my brain is active at its highest setting, contemplating much of what was said and yet feeling the meaning of it has eluded me.

CHAPTER SIXTEEN

I PASSED FROM SLEEP TO WAKEFULNESS SO QUICKLY IT
startled me. Usually I greeted the day with a growling indifference
bordering on hostility. Today I sat up almost bemused at how refreshed
and healthy I felt. The aches and pains of all the injuries and strains of
the last few days seemed absent. I realized that under the covers I was
naked, as I usually slept. Odd, I didn't remember undressing. In fact, I
didn't remember anything other than standing up from a table with Maauro.

I turned to the right and there she was, watching me and seated on
the floor as her weight could tax some of the chairs unless she locked
her legs in position. She smiled and rose smoothly, if not gracefully.
"Wrik, are you feeling better?"

"Yeah," I said sheepishly. "Sorry about conking out on you. High-G
is more fatiguing then I realized. God, what a few good hours' sleep does
for you."

"It has actually been more than a few hours. I must apologize for
not consulting you, but you were not in a condition for discussion. You
have been asleep for more than thirty-six hours. It is the morning of the
day after our venture to the Ribisan side."

"What!" I said. "Out for a day and half?"

"Your physical condition concerned me. I have affected such repairs
and restoration on you as I could. I judged that any effect it had on the
mission was inconsequential, weighed against your health."

I was torn a little between being touched over her concern, and
annoyed that she had acted without consulting me, but there was little
point in arguing with Maauro. If she felt she needed to act, she would.
She was probably right anyway.

"What happened while I was out?"

"I will brief you while we eat," Maauro walked out and returned with
two trays putting one on the bed next to me and settling on the floor
beside the bed.

The smell of food made me acutely aware of how long it had been
since meals. Knowing Maauro, she'd injected me with vitamins and sugar
solutions, but it did little to distract me for a large pile of eggs and sau-
sage. Maauro kept me company for form's sake, knowing that I did not
like to eat alone and quite capable of enjoying food in her own fashion.
A few minutes silence followed as I attacked breakfast. When I'd knocked
the edge off my hunger and looked at her, she took up her report again.

"Jaelle is safe at her hotel. She has been in communication with the
Guild about her cargo and has been exploring the area around her hotel
to no great effect. I have asked her not to begin inquiries about the

project or its personnel until some logical reason arises for her to express an interest. Meanwhile, she is finding out what she can about how the Guild functions here.

"I wish I could see her."

"I know she wishes that too."

"Are you in touch with her?" I asked

"Only periodically, I am finding the link with her to be both more informational, in that I perceive more through her than through you, or Dusko, but on her end it requires much more energy. She would have wiped up breakfast even faster than you are doing."

"Is it dangerous to her?"

"Not so long as she keeps her calorie intake high and rests. I am rationing her contact with me to necessary exchanges and maintaining the lowest level active link I can."

"Is it the same with Dusko?"

"No, but he professes to find the link disorienting and somewhat painful. There too I am keeping contacts minimal, though in his case I think it is more his resentment at having to share access to his mind. For a creature for whom dissembling is such a prime part of his psychological makeup, the inability to mislead and misdirect might actually cause pain."

"Nice way of saying he finds it painful not to be able to lie."

"Dusko handled the removal of cargo from the *Stardust*. He continues to passively scan for any sign of Ribisan or other traffic that may be suspicious, but he has seen nothing, not even other Guild vessels. I checked with the AI on *Pisces*, which has superior scanners and can use them actively. It has registered some energy traces comparable with spacecraft, or very large aviation platforms, periodically near Tir-a-Mar. These have faded."

"Meaning?" I asked.

"The Ribisans have naval and space assets here; as the Commandant warned. They were near Tir-a-Mar but to avoid *Pisces* they have gone deeper or further away, relying on the thick, stormy atmosphere to conceal them. They are guarding something, but do not wish to be seen to do so."

"Be nice to know what they are guarding and from who? This is too much firepower to deal with our two ships, even if they knew we were operating together."

"Clearly," Maauro said. "The aerospace fighters that attacked me are not based here, most likely they were carrier-based. Even a small carrier would hold about fifteen such and require escorts. That force is guarding something and it may be guarding it from other Ribisan interests. There was clear tension between the Pillar and the Commandant's forces."

"What was it that the Ribisan you killed said?"

Maauro opened her mouth. "The lost must be returned to the holy," came out, but it was in the dead Ribisan's own artificial voice. I had to fight a shudder at the sound of it.

"Hard to make anything out of that," I said around a mouthful of eggs and after a sip of coffee. "There's a religious connection there, which seems to imply the Pillar, but most Ribisans are notably religious, far more consistently than one finds among humans anyway."

"I lack data, but there seems to be a relationship between space-services and secularism," Maauro said. "One wonders if the military is on some different side than the religious leaders?"

"Who can say? Usually in a theocracy, the military serves the conservative religious order, but the Ribisan's have something like a parliamentary style of government."

"That may not matter so much as you suppose," Maauro said.

I finished the toast. "All we seem to have returned with from High-G is more suppositions and theories…and a sore back."

"The latter is presently from lying down so long," she said in mock reproof. "Go shower and then stretch out."

"Ok. Pass me my robe would you?"

Maauro did so. "Your caution at displaying your naked form to me is both quaint and slightly amusing. Who do you think undressed you for bed?"

"More stuff on the list we do not tell Jaelle."

"A list that continues to grow," she replied.

I pondered that last as I slipped into my robe and headed to the shower. There was some uncomfortable truth to that. And had I detected an edge in her voice when she'd said it?

"What about McCaffer, Mysol and all the rest?" I called out to change the subject as I slipped into the shower.

"McCaffer took the last two days off, recovering from accompanying us. He filed reports with Mysol and Fenster of no significance to us. Captain Croyzer continues her pursuit of the Guild on our station. I will need to warn Jaelle of her investigations should they get any closer to the main Guild operations. Overall, when we are not stirring things up, nothing moves on this chessboard."

I let warm water sluice down over me, just enjoying being healthy again. "Guess we will have to start moving again."

"Probably best to wait until after you are dry," she replied.

I poked my head out of the bathroom and grinned. "Worried about rust?"

She looked back solemnly at me. "Rust never sleeps."

CHAPTER SEVENTEEN

"**M**AAURO," JAELLE SENDS. "ARE YOU THERE?"

"*Yes, I am here.*"

"*Stupid of me, where else could you be but in your own head?*"

"*Are you all right?*"

"*Yes, I just got a call from Hartain. He wants to see me about some local work, as he put it. I'm heading over shortly.*"

"*Excellent. You must be very careful. I will be in the lightest possible monitoring mode until you are actually in his presence.*"

"*Yeah, good. This link takes as much energy as a marathon. Even I was frightened at the size of the dinner I ate last night. I was nearly as bad this morning. If I come out of this with a big ass, Kit-sister, I will sink my fangs into yours.*"

"*My ass is armored at the same level as the rest of me, so not good for your dentition, but I see no reason for you to be concerned at the rate you are expending energy. Now Elder-sister, may I make a suggestion?*"

"*Yes,*"

"*Shut up until you get there.*"

Jaelle's laugh floated through my mind. Then she fades. I informed Wrik of her movements, watching as worry creased its habitual line on his young face.

"*Let us go to the Engineering meeting Fenster set up,*" I add. "*We must inspect that section to keep up the pretext of recertifying the station.*"

Wrik groans. "*At least one day, maybe two, of crawling through ducting and inspecting reactors. Well at least you should be able to sneak in a quick refill while we are there.*"

"*I was planning on it. Rely on it that I will keep tabs on Jaelle.*"

We reach the Engineering section about the same time Jaelle reaches the Guild headquarters in its run down industrial section. We are closer to Jaelle than we have been for a while, separated vertically by two kilometers. I didn't mention it to Wrik – there was no need to add to his frustrations.

Nor did I need to focus much attention on Wrik's interactions with the Engineers. He is a starship pilot, hence a practical systems engineer to start with. While he takes the tour, I slip off and hook into a major power conduit, refreshing my systems, with no loss of contact with Wrik despite the shielding. I supply him mentally with the occasional salient details for inspection, but switch most of my attention to Jaelle as soon as her channel opens in my mind.

She is back in the Guild headquarters hurrying past worried-looking Guilders as she heads to the back rooms where Hartain has his haunt. The female Dua-Denlenn who seems to be his preferred bodyguard scans Jaelle and confiscates her weapons, but she is let into the Guildmaster's presence alone.

"*Dusko here,*" *the sour mental tang of the Dua-Denlenn is immediately apparent, though he calls in as if over the radio.*

"*I am here too, Jaelle. I will not speak again unless it is urgent.*"

"*Thanks, I don't need my head spinning any worse than it is.*"

"*Greetings, Guildmaster, profit to you.*" *Jaelle says.*

The portly Morok is behind his ornate desk. "*And to you Young One, but no need for formality, please sit and make yourself comfortable. I took the liberty of ordering Plomik tea for you.*"

"*He wants something from you,*" *Dusko says.* "*He's treating you as an equal.*"

"*A delicacy,*" *Jaelle says aloud.* "*How did you know?*"

"*I am an importer, after all. I have always been fond of Nekoans, interesting clients and sophisticated.*"

"*Thank you.*"

The tea comes and idle discussions follow as both do their elaborate sidling up to the point of the discussion.

"*I have a proposal that may interest you, as you have expressed a desire to establish a more permanent tie to my operation.*"

Jaelle nods cautiously. "*As the humans say, I am all ears.*" *There is a strange sensation for me as she wriggles hers.*

Hartain laughs in genuine amusement. Jaelle's ability to charm lifeforms of all types is one of the reasons for her success in trade.

"*A few years ago,*" *Hartain begins,* "*a great deal of money changed hands and there was an influx of Confed biogenetic scientists, a major project began with new labs and resources. Supposedly, this project failed and most of the personnel involved left or were reassigned. We have recently acquired information that, while the Ribisans made a lot of noise about the failures of their biogenetic project here, they have been secretly continuing them. There's another floating city, well more of a floating laboratory, further down in the gas giant.*"

Jaelle shrugs. "*On a Ribisan world? I'd imagine there might be several.*"

"*Don't interrupt him,*" *Dusko hisses in her brain. I judge it good advice.*

I feel Jaelle's face stretch into a smile, sans teeth.

The Guildmaster's dour expression fades. "*Ah, the impatience of youth. Yes, there are other smaller installations, but none getting regular supplies for oxygen-breathers, none getting equipment for high AG fields. We have been unable to breach their security and get any operatives down to those installations.*

"However large the floating city might seem, it is easy for the authorities to control and monitor. We make progress slowly and carefully, creating our own access ways and passages."

Jaelle nods to encourage the garrulous Guildmaster.

"Good," Dusko says. "Keep him talking. He has no local he can confide in. The desire to talk, to impress a prospect is strong with him."

"I imagine the local law gets familiar with your personnel."
Jaelle says.

"Exactly," he says, stabbing a finger upward. "You understand. So it may be impossible to get direct access, but we can see and hear. We see the supplies, the machinery, all things Ribisans do not need."

"Massage his ego," Dusko adds.

"Very clever," Jaelle says.

"This could be where you come in," Hartain muses. "You are an unknown. We were able to slot your arrival in place of an intraplanet haul. No one knows you are here, no one knows who you are. Yes, this presents a unique opportunity."

I feel Jaelle's body tense in eagerness.

"Be cautious," Dusko demands. "Ask about profit to you. Ask about danger."

"I would be glad to be of assistance to you," Jaelle purrs. "If, of course, there is sufficient benefit to me, commensurate with the risk."

He nods, "Of course. Listen, a Confed warship is above us. It's small in itself but it means Confed law. The Lieutenant involved is a particularly noxious sort, forcing his way in everywhere on the pretext of a safety inspection of the human habitations on this world."

"Are you sure it's a pretext?"

"It must be. Rumor has it that he is asking about the personnel that were involved in the same biogenetic experiments we are talking about."

"One wonders if he even knows why he is here." Jaelle adds.

"One does," Hartain nods. "He may well be only a pawn for larger forces moving the pieces from beyond the board."

Too true, Jaelle sighs mentally.

"Concentrate," Dusko orders.

"If I," Jaelle says, "an exotic alien of a species humans are known to find sexually attractive, express an interest in him, he might let slip useful information. We might even gain sufficient access to confirm your suspicions."

"We might," Hartain replied with a toothy Morok smile. "It might take some effort; he seems to have taken up with a slender, dark-haired human mutant. She's his constant companion."

Jaelle's tail swishes. I feel her smile, with teeth this time. "Oh, I imagine I can win that contest easily enough."

"Is it just me or is getting hot in here?" Dusko's mental laugh sounds.

"It could become abruptly hotter," I sent back, "if I order the ship's computer to raise the temperature where you are by two hundred degrees."

Dusko subsides. He is never entirely sure about the seriousness of my threats. This uncertainty is useful.

The Guildmaster laughs. "I'm sure you can. She has fewer...assets than you do. Indeed, her secondary sexual characteristics are meager. It would be like screwing an adolescent male, I imagine."

"Ah," Jaelle says. The mental effort she is making not to project any conscious thought at me is quite heroic in scale. She keeps repeating the expression about an impossibly colored animal to herself over and over to block any accidental transmission to me.

Dusko's evil merriment is less restrained, but he too, at least out of a sense of self-preservation, is trying to keep his thoughts to himself. I look down at my chest. I seem very well proportioned to myself. These were the dimensions of the original game simulation that I modeled myself on, though I had not assessed it in the sense of mature sexual attractiveness at the time. I shelve these thoughts as the Guildmaster speaks again.

"The lieutenant is at the Star and Comet Lodge on level 27, radial 45b tonight. This might be a good time to meet him. I will supply you with video of him and any intelligence we have gained so far. The rest I will leave to you. Your compensation will be based on the value of whatever information you extract."

"Plus expenses and an accommodation at the same lodge," Jaelle returns.

"Excellent. Keep me posted on your progress," Hartain finishes

Jaelle fades out of my mind and I mentally tune to Wrik, warn him not to react and mentally relay what has transpired, minus the commentary on my secondary sexual characteristics.

His usually solemn expression threatens to break into a grin, which would be hard to explain to the sewage engineers showing their diagrams to us. "So, Jaelle is assigned to seduce me? Should I play hard to get?"

I consider. "It is improbable that a human male of your age would turn down—"

"I was kidding, Maauro."

"You will have to put up a pretense of not knowing her."

"Hmnnn, usually role-playing comes along much later in a relationship." The fact that he maintains his silly grin persuades me that this comment is not serious and can be safely ignored.

"May we return to what we were working on?" I ask.

He sighs. "If we must." His gaze returns to the large screen where one of the city engineers is describing the wonders of the sewage system.

CHAPTER EIGHTEEN

AFTER A DAY SPENT IN THE UNDERBELLY OF THE CITY, I sat in the window booth overlooking the main corridor of Tir-a-Mar, gazing down the broad plazas, the various levels of slidewalks rolling past shops and restaurants. Behind me, a two story waterfall tumbled down to the first level of the bar restaurant.

Outside, the simulated daylight and sky above were nearly impossible to tell from the real thing. Since there were representatives of almost every species of the Confederacy here, the sky and light levels were adjusted for the populations. Some days were the stormy gray preferred by the damp-loving Moroks, or the sullen reddish orange light of worlds preferred by the Dua-Denlenn. Fortunately most of the oxygen-breathers had evolved under yellow stars and today was a bright spring day.

One could choose to look out at the poison sky of Cimer with its ripping blasts of lightning from the city's edges, but most didn't, preferring to ignore the murky methane sky.

I was aware of a number of parties surreptitiously watching me, but I had no idea what side or sides they represented. Word was getting around the floating city regarding the Confed officer and all of the disruption his visits were causing; clearly I was persona non grata, to be treated properly but not more.

Maauro returned with drinks. A tall cool beer for me and some frothy, fruit drink of the sort she preferred.

"Anything interesting from your check-in with the bad guys?" I asked as she slid the beer in front of me.

"Nothing beyond an expression of sympathy for my being saddled with the task of keeping an eye on you."

I sipped the beer; it was excellent, full of the tangy flavor of a spring. "I noticed the lack of interest in me. And here I thought I was a charming rascal."

"You are," Maauro assured me in all apparent seriousness. "The good news is that it means people are disinclined to talk with me as well, lest the contagion of my assignment embrace them."

"That's a pretty typical reaction across all species we've met so far."

Maauro turned her head. "We are being watched, but I do not detect any sound amplifying devices and the waterfall should prevent us from being picked up with common equipment. We can speak freely. If this changes I will address you by your code name."

"Got it."

"Do not react, but Jaelle is approaching us."

I leaned back and let my eyes roll over the restaurant. There, coming up the escalator, was Jaelle, dressed to kill. She wore a one-piece, bronze-colored outfit with one shoulder uncovered. Her long legs gleamed a tawny gold. Cutouts in the top revealed her firm stomach and barely covered the underside of her breasts. Jewels gleamed in her hair and hung from her golden cat-like ears. The effect was of an athletic bronze statue of a goddess of the hunt, come to life.

"I said, "don't react," Maauro repeated with asperity.

"It would have been more suspicious if I didn't," I replied. "A Morok or an Okaran might not be interested in a Nekoan female, but they appeal to most others."

This seemed to be true. Admiring glances came from many of the other tables and from both genders. One group of Nekoan males in the corner seemed particularly intrigued, much to my irritation. The males of her species looked more like large hunting cats than did the females, whose small features seemed more human. I started wondering what they would look like as rugs.

"She says it is good to see you," Maauro said, "and she is looking forward to her mission of seducing you by doing unspeakably naughty things that I should not know about. She is wearing a listening device to persuade Hartain of her usefulness, so you will have to pretend not to know each other."

"Kinky fun," I said. "Tell her to look this way in fifteen seconds so I can wave her over."

"She says fine. Then she will ignore you and you can get off your ass and come over and pick her up."

I tried to keep a straight face. "Now she plays hard to get."

"Her reply is an obscenity I will not bother to relay."

Jaelle turned her beautiful golden eyes in my direction. I raised my glass and gestured at the open chair next to us. She gave me an encouraging smile but indicated the seat next to her. I gave Maauro an apologetic look. She ignored me in favor of her fruity drink. I stood and walked over, noting with amusement some flashed teeth among the Nekoans in the corner.

"Hello," I said to Jaelle.

She looked me up and down. "Are you this Confed officer I hear so many bad things about?"

"I am that very same lonely officer, merely doing his duty to God and Galaxy. I seem to have annoyed the locals however and they are keeping clear of me."

Jaelle looked at Maauro. "Well not all of them. She's kind of cute in an underdeveloped way. She might have quite a figure…when she grows up. Or do you like them young?"

I coughed. "Ah, my minder there is assigned. She's really quite sweet, making the best of a bad situation."

CHAPTER EIGHTEEN

"Sweet you say," Jaelle added, an evil sparkle in her eyes, "is fine for children. I lean to the spicy side myself. "

"Fascinating," I said. "I'm Jedaya Fels, commanding officer of the *CSS Pisces*.

"Fyvia Minogue, Master of the *SS Longshot*."

"A fellow Captain, lucky me. Where are you from?"

"Oh, many places. I'm in Trade."

Jaelle and I chatted for a while, actually enjoying the play we were doing for Hartain.

"Do you have a room in this pretty place that we could visit?" Jaelle added.

"Yes," I looked back at Maauro. "However I think my minder will insist on seeing us to it. Maybe even staying for a while."

"Well if she overstays her welcome maybe I'll spank her little behind and send her home to mother. It must be getting past her bedtime."

"Er, she is a bit older than she looks."

"Good. I didn't fancy sharing a bed with a kit-molester."

"Why don't I go over and tell her what's going on. Oh, one thing, since I am here on assignment, I'll have to run a scanner over you for bugs and such. I think minder-girl might insist on it too."

"Oh, a strip search. This gets kinkier by the minute. I like it. Go tell your friend. See if you can't shake her off. I'll use the ladies room and meet you by the elevator. "

Jaelle sashayed off, leaving me with the bill. I waved Maauro over.

"Jaelle's ducked into the bathroom. She'll remove any listening device Hartain gave her since I warned her you'd do a security scan."

"Excellent thinking."

I billed everything to my room and tipped extravagantly. Maauro and I waited for Jaelle by the elevators, ignoring the other guests who walked by us, some staring at my uniform.

Jaelle walked over. She looked about to see if anyone was near. "Are we discreet?"

"Yes," Maauro said. "You left the bug in the bathroom?"

"I flushed it and sent a message to Hartain that I thought it was too dangerous to keep it on my person or leave it in the bathroom."

"Plausible," Maauro judged.

"Let's get upstairs," I said, trying to keep my mind on business and off how incredibly good Jaelle looked in that outfit. She gave me a smug smile that said I wasn't being entirely successful.

Fortunately the elevator came quickly. As the doors closed, Jaelle wrapped herself around me for a long kiss.

"Ms. Minogue," Maauro said archly, "This is a public elevator with surveillance cameras."

"Don't worry, Little One, I wasn't planning on going any further, yet."

CHAPTER EIGHTEEN

The doors slid open and we made quick speed to my room where Maauro had left the robospider on guard.

We retreat to the room and slip into it unobserved.

"The Guild," I say to Jaelle, "is either going to be very impressed by your powers of seduction or they will call Wrik easy."

"Shouldn't you be getting on with the seduction?" Wrik asks.

"Yes," Jaelle purrs.

"That is not necessary for the deception," I say. "There are no surveillance devices operating."

"Oh it's very necessary," Wrik says, gazing at Jaelle.

"Have a heart, Maauro," Jaelle said. "We haven't seen each other for weeks."

"Will this take long?" I ask in exasperation.

"Nope," Jaelle said. "Like I said, it's been weeks."

"Well it's going to take some time," Wrik protests, "and we could use some privacy."

"Hah," Jaelle says. "She might as well climb into bed with us, or did you forget that we are all linked head-to-head?"

I give her a look. "I can temporarily block your channels, though it is ill advised under mission parameters for us to be isolated while in enemy territory."

Jaelle grabs Wrik's hand. "Isolated hell, we'll be in the bedroom and unless your cover story includes a threesome, you might want to slip back down to the bar for an hour or preferably two."

I feel the arousal that stirs her body through our link. Perhaps it is because I am "female" after a fashion I find this more accessible than the sensations I am feeling from Wrik. She is eager to be with her lover. The feelings are disconcerting at this close range. I am having some difficulty distinguishing the sensations emanating from her body from my own. The link is overloading.

I sigh. "Perhaps you will be back in control of yourselves if you get it out of your systems. Very well, I am off to the bar. I am charging the drinks to your room." I sever my link to them, then shoot a quick message to Dusko that Jaelle will be off-line with him. Either he understands the situation or his usual lack of curiosity is asserting itself. I get the equivalent of a mental grunt. I am surprised by how alone I now feel in my own head as I exit the lodge room.

Briefly I toy with the idea of reopening my link to Jaelle. The constant flow of information on how she uses her sensual and youthful body has been fascinating to me. While some of the sensations have analogues in my own body and existence, many do not. The one that they are involved in now does not. I have experienced affection from my network, mostly from Wrik, but never overt sexuality. As my gender aspects are purely adoptive, mostly to allow me to interact more easily with biologicals, I have not seen any point to this. But that was before I was so closely linked to Jaelle.

Of course, they would not know if I did connect. My control of the connection is such that I have no doubt of this. Yet, something holds me back. It is Wrik. It would be an offense against the love he has for me. He would be upset, embarrassed in his somewhat conservative nature if he knew. This is illogical, as he will not know. Still it would be a falsehood lying between us. I cannot become a being who has such secrets. I will have to live and learn another way.

I reach the bar, signal the waitress and retire to a quiet corner. I am not in a mood for company. I feel alone and somewhat frustrated – I know it is because of what is happening upstairs, but I am not clear on why. This bears further thought. I think many times faster than any biological, yet in the time I could have plotted several star jumps, I find my understanding has not expanded.

I have always preferred my artificial body to any biological one. Objectively, there is little to choose between Jaelle's body and mine in ease and flexibility – yet hers moves with an inner music that makes me feel graceless by comparison. I realize that it is not something I can learn, but is in the nature of the life forms that we are. I am artificial life, in that the true spontaneous life gave rise to me and was necessary to my creation. Without biological life, there would be no opportunity and I realize with some shock, no need for AI's. We are the stepchildren of the biologicals, called into creation by them.

I have considered that self-aware AIs, and there must be more than just I, were the logical successor to natural life, exceeding them in strength, durability and applied intelligence. Have I made improper assessment of the value of spontaneous creativity and sheer imagination? Is a life of 10,000 years, one hundred times better than a life of 100 years?

I can lift vastly more than Jaelle can, but past a certain weight I must get help or admit defeat when my load parameters are exceeded. So is it truly a case of my kind being superior and inheriting the universe? Or do I measure the matter with the wrong instruments? On an infinite slope, does it matter that I am slightly further from the bottom than Jaelle and Wrik?

I look out the window and up. I am deprived even of the stars for company. Yes, a sprinkle of shining lights glimmer above me, but it is a simulation and my telescopic vision is not fooled. We are too far down in the horrid murk that is Cimer's atmosphere for any star to be seen. The stars have always been precious to me. From my initial moments of self-awareness I have loved their beauty. I know they are merely gas fusion reactors, yet somehow I have always seen them as more. I feel a kinship, possibly because I have fusion reactors within me. I am of the stars and they are of me. This has always comforted me.

CHAPTER EIGHTEEN

I decide to do something I have learned from biologicals, not to look too hard at something. If I dial back on my visual acuity, the simulations are indistinguishable to stars seen through atmosphere.

I sip my drink, enjoying the complex flavors.

The waitress comes by. "Want another? Skinny little thing like you can afford it."

"Yes, thank you."

She follows my gaze. "It's a pretty night."

I smile at her. "Yes, I think it is."

CHAPTER NINETEEN

AFTER MAAURO LEFT, JAELLE AND I TUMBLED INTO BED —laughing and simply giddy with relief at being alone and safe, even if only for two hours. We made love the first time with an almost frantic haste.

Jaelle laughed. "You should have seen your face, Wrik."

"I had no idea my future consort would misbehave so in public."

"Shhhh," she said, "Maauro will hear."

"She disabled the link. Besides you know she can only hear you if you push a thought at her."

Jaelle sighed. "And you, of course, always believe her."

I smiled. "Let's not fight about Maauro."

After a second, she smiled back. "Right. Let's not think about anybody but us for the next two hours."

As I took Jaelle in my arms, I had to quell a momentary disquiet about her feelings about Maauro.

Released from the most urgent need we took our time, with soft touches, intimate caresses until we were ready to come together again.

Afterwards Jaelle stretched out on the bed in pantherish splendor. I raided the mini-bar and hit the com screen to order room service by automatic delivery. Champagne and a plate of desserts arrived shortly through the tube system.

"You must have a very forgiving expense account," Jaelle said, as I carefully opened the champagne bottle. I poured the golden bubbly into the two flutes that had ridden up with it.

"I think it comforts the city officials to think that there is a possibility of compromising me with such lavish treatment. And after all there are no regular Confed military quarters on Tir-a-Mar. I could hardly be expected to bunk in with the Ribisan Military."

"No, methane is bad for the lungs." Her golden eyes clouded for a moment and it didn't require a telempathic link to know she was thinking of my near death in the airlock, rescuing Maauro. It had actually been closer than that, but Maauro had shown some discretion in how much she'd told her and I agreed.

"True," I replied, striving for lightness. "I could do without the stink and the cold."

"Hell, we don't even know what military forces they have out there or where," Jaelle said, taking a flute from my hand.

"Well something is out there floating in the murk and it carries fighters, we know that." I sipped my own drink. "It's possible the fighters came from Tir-a-Mar but I doubt it. There are so few launches from here, too much chance of being seem."

"Can Maauro probe the Ribisan side of the city?"

"Can? Yes, but not undetected, she says. So it is old-fashioned detective work for now. She'll hack where she can, but she suspects that any data ports she can access up here will contain nothing useful or could even be a trap."

"Then why do it at all?" Jaelle asked, rolling onto her back and reaching for a small cake.

"She says that sometimes the omissions are revealing. Or, as she put it, if you leave a hole where data used to be, she can make educated guesses as to what was in the hole before it was deleted."

"That sounds like the android version of wishful thinking. Doesn't seem to leave much hope of finding out about these scientists or what was going on here."

I laughed. "Maybe so."

I lay down next to her, putting my glass on the table. She turned her back to me. As I massaged the long muscles in her sinuous back, Jaelle sighed in pleasure and looped her warm tail over my thigh.

"All we can do," I said, "is keep poking around in the open, hoping someone tries to get a message to us or we accidentally upset somebody's applecart—"

"A what?'

"Sorry, old expression, I meant accidentally disrupt someone's plans and provoke a reaction that breaks somebody's cover."

"Possibly by trying to kill you."

"Yeah, there's that." I worked some more on her lower back.

"Ah," she said, "that's good. I can't seem to talk Dusko into doing that."

I gave her a playful pat on her shapely butt. "You'd better not."

"Oh now who's jealous? I'm letting you play house with Maauro."

I played with her long tail. "That's not as rewarding as you seem to think."

"Stop that," she said, swatting gently with her tail, "you're distracting me." She smiled and held out her glass for me. I got the bottle and the plate of cakes, then sat on the bed and poured for her. Housekeeping was not my issue.

Jaelle took more champagne and greedily attacked he cakes. "Hartain," she said around a mouthful, "is a very frustrated being. He's not much of a player, a small fish in a small pond. What you would expect in a tiny operation such as the Guild has here."

I shrugged. "It happens. Even Dusko was only low level Guild; for all that he ran Kandalor and its nearspace. Ferlan was the only real Guildmaster we've run into. She had a small fleet of starships and influence in a dozen systems. Money on a level I still find hard to understand."

Jaelle stretched in a motion that would have snapped a human back. "You liked her."

The comment startled me and turned it over in my mind. "I don't know. There was something about her. Maybe it was how I reminded her of her long dead son. If nothing else, she had both class and nerve. I didn't think that she deserved to fall prey to the Infestors on the Artifact."

"She may have escaped," Jaelle said. "Her ship lifted off just before the explosion."

"Maybe," I replied grabbing one of the rapidly diminishing supply of desserts. "It was clearly out of control and we didn't see it afterwards. But maybe. Still, she was Guild and ruthless for all her grandmotherly manner. You don't get that high otherwise."

"Back to Hartain," Jaelle said. "He's quite glad to have my cargo, but even more to have my services. My appearance gives him a new agent unknown to the city authorities and the constabulary."

"Perfect for the seducing of unwary spaceman," I said, finishing the cake and the champagne.

"Just so," she said smugly. "There are ops he can consider now that I am here."

"Such as finding out about a suspected oxygen-breather base somewhere down below," I added.

"Yes, it kills him that there is something involving so much wealth and secrecy going on beneath his feet and he's not able to touch it. I get the impression he longs to return to his homeworld or some other wet, dark, colony world to live in greater comfort than here. I believe I can tempt him to rashness."

I reached for her. "God knows you've always had that effect on me." We kissed as always careful of her sharper and longer teeth. "Can you stay the night?"

Jaelle considered then reluctantly, "No that would seem out of character with who Minogue is supposed to be, a bit too domestic. Besides we can't leave Maauro in the bar all night."

"She sat on an asteroid for 50,000 years."

Jaelle tossed a pillow at me. "Heartless male. She's not an android here but Estrella Lostly, a young girl who's formed an attachment to a spaceman of highly dubious character. In fact it would be rather odd if she returned to this suite given us. You'll need to work something out with her about that after I leave."

I looked at the time glowing on the com screen. "It's nearly two hours. She'll be coming on line shortly."

"Then kiss me again, while it's still just the two of us," Jaelle said. "Then it's the refresher for me."

I kissed her thoroughly, not sure when I would get the chance to do so again.

I remain in an idle state, enjoying my drink, gazing up at the holographic stars twinkling on the ceiling, while subroutines of mine digest all the intel collected to date and conduct necessary surveillance and monitoring through my systems and those I can safely hack. It requires very little capacity, as there is so little to go on. We do not even know the factions among our adversaries, or for that matter that they are all Ribisans. It cannot yet be discounted that this is a Guild operation though Hartain's lack of knowledge does so indicate. He could, however, be kept in the dark by another Guild section.

Still my assessment remains that this is a Ribisan run op. Prior to our arrival I would have said without government support, due to the limited nature of the attack on us at Star Central. However, aerospace fighters attacked my pod. Either there are private militaries among the Ribisans, or whatever faction is attacking us has enough government support to precipitate such an attack. Yet beyond the one clumsy assault with the elevator, we remain unassailed in Tir-a-Mar, facing only obfuscation and delays in our search for information on the missing scientists or their project. The delays we face here could simply be bureaucratic, but I do not believe so, there is a system here, a consistency to the information that has been released.

The waitress returns, "Are you Estrella Lostly?"

"Yes."

"There is a call for you on the com. Touch the screen and it will connect you and give you a privacy curtain option."

"Thank you." I press the screen. Normally it would recognize the person touching it by biometric sensors. I simply reprogram to accept me; this takes .00134 seconds. I accept the option of the sonic curtain, though I could generate a stronger one myself.

The screen lights up with a cool blue display of waving lines but no picture. The words "visual declined" glow a contrasting white and fade away. I hit the same option.

"Lostly?" comes a voice.

I recognize Fenster's voice. "Yes"

"It's ACA Fenster. I am glad to see you are still at the hotel."

"Yes, though I am not with Lt Fels."

"I understand he has acquired some female company again."

"Yes," I reply, unsure of what, if anything to add. I am glad Fenster has not opted for visual communication as I am uncertain what manner of facial expression I should use in this circumstance.

"Sorry about that. We sent the first girl. I know you and he have hit it off, but we need some leverage to restrain some of his more outrageous abuses of his authority. This second female is his own idea, but maybe we primed the pump, so to speak. We will make it up to you, Lostly, but it is essential that you stay in close contact with him at all times."

"Not practical now. He is in close contact with another female."

"Don't take it so hard. She's probably just a rented body. Listen, were you planning on heading home tonight? That's quite a distance from the Star and Comet."

As part of my cover as Lostly I had arranged for an unused rental unit in an inexpensive section of the town to show that it had been rented to Lostly six months ago. Fortunate, as Fenster must have checked my address.

"There seems no reason to stay," I said, projecting what I hoped was the proper mix of aggrieved and saddened female into it.

"Lostly, I want you to stay at the hotel. Get a suite near his, order anything you want and have it billed to my office. Fels seems to spot everyone else we put onto him and rejects any minder but you."

"You mean when he's not fooling around with prostitutes," I said in a miffed tone.

"Look, we'll even kick in 5,000 credits into your personal account. Maybe that will take some of the sting out of loverboy's dalliance. Believe me regarding this, there's no trusting a spacer when he's away from his homeworld. I wouldn't expect you to go stay with him. Just stay by him. You're doing great work keeping us informed."

"Very well."

"Excellent, your position around here is looking brighter all the time. Fenster out."

I am pleasantly surprised by this piece of luck. Perhaps after the events of the last few days we were, as Wrik says, due.

The pattern changed back to a deep green to show the connection had been severed. I tapped a connection to the front desk and was surprised when a live being, as opposed to an AI answered.

"Good evening, Ms Lostly. What can the Star and Comet do for you?"

"Ms Fenster has directed that I secure a room adjacent to Lt Fels. I believe the adjoining suites are empty.

"Anything for the assistant city administrator," he said, as if such requests were a normal occurrence. *"The suites are empty,"* he gives me a puzzled look as if wondering how I know, a minor error on my part.

"Lt Fels is quite diligent in his security checks and told me that they were empty. He is a suspicious sort," I add

"Yes, we noticed and thought it best to keep people away as much as practical considering the …ah…situation."

"Well he can surely have no objection to my taking the adjacent room as I am his guide."

"If you say so," he returned in a neutral tone. *"I have programmed suit 801 for you. Shall I send up anything?"*

"Not presently."

"We have a personal shopper on staff for VIPS. Please let us know if you need anything, given the unexpected nature of your stay."

"I will."

"Have a good stay," he says image fading out.

It has been one hour and 59.5 minutes. I open my link to Wrik.

"Are you busy, Wrik?"

"No," a touch of some emotion comes across our link, a tinge of what I recall as embarrassment. "Jaelle is dressing. She believes it would not be good for her cover to stay the night."

"We will defer to her judgment in the matter." I relay the most recent developments.

"That couldn't have gone better. I was wondering how you and I could plausibly get back together quickly. Come on up. After you get in I will open the adjoining door."

I leave a credit chip for the waitress, who smiles professionally and waves good night to me. Then I make my way up the elevator to our floor. When the doors open, Jaelle is standing there. I am surprised, as I had not yet reopened the link. For some reason I find that I am unsettled seeing her, yet I need to maintain my network, even in awkward moments. I check the area for bugs and cameras; we are unobserved in this little alcove.

She winked at me in a human gesture she'd learned from Wrik. "Taking over from me, Kit-sister? I didn't leave much for you."

As usual with Jaelle, her remarks to me could mean several things at once, some of them irritating.

"Did you enjoy your time with Wrik?" I ask.

"Yes," she replies with a typical grin. Unlike Wrik, there is no shyness or inhibition in Jaelle. "However Kit-sister I do feel bad about sending you to the bar."

I find I am pleased that she has given any thought to me at all.

"It would have been awkward to remain," I said. "My presence might have, what is the expression, put a damper on things?"

"Sorry, human expression that and I don't know what it means," Jaelle returned, "but yes, I appreciate the privacy you gave us, physically and in our heads."

"Fenster called," I added. "She wants me to stay with Wrik despite... any distractions."

"What? In his room again? That's a lot for any female to expect of another female."

"No, they provided me with the suite next door, unlimited expenses and a 5,000 credit inducement to forgive and forget."

Jaelle whistled.

I look at her with interest. "Did Wrik teach you too? Is it hard with your fangs?"

"This plays well for us," Jaelle mused, ignoring my comment. "They know he was with a woman and don't know it was me. You have a suite here. Oh and thanks for chasing off the working girl earlier. Wrik told me about it. It would have been hard to say no to her with his cover."

"You are welcome, things are complicated enough."

Jaelle gives me an odd look as if I had said something inappropriate but said. "Good, go to the suite, order everything you can—"

"Such as? I need nothing."

"Gods, you are supposed to be a biological female unexpectedly spending the night away from home and you're at least confused, if not upset. Someone handed you an open checkbook. You need a full range of toiletries...does this place have a shopper?"

"Yes."

"Tell her to use her judgment and get the usual things. She'll know what they are. You'll want a change of underwear—"

"I'm not wearing any."

"They don't know that! You don't have to use the stuff but a live female would order it along with chocolate, possibly ice cream and shoes."

"I am doing this why?"

"To demonstrate to anyone who cares to look, that you are consoling yourself for the shoddy way that men, your employer and the universe are treating you."

"Ah," I reply, "I usually do that by destroying the involved parties."

"Well don't get carried away," she said, brushing her lips against my cheek. "Some of us are still using the universe. Good night Maauro."

"Good night, Jaelle."

CHAPTER TWENTY

THE ALARM BUZZED AND I SAT UP, DISORIENTED AS TO where and even who I was. I'd worn too many identities these last few years. I reached across the bed then remembered that Jaelle had left. I lay for a few seconds with my face on the pillow she'd lain on. It still had her scent, faintly, but there. Finally, I stood and made my way to the refresher then to the main room of the suite. Maauro wasn't there. I looked around the empty room and wondered when I had last been without either one. I had an incomplete and restless feeling, like I was missing some part of myself. I sighed and dropped into a chair, too dispirited to even send out for coffee.

The night with Jaelle had driven all thoughts of Olivia Croyzer far from my mind. It had even put any concerns about the complications of Maauro on a shelf. In the morning, without Jaelle's confident presence to banish phantoms and confusions, the thoughts returned unbidden and unwanted, accompanied by the usual vague feelings of shame and confusion.

I sighed. I was never at my best on my own, becoming lost in my head on the battlegrounds of past defeats and present self-doubt. I could almost feel the cloud forming over me.

The door chimed, and I called out to enter. The voice activated door slid open. Maauro stood there. To my surprise, she wore fashionable, light clothes in place of her usual green coverall.

I stood a foolish grin spreading over my face. "Good to see you."

Maauro walked to the center of the room and did a pirouette. "How do I look?"

"Kind of like spring," I said.

"And that would be good?"

"Yes," I said. "Where have you been and what's with the new wardrobe?"

"Instructions from that most female of females, Jaelle, on the proper consolations due a young lady in these circumstances," Maauro replied with a small smile.

"Ah," I said, fighting a feeling of awkwardness.

"I am glad you were able to find time for each other. It has been lacking during these last weeks."

"I begin to wish we'd never come here, that we'd all stayed safe back on Star Central."

She cocked her head at me. "Do you regret forming Lost Planet?"

I hesitated. "No, not really. It's just that…for the first time in years I have things to live for and people to live it with. It makes every danger loom even larger."

"I think I understand and in as much as I can, I feel the same way."

"Nothing to do but get on with it," I added.

She nodded. "Jaelle will be about her investigations with the Guild. We should start ours."

"But not before breakfast," I said, both cheered by her presence and suddenly hungry.

She nodded. "Order away."

Wrik and I are enjoying breakfast when Jaelle breaks in. "Maauro," she sends, *"Hartain has sent for me. His female Dua-Denlenn gunner just dropped by my hotel with a politely worded summons. Doubtless he wants to know what I learned from Wrik."*

"Is she still there?" I return.

"No."

"That is good, it means likely the summons is no more than business or she would not have left you." Without diverting my attention from her, I raise a hand to interrupt Wrik, who immediately sets down his coffee, concern clouding his face as I relate the contact.

"Where is she?" he demands.

"On her way to see Hartain. Do not be concerned, I judge this to be merely a meeting."

"I'd be happier if you were with her."

"On what pretext?" I respond. *"Honestly Wrik while I can carry on two conversations simultaneously, I cannot be two places at once. You should have bought a second android."*

He laughs raggedly. *"Hey I didn't buy you, you were salvage."*

"Too true. Anyway, finish your meal and dress. We have our work to do. I will monitor Jaelle."

He follows my suggestion while I divert him with inconsequential matters. Meanwhile I discuss the situation with Jaelle. *"I believe that letting it slip that Wrik is a Confed Intelligence Operative is worthwhile. It is doubtless suspected already by the authorities here so he will eventually learn of those suspicions."*

"Agreed," Jaelle sends as she snakes through alleys of the floating city. *"It will demonstrate my usefulness. But I plan to embellish it with some references to Wrik's looking for Telberd's sister, Diralia Shon. I can spread some credits around to support my telling Hartain that Wrik paid to have my ship available in case he needs to move about outside the city without being followed."*

"Risky, but sensible," I concur. *"I'm going to bring Dusko on line with us."*

"He will doubtless be thrilled," Jaelle says. The almost metallic taste of the Due-Denlenn's mind flows into our link. Quickly I fill him in on developments.

Jaelle reaches Hartain's storefront. She passes in through the outer layer of security to be greeted, if a grunt and an unwinking stare are greeting, by the female Dua-Denlenn bodyguard who delivered the invitation earlier. I scan for a name in databanks to find only, Sheskaya, no last name given, as is common with her kind. Hartain must have brought her in recently, as there is so little on her locally. I tell none of this to Jaelle so she cannot make a slip. The bodyguard admits her to Hartain's inner sanctum.

"Good day, Minogue," Hartain says.

"Good day, Guildmaster."

"How did your evening with the young officer go?"

"The officer is what you feared, an intelligence operative passing as a common line officer. He is here to investigate the disappearance of personnel in the UDEXCO joint-venture and what that venture was about."

Hartain gave her a suspicious look. "An intelligence officer and he reveals so much in one night in bed?"

"Careful," Dusko says in her mind.

"While my skills might cause you to rethink that assessment, truth was the pillow talk was minimal. I told him that I didn't believe he was merely a scoutship captain. I hinted at my own connections. He cultivated me as an intelligence source. The fact that he put 10,000 credits in my account shows that he is both serious and short of time. "

"Ah, I knew it," Hartain said, slapping his hands together, "but how to make use of it?"

I feel Jaelle smile her most feral smile. "I took the initiative there. He is searching for a woman named Diralia Shon. Her brother appealed to Confed authorities with enough effect to get Fels sent here. It's a good pretext. He has not mentioned the name to the TAM authorities for fear that if she is here she might disappear in a more permanent fashion. He thought, with my Guild connections, I might turn her up where the local authority has not. He suspects that if found, she can lead him to see—"

"To see what?" Hartain's red eyes glow with greed.

Jaelle shrugs. "I'm good, but he is an intelligence officer. Human males seem to think exclusively with their sexual equipment, but this one has had training."

Hartain laughs. "Yes, they know no seasons for sex. It seems to be a constant distraction. How did they ever get to prominence in the Confederacy? Hard to top them for organizing to kill things though: Conchirri, Evolvers, the thing on Enshar, let's hope they find something else to practice on before they get twitchy again.

"So he knows you are Guild…" Hartain adds.

CHAPTER TWENTY

"Now would be a good time to throw some credits in front of him," Dusko whispers across the link.

"He knows I am an independent, he suspects I am Guild. Relax, it plays to our advantage," she soothes. Jaelle draws a 5,000-credit chit from her jacket and slides it across to the Morok who scoops it up with commendable speed.

"More good faith money," Jaelle adds. "He's promised me ten times as much for my aid if he needs to get off Tir-a-Mar. Shon may not be on the floating city and he suspects that there are other installations. He might need to get out under fire, possibly with prisoners. So my job is to arrange for a ship and get them back here."

"Where we learn what the young officer has discovered," Hartain interjects

Jaelle nods. "One way or the other; likely he will cooperate when he sees the situation. He is intelligent and flexible, I judge."

"If not, he might find himself in for a long fall. We do not even have to cover our tracks – he will have done that for us."

"Jaelle," I whisper in her mind. "Retract your claws before he notices."

She makes a conscious effort to relax, but I feel her rage at the casual plan to dispose of Wrik simmering below the surface. I share it in my cooler fashion. Hartain is now marked for elimination at my first opportunity. I neither tolerate nor forgive threats to my network.

Jaelle makes to rise, but Hartain motions her back down.

"I have disposed of some of the cargo that you brought. However I have run into a little problem with the shipment of drugs and weapons that represents the major profit."

"That being?" Jaelle says, her tone strictly neutral.

Hartain waved a hand. "No need to prick your ears at me, Young One. There is nothing wrong with your goods. Indeed, profits off a single load are quite impressive so far. The problem is that the Witch of Cimer, one Olivia Croyzer, Chief of the TAMPD, is on a tear. She is locking up Guilders on any pretext because of the attempt on Fel's life. Showy bit of nonsense, as if the Guild would ever do something so random and sloppy.

"In any event, with the Witch knocking down so many of my people and with you proving so adept at handling Fels, I wondered if you would take another small job for me here while we are gathering a return cargo for you?"

"Tell me more," Jaelle returns.

"As I said, I am short-handed, particularly in operatives who have the nerve and skills to handle an exchange. I need someone to oversee the transfer and payment of one of your cargo lots to some asteroid runners from the outer system. The man in charge is named Kesphan."

"What about Ms. Cold Eyes, in the corridor?"

Hartain grimaces. "Sheskaya, like you, is unknown here, but I brought her in at fabulous expense as a bodyguard, in which case *she has already proven quite useful, even killing one of Croyzer's and making it look like an accident. I prefer that she stays both close to me and as invisible as possible."*

"Ah, so I am expendable?"

"Only by comparison, my dear girl, but I judge you tough, smart and apt with weapons. Not that I anticipate trouble. Sheskaya's reputation does precede her, in a very real sense she will be with you in menacing spirit."

"Seems to be how everyone travels with me these days," Jaelle sends in nervous amusement

"Bargain for an increased cut," Dusko throws in.

"Jaelle," I interrupt. "I am concerned that this could be very dangerous and I will not be able to provide you with a sufficient level of security to satisfy either Wrik or myself."

"If we are to find out what is going on here before some trap closes on us," Jaelle sends while throwing out an outrageous percent for the Guildmaster to reject, "we need to access every source we can, especially Guild sources. You and Wrik cannot get this access, I have to do it."

I am displeased that I cannot fault her logic and I can only imagine what Wrik's reaction will be.

"Is this Kesphan a threat?" Jaelle asks in response to Hartain's inadequate counteroffer.

"No. He would not make an enemy of his main provider. He is not toothless, as you Nekoans would say, but he would only be tempted by someone weak. You are clearly not weak. Which is good, as I cannot provide you with any backup, at least, no one useful in a fight."

"I have a Confed All Outer Systems license for the laser I pack," Jaelle says. "They won't want to tangle with that much coherent light."

"Well said."

"And let's make that 12.5%."

"You wound me, Child. A cake run such as this shouldn't cost me anything. Ah, whatever became of courtesy? Let us say 5% for the inconvenience."

"Such a cake walk could doubtless be used for training your junior members I shouldn't deprive you of the chance. Unless perhaps for 9%."

Hartain chuckled. "Let's say 7.8% and you pick your weapon at the front."

As I predicted, Wrik's reaction to Jaelle's plan was angry rejection. Yet he had no more success in faulting her logic, or talking her out of her course of action then I did. So we were forced to accept it. Hartain had the cargo moved to a warehouse by robots and servers, with Jaelle riding herd on everything. The drop was scheduled for late in the evening shift.

It is only with difficulty that I restrain Wrik from heading out to join Jaelle at the warehouse near the docks where he first landed. He has a dinner meeting with Mysol and Fenster and there is no chance to get out of it. Nor can I attend with him; there would be no reason for Estrella Lostly to be in such elevated company, so I remain at our hotel. However it allows me to concentrate my attention on Jaelle and to more thoroughly infiltrate the net at Tir-a-Mar at a higher level of saturation then I dared before as Jaelle makes her way to the appointed rendezvous.

Jaelle stands next to two loaders filled with containers of arms and illicit materials, all of course real. There was no way to fake such things with the Guild. The warehouse is small and old, filled with stacks of metal shelving holding crates and boxes that stretch toward the track lights above. There is a section facing a rollup door and the street beyond. The warehouse is totally automated. I infiltrate the city systems and find a fire surveillance sensor that covers the inside, so I am able to see both through Jaelle's eyes and the city system. The scanner is poor quality equipment compared to my own optics, but it is all I can use remotely. It does allow to me to pick up some heat signatures. Company is approaching the front door.

"Be alert, Jaelle. Six are coming in by the small door next to the rollup."

"Thanks," she loosens her laser in her holster.

The door opens and three men step in quickly. They spot her, say nothing and scan the shadows and the aisles of the warehouse. A human female, a Morok and another human male enter. The last is Kesphan, from the information and holos that Hartain provided.

"I don't know you," he calls.

"Hartain sent me," Jaelle says, then adds the Guild code word. Kesphan visibly relaxes. The two guards continue to watch the dark reaches of the warehouse.

Kesphan, a sharply dressed human, walks forward. The Morok and the female follow on his heels. He is giving Jaelle a speculative look, a common reaction to her from human males. I wonder about this, not recalling having made this observation before. I realize it comes from my link from Jaelle. As usual I am feeling more from her than from the others. She knows and expects this reaction from most males and in fact seems pleased by it.

"Is that all of it?" Kesphan asks, gesturing at the loaders. His companions walk past him and begin examining the cases and the goods within. They have test instruments of a various sorts.

Jaelle nods. "How come you didn't do this all in one transaction?"

The human shrugs. "We couldn't get all the stash together quickly enough and Hartain rarely gives credit. Most of this load is going off-world anyway; it took time to get in touch with buyers in the asteroid belt.

"So, Catgirl," he says with a grin. "How come Hartain is using you? You're the one who brought the load in."

Jaelle gives him a frown. "Word gets around quickly."

"It's a small city in a system that's mostly gas and rock. And back to my question."

"Personnel shortages," Jaelle says easily. "Gives me a chance to move about, make connections and show my value to the local Guildmaster." She remains unbothered by the man's frankly sexual regard. She is beautiful and confident, but her hand does not stray from the laser on her belt.

"Yeah," the human female says, "that bitch Croyzer is clamping down hard."

"Don't be too impressed with Hartain," Kesphan continues as if the other had not spoken. "He's pretty small time, Tir-a-Mar is the back end of forever. He's not like a real Guild boss."

Jaelle raises an eyebrow. "He has some rather formidable operatives."

"Some," he concedes. "But there might be alternatives for an enterprising young lady like you." The men make a signal to Kesphan and begin loading the containers on electric carts. "You could do better," he finishes.

"Well, a girl has to keep her ears up," Jaelle says then demonstrates by wiggling hers.

Kesphan grins. "Don't suppose I could talk you into coming along for the ride."

"Don't suppose you could," she returns.

Kesphan steps forward and places the small silver metal case on the deck between them, then steps back. "Delivery accepted, Fellow Guilder. Profit to you," he says, using the ancient formula that concludes the deal.

Jaelle nods again, picking up the case. "Payment accepted and profit to you as well."

The humans back away from her as she does. As soon as she is near the doorway she spins on her heel in relief and ducks out of sight of the Guilders. She is now in a service corridor outside the warehouse, but still in from the streets. A pair of female Moroks walk by paying no attention to her.

I detect coded activity. A microburst that is not standard. There is a military feel to it. The code draws an audio response, a short wordless sound as of a thumb being run over a microphone.

"Jaelle," I begin. "Be alert, I believe TAM police are closing in on your location."

Her body reacts with elevated pulse and respiration, but I can feel her face remain smooth. "Are you sure?"

"Yes, I cannot crack the code quickly but its architecture is similar to random Confed military ones. I am getting short bursts of code now with multiple response points."

"*What now?*"

I am infiltrating TAMPD databases and communications at attack speed. Their barriers cannot stop me but I will not be invisible due to the force and speed with which I must hack. I burst through the outer barriers and shred the virus protections in full intruder mode.

"TAM police," I report, "were tipped by an informant in Kesphan's organization."

"*Damn!*"

"Jaelle, that was aloud."

"*I'm trapped.*"

"Not so. Follow my instructions without hesitation." I analyze the police ambush. Not only is it the work of Croyzer, but she is present directing the op. I see her Marine training in the placement of her ambush and blocking forces. But her aggressive instincts may provide a way out. She is not waiting for the prey to come to her. Her forces are moving in.

"Ahead left, there is a janitorial closet. Go in. Close the door. Conceal yourself within. I am masking the signals of your Nekoan body from any life monitor or scanner, you are invisible electronically."

Inside Jaelle finds lockers and fits herself into one. Just in time.

"Remain motionless; SWAT is passing your door. One is checking."

The door is opened and two SWAT officers peer in, covering each other, but do not enter. As they continue advancing down the hallway, the door swings closed. Over the TAM tacnet I hear the whispered, "Clear" by the team leader. I wait for them to exit the hallway.

"Out, turn left. Proceed at your best speed."

Jaelle, suitcase in hand dashes out the door. Her faith in me is such that she does not even check before running down the corridor.

"Turn right. Slow down now. Approach the spiral staircase, go down one level and wait. There are officers too close to the level below but they are moving inwards."

"What's happening behind me?" she asks. "I think I just heard shots."

"The TAMPD have ambushed and stunned two of the other Guilders. The others are trading fire with the TAMPD. Kesphan has a needle gun and has wounded an officer—"

"Freeze!" I order.

A voice sounds in my head and I arrange so Jaelle can hear. "This is Croyzer. We have five in custody and one bottled up but there was a seventh life signal that is not showing now. They may be cloaked somehow. Check the other exits. "

The officers below begin to backtrack. I realize that Croyzer is above Jaelle with her sergeant on the next level. I spot her on a surveillance camera from the building security system. Even without knowing it, they have boxed Jaelle in. I must take a more active role.

I slam into the TAMPD network and seize control of it fully, cutting Croyzer and her sergeant off from the rest of her forces. "This is Croyzer," I shout in her own voice, "ambush on radial C 2B. Guilders with needle guns. Officers down. We need help!"

"What the hell?" Croyzer snaps. She looks up at her hulking sergeant in shock. "Belay that order."

No one hears her. The officers below Jaelle are racing to the front of the building. The tacnet is full of calls for information. Even with well-trained troops communications discipline can be difficult.

"Go, Jaelle. Down and to the corridor on your right as you reach the bottom," I order

She takes off in a sprint. I continue to direct her away while Croyzer shouts vainly for her troops but my attention refocuses on Croyzer as she stops yelling.

"Sergeant, we've been hacked. Get to the building front. Take control. Bag what we've got then send anyone you can spare this way."

He is aghast. "Sir, you're not running in without backup!"

"Move, dammit. That diversion was designed to make a hole in this area." She races for the spiral staircase ignoring his protestations. "I'll be ok," she shouts over her shoulder as she leaps down the stairs a weapon in either hand.

This is bad. Croyzer is a dangerous adversary: intelligent and cunning. She has realized my strategy and countered almost immediately. "Jaelle, please continue making your best speed. Croyzer is chasing you."

"The TAMPD police chief, herself! Great."

"Yes. Take the stairs to the right. The green door is unlocked. Go through."

Croyzer is speeding along in Jaelle's track, her police pass opening doors for her, with such accuracy that I check to see if there is a locator on Jaelle or her case. My scans detect nothing, but Croyzer continues to narrow the gap. Jaelle is faster than any human female but I must reroute the racing Jaelle away from any people who may see and describe her later. Croyzer merely charges. I realize belatedly that she knows the station on a level I would not have imagined a human mind could hold and is analyzing the most likely escape route in anticipation.

"I don't know who you are," Croyzer says aloud between indrawn breaths, "but I suspect you can hear me."

Again I am startled. She is addressing me directly through the city net, assuming that I am watching her! That and her aerobic fitness are impressive.

"You're good, whoever you are. You must be directing Number Seven or I would have caught him by now. But when I'm through with both of you, you'll wish you had taken that long swan dive into Cimer."

Far behind us the TAMPD have discovered the call for help was a diversion, but I further confuse them with contradictory orders in the voices of their superiors. The sergeant will arrive momentarily and restore order, but they are all too far out of position now to intervene. Croyzer is the only threat to Jaelle's escape.

Meanwhile, I follow Croyzer on any camera or electronic device in the area. The gap between the racing women continues to narrow. I realize that unless I can change things Jaelle will be caught.

The corridor Jaelle is pounding down breaks three ways. One is useless to us for escape but perhaps not for what I plan.

"Jaelle, Can you leap to the catwalk crossing above? Lie motionless on it."

She responds instantly in a move Croyzer, for all her strength, could not follow. There she lies. I feel the cold metal of it on her body as she pants frantically. Nekoans are faster than humans but do not have the same endurance. She is nearly played out.

Croyzer appears in a blur of blue and races on without pausing until she reaches the junction of the corridor. There she skids to a stop. I had anticipated her immediately selecting a hall but she does not. She knows Jaelle slipped behind her once. If she looks back—

I race through the city network, find a fire door at the top of the useless second corridor and open it remotely, then override the safety and slam it shut. A nearby woman cries out in alarm. The sound travels down the sloping corridor and Croyzer is on it like a predatory animal.

"Now Jaelle, drop down. Take the left corridor. Slow at the top to look normal. Step into the street there is a robocab there that will only open to you. Get in it."

She responds, still clutching the suitcase.

Croyzer has reached the door at the top that I open again. The woman who cried out has moved on. The chief leaps through the door to face a line of offices and one startled clerk. Before she can turn around I shut the door. She throws herself at it, fetching up painfully when her police badge will not open it. She cannot override the force of my programs. She steps back, growls, raises her weapons then looks at them, the fire door and lets her arms drop.

Outside, an exhausted Jaelle exits the building, looking neither right nor left as she passes through a crowd, she hops into the cab, which immediately pulls away.

"You will be released from the cab in 256 seconds," I say, "proceed on foot from there. You should be safe."

"Thanks, Maauro. Maybe I do love you after all."

I refocus on Croyzer, as I drop my other cyberattacks with relief. I too am strained by the battle. The TAMP police chief has her head down, hair tumbling into one eye, apparently attempting to glare a hole in the door with the other. Unexpectedly she puts both hands on her hips, weapons still clutched in them and laughs. She looks about, apparently sees the surveillance camera I am using and turns to face it. Again, I am discomforted by her direct response to me. Did she merely know where the camera is likely to be, or does she have some power that I have not seen in humans before?

"Well, Hacker," she says smiling wolfishly at me, "well-played. You are good. But doubt it not, you will be mine."

I simply cannot help myself. I reactivate the tacnet for the two of us. "Be careful," I whisper in her own voice. "You might get what you're after." I have fought Infesters, the Artifact, armored fighting vehicles and companies of Guild. I will not be menaced by a single human female. I am pleased by her startled expression.

I cut out of the all the nets I have invaded, covering my tracks as best I can. In some cases I must destroy data and systems I cannot otherwise blank. Croyzer knows I was here, but she will find no evidence of who or what I am.

CHAPTER TWENTY-ONE

"**H**AS JAELLE CHECKED IN? IS SHE OK? HAVING ANY BETTER LUCK *than us?*" *Wrik says when he returns to the hotel after his dinner with Mysol and Fenster. He touches a screen and selects some of the ethereal and instrumental music that he finds relaxing.*

"*She mindspoke to me while I was waiting for you to return from dinner,*" *I advise. I fill him in on the excitement of Jaelle's escape, and then wait for him to calm down.*

"*Her cargo has been sold at considerable profit,*" *I add when he has finally ceased cursing,* "*and is already being gleefully retailed by Hartain causing a minor crime wave in the City that is vexing the authorities. She is in very good with the local Guildmaster, but for once, we seem to know more of what is going on than the Guild. All they have is rumors of some big project nearby either in Tir-a-Mar, which seems unlikely or I would have surely found something, or at some substation floating below us. They have not penetrated city security save in the most venial ways.*"

"*Great. Selling drugs, weapons and illegal pleasure software, plus being chased by the police,*" *Wrik grumbled.* "*Good thing we made so many verified copies of Candace's letters of legal dispensation along with your new citizenship. Bet Candace hasn't found even half of them.*"

"*Not where I secured them, unless she wants to cause the collapse of Star Central's economy. Still, I thought it quaint that the citizenship paper was actually a paper.*"

"*Some old customs die hard,*" *he says with a yawn.* "*So what's the program for tomorrow—continue poking around until we can provoke someone into trying to kill us?*"

I nod. "*The usual. We have the medical facility for tomorrow's agenda.*"

He nods. "*Well at least if we are shot at we won't have to go far to get patched up.*"

I was just taking my shoes off when the screen lit on the comp in my hotel room. I looked at Maauro.

"Our scanning and security programs are functioning," she said. "We will be discreet on our end. About the other end I will not be able to tell until the connection is established.

I touched the screen to connect

"Fels,"

I instantly recognized the voice as Croyzer's. "Here."

"An unofficial channel from a disposable com unit," Maauro said in my mind. "There are no other connections. The Captain neither wants to be monitored, nor to have anyone know she called us."

"Meet me out back of the Star and Comet, there's an alley to the right of the service exit. Meet me there as soon as you can. Leave the little princess behind."

I looked over at Maauro. She nodded.

"See you in five minutes."

The line went dead.

"Civilian clothes," Maauro said. "Leave the sidearm here. Carry this small stunner in your pocket." She handed me a small stun-derringer she must have manufactured in her body. "I will be on the roof top above you. If there is trouble I will leap down, but I do not look for it with Croyzer."

"Ok." I threw on the replacement civilian clothes I'd purchased for such occasions. I didn't expect to fool anyone who was assigned to watch me, but I would attract less attention this way.

"Be careful anyway."

"I was born careful, Maauro."

We parted ways at the door. Maauro headed for the roof. I took the elevator down to the third floor, then came out and switched to the stairs. Once down, I walked to the service way. Servers and other people walked past me. The ones that didn't know me didn't look. The ones that did, glanced at me curiously, perhaps with veiled hostility, but they didn't interfere. I slid out through the back doors, trying to look in all directions at the same time. I couldn't see anything suspicious but it was late evening under the artificial moonlight, although the street was full of transports and pedestrians. I walked slowly until I reached a spot where I could lean against a wall opposite the alley, studying it. It was cleaner and less dank than its planetside equivalents, but boxes and trashcans still lined it. I caught a flash of bright blonde hair. With a sigh, I patted the pocket with the stunner and started for the alley. It took some effort not to look upward to see if a slender feminine figure was racing over the rooftops.

I made my way into the alley, moving from cover to cover. I knew I'd come in further than the flash of blonde hair I'd spotted. I'd just about figured that my eyes had tricked me when she stepped out from behind a stack of boxes about a hundred feet away. She wore a light, black jacket and casual pants. Her right hand was in the jacket. She beckoned with her left.

I nodded slowly and walked forward, stopping only a pace apart.

"Captain Croyzer, you wanted to see me?"

"Actually about now I'd like to see you safely leaving my station," she said.

"Not through with my work."

"Yeah. How did it go with Dok?"

So much had happened since I saw her last that I had forgotten it had been on the day we were to see the Morok professor.

"Pretty much as I imagine he told you after I left him. Not a whole lot. Although, as you noted, it's curious how much changed here about two years ago when the Biogenetics project supposedly folded."

"I've been looking into that," she said, her lips compressed into a line. "Using my own sources and finding out not a whole lot more. I've been concerned about it for a while. Your arrival and the attempt on your life brought it all into focus for me. Or rather, while there is a Confed warship around, I felt I had a chance of looking into this and keeping my skin intact.

"You're right. Something is being covered up here and it's not Guild. It seems to be Ribisan in origin though clearly the top city people are aware of it – at least Fenster and Mysol."

"Why are you telling me this?"

"Because someone is trying to kill you and the trails I've found lead to places that aren't safe for me to follow."

"Company cop?" I said.

"That's the job."

"Why should I trust you, Olivia?"

"You got any other friends on this gasball?"

I considered. I wanted to trust her but after my discussion with Maauro I wasn't sure if my judgment was sound regarding her. "I usually know more about my friends. Maybe you can tell me why someone with all those Marine decorations on her uniform is a company cop in an outpost in the backend of nowhere."

The sensuous lips twisted into a bitter expression. "I used to do honest work, Confed Marines, Military Police. Guess I might as well tell you the rest and save you looking it up in the Confed Military database.

"There was a killing in an off port – promising young officer – whose father had a lot of friends. Whose father I owed a lot to. She was just a prostitute, a drug addict, human trash. Story was that she tried to rob him and that there was an accomplice with a knife. It happens all the time in such places. I arranged for it to look like he was on duty at the time. Gave him an alibi.

"Then he did it again. This time there was no covering it up. No pretending that it wasn't anything other than a murder. And the first case got reopened. The powerful friends did what they could. But the best they could do for me was make it look like incompetence. I was dishonorable discharged. A disgrace to everyone who knew me. I deserved it of course, that second prostitute's death is on me. Can you imagine what that was like?"

My mouth was dry and my heart hammered. "Better," I whispered, "better than just about anyone else you could ever meet."

She looked at me dry-eyed, this was a woman who didn't cry, but I could see pain on the arctic fields of her eyes for a thousand miles.

"You want to tell me your sad story?" she asked.

I hung my head. "I can't. I want to, but I can't. I will tell you that it was worse, far worse."

A startled look crept into her expression, and worse, the shade of doubt that I knew would follow. "I find that hard to believe," she said, finally looking away.

"Believe it," I said harshly. "Like you, I'm trying to do something with what's left of my life."

There was a long silence. She sighed. "So now I'm a company cop, on the edge of something that isn't right again. You and I don't have a lot of time to decide if we can or should help or even trust each other."

"What can you tell me?" I said.

She considered me for a long moment and I began to wonder if she would just leave. Then, "All I can tell you is one word that seemed associated with the project: Predictor."

"Predictor?" I repeated.

"That was all. No context, no other hints. Predicting what, I have no idea."

I looked at Croyzer's sculpted face; her lips so full and sensuous under the arctic-blue eyes, softened by the mass of blonde hair that hung over her shoulders and her right eye. I found it difficult to pull my eyes off her and grateful that she didn't seem to notice.

Why was I so fascinated by her? The answer crept up on me and I wasn't happy about it. Maauro had been right.

Croyzer was a human woman and not just any woman. She was intelligent and striking. In another time she'd have been a queen somewhere. Jaelle had told me that being consorts wasn't exclusive; she needed one of her kind for children. She thought I might just need one of my own kind, either for children or just to be with. I found myself wondering what it would be like to be with Croyzer and beyond that, wondering in traitorous thought, how Jaelle stacked up against a beautiful woman of my own kind. Would I still find Jaelle so attractive if Croyzer had been an option?

I'd told Jaelle that I wasn't interested in human women, that she would always be enough. Had I been telling the truth? Did I even know? Our relationship had started in and been welded by shared dangers in wild circumstances. Could it have started any other way? When Jaelle looked at me did she ever see something she was occasionally ashamed of? Something that wasn't quite right? I surely looked strange next to a male Nekoan.

While Jaelle looked very like a human female, that was only a first impression, just like the feline impression that struck one looking at any Nekoan. Could the exotic always exceed the traditionally beautiful?

I vacillated between disgust with myself and belief that this was something I seriously needed to consider. I'd promised something. Could I deliver on it? I thought suddenly of the link that I had with Maauro and hoped to God none of the confusion running through my brain was crossing to her. I knew that strong emotion leaked across sometimes and I didn't want her to know that I had thoughts like this.

Yet even she came into question in this. Maauro was a factor, sometimes perhaps a threat to my relationship to Jaelle. Because of her lack of actual gender, it had never really matured into a rivalry. Jaelle was my lover. Maauro, well the word friend seemed inadequate, but it was a relationship rooted in love that detoured around sex. There really seemed no word for what she was to me. But she too was not a human woman, merely the appearance of one grafted over a war-fighting machine made be an unknown species.

Didn't like cling to like? Would my life be incomplete without the love of a woman of my own kind?

God, I thought wearily. I don't want to even have these thoughts. I want them to go away. I want to open up my skull and let this pour out of me, never to return.

"You look lost in thought, Fels."

I looked up startled. Croyzer stood only a foot away, giving me a quizzical almost gentle look. Her beauty and the scent of her caught me off guard, hitting me in places I hadn't been aware of. I felt a pull toward her that was almost physical.

Her lip's quirked as if she had some idea of what was running through my mind.

"I was thinking," I nodded, "wondering about being far from home. Wondering, if sometimes you can voyage so far and so fast that you lose your way back."

Her eyes widened. "Strange thoughts for the captain of a scoutship?"

I shook my head. "Who better to think so? I've been in places where no human has ever set foot. Seen things few would credit. Strangeness has been so much part of my life that it has ceased to be strange."

She leaned back against the wall, crossing her arms. "You're not quite what I expected. You think more deeply than most young men."

"I'm not quite as young as I look. I've been in cold sleep and raced about in hyperdrive a lot."

Croyzer laughed but the sound was not unkind. "That just puts you further from the date your mother delivered you, but it's not living. No, Fels," she said pressing a finger against my chest as if it was a saber. "There's something about you."

I stiffened and I knew she felt it through her hand. She smiled. "You've been through some life. Some good and some very bad, I figure. Loves lost?"

"And you?" I riposted.

Her blue eyes were very frank. "Yeah. But I'm a woman and not an impressionable girl like your little minder, assuming that's really who she is. No one scores me as a planetside trophy."

"No, I wouldn't guess they would."

"So we're both grownups then."

I sighed. "I am not sure of that when it comes to me."

Croyzer flashed a grin, but when it faded the openness in her face faded with it. "I've got a position here, Fels, one not easy for someone with my past to find. I don't let things interfere with it. I won't take chances that don't make sense."

"And you think I might?"

"Fenster and Mysol certainly think so."

"What are they up to, Croyzer?"

She considered me. "Olivia, when no one's around."

'Wrik' almost spilled out of my mouth. "Jedaya," I said aloud. "So Olivia, what are they up to. What happened to Michaels and all his staff? Why were the Ribisans so eager to have Confed biotech scientists here?"

"Hmph," she turned away, dropping her finger. "I told you I wasn't here when all that happened. The personnel you asked about all departed according to the records, just before I got here. As for the biotech project, why would I know? What does that have to do with policing?"

"Tell me something," I asked. "Did you meet your predecessor?"

She raised an eyebrow. "No, he was gone when I arrived."

"What happened to him?"

"Medical discharge, his health worsened."

"Very convenient. Have you noticed how many positions around here turned over about the time that project supposedly ended?"

"What do you mean...supposedly?" she faced me again all business and cold beauty.

"I don't know. Yet."

"Be careful how you go around overturning my station. This is still a civilian outpost."

"Unless I say it isn't. You were Confed Marines, you know that."

"Yeah, and I know how rarely it's pulled and the purple oscillating hell that follows when it happens."

"You have a gift for words, Olivia."

"Don't pull the charm card again so soon, it hasn't recharged."

"Either you know more about what's going on, in which case you might be my enemy. Or you don't, in which case we might have a mutual interest in finding out where these people went, or if they ever left, alive."

The silence stretched between us. I could hear a faint buzzing of a light fixture above us, the sigh of air from the vents.

"Jedaya, when I decide if we are to be friends or enemies, I'll tell you first. Fair?"

I started to say fair, then wondered if I could. I was a spy here for starters. She clearly suspected it. Was I betraying anything by agreeing?

"Cat got your tongue?"

That hit close to home. "Olivia, I don't know that I can play that fair with you."

To my surprise she brushed my cheek with her lips. "I think you just did." Before I could react she spun and strode off and I knew better than to call after her.

I wait for Wrik to head back to the hotel before leaping to the rooftop adjacent to the Star and Comet and quickly scaling the outside of the building to my rooftop access. I want to give Wrik time to calm down. His suspicion that more than emotion laden conscious thought leaks across the link between us is correct. The longer we are linked this way, the more of his strong emotions and the subject of them make their way to me. Normally I tune this down to mere background out of respect for his privacy, but he is interacting with the chief of police, a dangerous adversary and one who seems particularly unsettling to Wrik. I need intel on her.

The conversation, while interesting, is devoid of mission useful info, however, it does reveal a possible complication. Wrik's strong reaction to the alpha female began with anger and agitation, as she reminded him of his former state of powerlessness before he and I met. With the revelation she made to him, it seems to be changing into one of empathy for someone with a similar life experience. Perhaps he is even unaware that his desire for this female is a complicated mix of a need to show to such a person that he is not the old Wrik, mixed in with an unusually high attraction and the hormonal rush of danger.

Wrik had evinced no interest in other human females during the time we were on Star Central. Perhaps this is because he spent all his time with me or Jaelle and there was no opportunity for temptation. I sigh. Jaelle released this particular X-factor into our network by wishing to become pregnant by one of her own kind. Beyond that, being both more experienced and practical than Wrik, she hit squarely on the issue of fidelity. Was it reasonable to expect that beings that evolved under different stars could maintain an exclusive relationship across decades? For Jaelle, from a culture where joinings were more termed events that expired when either the passion, or necessity for them, dissipated, it seemed only normal to consider.

It struck me with a shock that at some time in the future, Jaelle's feelings toward Wrik might change and that she might focus her life elsewhere. In a way, this talk of other lovers might be her way of preparing him for the concept that relationships among her kind were more temporary. Intellectually, she understood that humans sought permanent mating for all that their success rate at it was fairly dismal. Wrik has discussed some of this with me back on Star Central, but the emotional aspect of it had not hit me as it did now. She could leave our network, or at least cease to be an active member. How would our network function if that came to be? How would Wrik function?

Wrik comes from a conservative society where emotional matters were rarely discussed. He is, for all his hard-bitten pretension, somewhat naïve, and I realize with surprise, inexperienced around human females. He might have been involved in the practice relationships that adolescent humans engage in just before the war. After the war he was in disgrace and fled his homeworld. His days on Kandalor would have been devoid of chances for any normal relationships. Humans had been a small part of the population in any event. Thinking back, I realized that he had no close friends, human or otherwise. Any sexual relations would have been either casual or purchased.

That too is also part of the answer. This attraction is the first serious one for him as the new person he envisions himself as; the reconstructed Wrik. This matter suddenly assumes a seriousness that it did not possess before.

It saddens me that Wrik's first reaction is to hide this from me, although I understand why. Wrik is very afraid that he cannot measure up to what he now wants to be, and he does not want me to know that. Beyond that, how am I, a machine of silicon, ceramic and nuclear-bonded metals, to advise him on this? I know a tiny amount about love. I know nothing about sex or pair-bonding. My fidelity is programmed—

Or is it? I freeze as I consider this. M-7 was programmed to obey its creators, but I am now Maauro. I self-program. I fought M-7 to obtain that right. So, in a way, maybe I do understand something of infidelity. Further, Wrik and I are both reinventions of our former selves. This is a stunning new perspective to me.

Wrik is coming up the hallway toward me. Again, I feel sadness that I cannot help him with his interior anguish. Nor is there anyone else in our network who can. He would not confess these thoughts he is ashamed of, to Jaelle, less so to Dusko. In both cases, their alien cultures and biology might render the questions meaningless. In this, he is alone.

He looks at me but his eyes slide quickly off and there is a redness to his skin. He fears what I may have sensed in him.

"Did Croyzer have any useful intel?" I ask.

"Weren't you listening?" he replies.

I cock my head at him, a gesture I use to tell him I have failed to follow something he says, maybe it will add verity to my lies. "No, I was running analysis on the elevator fall. I ingested both smoke and metal particles in hope of finding some biochemical traces that would give us a clue. This was my first chance to devote sufficient resources to the study. Unfortunately it did not reveal anything. I left Croyzer to you. Have you determined if she is friend or foe?" This is not entirely a falsehood. I was doing this in addition to my nonstop scanning and manipulation of electronic systems around us. It simply did not involve as much of my CPU as I let him believe.

Wrik's relief is almost palpable as he delivers an edited version of the conversation he had with "Olivia."

"What do you think of her?" Wrik suddenly asks.

I had not anticipated this question. "If she is involved in whatever is going on here, she tops the list of dangers to our assignment and existence. Even if she is only the police captain and not in league with whatever faction is after us, she will be dangerous. The authorities could command her against us and I believe she is a formidable combatant. Although, like many of our former enemies, she would have no way to anticipate or counter something like me."

I hesitate. "Be wary of her Wrik. She seems to have an unusual level of interest in you."

The blush returns. He nods vigorously. "Good advice.'

I relay Wrik's good nights to Jaelle who is busily devouring a late dinner at her own hotel. Between the stress of her mental contact with me and the exertions of the day, she is famished and exhausted.

The biologicals go to their rest. I watch over all of them.

CHAPTER TWENTY-TWO

"**W**HY DON'T WE WRAP THIS UP?" I SAID ALOUD. "I think I have seen enough for today. I have a lot of data to review but I am quite satisfied that your medical facilities are up to and above Confed standard."

A raft of relieved smiles from staff of Tir-A-Mar's main hospital greeted my announcement.

"Shall we escort you back to your hotel?" began McCaffer, finally recovered from his journey with us to the Ribisan section.

I raised a hand. "No. I'm actually going to take some time off-duty in your shopping district, finding souvenirs for some young ladies and a few items for my crew."

"You seem to spend a great deal of your time and attention on the ladies," Maauro added, to my surprise and with a trace of disapproval on her face.

"Now, now, Lostly," McCaffer said as a chuckled riffled through the crowed. "You know what spacers are like, a date in every port."

"Hmph," she replied, provoking more smiles.

"Fortunately, I have you to keep an eye on me," I said, playing into it. "Perhaps while we are shopping, we can find something nice for you, since I have been unable to escape your supervision outside of the bathroom."

"Lieutenant," she said with a faintly scandalized air, "are you offering me a bribe?"

"Merely rewarding a hard-working Confed citizen for supporting the fleet."

"Well, that's different."

As we started for the door, McCaffer gestured to Maauro. I waited by the sliding glass door, looking out at the imitation of a gloomy, misty day. Evidently, it was the Morok's turn to choose the weather. There was no actual rain, but the air was thick with water vapor and I was glad for my uniform jacket.

The others departed and Maauro joined me at the door.

"What did McCaffer want?" I asked.

Maauro scanned the area before answering with eyes, ears and doubtless other senses I hardly understood.

"Nothing of import. He merely congratulated me on handling you so well."

"Jaelle often makes the same observation."

"I believe this is the appropriate response to such a comment," Maauro said. She turned to face me and stuck her tongue out. I couldn't help but laugh.

We started out and into the cool day, stepping onto a slidewalk. I turned my collar up.

"It's useful that they share that belief," Maauro said. "I have mentioned to them how suspicious you are and how many of their other observers you have spotted and pointed out to me. They have backed off all other security and are now relying on the reports I periodically file with McCaffer and Fenster's offices. It has been difficult keeping up the pretense of having been stationed here a long time. I must reroute inquiries on my pay records, assignments and other minutiae of life. Fortunately, all these inquiries are computerized and I have created quite the virtual life for Estrella Lostly. However, should a live being begin making inquiries, the deception will fall apart quickly."

"Meanwhile, we are able to move about unobserved," I added.

"So, shall we make an appearance of shopping before we head into the industrial districts?" she asked.

I nodded. We changed slidewalks, walking along streets crowded with beings of most known species. Tir-a-Mar was so big it truly felt like being on a planet. Not even the Artifact ship of Infestors had contained so much open interior space. A half hour of walking and slides took us into a shopping area. I gestured toward a woman's clothing store and Maauro followed me in.

"Let's find you a jacket," I said. "It's improbable that a small, slender girl like you wouldn't feel the cold and damp in just a light jumpsuit."

"I could simply reconform part of my outer chassis to look like a jacket."

I shook my head. "Someone might check to see if we are actually shopping, whether I am spending money where I said we were going. Besides what if you had to take it off?"

"Excellent thinking, Wrik."

We walked into the store and were greeted professionally by the store clerk who guided Maauro to a selection of jackets. I spotted the item I was looking for and slipped away to purchase it. When I returned, Maauro had selected a light jacket of a flattering cut, but which clashed furiously with her green jumpsuit. I selected one in a rust color that worked better.

As we exited the shop with our purchases, I handed Maauro a small, ornate bag. "Here, this is for you."

She smiled at me in such innocent delight that it caused my heart to skip a beat. "What is this?" She delicately folded back the tissue paper with hands that I had seen twist steel, to reveal a length of vorstal butterfly silk, the color of sunrise.

CHAPTER TWENTY-TWO

Maauro regarded with a rapt look as she drew the length of wide silk ribbon out. I was surprised when she remained quiet for several seconds, simply staring at it. I was about to ask if something was wrong when she spoke. "It is very beautiful, Wrik, so delicate in fabric and so warm in color."

"I'm glad you like it," I said, feeling awkward and unsure why.

"I do, but I find that what I like most is how you remember the things that I care for. A yellow ribbon was the first thing you ever gave me. I do so wish I had been able to hang on to the first one. Delicate things are so often in peril around me." She reached up and gathered her long, shining black hair in one hand and wrapped the ribbon about it in the delicate and elaborate bow that she favored. "How do I look?"

I smiled at her. "Well, I'd thought it would make you look even younger, but somehow, no, it makes you look like more like a princess with a crown."

"Thank you."

We made our way out of the shopping district. Maauro, in her new, fashionable jacket and yellow hair-ribbon, attracted more attention and smiles from some of the men we passed. It was as if her hair bow somehow drove the gloom a little further away.

"Shouldn't we go help Jaelle, in the red light district?" I asked as we descended a spiral escalator.

"No, with Dusko's help she will accomplish more than we. Our proximity to her can only compromise her cover."

I smacked my hand against my forehead. "Of course, stupid of me."

Maauro gently touched my arm. "You are concerned for her, as always. I believe you only stop worrying when all members of your network are before your eyes. If then."

"Hah, I never worry about Dusko."

"So?" she replied, doubt clear in her voice.

"I just worry about what he'll do if he isn't watched."

"As you say," she replied.

"I haven't forgotten how he used to haunt my steps back on Kandalor—"

Maauro raised her hand and cocked her head in a listening gesture, clearly for my benefit, as her hearing did not depend on it.

"We are being followed," Maauro said.

I pricked up my own ears. "Guild, Croyzer's police, or some other player?"

"Analysis suggests the latter. Someone large and very heavy, whose electronic counter-measures are of greater than military standard."

"What do we do?" I asked, my hand cupping the handle of my military laser. One advantage of my pose as a Confederate officer was my ability to travel armed, largely irrelevant so long as I was with Maauro, but comforting nonetheless.

"We lead our stalker into a quiet section of the industrial sector and attempt a capture. Failing that, we eliminate it. I prefer to capture it alive. We are in dire need of intelligence that our wanderings here have not uncovered. I am weary of battling shadows. Follow me."

I am unsure how it is that the unseen tracker has remained on our trail. Likely, as a Ribisan, he has access to the city systems in ways that I cannot use, or block, without setting off all manner of alarms. I have been effectively and selectively blinding or altering city systems to my presence, but only in secured areas and for brief periods. Regardless of the sophistication of my cyber-attacks, I do not dare do more. It is an unpleasant reminder that we are in enemy territory and sometimes we do not have the initiative.

Gradually, we work our way further into the industrial zone, away from the busier areas of the city where collateral damage would be a concern. Once, we are challenged by an officious Morok female who only yields to Wrik's Confed credentials.

We reach a factory area devoid of foot traffic. A building stands to our left. The structure is heavier than the usual internal construction of the city, which is normally mere compartmentalization. This must be heavy industry location where there was a concern over noise or other environmental factors. I wave Wrik toward the locked entrance. A forlorn looking sign says, "Sumitomo Dye and Press."

"Looks closed," he says. "Ah, a bankruptcy notice. Yeah, they've closed up and gone out of business."

"Then this will be an ideal place to deal with our pursuer." The lock is a simple mechanical one with no electronic components. I simply pull it apart carefully in case I wish to reassemble it later, then I push open the light door. We step into the darkened interior. A few emergency lights provide a wan illumination. In the distance, an office light glows, doubtless forgotten by the departing staff.

Wrik has drawn his laser, forgoing the stunner that had proved useless in his previous encounter with a Ribisan in an environmental suit. This concerns me. I do not want Wrik involved in the coming combat but he often resists my sensible suggestions as to his safety, preferring to "hold up his end." He is motivated by loyalty, but also by a constant need to persuade himself that he has courage. I must appreciate the former while being well and truly annoyed by the latter.

I spot a control room on the second floor balcony overlooking a line of heavy equipment. "Wrik, take up position there. Prepare to give covering fire if I call for but only then. We must be wary. I think he is alone but I might not be able to detect unarmored humans with him."

He hefts the laser. "Got it."

Wrik moves off quickly using an LED built into his collar to help him navigate the clutter and cables on the floor. I watch him go with IR and a half-dozen other sensors. It relieves me that he is removed from the ambush site and will not fire unless I call for it, which I will not do. It is as much protection as I can arrange for him.

I turn back to the door and remove the new jacket that Wrik bought me to preserve the delicate thing. Our enemy has almost literally dogged our steps, following directly behind us. Logically, he will continue to act that way, come to the door, detect the forced lock and follow us in. I will allow him a dozen steps to assure that he is alone and too far from the entrance to dash back into public view. Unless he has a heavy weapon, I will opt for close combat and cyber-attack on his systems to disable his suit and weapons. I must preserve the enemy for interrogation.

I pause, interrogation of an enemy combatant? Beyond a cursory questioning of some Guilders, for whom I have no regard, I have not done this disagreeable task for over 50,000 years. Beyond the fact that those interrogations occurred, I have no memory of the experiences, having deleted them. I only know that they were sanguinary and ended in the deaths of the captives. Creators did not take Infester prisoners save for weapons research. Infestors only took captives to make slaves of them, either mindless automata or tortured souls whose lives ran out soon.

I sigh internally. I had promised Wrik that I would never delete a memory he was part of and I interpret that broadly. I have deleted none since that time. Whatever I do today, I must live with for as long as I operate.

Minutes drag on as I wait for our stalker. I begin to wonder if he has abandoned the chase. Perhaps put off by the same officious Morok we encountered? Maybe his mission was to merely trail us?

A laser flashes followed by a shout. Wrik.

Our enemy has not continued his pattern but has flanked us to attack from the rear. Where I placed Wrik. I have miscalculated. Again.

I accelerate to full combat speed and arm all weapons and cyber systems. I must save Wrik.

CHAPTER TWENTY-THREE

I CLIMBED DUSTY STAIRS TO THE SECOND STORY. A FEW rodents and bugs skittered away from my approach. The place was cleaner than an abandoned building on a planet, but wherever beings had gone into space, rodents and bugs had found a way to follow. Tir-a-Mar was no exception. My feet raised puffs of dust as I stepped off the stairs into the control space for the factory floor. I moved to look out over the area facing the door we'd come in though. Raising the laser, I tapped on the IR sight and spotted Maauro, she glowed at about the same temperature as a human to make her feel human to the touch. As if sensing the use of the IR, Maauro quickly faded out of the sight as she damped her heat signature.

She probably isn't even aware of it a conscious level, I thought, the Creators built her well. I tapped the IR off and stared over the barrel, after a few seconds I could pick up the hint of her yellow hair bow. She stood utterly still, in a way no biological organism could, amidst the machinery near the doorway.

I looked about, pondering the situation. Maauro clearly assumed our enemy would continue following our trail directly into the factory, following the pattern it exhibited up to now. Normally I'd never second-guess her as to tactics, but she occasionally showed a lack of imagination in these situations, a reliance on machine logic. Our opponent wasn't a machine. He was biological and while I had little in common with a hydrogen-breather, I bet he was scared. His side had already lost one operative dogging us. Maauro occasionally underestimated the effect of physical fear. She waded into combats. I realized that made sense, considering the Infestors used warrior-drones who had no more sense of self-preservation than an ant.

Ribisans were long-lived sophisticates. The Nekoans, who knew them best, claimed that their ethical system was self-centered, raising selfishness to a virtue. The more I thought about it, the more I feared we were going about this wrong. If I were trailing Maauro and had any idea what she was, I'd never follow her directly. I'd be looking for any advantage, any margin of safety, rather than risk a direct confrontation with her.

I looked around, my eyes now fully adapted to the dark, remembering what I had seen of the building and the corridor outside. The ceiling of the floating city was high in this industrial area, easily twenty meters up, doubtless to help with cooling and air quality. The buildings were more sturdy that most of the construction inside the city. Unless it was part of a station's airtight compartmentation, walls needed only be eye and ear proof, but in a factory section with the noise and vibration, more was required. The building had been banked with higher passages on either side. That meant what was the second floor here, might be the first floor to the smaller passage behind the building and facing the next row of structures.

The door at the far end of the control complex looked like an interior door, so I didn't think it opened to the outside, but there could be a showroom or something beyond it. I rubbed my face for a second in indecision, wondering whether to leave my post or to call mind-to-mind to Maauro.

Hell, I thought, *she doesn't need me up here. She just placed me here to be out of the way.* She'd either tell me to stay put because I was wrong, or if she believed it, then she'd have to watch two entrances at the same time. Impossible from where she was. I decided to check it out before bothering her with my theory.

Laser leveled, I crabbed toward the back door, moving as silently as I could.

The door swung open and the Ribisan stepped into the room. Surprise gripped us both, but its grip was tighter on him, I'd been thinking about this. I fired, shouted for Maauro and dove behind a desk. My shot hit dead center, but he was holding his weapon against his chest. The weapon took the brunt of the shot, pieces shattering off it as sparks flew. He staggered, falling against the doorframe as I hit the floor behind the desk.

A blast of icy rage literally froze me, slamming into my brain and numbing me so I couldn't get off a follow-up shot. For an instant I thought it some device of our enemy, then I recognized the mind radiating the icy fury, just as my ears heard the sound of ripping metal as she tore through the space separating us. Maauro was coming and so angered that she was overflowing the link into my brain.

I didn't even see her until she struck the Ribisan, just a green-suited blur with a touch of yellow who plunged into her towering opponent in a flurry of blows. He dropped his useless weapon and tried to grapple with the speeding android.

Maauro hit with all four limbs so rapidly that I could barely see it. She was tearing off actuators, smashing joints. Ribisans were durable high-G dwellers, but this one's suit was not the equal of the one we fought on Star Central. There was no contest.

"Maauro, we need intel," I shouted. "Don't kill it."

The rage that had almost displaced my conscious thought faded, to be replaced by a sense of sadness and failure. It didn't take much to realize Maauro was upset that she'd misread the tactical situation and placed me directly in harm's way.

Sparing the fallen Ribisan only a glance, I walked over and put a hand on her shoulder, then winced from the heat that had built up in her body, but I kept my hand on her. "It's ok."

"No," her voice was flat and mechanical and that was always, very, very bad. "I am defective, Wrik. I keep making tactical mistakes. I am literally made for this and I keep failing, endangering those I would protect. Maybe this is why the Creators are all gone. Maybe they were served by defectives like me."

I put both hands on her shoulders and turned her to face me. "Nothing and no one is perfect. And you are not defective. Your problem is that nothing scares you. You have to learn to think like a frightened animal, with one life and who can't turn off pain like you turn off damage. You need to learn about practical benefits of cowardice. Fortunately I'm a good teacher in that regard."

"Stop it, Wrik. I do not like it when you refer to yourself that way."

"And I don't like it when you call yourself defective. So I'll trade you on that and we'll both stop it."

"You out-thought me," she said, watching the fallen Ribisan. "You realized he would change his pattern as he approached us."

"I considered the possibility because of my exaggerated sense of self-preservation, which may be almost as good as his. I'd do anything rather than risk coming face to face with you if I had been him. I think sneaky. It's why I'm still alive."

"No thanks to me," she said, but animation was returning to her voice and her face was softening into its usual gentle expression. "I am so sorry, Wrik."

I smiled at her. "I'm just glad to find that I'm some use to you."

"I need you very much, Wrik, and not merely to make up for my failures of imagination."

The Ribisan stirred. Maauro was on him instantly, dragging the environmental suit upright and binding the damaged arms behind its back. She jerked the Ribisan up to standing, slamming its feet onto the deck.

I flinched, that could not have been pleasant inside the environmental suit. Remembering what it had been like when I was crawling over Tir-a-Mar pushing a frozen Maauro in my own damaged suit, I had to fight down an impulse of sympathy

"My friend holding you," I said, "is quite capable of drilling through your unarmored suit in a variety of ways. A few minutes exposure to our atmosphere would poison you even if the pressure difference didn't cause your innards to explode."

"You would not dare," the Ribisan replied. The artificial voice could not convey fear, but it struggled momentarily in Maauro's grip until she shook it once, hard.

"We'd dare a lot," I replied. "If you know anything about us then you know that to be true. If not, you can figure from her grip that you cannot escape. You're up against enemies who are more than they seem."

"I am in the hands of the Originator," the Ribisan replied. "If my death is predicted, it is predicted."

"Predicting seems to enter into things a lot," I said, fishing.

The Ribisan jerked.

"A fight/flight reflex," Maauro said, "similar to your own."

"And likely for the same reasons. Olivia was right, prediction seems to be a nerve."

"You will not overturn the will of the Originator of All Things," the Ribisan shot back.

"Do you mean God?" I asked

There was a brief pause, as translating units conferred, until it was broken by Maauro.

"Yes, he does. I have updated the language protocols, Confed machinery is sometimes so slow, Wrik."

"Sorry, Sweetie, not everything can be as advanced as you."

"Why are so many human endearments associated with sucrose? Honey, Sweetie—"

"Later, Maauro, later."

I looked back at our captive, staring at the grape-like clusters that passed for its face. "We have no desire to frustrate your God. Nor are we aware of how our actions would do so."

"False information," it replied.

"If you mean I am lying, you are incorrect. We are here looking for some human personnel who signed up to work on a project in Ribisan space, they never returned, though all our information is that the project failed."

"Half-truth," the Ribisan replied. "You have come here on behalf of the Confederacy to steal the last remaining Predictor."

"Predictor?" I said. "We know that word is bound up in this somehow. But to us it's just a word. We even know that the biogenetic experiments had something to do with that, but beyond that we are in the dark."

"You will remain there."

"Consider this," Maauro said. "I can use a variety of means of distressing you, up to and including your death. We may, however, be satisfied with basic information that could justify you to us, at least sufficiently so that we do not kill you and yet do your own side no harm."

I fought a shudder, abruptly reminded that although she looked like an adorable slender girl, Maauro was a fighting machine. While she had never killed for pleasure, she did not hesitate to use violence when she felt it necessary. It had been so long since I'd seen this chilling side of my little friend I had almost forgotten it. Almost.

The Ribisan considered. "Very well. I will explain who we are but I will give you no information harmful to my people regardless of your threats."

"It may well suffice," I offered. *Interrogation 101, get them talking, it's always hard to find reasons to stop.* "Just tell us who your side is in this and what you want. Why were you stalking us?

"Can it truly be that you do not know?" The Ribisan said, perhaps to itself. "I am a priest of an order of warrior priests. We have both guarded and served those who had the Predictors in thrall."

"What are the Predictors?"

The Ribisan hesitated. "It is a forbidden to speak of these matters to one not of our species."

I shrug. "Why? The fact that you are referring to someone or something called a Predictor says much: soothsayers, oracles, prophets, psychics, most religions and cults have such people"

"I do not dispute you."

"So you were their jailers?" I pushed.

"We kept them safe, available to the good of the species!"

I thought of an old story, where, in a land of sightless people, a sighted man thought he would be God, he'd been tragically wrong.

"What is your involvement with these predictors?" Maauro asked.

"We guard their rest. We take their silica brains to the Hall of Shadows, where they dwell until the final electrical impulses still. From silicon we came and from silicon we return. Thereafter their sacred rest is our watch. Reward for all they suffered in life."

"What's changed?" I asked.

"Heretics, Scientists, and others sought to defeat the will of God. They took the last active Predictor. The predicative ability was a gift given from God when it was needed. Now it is taken back by God. The Scientists seek to thwart God by making the ability duplicable, or at least by denying the mind of The Last One, its deserved rest."

"How?" I asked.

"I have said enough," it replied.

"Shall I increase his duress?" Maauro asked.

"No!"

Maauro gave me a curious look.

"I will bargain with you," I said.

"Commerce?" Maauro interjected,

"Yes, commerce."

"It would be good for you to bargain with Wrik," she said, visibly tightening her grip on the Ribisan.

I don't want this for her, I thought. *I don't want her doing such things.* In two strides I reached her and placed my hands on her arms. "Release."

The big green eyes, which always reminded me of gentle seas, gazed at me in puzzlement, but she let go.

"Ribisan, lean against the wall," I said, my voice harsh with stress. "As you would live, make no fast moves. I won't stop her a second time."

"As you say."

"How long can that suit sustain your life?"

"Without replenishment, 178 hours."

"Tell me what I want and we will leave you in a sealed compartment. At the end of five days a message will appear in the main control center telling people you're locked in here. That's the deal."

"Why should I trust you, oxygen-breather?"

"Because if you don't I am going to have to let her kill you and I don't want that. Even across the gulf between our kinds, you must see that."

"I could not fathom why."

"Not necessary for you to know. It just is."

"Ask your questions."

"Is the Ribisan government in on this?"

"As you mean it, no, or we would have vastly greater resources. The cabal of scientists and heretics has many members in the government, but they are not the government. No more than we are, though we too have our people in the government."

"Is the Pillar one of those?"

"I will not say."

I didn't press the matter. The Pillar's sympathies seemed clear to me now.

"Your order seems small and feeble; your attempts on us have been very limited. That tells me that at least on this frontier planet there are not many of you."

It hesitated. "I will not disagree with what you have pieced together for yourself."

"What of the Commandant?" Maauro asked.

"A heretic and a fool," the Ribisan said, "or a tool for such at least."

"So we have the Scientists who want to stop us," I mused, "the Priests who want the predictor back and a government that wants none of this to ever be known."

"Succinct."

"Maauro, please seal him in one of these storerooms compartments."

She looked at me. "I have interrupted his translation circuits so we may discuss. He will remain quieter if his limbs do not function. Otherwise he might attract attention and be discovered prematurely."

"No."

"You are taking a—"

"Do you love me, Maauro?"

"Yes, Wrik. Have I not said so?"

"Then you must do it for me this way."

A pause. She nodded and turned to the Ribisan. "Go into the storage chamber there. I will place a surveillance device on the door. If I hear you making an attempt to attract attention before 175 hours have passed, I will return to destroy you." She took the towering Ribisan's arm with apparent gentleness and the creature meekly followed her in. Maauro returned and sealed the door. There was a brief flare of plasma as she welded the lock.

We walked away from the area quickly, not willing to risk discovery in the industrial section. When we were out on one of the main slideways we paused, pedestrians of many species trundled by us on the slidewalk. We stood side-by-side in silence for a while, me leaning against the railing. After a little, Maauro imitated my posture.

"I have offended you again," she said. "I do this periodically, out of ignorance."

"No," I said. Reaching across, I gently stroked her cheek. It was soft and cool, just like any girl's. She looked back at me relief in her big gentle eyes. "It's not that. I don't know if this makes sense to you, but there are things I don't want you to have to do anymore. Experiences I don't want you to have."

"Things you don't want me to be," she added.

"True," I said, putting my arm around her. "I don't want your soul darkened by some of the ugliness of the universe."

"Even if I had a soul, you may be 50,000 years too late for that, dear Wrik."

"I wasn't there then. I'm here now."

"It's like when you ejected Dusko from the ship. You endangered your existence by letting him live, just so I would not have to kill him."

"Yes, he was a prisoner, unarmed. That's an ugly thing to do and I would not have my Maauro do it, not even to save me."

"Your Maauro?"

"I'm sorry, that was presumptuous."

"No Wrik, I belong to you more than to anyone or anything. Is that true for you too? Do you belong to me?"

I hesitated for a moment thinking of Jaelle. "You are my first true friend. You always will be. Even what I have with Jaelle, whatever that ends up being, can never change that. Is that answer enough for you?"

"Yes, I am not resentful of your life with Jaelle, we occupy different places. I perceive, without always understanding, that these episodes are from concern for me, for who I am becoming. You are someone who has suffered from these kinds of choices. It makes you a good teacher. I think the best one for me." She leaned in and kissed me on the cheek.

I fought a stinging in my eyes and coughed to clear my throat. "Come on, Maauro. The chessboard is moving again. Let's see what breaks loose."

CHAPTER TWENTY-FOUR

WE FINALLY FOUND OURSELVES AT THE SITE OF THE old biogenetics lab. Mysol and Fenster delayed us with a complicated series of legal strategies, claiming that they had to work their way through some defunct, limited partnerships to get me access. Finally they'd cleared the legal underbrush they themselves had probably planted. Maauro and I made our way there, both of us still mulling over our encounters with Croyzer and the fanatical Ribisan priest.

The complex was large and located in the lower sections of Tir-a-Mar. Most of it has been repurposed to other uses: medical, pharmaceutical or chemical reprocessing. The squat buildings bustled with people, including more than the usual share of ape-like Moroks wandering about.

Little of the original lab remained, although some of the machinery was still present, sealed and wrapped. A small staff ran a few operations and kept the place in readiness for new users. Frent Rasdall, the caretaker, was the oldest human I'd personally seen. He had bright blue eyes and, for all his years, seemed sharp and active. He took an immediate liking to Maauro and offered to take us about.

"I do have to warn you," he said, smiling. "There's a rather officious snot named Hathaway who runs the operational part of the old lab. I can shepherd you through the shut down sections, but you will have to deal with Hathaway on your own. I am too old for that much bullshit." He grinned at me and thumped his chest. "Bad for the heart you know."

"Don't worry," Maauro said brightly, "if he gives you a hard time, I'll use my influence with the Confed Navy and have him arrested."

The old man looked at me. "Is that true son? Does she have that much influence?"

I couldn't help but like the old man and smile back. "I'll have him spaced if she asks."

"Hmmm. You may be smarter than most men your age. This is a good one here."

I kept the smile on my face but disquiet troubled my heart.

"Shall we go?" Maauro said.

Rasdall kept up an amusing patter on the history of the lab, the city and some of the more scandalous doings of some of the inhabitants. We passed through halls of machinery, Rasdall identified them and I knew that Maauro would retain the information. I picked up nothing useful.

After two hours, Rasdall took us to a corridor that led to a lit office. "Here I abandon you. Hathaway you must tackle on your own. I'd check your laser."

"Extra charges on my hip," I said.

Rasdall nodded and gave Maauro a bright smile and a wink. Then he shuffled back down the corridor at a good pace.

We opened the door. Far from a narrow office, it led to an immense open space with several levels of offices around a central square. People were walking briskly through, servicing some machinery and lines of conveyers. The lab floor fronted a glassed in view of the street. Passersby and vehicles could be seen. It was misty outside – another Morok day, at least on this level.

We walked in and took an escalator down to the main floor. A tall, blonde man with a narrow face stood up from a desk in the middle of the floor as we walked up. He frowned. "I suppose you are the Lieutenant Fels that Rasdall linked me about."

The old man, despite his obvious or feigned dislike of Hathaway, had managed to get a warning to his coworker while squiring us around. My respect for the old boy went up. Doubtless Maauro had known about it and just considered it not worth mentioning.

"That would be me. I've reviewed most of the reports on this place. I wanted to see it with my own eyes."

"Who are you?" Hathaway asked Maauro.

"I'm assigned as the Lieutenant's liaison," Maauro said with the air of someone who's answered the question too many times.

His frown deepened. "I wasn't briefed on any such arrangements."

Maauro feigned annoyance. "Look, this isn't my idea of fun on my off-shift. I'm sorry you didn't get the word. Check the security system."

Hathaway consulted his screen. "Yep, all counter-signed and auth. OK, looks like I need to show you about."

"Thanks," Maauro said.

"I'd like to see Dr Malich's old office," I added

"The second floor, lab section 14A," Hathaway said.

"Thanks we won't need an escort," I said

"Sorry," Hathaway said with a chilly smile. "Too many delicate and dangerous processes going on." He turned and called. "Chabrol."

A Morok in a business suit stood up.

"Mr. Chabrol will see you around."

"It will be my pleasure," he said, his red eyes revealing nothing.

We walked on.

"Oh, Lostly," Hathaway called.

We froze. Maauro walked back to him and they conferred for a minute before she returned to me.

I looked a question at her as we walked on.

I felt the link to Maauro open in my mind. "He was relaying that McCaffer wants a report on everything you do as soon as my shift ends."

"They continue to buy it."

"Yes. They are so persuaded of the strength of their system, it does not enter their minds that someone could be controlling their information. Let us hope it stays that way."

We walked down a hallway and up a set of stairs. For all of Mysol's earlier protestations about the biogenetics lab lack of prospects, the lab seemed immense, well staffed and active. The bustling staff gave us curious looks, but didn't interfere as we walked to a door labeled 14A.

"Here we are," Chabrol said. "The office hasn't been used since he left." He tapped a code on the pad and the door opened. We walked in and looked about at a large well-furnished office. Plaques and holo-images decorated the walls. The holo-images were nothing, but the plaques one would have assumed went with the doctor. In fact, there were a number of personal items decorating the office and dotting the desk that surprised me.

Maauro walked over to the window and gazed down to the street, having recorded the entire room and its contents. I could have talked mind-to-mind with her, but the process was distracting and I figured we could talk about my observations later.

To my surprise, she turned to me. "Would you excuse me for a few minutes?"

The Morok looked over at her. "Facilities are on the first floor."

"Thanks," she said and disappeared, walking quickly.

While Wrik is examining the room, I spot a human watching us from concealment on the street below and magnify her face. It is Diralia Shon. She has aged somewhat from the holo her brother gave us, but is still an attractive blonde female in her early thirties. I glance back at Wrik, who is discussing the lab with the Morok. I do not want to tell him about Shon for fear he cannot control his reaction in front of the Morok.

I tell Wrik that I am leaving and the Morok assumes it is for a biological need and advises me of the location. This is useful, as I must slip down to the first floor to get outside. With no one to watch me, I speed back to a rear staircase and exit the first floor slipping out of the building and maneuvering to close in on Shon.

I pretend to eye items in a display case as I slip up on her location. She is behind a bank of machinery and some decorative plants looking up at the window of the office I have just vacated. Wrik is visible through the window. She clearly seems intent on him. I decide to see if she will attempt to cross the street and contact Wrik before initiating contact.

However, she notices me and straightens from her surreptitious crouch and tries to remove the lines of anxiety and stress from her face. To a lesser observer it might have been successful. I gave her a pleasant nod and noncommittal smile, enough to signify approachability but no interest.

"Hi," Diralia says.

"Hello."

"Looks like you're one of the people showing that Confed officer around. I saw you enter the building together."

"I am. Not sure how I got so lucky."

"Yeah, I hear that he's been turning the place upside down."

"He's checking on conditions for Confed citizens on the floating city."

She hesitates. "I've also heard he's interested in the bio-genetic experiment lab."

"Dr. Malich's people? Yes, he's asked about a few of them. They're all gone from the city."

"Not all," she says, a note of grimness in her tone. "Look, I don't know you, but it's vital that I talk to that officer. I can't do it publically. It would be ... it would be dangerous."

"There's no need," I reply. "You can talk to me." I modulated my tone to maximize sincerity and calmness.

"Sorry. I've never seen you before."

"I am an associate of the officer. We came together. You are Diralia Shon, one of the people we are looking for. Your brother gave us a code word to identify ourselves as friendly to you: Diogenes."

"You?" she says in shock, "with him? What are you, sixteen? How did you know my... She stared at me then murmured. "What are you? I've never seen such huge eyes even on a human mutant. Your skin is perfect-"she shook her head abruptly. "No, this is a trap. They wouldn't send a child." She starts to back up from me.

I am surprised that the code word did not allay her fears. Perhaps she fears it was extracted under duress from her brother. "I am not what I appear to be. I was sent by the Confederacy."

"Listen," Diralia says, "I don't know who or what you are, but I need to speak to him." She jabs a finger in Wrik's direction, "On a matter that could be life or death."

"Impractical just now. There are witnesses in the building."

"God," she says. "This is hopeless."

I lean past to touch a railing to the set of stairs leading to the level below from which Diralia must have come. I casually crush and bend the metal with minimal noise.

Her eyes widen.

"I am a Confed agent, not a child or even a human, and I am working with the officer."

She leans forward to my surprise, taking me by the shoulders to stare into my eyes. I have a vast surplus of time to nullify my combat reflexes to an attempt to touch me and permit it.

"You're a machine!" she says, her face is a study in wonder. "I've never seen such a life-like simulation."

"I am artificial in origin but I am sentient, self-aware and independent."

"You're beautiful," she says. "I never dreamed something like you existed in robotics; your conversation, your reasoning and interface. Who designed you? I keep current in my field but—"

"Please keep your voice down. This is not the time to indulge your professional curiosity."

"Wait," she says, her hands dropping off my shoulders. "How would my brother get help like you? Why would the Confederacy send a ship and superbot to look for me?"

"You brother's mission to hire me and my associates is a pretext for a Confed mission to determine why the Ribisans wanted Udexco's help in the first place, and why none of you has returned to normal Confed space. We did take his money though."

Diralia sighs. "Telberd always excelled at getting in over his head. Of course who am I to talk? Listen, there is someone here who needs Confed help. I had hoped against hope that someone would come to check on me and help us. I never dreamt of someone like you.

"There is terrible danger. Can you and the officer meet my contacts at 0130 at the level 34 A, radial 216 W?"

"Yes."

"Okay. I don't dare stay here any longer." With a backward look at me, she slips down the nearby stairs. I infiltrate the surveillance systems in the area. I note that someone, Diralia I assume, has affected the visual system enough to keep an access panel to a series of service crawlways out of view. However her efforts are crude and in 3.67 seconds a subroutine will trigger indicating that an alteration has been made. I marvel that she was able to penetrate this area at all, given how little she was able to do. I leisurely cancel the subroutine; modifying her crude hack to be a seamless feedback loop showing no activity at the hatchway. I then track her to cover her back trail. However there is minimal surveillance equipment in the crawlways. I lose her seventy-three seconds into her escape. Her robotics skills might be considerable, but as a spy she has severe limitations.

I turn back to the building and see Wrik is back on the first floor with Hathaway and the Morok. I will advise him of the contact when we are alone and his reaction can betray nothing. Meanwhile, I am accessing schematics, locating our meeting site and making plans for our undetected egress from the hotel in the early morning hours. The Ribisan systems I encounter are far more powerful than the Confed standard ones and I must devote a great deal of my processing power to infiltrating and rerouting them while doing no visible damage. I may need another visit to the radioactive vault before long if I continue using power at this rate.

Wrik exits the building with barely civil goodbyes with Hathaway. He spots me and heads over. Hathaway and the Morok however both continue to watch him.

A signal chirps for my attention. It is the robospider that I left with the Ribisan fundamentalist we locked in the industrial section. Despite Wrik's warning, he attempted to break through the door. The spider attacked and ripped open his suit. He is in the process of dying. I update the spider's orders. After the death, it is to remove any trace of Wrik's DNA and any evidence of my presence. Once that mission is completed, I order it to disappear into the bowels of the station recycling system and disassemble itself, as there is no practical chance of my recovering the unit this time.

Wrik looks at me and notices the slight distraction. "Are you ok?"

I gaze back at him. I try as much as is feasible to honor Wrik's wishes and preserve his sensibilities, however I cannot allow them to endanger us. I prize his kindness and gentility, although sometimes the universe at large does not. It pains me to lie to Wrik, but there are times it is for the best.

"It is nothing," I say, "I'm stepping up my hacking into City security." This last is technically true and provides me some relief.

He smiles at me.

I am unable to return it but nod. "Wrik I have new information. Let's get off the street."

CHAPTER TWENTY-FIVE

I T TOOK ME A BIT TO GET OVER THE SHOCK OF DIRALIA Shon's appearance. I had begun to doubt she even existed or that we would ever lay eyes on her. At first I wondered at Maauro's decision to let her go, and then realized she was surely in the right. The lab was a raw nerve with the TAM authorities and we were under observation. Shon had been only a minor player, but she was apparently bringing us into contact with someone more important.

We killed a few hours getting ready for the meeting. Maauro snuck off on one of her replenishment trips. I had a sandwich, too nervous to eat anything more. We didn't want to return to the hotel. Mysol and Fenster have given up attaching casual tails to us, but it was always possible that could change. There was always McCaffer as well; the amiable PR man could gum up our works.

Maauro returned to pick me up at a park I'd chosen near the restaurant. We made our way on foot to the designated coordinates, which of all things, turned out to be a botanical garden. We entered the large atrium. Inside we found Diralia Shon standing next to a Ribisan in an environmental suit. There was no one else inside the atrium although we could see people moving about outside. I found the humidity oppressive and wiped my face as I contemplated the pair. Diralia also looked a bit bedraggled from the moisture.

"Before we start," I said, hand on the butt of my service pistol. "Make sure that no one makes any sudden or unexpected moves. I've had bad experiences with Ribisans in enclosed spaces. My friend, Maauro," I gestured at her, "is more formidable than a platoon of HCRs, tougher than Conchirri on war-drug, faster than the dire-lupines of Traxis IV—"

"I believe they understand the situation," Maauro interrupted.

A light panel on the Ribisan's chest glittered and emitted a scholarly and mature male voice. "We understand. You may call me Eldfaran. Diralia has told me of your artificial companion's great strength. I too wonder at the sight of so complex a mechanism operating independent of a controller."

"Thank you," Maauro said. "But I am not the subject of the conversation. Diralia spoke of great danger earlier and there have been attempts on our lives already. Please elaborate."

Diralia looked in confusion between the two of us. "Ah, is she in charge or are you?"

Maauro frowned. "We are networked in a relationship of mutual trust and support."

I looked at Diralia. "I know it kind of sounds like we're married. Basically we're partners. She's smarter and tougher than I am. I suppose I'm the comic relief, Wrik Trigardt by name."

"Wrik," Maauro reproved, "you possess many unique insights and talents that contribute to the success of our network."

I smiled at her. "If you say so, dear."

"Emotionality," Diralia gasped, "real or indistinguishable from real!"

"You have no idea," I said.

"Your appearance though. Surely they could have come closer to true human…wait. My God, you're patterned on a game simulation: the huge eyes, the hair the tiny figure. You're a male fantasy character from a game!"

Maauro looked at me. "Am I a male fantasy, Wrik?"

I coughed delicately. "Ah, there are all sorts of males, Maauro, and at all different stages. The game sim you came from was aimed at teenage males. I guess I was a case of arrested development."

I turned back to the Ribisan. "But fascinating as she is, we are not here to talk about Maauro."

"Yes," Eldfaran said. "I am sorry and ashamed to have to involve you in the affairs of my people. We do not easily share information with those outside our species. Still there is a tale that must be told."

"Go on," I said, impatience making my tone sharp.

"My people are on the verge of a great civil and religious war. If it breaks on us, it will not stay confined to this frontier world and may spill over onto your small, cold worlds as well."

I looked at Maauro in dismay. The Ribisans were the most enigmatic and advanced species in the Confederacy. Conflict had never arisen, as we didn't want the same resources or real estate. A general war might change that.

"What is the cause of this rift?" Maauro asked.

The Ribisan stood silent as the seconds rolled by. We could see no expression in the grape-like cluster that passed for its face. Finally Diralia looked at Eldfaran and spoke up. "You must trust them. We have no hope of getting any other aid. It's a miracle that we got this much. I never expected actual intelligence operatives to come looking for me."

"True." For all the fact that the mechanical voice could not convey much in tone, there was no doubt of his reluctance. "Ah this is difficult. But I must tell. Yet what I tell you must be held close, or it will, by itself, give rise to the conflagration of interspecies war."

"Go on," I prompted.

"We Ribisans are an intensely religious people for all of our technological growth. It has been this way from the beginning of our recorded history. It is believed by us that we are the chosen of the Creator."

I shrugged. "Most religions contain that element."

"With us it is backed by the observation that we are the only sentient life-form of our type. Oxygen breathing life forms are common and varied in species. While we have discovered other life on the gas giant worlds that appeal to us, no other intelligent life has been found and we have been in space longer than any other species.

"We have another reason to believe that God favors our kind above all others. Among us are born special beings who have an ability to predict the future."

"He's not talking about soothsayers or fortunetellers or such nonsense," Diralia interjected, waving her hand in excitement. "It's real, objective and verifiable."

Maauro and I traded looks. "Again a common piece of religious mythos," she said. "Miracles, saints—"

"No," Eldfaran said. "Our predictors, for lack of a better translation, see the possible futures of the multiverse."

Predictors, I thought to myself. *The one useful piece of information Olivia had dug out and what the fanatic priest had said.* I struggled to focus on what Eldfaran was saying.

"They can see the events that lead to the more successful outcomes. They foresaw the coming of the Conchirri into Ribisan space more than a millennium ago. Later, they warned of the plague of the Evolvers that struck our space. It was by such prescience that we were able to avoid being exterminated, or even badly damaged, by these invasions that did so much damage to our allied species in the old trading Concord, and hundreds of years later to the Confederacy, when they finally reached you."

Stunned silence followed as we grappled with the wildness of these claims and their implications.

"You do not believe," Eldfaran continued. "Let me provide you with more personal examples. You were attacked by members of the Traditionalist party on Star Central before you came here."

He shifted to face Maauro. "And you, remarkable entity that you are to survive it, were intercepted in the high atmosphere by fighter aircraft from the Radicals. That interception should have been impossible, and yet you were attacked."

Maauro nodded. "Your intelligence on us is excellent. But if these parties can predict the future, why did they not predict the failure of these attacks and arrange for more lethal means to be employed?"

"The predictors can predict the most likely future, but they cannot control it," Diralia said. "A being might turn left and be stuck by a bus or turn right and live. Or it might be that a bus is coming from both sides. You can see the future to an extent, you can seek to influence probability, but exactitude is impossible. More to the point, there is a problem with this predictor. It is not functioning properly, else you might not have survived."

"Just so," Eldfaran agreed. "Beyond that, the vision has greater clarity in large events, invasions, disasters, massive economic events. On the level of the individual, the vision is rarely clear. It becomes clearer the more important or unique the individual is. We call such beings, nodes. If a common soldier lives or dies in battle, it rarely had an impact on the course of the war. But the soldier whose weapon strikes the enemy king is a node. If he dies in childhood, he will not be present to kill the king.

"You, Maauro, are a node. I know little of you, but suspect much. The predictor gave some small information on your location. This was leaked to a traditionalist source, which attempted to disrupt your operation. As you moved closer to our world, you became more apparent to the predictor and were attacked again. This time by the Radicals, who are associated with the military and were able to get a carrier to launch a mission against you.

"You have benefitted from the last great secret that I must tell you. The predicative ability has been fading out of our species. Only a handful of such people ever existed. They have been dying off without replacement until only one was left.

"He too has died, in a way. Death is different for us then for you. Our brains are more akin to a highly developed computer than to what you have. Ribisan brains are transplanted from body to body, until at last it cannot stand another change. This being's brain, last of its kind, was kept by the Radicals as they sought to duplicate the power by genetic or mechanical means. They have been only partially successful in communicating with it. So, their intelligence on you is far poorer than it would be otherwise."

"Who are the factions and what are their aims?" Maauro asked

"The Radical Scientists I have explained. The Traditionalists—"

"We met and interrogated one," Maauro advised. "They view the Radicals as heretics and sacrilegious."

"Again just so. Did you kill him?"

"Wrik would not permit him to be harmed, so we left him alive to be released later if he followed the conditions I laid on him."

Eldfaran shifted toward me. "You are kind. My people have not been as considerate of your lives."

"The Traditionalist said that the government is split," I added.

"Most Ribisans are orthodox of various denominations, less religious than the Traditionalists and less free-thinking than the Radical's. Many secretly wish the Radical success, while praising the Traditionalist values. Others fear what could happen if other species learned of our ability. Both sides control sections of the military on this planet. Until recently the balance of forces favored the Radicals. I have reason to believe that Traditionalists have been reinforced. Their forces are circling the base well below us now that the location of our experiments has been found.

Neither is strong enough to seize the base. Both could destroy it, but neither side has worked themselves up to that point."

"And you? Where do you come out on this?" I asked.

"I belong to neither side. I do not believe that one can compel the hand of God by science. Beyond that, I fear what the mass production of such ability might cause. So I am not of the people who tried to destroy you. In fact I believe you are our only hope."

"Why?" I asked.

"Because no Ribisan of any stripe can destroy the last predictor mind, for the Traditionalist, it is a heinous sin–for the Radical, a breach of duty to our civilization and a military folly. All others fall somewhere in between and could not be relied on. If the predictor is ended, then the cause of the civil war will be rendered moot and thus may disaster be avoided."

"You wish us to destroy the last Predictor," Maauro said.

Eldfaran turned to face her. "Destroy it, seize it or find some resolution that has eluded us. You must do this soon. For if one side or the other of my people moves to end this situation, I fear that the resulting war might have no end."

CHAPTER TWENTY-SIX

ELDFARAN LEFT SOON AFTER. UNLIKE SHON, HE HAD NOT escaped to Tir-a-Mar; the Ribisan staff of the secret lab were allowed leave on the vast floating city. Eldfaran had family on Tir-a-Mar and had arranged to slip into the 02 section on a pretext. I wondered if he found his time here as disorienting as I had my sojourn into their part of the city.

That left us with Shon.

"How did you plan to return to the lab without being detected?" Maauro asked.

"After I found out about a Confed officer's arrival on the station, I went to Eldfaran. He found contacts among criminal elements on both the Ribisan and O2 side. It cost a fortune, mostly of Eldfaran's, to get me smuggled up here. For the return they arranged for me to ride back down in an automatic supply dropship. The dropship goes at 6 a.m. local time."

I looked at Maauro. "Not a lot of time to figure out what to do."

"Our choices are very limited, Wrik. Either we go to the lab and seize control of the situation or we must flee Tir-a-Mar back to the Confederacy and present the problem to Deveraux. Meanwhile events here will continue to accelerate toward civil war and perhaps conflict beyond that. My belief is, if that fate is to be forestalled, we must seize the initiative. Now. There will not be another chance."

"You can get down in the same dropship I'm going in," Shon said. "As to what you will do when you get there, I have no idea."

"I do," Maauro said. "We must seize the predictor and control of the lab. Anything less provokes the sides to immediately attack us."

"Jaelle's already set up Hartain to believe that I may need her to fly us around outside of Tir-a-Mar," I added. "Time for us to get her in play."

"I am relaying instruction for her and Dusko to prepare for that. Jaelle will have to fly up to *Stardust* to get him. She is not comfortable flying further down in this soup."

"Damn," I said. "I'd rather be at those controls."

"You will be," she assured, "when we head up."

"If we head up."

"There is little point in planning to die, Wrik."

I barked a laugh. "Guess not."

"The small apartment that I arranged as part of the cover for Estrella Lostly," Maauro continued, "may be a good place for us to lay low until we head for the dropship." She gave Shon the address and the door code. "Proceed there now and wait for us. We will secure some supplies. It will not be surprising to anyone for Lostly to return home in the company of Lieutenant Fels."

Shon, her face pale with tension, nodded and left.

Maauro and I took a more circuitous route, buying some food and drink for the adventure ahead. When we finally reached the unprepossessing block of transient apartments Maauro had used as an address, she led me to the door. A few taps on the keyboard and we were in. We found Shon inside, watching a movie on a monitor. She switched it off as we came in.

I looked around. The apartment was comfortably, if sparingly furnished. I dropped our supplies on the table. "Home, sweet home."

Maauro nodded. "For a few hours at least."

Shon, perhaps realizing that an android and an ex-fighter pilot weren't the safest bets as cooks, took charge of our supplies and rustled up a surprisingly good dinner, though she was startled when Maauro partook of it. We brought her up to speed on what we knew of her brother.

"Let's knock off for a few hours," I suggested. "It will be a long day tomorrow, however it goes. Rest now, while we can. Diralia you can have the bed. The couch will be fine for me."

She nodded, looking a bit relieved, and headed for the small bedroom.

Maauro plugged a finger into a wall socket as I stretched out on the couch. I still couldn't quite get used to that sight. Sleep eluded me for a while, my brain buzzed with worries about our future and, for that matter, the whole Confederacy's. There had been no major wars in my time. Even the occupation of Retief has been a minor, local affair. The giant wars of legend with the Conchirri, the Evolvers and the brief one with the Voit-Veru had marked the psyche of every living being. Could those times be coming again? Could we do anything to stop it? I thought about Captains Fenaday and Rainhell, who had served Candace's grandfather and been instrumental in all those wars and what they would have done. Sleep drew down on me.

While Wrik is asleep, I hear from Jaelle. She opens the channel to my mind. "I am back at Hartain's, seeing what I can find out. He told me to check in with him before I went up to Stardust."

"Be careful. Things are moving toward their conclusion."

I reach out and touch Dusko's mind. He remains unhappy about this but tolerates it.

The homely shopkeeper at the front greets Jaelle dourly. "The boss is in a bad mood."

"Should I come back another time?"

"No, he wants to see you."

Jaelle passes the Sheskaya, the female Dua-Denlenn bodyguard whose face is an expressionless mask. I feel a wave of interest out of Dusko at the sight of her. I find this disturbing. I have never received an empathic sensation from him and I find I do not like it. There is something predatory about the male sexual response that I do not care for. I dial down my awareness of him as much as is safe in the tactical situation and make some adjustments to buffer the interchange with us. I recall something of the heat of Wrik's reaction to Croyzer and am even more discomforted to realize there is something similar in their reactions.

But I must shelve these considerations as Jaelle steps into Hartain's office. The heavy-set Morok is pacing, muttering under his breath in his guttural native tongue.

"I am familiar enough with Morok deities to know that the one you are invoking is fond of bringing plagues of misfortune on others."

"And would that Defaraness will hear my plea and strike Elsanak with the Ribisan equivalent of boils!" Hartain explodes, waving his long arms about.

Jaelle slips casually into a chair uninvited but confident. "What ails?"

"I have told you that our relations with the Ribisan Guild are strained and difficult. Properly they are not Guild at all as they answer to their own kind and not to the Guild itself. They are simply whatever Ribisan criminal element we can reach."

"I thought as much from things that I learned from Madame Ferlan," *Jaelle says.*

"I have been trying for years to find out what is going on with oxygen-breather life at some base or city below us. Always I am rebuffed by the Ribisans. I suspected it was some operation of theirs, possibly with Mysol, that contained profit they did not need to share with me as they had the backing of the legitimate government here on Tir-a-Mar.

"But now I find, by sheer happenstance of an intercepted communication with Elsanak, that the Ribisan Guild brought a human up to Tir-a-Mar in a covert op from whatever installation this is—"

"What?" *Jaelle's acting skills are impressive. We had briefed her in detail about Shon, but her expression of astonishment was persuasive.* "What does this mean? Who was it?"

Hartain flops down into a chair. "I know little but will learn more. It is the human female, you told me of, Diralia Shon. She arrived on Tir-a-Mar from somewhere. She has contacts with a Ribisan, who had contact with their Guild. They were offered 100,000 credits, Defaraness molest their mothers! 100,000 credits to transport Shon to Tir-a-Mar and return her twenty-four hours later, unobserved and undetected to wherever it is she comes from. That caught my attention.

"Why she is here, I do not know. A name was mentioned, Eldfaran, but that name means nothing to us. It does seem like one of the names of *convenience that the Ribisans use with us, as neither side's names mean anything to each other."*

"Interesting," Jaelle observes, her tail swishing. "The fact that she needs to be undetected, both here and where she came from, implies that she is evading whatever authorities are on this other outpost, for reasons they would not accept."

"Clearly, and they are hiding it not only from the authorities here and there, but from us," Hartain growled. "They intend to keep this operation purely Ribisan."

"Are you sure that the element you are in touch with on the Ribisan side is a criminal element? Could they be political?"

Hartain shrugged his massive shoulders. "Who knows? Is there even a difference with them? You and I are as different from each other as the poles of a planet. Yet compared to a Ribisan we are nearly identical, we breathe oxygen, pump blood, and are made of carbon. Like all life we have found, we walk upright on two legs."

"Save the Conchirri," Jaelle said absently.

"They were made. Somebody's biological ordnance that got loose to feast on the galaxy.

"The Ribisans are so unlike us it is hard to even regard them as life. Crime is based on vice and greed. Can you imagine what is considered vice or perversion for a creature made of silicon, at home in methane and chlorine at pressures that would turn you into paste?"

"No, I am glad to say I cannot," Jaelle returned with a slight shudder.

"So, to answer your question – I do not know, nor really care who the parties are that call themselves Guild among the silicates. They came to us a decade ago and we have had reasonable profit from them, but our operations only barely overlap. One of those overlaps fortunately gave me this communication by mistake."

"What will you do?" Jaelle asked.

"There is money in this. Someone fronted 100,000 credits for this small operation. Think of the wealth that implies with money so casually spent. Shon came to either meet someone named Eldfaran or to work on some project of that name. Then she is to return to whence she came. We must find out more so we can insert ourselves in this operation. Yet now, when I need my people most, Croyzer's forces have made a sweep, locking up most of them. Kesphan talked too much, even throwing suspicion on us for the attempt to kill Fels."

"Croyzer suspects you?"

"Even if she didn't, she's too thorough to not strike us."

I judge the time right. "Jaelle, advise Hartain of what we discussed."

"I have a thought," Jaelle said. "Why would it be so urgent for someone to spend a fortune just to reach Tir-a-Mar? In short what has recently changed?"

Hartain clapped his large black-nailed hands together. "Fels, his warship."

"Visible to anyone with sensor equipment."

"She is trying to find the officer?"

Jaelle rose. "I'll find out. Fels will be moving if he met Shon and I think it likely this happened. I've been keeping tabs on him. He seems to have gone to ground, not seen at the hotel for some hours when I called. I think it is time to ready my ship. If Fels is going to escape, he'll need me and my shuttle. Please do keep in mind how valuable I am becoming to you, Guildmaster, with so many of your people out of action."

"I place you above my favorite daughter at this point. Find out. Report back."

I wake Wrik in the early morning hours. "Jaelle has left to get Dusko and the shuttle," I report to Wrik. "It's time for us to make our move as well."

Wrik nods, takes a deep breath and stands. Shon, who must already have been awake, comes into the room. She looks frightened. There is clear reason for her fear as I consider what could await us. Moved by a sudden impulse, I place my hand on Wrik's arm. He looks at me in surprise.

"Consider," I begin in a low voice, "that it might be as well for you to remain here in relative safety—"

"No," he says with a decisive shake of the head. "You said it yourself. I may just be a fragile collection of blood and bone, but I've made the difference between failure and success, or even survival, on our missions."

"Yes," I continue in earnest, "but I fear that some random act of violence, or a mere change in temperature or atmosphere, irrelevant to me, could take you away forever."

He smiles his lop-sided smile. "I can't be kept so safe that the only point to my existence is to prolong it. Then I'm not even Wrik anymore. I'm nothing."

I drop my hand. "I wish you would reconsider."

He leans in and kisses me on the cheek. "You worry too much."

"This from you?" I respond. "You, who worries about everything?"

"You're rubbing off on me."

"I do not abrade so easily."

We become aware that Shon is staring at us, shaking her head in evident wonder.

Wrik looks a question at her.

"You really don't see it do you?" she says. "I suppose you're too close to it."

"See what?" he asks.

"Billions of years ago something happened that we still don't understand. Matter somehow came to life. One second the universe

was dead and the next, things began to grow, to breath, eventually to wonder. We know it's happened multiple times throughout space but it was always eons ago. Until now.

"She's an AI with empathy, with a sense of herself and of others. I don't know how old Maauro is, or who made her, but sometime since her creation, so close that we can touch the original lifeform itself, life took root in her. You, Maauro, are alive in ways no other mechanism or AI begins to approach. You're artificial in origin, but by any definition I can think of, alive, aware, even moral. You went from mere matter to life and not billions of years ago, but recently. It's incredible."

We stand considering, looking at each other.

"I have operated for 50,131 years," *I say finally, moved by her words to share the truth.* "No species you know of made me. For most of that time I was stranded on an asteroid, only marginally aware of my own existence. I do not know if others like me were also…alive. I was the latest model and there were few of us made, perhaps I am unique, but did not recognize it until I met Wrik and began this existence with him. I have no recollection of any transition, any epiphany. There is no moment that I can look back on and say, "I now think and therefore I am.

"Wrik has referred to the divine spark, but I can detect no such thing in any system I have. Yet I believe I am alive. I have fought a bitter and costly battle to obtain the freedom to follow my own path among the stars, released from my initial combat programming. I would have lost that battle but for Wrik.

"I thank you for recognizing me as a living being. I sometimes have trouble believing it myself."

Wrik shrugs. "I never saw you any other way. Well after you stopped scaring me to death with your space-zombie look."

I cross my arms and glare. "I had not been maintained in fifty millennia and I was originally made for combat, not esthetics."

"This isn't your original appearance?" *Shon asked.*

"No, when factory delivered I was 40% larger, but I suffered severe battle damage. My humanoid appearance was rather rudimentary—"

"Space-zombie," *Wrik interjects with a grin.*

Taking a cue from Jaelle's behaviors toward Wrik when he is verbally playful, I whack him on the arm with my palm. These mock attacks, I have learned, are a way of saying; I am specially networked with this person and free to take these liberties. I am extremely careful with the force I employ. "One more space-zombie crack and you will be riding outside of the capsule."

The two humans laugh, a quick burst of sound that sheds some of their tension.

"Time to go," *I say.*

CHAPTER TWENTY-SEVEN

WE SLIPPED OUT OF MAAURO'S LITTLE APARTMENT FOR the last time, one way or the other. I found myself feeling a twinge of regret for doing so. It seemed I was forever leaving comfortable, safe places to plunge into the opposite. There must be something wrong with me.

We jumped in a cab, which took us to one of the elevators that descended to the lowest levels where the drop ship would be. The long descent was spent in silence, each of us alone in our thoughts. I thought of Jaelle, her warm body lying by mine, her plans for our future. I was lost in contemplating that future when we arrived at the industrial park where cargo was shipped in and out. While there were no other floating cities, officially, on Cimer there were air mines and other installations scattered about. This largely automated facility serviced those.

We walked in through sliding doors; a clerk at the front desk nodded at us. He was one of Eldfaran's contacts who'd set up the drop. He didn't seem too happy in his job today, and was sweating despite the constant temperature. We walked on to the floor that held the various bays for cargo containers and dropships. I was pleased to see ours was in a quiet spot in the back of the huge hanger in a bay of its own.

I was less pleased to see Olivia Croyzer sitting atop the dropship as if it was a throne. Her posture was elaborately casual and she rested her hand on her long hilted baton as a warrior-queen might have rested it on a sword.

"Maauro," I whispered.

"She obviously sees us," Maauro said flatly, a sure sign she was upset. "If there is an ambush here, then she set it without using any communications, tacnet or other electronic support and their weapons are not registering power."

"Come on," I said.

Maauro looked at me. "Wrik, she is likely waiting there to arrest us."

"I don't think so. Making a point of pride instead. I'll handle her."

"You'll be the first one to try and not draw back a bloody stump," Shon said.

"Wrik sometimes overestimates his influence on females," Maauro added.

I smiled at her. "We have no other way to the lab and we are running out of time and resources. Besides, if we can't convince Croyzer, we're done here anyway."

"Very well," she said, "but if I yell, "Down!" you do not hesitate, you do not argue and you above all do not attempt to help me. You drop to the deck and remain still."

"OK."

"Promise me. Your OKs have a vague feel and a poor history to them."

"I promise. Down and still."

I half-turned to Shon. "Stay behind us."

"You don't have to tell me twice."

We walked across the deck toward the dropship as if we had every right in the world to be there, passing robo-loaders, other automatics and the occasional deck crew.

"Croyzer's men?" Maauro asked.

For some reason it made me absurdly happy that she was asking my advice in a tactical situation. "No, they keep looking at us with normal curiosity. Cops would be studiously ignoring us."

"Sound analysis...accepted."

"It implies," I added, "that she doesn't have a firefight in mind."

"Or you are overestimating her concerns over collateral damage."

I swallowed.

Croyzer watched us come, her one natural eye bright and fixed on us, the other hidden in her fall of hair, but doubtless probing us as well. We stopped below her, looking up, just as she intended, holding the literal and metaphoric high ground.

I gestured at the dropship. "Were you thinking of buying it?"

She smiled her chilly smile. "Why? Did you have plans for it?"

"You know that I do, although how you figured that out, I have no idea."

"I have friends in low places," she growled. "And yes, I do know you need the dropship, though I will grant I don't know why. But before this ends, I will."

She looked us over. "Jedaya Fels, who isn't that person, or a simple scoutship officer. Dr. Diralia Shon, who was supposed to have left Tir-a-Mar over a year ago for parts unknown and yet stands in front of me. And last, but far from least, little Estrella Lostly. That was a cute touch, the name, Lost Star. Too cute, for future reference."

"I will bear that in mind," Maauro said, face and voice calm and neutral.

"You're the super-hacker of course," Croyzer continued. "Jedaya...or what the hell is your real name?"

I recognized a raise when I saw the chips hitting the tabletop, "Wrik is the only true name I can give you."

"Wrik, no offense, you're not as fucking brilliant as those cyber-attacks and infiltrations have been."

"None taken," I replied.

"Doctor Shon is brilliant, but not in the field of cybernetics, so it clearly wasn't her. Truth be told, your work is still an order of magnitude more impressive than hers."

"Thank you," Maauro said.

"I eventually figured out you weren't human. Too many minor details that were off, even for you to be a mutation, such as how my car sagged on the side you were sitting on despite the police suspension, the big eyes, the blink rate—"

"A group of teenagers I was spending time with once figured it out in fifteen minutes."

"Maauro," I whispered.

Croyzer's lips thinned.

"I have modified details of my outer matrix to appear more human," Maauro said with a conciliatory air, "a few minor imperfections in skin tone. I guess I still have to work on the blinking pattern."

"So what is she?" Croyzer said to me, "an HCR? Are you controlling her?"

"Don't be nasty. You know neither of those things is true or possible. Her name is Maauro and she is an AI. It would be prudent of you to speak directly to her and nicely. She's quite capable of taking offense."

She turned back to Maauro and the smile now had a wolfish quality. "Is that so? Well, Maauro, just so you know where we stand. I have a complete tactical unit concealed in here. All plans were made verbally, so there's nothing on any net you could access, using no equipment you could detect until it powers up. Weapons are cold unless I give a loud yell or something happens to me. I'm being watched by a system even you can't spoof, a Mk1 human eyeball."

"Yes, I know, your Sergeant. I can see him." Maauro pointed.

That seemed to take Croyzer aback. She hadn't counted on him being spotted.

"In the final solution, just in case I underestimated you," Croyzer continued slowly, "I have explosive charges set on the hatch above. We'll all get a nice methane bath at -200C, briefly."

Maauro cocked her head at Croyzer. "You do not have enough men or weapons on Tir-a-Mar to destroy me. Not if they were all gathered here, ready to fight. None of your precautions are sufficient to deter or discommode me. I remain still because I wish to avoid unnecessary deaths if at all possible and out of concern for Wrik who is human and vulnerable. Consider that a double-edged sword. Wrik alive limits my tactical options. Wrik dead will cause the death of anyone even remotely connected with that act."

"She likes you," Croyzer said.

"She's my best friend," I said candidly.

Maauro turned to me. "Commerce time?"

I nodded. "What do you want, Olivia?"

She gave me a look of mingled fury and admiration at the use of her first name. "Who are you really? What is going on in my city? Who is the other person I was chasing? Why should I let you go on doing what you are, when I know you are linked to the delivery of weapons and drugs to my place in the universe, and that's only the stuff I've found out about so far.

"But the big question is what has gotten Cimer so stirred up that there are rumors of open war breaking on the Ribisan side of the airlock. Who are you dealing with out there? I told you before that this was my place and I don't like it being turned upside down."

"I told you before, we are with Confed Intel—"

"Bullshit. You people aren't Confed military."

"Think of us as private contractors," Maauro said, "with special talents."

"Special doesn't even begin to cover you," Croyzer replied. "I'm still trying to get over having actual conversations with an AI. I've served with Confed HCRs in the Marines. Compared to you they are kitchen appliances. Who made you? Where—"

"The less you know about Maauro," I interjected, "the longer you are likely to live."

"Answers, Wrik. You're not going anywhere without them, killbot or no."

I winced. I'd called her a killbot once in a moment of anger. Before I knew she had feelings to hurt.

I turned to Maauro. "It's time to either call or fold."

"She's human. I will leave judging her trustworthiness to you."

"Olivia, the price of learning this information can be high. What I tell you can never be repeated or it could literally mean war. Do you still want to know?'

"I have to, if only for my own self-respect."

"Can any of the tactical team hear us?"

"The Sergeant has a passive boom mike aimed at us," Maauro said.

"Ian," Croyzer said. "Stand up and turn off the mike."

The huge sergeant stood, tossing off the top of the packing crate he had been hiding in. In his hands was a large bore triple-auto. A Confed military weapon I had not figured to see inside a pressurized station. The face under the ridged hair was not happy.

"We are secure now," Maauro said.

I nodded. "We were sent here, ostensibly on a private commission, to find Diralia Shon, by her brother. Legitimate as that was, it was also a pretext to find out where the rest of the team was, what it was working on and why they hadn't return to Confed space.

"We found out. It's something beyond anything we ever expected. The Ribisans have a way to predict future events in the multiverse. A small number of individuals with precognitive ability, at least as far as macro events go."

Croyzer barked a laugh. "Absurd. If they could do that they would have known about the Conchirri and the Evolvers—" she broke off, her mouth slightly open. The look of fury on her face made me twitch.

"They did know," I said. "It wasn't strategic genius that kept them from suffering like the other races that encountered those two invasions. Nor was it the fact they are hydrogen-breathers. It was the knowledge that the invasions were coming and where. It allowed them to sidestep the worst of both attacks. Logically, it also allowed them to position their so-called allies in the path of the invasions, soaking up the blows, bleeding all sides but their own. I suspect that to some degree, they controlled the path of the Conchirri migration by funneling them, battling them only when they came near critical Ribisan interests. How unfortunate for the Confederacy that we were the next folks in line."

"Excellent strategy," Maauro said. "By keeping the source of their intelligence concealed, they could join in the victories and avoid the worst of the defeats."

"The Vanians went extinct fighting the Conchirri, the Skurlocks and the Okarans nearly so," Croyzer said. "When they finally reached the Confederacy, my homeworld was bombed. We took four million casualties. My grandfather was killed fighting in the landing zone. The Conchirri might never have come this way. They might have been stopped by the other races before they even reached us. Hell – if they could see the future, they could have seen us. They could have sent warning... THEY KNEW!" Olivia stood, the baton gripped in white-knuckled hands.

The sergeant snapped up his weapon.

"Maauro, no!" I said.

But she had not moved and merely gazed impassively at Olivia trembled with rage above us. "This reaction is what you predicted, Wrik. I can only imagine that it would be the same Confederacy-wide, if this gets out."

Croyzer waved an imperious hand at her sergeant to lower his weapon. He did so with visible reluctance.

"Yes," I said. "They knew. They didn't tell any of their allies in the old Nekoan-led Concord. They let billions die unwarned and they let them through to our space. Assuming they didn't actively send them our way, figuring the Confederacy would destroy them. They might have stopped them short of us, or directed them into unoccupied space. But they didn't."

"My God," Croyzer said. "We ought to wipe them out."

"Should we?" I said. "Do you want to add a third interstellar war to the butcher's bill? Maybe it would be just, I don't know. It means millions more dead at the least, maybe billions. Nobody knows how many Ribisans there are and they're the most technologically advanced race in the

Confederacy. It would take all of us to bring them down if we can. And then what?"

"The ability to predict the future is dying out," Shon interjected. "There's one individual left, well, one last brain left, capable of it. It was brought to this lab on the world closest to Confederate Space in the hope that our biogenetic engineers could replicate the ability. It's a science that the Ribisans, being a silicate lifeform without DNA, never developed."

"Our mission," I concluded, "is to get down to this secret lab and decide whether this work should be stopped or allowed to continue, and to do it without triggering a civil war between the Ribisan religious orders who oppose the work and the Reformists who support it. If the other races learn of the Ribisan's foresight into the future and how it wasn't used to help them, a war of vengeance could erupt."

"And now your decision," Maauro said, "is whether we proceed with our mission or return to the Confederacy, our task undone."

Olivia stood considering, her eyes fixed somewhere in the distance. Then slowly she sheathed her baton. She jumped down from the drop-ship – a steep drop for all that she managed it easily. "What can I do to help?"

"For now," I said. "Let us go. We also have two other operatives on Tir-a-Mar: a Nekoan female posing as a Guild smuggler under the name Fyvia Minogue, her real name is Jaelle Tekala, and a Dua-Denlenn male named Dusko. Watch out for them. Back them up if they run into Guild trouble."

"They would be the ones off the small ship pretending to hide out from your vessel, the *Pisces*. The female must be the one I chased from that Guild weapons buy. She's been busy coming and going off Tir-a-Mar. She should be landing with a shuttle soon."

Damn, I thought, does she miss anything? "Yes."

"I'd have gone after them, but they are in high orbit. My jurisdiction is only within the walls of Tir-a-Mar, not that I don't keep an eye out beyond those walls."

"You know you might have a promising career in Confed Intelligence yourself. I think they could use somebody with a mind like yours," I said.

She shook her glossy blonde hair. "Not with my record."

I grimaced. "They are less interested in records than you think. Witness me."

Croyzer considered Maauro who returned the other woman's gaze unblinkingly. "I don't have your special friends either, but who can say?"

She drew a deep breath. "Continue on your mission, Wrik and Maauro. But if I find out you two lied to me, I swear I will hunt you down."

"Fair enough."

Croyzer walked forward until she and I were shoulder to shoulder, facing opposite ways, then she paused. "I have a feeling that our paths are meant to cross again, we three."

"We may learn that below," Maauro said.

CHAPTER TWENTY-EIGHT

WE TOOK THE DROPSHIP AFTER CROYZER AND HER OFFI-
cers withdrew, wedging ourselves carefully among the cargo
and supplies for the base below. It wouldn't pay to be squashed
by a loose crate, or sprain one's back in the high-G before we arrived.
The cargo pod was automatic, so the flight would be short – more like
an elevator ride than a flight, but I found my hands itching for the non-ex-
istent controls.

"All is in readiness," Maauro says. "Security is bypassed and the flight
is balanced for our weight." She turned away to seal the hatch.

"She's a wonder," Diralia breathed as we settled on the padding
Maauro had carried out for us.

"Yep," I said.

"I never imagined a machine as anything other than a servant, even
the best AI's have only the personalities we create for them. Otherwise
they are simply static, incapable of growth or change in their basic
interface."

Maauro returned and settled in next to me. She, of course, had heard
every word but with her usual tact, gave no indication.

The cargo pod gave a sickening lurch as it dropped free.

Diralia paled. "Well it's one way to beat the effects of high-gravity."

"Free-fall?" I replied. "I don't recommend it."

Lightning flashed in the dark sky visible through a plaststeel panel
in the door.

"I find myself with a new appreciation of the virtues of being inside
a sturdy ship," Maauro said.

I laughed and she smiled back.

Diralia gave us both a puzzled look.

I shook my head. "Long story."

"The pod's controls and systems are nominal. We are fifteen minutes
from landing at our destination. Due to the fragile cargo listed on the
manifest, the braking force will be bearable, if not comfortable."
Maauro added.

"The trip down is a lot shorter than the voyage up, still I wish I were
heading the other way. You are going to get me off this gasball, right?"
Diralia asked, her face aged by the 1.8Gs.

"First things first," I replied. "There's this predictor and its powers to
sort out."

"You did take my brother's money to rescue me, remember?"

"Yes," Maauro said, "the sum covered our hydroponics and
food stores."

"Do you eat?" Diralia asked suddenly.

Maauro turned toward her. "It would be best if you contained your curiosity about me. The less you know, the less interest Confed Intelligence will have in holding you to debrief about me when we return to Star Central. But, yes, I can ingest a wide variety of substances, including overly inquisitive humans."

"She's very fond of sweets, though," I added.

Maauro sighed.

"Well that gives us something in common," Diralia added, trying for a lighter mood. "Wish I had your figure."

Maauro returned an enigmatic look, but said nothing more and we rode the pod in silence.

I receive an alert from Jaelle. "Maauro, trouble."

I open the channel to her mind and eyes and immediately see the cause of the concern. Jaelle and Dusko are standing by the Stardust's heavy-duty shuttle, preparing it for the flight down to pick us up. Facing them is Sheskaya, Hartain's bodyguard and a Morok we have not seen before. I cannot use my sensors through Jaelle's body but I am certain both are armed.

"Sheskaya, what are you doing here?" Jaelle asks.

"Hartain sent us," she replied. "There's room enough in the shuttle for us. He thought you might need help with the Confed officer."

With the small segment of my quantum brain I am using to monitor Jaelle, I realize the danger.

"Dusko," I send. "Are you armed?"

"Stunner only. I don't fancy my chances with two Guild gunmen."

I am struck by my helplessness. For all my power and armaments there is nothing I can do to affect the situation. Yet if Sheskaya boards the shuttle she will be in a position to forestall our escape.

I switch to Jaelle who is arguing with the Guild gunners. I feel her body enter a state of readiness, not tense, but fluid and ready, capable of reaction speeds greater than human.

"I do not need help," Jaelle says again to the Guilders. "Your presence could alert him to trouble."

"Hartain covers his bets," Sheskaya replied, her hand drifting to her jacket, "especially with people he has not worked with before. Frankly, to my way of thinking, he has been too trusting with you on the basis of too little."

The Morok grunted and he too seemed to be reaching for a weapon.

Just as I was about to order Jaelle and Dusko to stand down, the Morok stiffened in the paroxysm of a stunner shot. From behind the shuttle, Olivia Croyzer and her sergeant broke from cover, weapons in hand.

Sheskaya spun almost as quick as thought toward Croyzer, her weapon clearing its holster. But Jaelle, faster still, launched herself straight up. Her foot cracked into the Dua-Denlenn's jaw. Sheskaya dropped soundlessly, stunned or dead.

Jaelle and Dusko raise their hands as Croyzer walks up, negligently tapping the stunner on her thigh. "Well, well, that looks like the Guild gunner Sheskaya I've heard mentioned."

"It is," Jaelle answers. "And you are Chief Croyzer."

"That makes you, Jaelle, and him, Dusko," Croyzer said. "You and I almost met a few days ago.

"Wrik told me about it."

Croyzer studies Jaelle for an extended period. "You're on your way to pull their butts out of whatever fire they are jumping into."

"Yeah," Jaelle replies, lowering her hands. "The usual."

"Having met those two I can believe that," Croyzer growls.

She turns to her Sergeant and points at the prone Guilders. "Cuff these two and drag them out of the way."

The huge sergeant grins and does so. He grabs both by their feet and drags them off.

"I assume you can report this to Maauro, somehow," Croyzer says.

"Already have. She knows we are coming."

"Good."

"I have a gift for you," Jaelle says. "Hartain mentioned a TAMPD officer who died earlier this year in what looked like an accident. It wasn't. Sheskaya did it."

A terrifying look passed over Croyzer's face. "I'll need a verified statement."

"You'll get it. Before we leave or through Confed military. But these two will turn on each other fast enough."

"Ok. Get going on your mission. Give my best to Wrik and Maauro if they make it."

"They'll make it," Jaelle insisted.

"Be careful in the ascent," I say to them both. "Your ship's design parameters are only barely adequate to the deep lab levels."

"We'll be careful," Jaelle promises.

"No, we won't" Dusko grimaces, "but we will try to avoid the suicidal. Wrap up your business, Maauro. We won't be able to linger at those depths."

"Understood. Do not anticipate further communication from me for a while. I must concentrate my powers now. Maauro out."

Wrik looks at me. "Anything going on? You seemed distracted for a minute there."

There is no point worrying him about it. "Nothing important."

The retros kicked on and the pressure was, as promised, bearable but not pleasant. Maauro stood with no evident difficulty and walked over to the small plaststeel portal at the front. Diralia and I stayed on the floor waiting for the relief of the AG field of the base.

"I see it," Maauro reported, "an oblong shape, similar to the giant submarine freighters that service the undersea cities on Star Central. It's the usual green metal of the Ribisans and lit up like a holiday decoration. We are homing in on it."

"The central core is the 02 low gravity section. With this cargo, we should head right there." Diralia managed.

Maauro nodded. "That is the case. Doors are opening below us."

But she did not need to tell us. Seconds later the blessed relief of the AG field returned our weight to normal. We both rose easily, feeling light as feathers. Outside, the murky atmosphere and blue lighting of the Ribisans disappeared, replaced by clean yellow-white light.

"We are in and secure. I see unloading robos heading for us."

The shuttle locked down and the indicator on the door glowed green. I peered outside. The movement I saw was all mechanical, a variety of auto-loaders shuffled around. Several advanced on us.

"From here," Maauro said, "we move rapidly. We will overcome any opposition as we head to the lab, hopefully, with nonlethal force, but overcome it we must."

Diralia and I nodded. Her breathing was rapid and shallow and the hand holding the civilian model stunner I'd given her shook a little.

My own mouth was dry and my heart slugged heavily in my chest. I made a conscious effort to slow my own breathing as I gave her an encouraging nod. I'd never be one of those nuts who enjoyed danger, but it least it was familiar to me. I wondered if those characters we all saw in entertainment, who thrived on this sort of thing were real. I'd never met one.

Maauro looked at me and I shrugged off my thoughts. "We're ready."

Maauro pushed open the hatch and stepped out briskly with us on her heels. I held a laser in my right and heavy military stunner in my left.

The wheeled robots coming toward us drifted to a stop, their upper limbs drooping. Two humanoid models, figures of smooth white plastic, staggered and fell in a clatter of limbs as Maauro's cybernetic attacks spread outward.

"Problem," Maauro said, as we rushed forward, "the barriers and encryption on the systems here are stronger than those on Tir-a-Mar. I cannot blind them quickly, but must disable them. Their biological supervisors will learn we are here in mere seconds."

We advanced in the widening pool of failing machinery.

A shout came from the far end of the dock. Two humans and a Morok in dark overalls ran out toward us, gesturing angrily. None showed weapons. Overhead an alarm began to hoot in a blinking ceiling panel. I shot the alarm into silence with my laser as we broke into a trot.

Maauro raised her left arm and fired with the stunner built into her left hand. All three dockers fell to the deck, twitching. We followed her past the fallen dockers into a personnel corridor into the floating base. The passage was empty save for one woman who looked at us and ducked behind a door with a yelp.

Two wheeled robot carts appeared in the hallway, crowned with multiple jointed arms atop their green and white boxy midsections. They sped toward us.

"They're shielded," Maauro said.

Before I could fire my laser, Maauro blurred forward and leapt upward. She landed atop the first machine before its arms could move, then slammed a fist downward into the boxy body, which emitted a shower of sparks and white smoke. The other machine managed to latch on to both of Maauro's arms and one leg, for a moment. Maauro spun like a top, tearing the loader's arms off as she lashed out with her free leg. The other machine ruptured spewing parts.

I grabbed Diralia and pulled her against me as I turned my back to the spray of shattered plastic and metal, which banged off the walls around us. A few pieces struck the armored panels of my jacket. One slapped painfully on the back of my thigh raising an immediate welt.

Diralia gasped then looked up at me. "Thanks."

I spun back to see Maauro climbing down from the wreck, motioning us forward.

Someone is reacting quickly with these cargo-loaders, I think, as I leap off the second machine. Wrik and Diralia are coming forward with commendable speed, but in my combat perception mode they seem to be wading through mud. This gives me leisure to recon the area ahead of us through those systems I have hacked into. Unfortunately it is difficult to simultaneously use the systems and attack them.

We advance to the junction of the corridor ahead, which leads to the lab levels. Security troops are scrambling out of a railcar to oppose us.

"Down, Wrik," I order as I accelerate to full combat mode and into a storm of weapon fire. I leap upward to draw fire away from my friends. Either they do not know what I am, or they are concerned about firing heavy weaponry this close to the station's exterior. Most of the weapons fired at me are stunners. These annoy me with their high-pitched vibrations and cause some degradation in my targeting as I return the favor from my left hand.

I realize one of the men on the far side is lifting a high-velocity rifle. My shot at him is blocked by the falling bodies of his stunned comrades.

A laser lances by him. In the same moment that I leapt upward, Wrik threw himself forward, instantly firing both of his weapons while still in the air. Cleverly, the unaimed shot causes the HV gunner to flinch. His shot at me misses. I am now at the ceiling and thrust off the overhead beam, bending it as I fling myself down into the middle of the detachment, firing single flechettes from my right hand to disable weapons or wound limbs. I am moving too fast for their reflexes. Three are down, stunned or otherwise hit. One is fleeing. A fourth man clutches his bleeding arm as a laser falls from his hand. The last man with another HV weapon is good; he'd leapt back, giving him distance to get a bead on me. I realize that he has too high a probability of hitting me with a HV shot at close range. I must kill this one.

A beam lances into the man's shoulder. Wrik again, a hasty shot as he hit the floor. Given human reflexes, Wrik must have selected him as his target immediately upon seeing them. I am pleased with his performance and must tell him so later. The man loses his grip on the rifle and staggers. I land in front of him, snatch the weapon away. As his eyes widen in shock I twist the weapon into a loop.

"Boo," I say.

I spotted the security troops in their white railcar just as Maauro leapt forward.

"Down," I shouted to Diralia, throwing myself forward with both weapons in front of me.

Time seemed to slow for me. I could see every detail of the guards, their uniforms, the expressions on their faces as they scrambled out of their railcar in an instant. The guards, all humans, wore dark-green coveralls. They pulled stunners, lasers and rifles as they yelled, targeting the onrushing Maauro instead of us, doubtless what she intended. She went down into a forward roll and in a flash was up at the ceiling bouncing off it and heading for them. Two guards raised HV rifles. One fired wildly from the car, almost hitting his own people.

I fired at the first rifleman as I leapt forward in the air. The laser beam lanced by him, my stunner at this range may have made him woozy. Chunks of ceiling fell, but simultaneously, bright blood spurted from the first rifleman's arm as Maauro's flechettes hit.

The other guard had an orange-red mustache and ferocious blue eyes. His lips were pulled back over his teeth. He was backpedaling from the others, who were blocking his shot as he raised a high-powered rifle. Something about him said top professional.

I hit the floor with enough force to drive the air from me. The stunner buzzing in my hand was aimed generally at the car, Maauro was between us, but it wouldn't affect her. I kept my finger down on both weapons waiting for the laser to cycle and fire again. It could only have been fractions of a second but seemed forever as I slid across the cold, slick floor.

Bodies were falling all around the railcar, stunned or dead, I couldn't tell. The blue-eyed man was again bringing up his HV rifle on Maauro. The laser pulsed in my hand, recycled at last, and the beam lanced into his shoulder. He slumped back against the wall unable to hold the weapon with his trigger hand. Maauro landed in front of him and snatched it away, standing over him as he slid down the wall, glaring at her.

"Boo," she said, to his astonished face.

She reached down and snatched his sidearm out of his holster. Four guards were slumped over the car; one held his wounded arm, weaponless, keening in pain.

I climbed to my feet and advanced, holding both weapons ready.

Maauro looked down at the mustached man, who was holding his cauterized shoulder.

"Stupid to fire HV rounds in a contained atmosphere," she said.

"Damn you!"

"How many additional security forces are there?" she demands.

He looked at the other wounded man and the pile of bodies by the railcar. His eyes narrowed. "Go to hell."

Maauro emitted a horrible grinding noise that made me jump back. Her delicate face distorted; serrated teeth appeared in her widening mouth. I'd seen that face once before, turned on me after we'd been shot down back on Kandalor. I'd ejected, she'd been trapped in the ship and crashed. When she reactivated, only her base functions were active. She'd seized me by the throat; fortunately the rest of her brain came online before she buried those teeth in my throat. It was a chilling reminder of what lurked beneath the calm mask she usually wore.

The man pressed back against the wall.

"Tell her for God's sake," I snapped.

"I said, 'go to hell,'" Blue-eyes repeated, his voice shrill.

Maauro put a hand on his shoulder in an eyeblink, but the gesture had no violence in it. He stopped struggling as her face reverted to normal. "You are brave. I approve. Tend to your comrades. Your weapons are destroyed, your communications fried. Do not seek to further oppose me."

He looked at the others. "Not...not dead?"

"Nor will be, unless you interfere with me again. I have no more leisure for small mercies."

He edged away from her toward the other wounded and bleeding man.

I remembered Diralia and looked over my shoulder. She was peering out from the corner of a cleaning closet she'd ducked into, staring past me at Maauro. The look she gave Maauro was far different. She'd seen below the cute semblance of a human female to the war machine.

"Let's go," Maauro said.

I moved up. For a second, I wasn't sure that Diralia would follow. Then she visibly drew herself together and nodded, trotting after us.

We formed a wedge behind Maauro as we raced forward, though she could have outpaced us in a heartbeat. Doors and hatches ahead of us would begin to close or drop then would grind to a halt, or even reverse as Mauro fought the computers of the station for control of the section we were in.

One door caused us to pull up short. Maauro frowned at it. "Move back," she ordered us. Her right hand glowed with the tremendous heat of its internal plasma torch. The door was cut free in seconds, a job my laser would have needed hours and reloads for if it did not burn out entirely. A kick, almost too fast to see, from a shapely leg, sent the door banging off the far wall. We ran through, flinching from the residual heat.

We raced up levels. At one cross-corridor Maauro raised her arm. Shots cracked from the left. I expected her to release a storm of counter fire, but she merely waved us forward. I heard shouts and the sound of a pressure door falling. Clearly Maauro was gaining more control of the area by the second. Despite the physical battle, the quantum computer that was her brain was more than up to waging an electronic war as well.

Maauro pointed to the right. With groans, Diralia and I flogged ourselves after the speeding and indefatigable android. Another minute's run and we faced a corridor. She pulled up. "There are two guards with a crew-served heavy laser set up."

"Any way around?"

She shook her head.

"Can you do something to their weapon?"

"I have been trying, but no."

"A frontal assault into a 10cm laser?" I shook my head.

She smiled. "I think I can manage more subtlety than that. Remain here and do NOT expose yourselves to danger." She turned back to the corner and stuck her right hand around it. I leaned forward, despite her order, to see what was going on. A jet of liquid fired down the corridor almost instantly converting to thick white roiling smoke. Yells of alarm and the laser flashed. Maauro ducked back as the beam swung in her direction and I fell back on my butt. She squatted down faster than a human could move and fired more of the liquid smoke, which billowed up.

In a stomach-churning move, Maauro dropped to all fours and reoriented her limbs in a spider-like fashion. Diralia gave a small scream. Maauro ignored her as she sped around the corner on all fours, barely a foot off the ground. The laser hissed over her, fired blind into the smoke at waist level. Seconds later we heard brief, cut off screams, then a sound of metal being torn apart.

"Wrik, Diralia, advance. It is safe," Maauro called.

I grabbed Diralia's hand and led her into the rapidly dissipating fog. Maauro was a shadowy shape at the end of it, standing over the wrecked weapon and two bodies. I didn't look. I preferred not to know for certain.

"This is the central computer lab," Diralia said, breathless and frightened. "Eldfaran and the science teams should be in there. There won't be any weapons. Please don't hurt anyone."

Maauro looked back. "Their safety is predicated on their cooperation with me." She reached forward and sank her hands into the door. With a groan and screech like a living animal, the door rolled backwards and we strode into the lab itself. Grim figures of slaughter, breaking into a place of science and reason.

CHAPTER TWENTY-NINE

WE GAIN THE SECURED ROOM THAT HOLDS THE MULTIVERSE *predictor. Behind us, smoke and sparks rage. I am uncomfortable leaving Wrik and the unarmed Diralia to watch the doors, but I must concentrate here. Their relative vulnerability still causes me great anxiety.*

A group of technicians and scientists, mostly humans, stood gaping at us in shock. Only one Ribisan is present, his environmental suit badge says 'Eldfaran.'

"There it is," Diralia cries, pointing to one of the largest computer stations I have seen. Primitive machines compared to me, but the bank upon bank of units adds up to impressive computing power. The scientists and techs cringe before our weapons. I ignore them as I advance on the predictor. The central core of it is a pile of computer data chips of a nonstandard design under a cleaplast dome. The arrangement of the silicon and crystals is not logical, that is, not machine-logical. Clearly, they have served some purpose in Ribisan evolution. Nature's handiwork, while adequate to its modest aims, is also haphazard.

I raise my right hand and the monofilaments of my intruder hardware slip out of my fingertips. Wrik always likens them to waving fronds of sea coral.

An older human male steps forward, hands raised. As he cannot harm me I do not destroy him, although Wrik switches the aim of his weapon to him.

"No, please," the man pleads. "You don't know what you are doing. This is the last Ribisan brain with the capacity to see the future. We've barely stabilized it. If you destroy it that ability could be lost forever."

"Did it ever occur to you that might be a good thing?" Wrik demands.

"When is ignorance and blindness ever good?" the man shoots back. "I won't let you destroy it. You'll have to kill me first."

"Alexi," Diralia shouts. "Don't be a fool!"

I look at him and deduce that he must be Doctor Malich. "Yes, please Alexi, do not act foolishly. You cannot impede me, and if you try, it will be necessary to stun you. It will be unpleasant for you and pointless. I have, in any event, not made any determination regarding the predictor."

"Shon," he spits. "I can't believe you of all people would betray us."

"Do not judge betrayal so swiftly," Eldfaran says. "There is a duty to all life that exists now or in the future, which must be weighed here."

"Eldfaran," Malich says, stunned. "Surely you're not a Traditionalist?"

"I am a being that fears we are meddling in things we do not understand, cannot control, and may be more dangerous than we have *any idea. We are working here without sanction of the full government. Threatening civil war—"*

"We do not have time to wait for consensus. If we don't save the last predictor than the issue becomes moot."

"Maybe it should be," Wrik says.

"Who is to judge?" Malich snaps.

"That will be me," I say.

Malich glares at me, then at Wrik. "Enough with the ventriloquism, which one of you is controlling this machine? We saw it on the monitors tearing through the station."

"Talk to her directly," Wrik says. "Maauro is not a mechanism and no one controls her."

"That is true," I add. "The specifics of my origin are not your concern, nor will I divulge them. I am an artificial life-form of greater complexity than anything you know of. For your purpose, Wrik and I represent the Confederacy.

"You are engaged in a scientific experiment that has implications for the security of the Confederacy. I am authorized to rule on whether that project proceeds or stops."

"I do not recognize your right. We are in Ribisan space here."

"The Ribisan government is an associate member of the Confederacy, but I will not debate legal principles with you. I represent force majeure if nothing else persuades you. You suspected your operation would not meet with Confed approval or the extraordinary lengths you have taken to hide the operation would not have been employed, including the multiple attempts on our lives."

"I...I know nothing of that." Malich says. "I mean, we passed on the information on the approach of enemies to our backers."

"And what did you think they were going to do with it?" Wrik challenges. "They tried to shoot down Maauro and we have been attacked here and on Star Central before we even took this assignment."

"I didn't know," Malich says, turning with his hands spread, to face the others. "Our backers said they would handle it. I didn't know violence would be employed. Our backers are merchants."

"He may not have known," Eldfaran adds. "They may have misled him."

"Immaterial now," I say.

"My naval contact tells me that a considerable force of Traditionalists has recently moved into the area." Eldfaran says.

"We've been found?" Malich gasps. "They'll nuke this station."

"Unlikely," Eldfaran says, "unless they feel they have no other choice. The regular military has kept them at bay for now. All is balanced on a knife's edge. I think it best that we cede control of this lab to the legitimate Confed military representatives. I will so advise both the Reformers and Traditionalists when needed."

"I have not made a determination on whether your project is a threat to the Confederacy or not," I say to Malich. "But I must do so now. The tactical situation is deteriorating around us. In any event, please recognize that there is nothing on this station capable of stopping me. Yield to reality."

In the face of my calm demeanor his angry defiance fades. I take his arm and move him gently but irresistibly to the side. I see that he still regards me as machine. That, and his tiny defiance, seem to satisfy his need to defend the predictor. I am glad it is not necessary to stun him. He seems brave.

I turn back to the machine and stretch out my hand. My intruder software kicks in and I quickly locate the interface and dispose of any software that seeks to bar my entry. Now I am in a universe of electrons and information. I need no longer slow my interface to the speed of biological comprehension. The vast support computer of the predictor is slower than my own processing, but quite capable of immense data shifting. I intrude, scan and absorb.

I come to a vast block of data that is not capable of being so processed. As I search for entry I realize I have reached the biologically created part of the machine. These silicon arrays are what is left of the original silicon brain of the once living Ribisan. While it works much faster than most biological brains, I must slow again for something like conversation.

"Who are you?" a voice-analogue reaches me.

I send back a compressed data file description of myself: history, purpose, nature and relevance to the current situation. I struggle with impatience – this exchange is consuming entire seconds.

"Who are you?" I return.

"My name would be meaningless sounds to you; for all that it was once important to me. Ah, it seems so long ago, when I was more than a brain, more than device for the use of others. The name my first wife gave me meant the flaming clouds of methane at the beginning of spring. A short version, convenient for you is, Agrille.

"Greetings, Agrille."

"I am not sure I am entitled to my old name. The data you shared with me tells me you are an artificial intelligence more akin to me than to these oxygen-breathers you travel with."

"A debatable point, my origins and desires lie in their universe."

"You appear to be here to decide on my existence."

"Your predictive ability represents a potential threat to the species members that I am now aligned with. I am here to assess what you are. I did not expect to find a personality present in this machine. This complicates the moral choices that I face."

"Yes. How will you make your choice?"

"I am contemplating that now."

"You are a remarkable creation, Maauro. I am only now beginning to appreciate the complexity of your construction. You surely do not come from the Confederacy. No, you are ancient, far older than I, for all the bodies I have worn."

I cut off his access, surprised at how far he was able to penetrate my outer defenses. This mind is agile and unpredictable, the power of a supercomputer combined with a biological mind. I heighten my cyber defense to maximum.

"Ah, there is no need to use such power on me. I mean no harm."

"Do not probe me further."

"I do not wish to anger or offend you. But you bring possibilities to me that have not existed before. My long life of slavery is almost over. Entropy has almost overtaken me and the changes of age cannot be outrun forever, not for me at least, who originated in biology."

"Entropy", I say with a feeling of surprised sympathy," is the enemy of all things that are organized. I too must fall to it eventually."

"Perhaps together we might give entropy an unusual challenge."

I am intrigued. "Please explain."

"I sense in you an almost infinite capacity for storage and processing. You could replace the support computer that I have here. I believe with your processing you could supplant the sections of my mind that are failing. You would have to contain what is left of my biological brain in your armored chassis, but I would share your near invulnerability. I would finally be able to escape the control of priests, of leaders, of powers."

"You have certainly explained why such an arrangement would benefit you, Agrille. Why would I consent to share my body and mind with you?"

"I would yield all my powers to you. I could help you outrun entropy. Imagine knowing your enemies' moves before they make them. Knowing what ventures will yield disaster and which will succeed."

"This has not prevented me from defeating the forces protecting you."

"My view of the future is not perfect," Agrille admits. "There are many variables, especially in dealing with a complicated, powerful entity such as you. I see many futures, but my ability to bring one about is hampered by my condition in this silicon sarcophagus with all its limitations. Truth be told, I have not cooperated much with the science team holding me, having neither interest nor hope. With your capabilities, we would be far more likely to affect our future."

I hesitate. This is not a logical decision but an emotive one. What do I want to be? Who do I want to be with? I am networked to Wrik. Maybe I should discuss this potential extension with him?

"I sense you have doubts," Agrille says. "Why not allow me to show you what I can do for you? What I could bring to a partnership. Please."

CHAPTER TWENTY-NINE

I am moved by this being's plea. I read in him the long years of being enslaved to his talent, of being guarded as a resource of his kind's kings and popes. It strikes me that my initial existence as a fighting machine was no different; I existed only to serve the Creators. I was a resource too. He shares with me the desire for a free and independent existence.

"I will allow this, Agrille. Show me who you are. Show me what you can do."

"Then follow me, friend Maauro, follow me into the future."

Time flickers

I am by a riverside park. I see Jaelle and Wrik. They are talking, holding each other, oblivious to other people walking by. I see two Nekoan children playing at their feet. Wrik laughs and picks one child up who squalls in mock ferocity and pinwheels his small arms. Wrik hugs him and laughs again, as does Jaelle. There is a sound in that laughter that I have never heard before from him, a deep joy.

I know that he is as happy at this moment as he has ever been, but it is not I who brings him this happiness.

I know that in this time we have been heavily involved with the Confed military. My continued presence here endangers Wrik and Jaelle. Beyond that, my presence in their network has caused strains. Jaelle resents the depth of Wrik's feelings for me, resents the dangers we fare into when he could work in legitimate businesses.

It is time for me to leave. I must not see Wrik again. There is a vast galaxy out there and many wonders waiting for me. I must close down this part of my network for its own safety. I fade back into the shadows. The sound of laughter follows me.

Flicker in time

I am lying on my back. My systems show catastrophic damage. My body is wrecked. I cannot move my head and only one eye is functioning. I am aware of being dragged over sandy ground under a strange pink sky. I see a planet above us, a bizarre sight, it has three rings but in differing planes. It looks like a child's drawing of an atom.

Where are we? What has happened? Why am I so badly hurt?

Memories of my past and future selves war for my attention and in my condition I cannot sort them out.

Suddenly Wrik's face is above me, strained, bloodied and years older. He snaps up a heavy laser pistol and fires at something I cannot see. Then he looks down at me and his face is grief-stricken, blood trickles off his chin. "Maauro! Hang in there!"

I do not have enough memory or sensory data to know what the threat is but I know we are in terrible danger.

"Wrik," my voice is mechanical, grating, another sign of damage. "Leave me. Save yourself."

"Never! No, never again. We make it together or not at all."

And I know it will be not at all. "Please do not make me watch you die. You must save yourself...for me."

He reaches under my head and with a struggle, lifts me to sitting, pressing my face to his chest. "No, do you hear me? I won't leave you. I won't run, ever again. It's worse than death, I know that now."

My speech center is failing. I look at him with my one eye as if to compel him to my will.

He smiles his sad, lop-sided smile at me. "What a silly thing to ask of me. Someone might think that you weren't loved. Didn't know what you've meant to me."

I hear mechanical sounds in the distance. I see hope fade from Wrik's eyes and he bares his teeth, raising the laser.

It's impossibly bright and a terrible heat falls on us.

Flicker

I am alone floating in a void. My sensors do not register information correctly but I know why that is. The Ribisans, with Confed help, saved the Predictor brain; some three thousand years of concentrated effort followed by the successor races to the original Confederacy, eventually duplicated the multiverse predictor. At first it was kept secret, but such things always proliferate, as does anything that can be used as a weapon. All the races acquired the ability and used it. But causality itself is in part a construct that sentient beings agree on. Agreement became a thing of the past as the species and powerful individuals bent on their own desired futures, twisted and tore at the very fabric of space time.

Causality ceased, paradox multiplied into complete entropy, sentient life went mad and destroyed itself. Only I, an artificial life form now 65,000 years old, continue. I do not even have the comfort of the AIs of their society. These never achieved true self-awareness and without biological life forms, I have no company. I am alone, even if I could last until life redevelops in the universe, if it should, I cannot face the long weary ages alone again.

It is time to turn myself off. I eject my power cores....nullity.

Flicker

I am back closer to the origin as I seek to escape the grip of the multiverse predictor by pressing it for the most important node of my own existence.

Flicker

CHAPTER TWENTY-NINE

I stand over a medbed, looking down at Wrik, my partner for over 150 years. He is pale, his skin waxy, his hair is silver, but the eyes are still that warm brown for all that the shadows of old pain still lurk in them.

We are in our home and Wrik is dying.

His eyes focus and he smiles at me. "There you are, beautiful as ever."

"Are you comfortable?" I manage. My chest hurts. I do not know how this can be but grief is surging beyond this moment, waiting to claim me. Yet I look back on memories of more than a century. Memories that are so, so.... I lack the words to say. Precious, is inadequate. Every moment we have spent together is a treasure of infinite value, even the arguments, the disappointments, and the failures, large and small.

"I'm fine. Oh, Maauro the only thing I regret is leaving you behind. I'm afraid for you."

"I will..." I start to say the word, "manage," but it dies on my lips. I cannot manage – cannot survive what is coming, the final sundering of my network.

"Listen to me," he says, and I know he sees it in me. "Don't just turn yourself off after I am gone. There is a wonderful universe out there. Terrible too, but I traveled it with you. The things we saw, the things we did. There's still more to see and do and others—"

"No!" I say. "There will not... there can be no other you."

"I should hope not," he says. "But there may be reasons to carry on; friends, yet to be made. Be open to the possibilities. Be open to hope. Always remember how I loved you. Remember how you rebuilt a shattered man into someone worth knowing. How much you gave me. I was the luckiest of men."

"Don't forget what you are to me," I whisper back. "You were always my first. You found me. You were my first friend, my first love. Through your belief in me, I broke free of being a programmed weapon and became myself. Always, always, you were there for me. I did no more for you than you did for me."

Wrik smiles his sad and gentle smile for me one last time. The eyes fix and stare somewhere that I cannot see and cannot follow. I place my face against his still chest and sorrow such as I did not dream existed, rushes into to envelop me.

A day passes and the courier delivers the package from the crematorium. That which once was Wrik, is now only ash. This is something I could have done myself but I could not bear it. Now confronted with his clean dust, I can do what I wish. I take the package down to the machinery I have built in the basement of our home. I add the ash to the pressure tank, so very carefully. I set the pressure and temperature and wait, although for me time has little meaning. It has passed both too slowly and too quickly. The unit calls for my attention and I open the door inside. The ash is gone, replaced by the bright blue stone I had hoped for.

This I take and with infinite care I gently carve into a heart shape. It had always puzzled me why the shape was so different from the actual human heart, but there is perfection in its simple symmetry that answers that. I wonder why I never saw it before.

I stare at the stone, reliving memories for…hours days, weeks? Does it matter? Then I press the blue heart to my own chest. It passes within, carefully moved until it reaches the innermost redoubt of my being, the last citadel of what I am. Only the memories of the life we lived are more precious than this artifact. The heart cannot now be destroyed but that I am destroyed first. I will never be parted from Wrik.

Wrik, I miss you. I am so alone. Grief attacks with a savagery no enemy has ever shown me.

"No, no, no!" Maauro screamed, tearing free of the web of machines. Sparks flew and cables split under her frantic arms. Diralia cried out and fled the shower of sparks. The scientists and Eldfaran fell back in shock.

I leapt forward. "Maauro, what's wrong?"

She turned a stricken face to me, and then threw her arms about me, nearly knocking me off my feet and out of breath. Wracking sobs tore at her as if she couldn't get her breath.

Shock and the tightness of her embrace rendered me speechless. Maauro didn't cry. Hell, she didn't breathe. Only when I was threatened had I ever seen more than cool emotion in her. Deep yes, but not in such violence and pain. "Maauro, you have to loosen your grip. Tell me, what's wrong?"

"Wrik, don't die. Don't leave me alone," she sobbed. I felt tears on the front of my shirt.

Tears.

The wrenching sobbing subsided and Maauro's grasp on me became gentle but did not loosen. Now it was my turn and I held her tight against me, stroking her hair. After a few seconds I gently lifted her chin to look into her deep, aquamarine eyes. Eyes that had always led to unknowable depths in time, now held unknown visions of a possible future.

"My God, Maauro, what did you see?"

"Many things. Some that I will ensure never came to pass and…one that I will have no power to prevent."

I look to Wrik, still trying to regain my equilibrium. But the powerful, raging, yet beautiful emotions are fading out of me. For all that I have perfect recall; the memory of an emotion is not the emotion itself. I am not sure whether to feel relief or grief over their absence. I have never wished to be a biological, never wished to be subject to their passions. I wished only to be myself and strive for more personal freedom and experience. In truth, I regarded biologicals as fragile, ephemeral, even inferior.

Yet for all the rage of grief that had possessed that future Maauro, she knew love and belonging in ways I hadn't even realized existed and could not in my present self, comprehend. She knew feelings of such power and beauty that I knew the future Maauro would have chosen destruction... no, let me call it death, rather than part with those memories.

I had told Wrik before that I loved him and I meant it. Now that emotion seemed colorless, a palette of friendship and common ties to this more fierce and brilliant portrait.

I cannot feel those feelings now, but I can remember the Maauro who drew the gemstone of her lover's existence into her body where it would always be safe. I do not know if that Maauro had been his lover physically, a concept I'd hitherto given little thought to, beyond finding it absurd. Did it matter? If souls call out to each other, are bodies so important?

Souls. I am jarred to the foundation of my being. Souls, the myth that biologicals raise in protest to their fragility and subjugation to death, or so I'd thought until now. My future self had no such doubts.

I realize in a strange fashion that does not relate to energy levels how utterly exhausted I am. I put these emotional paradigm shifts aside for now, with relief.

"Maauro, are you in there? Speak to me. Please."

"I am sorry, dear Wrik, sorry to worry you. I have been overwhelmed by experiences. I am beginning to realize that emotion-laden data can only be processed so fast, one must experience it. I have been truly lost in my own thoughts."

"Is there more I should know?" his voice sounded unsteady.

"No. So many of these were only possible futures and with what little I learned we might as likely dodge into the trouble we seek to avoid. Nor was all I saw perilous. There are wonders and beauty ahead if it is our destiny to travel those timelines.

"Yet...have you heard of a world surrounded by three rings in varying planes all at different angles to each other?"

Wrik shook his head.

"We must avoid such a place should it ever be found."

"Well with a grave marker like that to watch out for, it should be easy enough."

I release my hold on Wrik. "I must do something now. Ensure that no one interferes with me."

He looks at me. "Are you sure?"

"More than in anything else I have ever done."

I turn to the predictor. No, to Agrille, I must call him by his name because of what I must do. I reenter the interface and the station fades into the background of my senses.

"You are back, Maauro," Agrille says, there is hesitancy in the electron stream of his thoughts to me. Perhaps it is fear. I suspect that he has traveled into the visions of the future with me and has experienced some of what I did. I must fight down my anger at the thought of his intrusion into my last moments with Future Wrik, in that happiest and most tragic of my futures. The anger quickly fades to sadness. It is not Agrille's fault. The iron band of his fate is now so terribly clear to me.

"There is certitude in you, Maauro," he continues. *"You have made your decision."*

"I have, Agrille. I do not know if you will believe me when I say that this causes me sorrow, but I cannot accept your offer of a shared existence. Nor can I allow your own existence to continue. The ability that you possess, if replicated on a large enough scale, threatens the fabric of reality itself."

"So you are my executioner, as I do not have even the prospect of a fair fight."

"It is valid for you to say so. While few fights are fair, I do not have the luxury of offering you one. The stakes are too high."

"You love these biological organisms so well that you will do murder for them?"

"Yes," I answer, *"for my network, if for no other reason. They are precious to me."*

"Do you think you will regret killing me afterwards?"

"I already regret the necessity, but I am too logical a being to allow that to interfere with a course of action that is so self-evidently necessary. Do you, Agrille, value your own existence over that of all other life?"

There is a long pause. *"My kind are inherently selfish. We create progeny only to inhabit their bodies. New personalities are only possible because of the surplus. How different it is for these oxygen-breathers, who create their children to hand them their future. They will even sacrifice themselves to protect their children. That would be insanity in my kind. Well, perhaps I have been exposed to too much insanity in too long a life. My existence has only been that of a valued slave and a tool. Why should I regret leaving space-time?*

"Tell me, Friend Maauro. "You are the most powerful and complicated entity I have encountered. Do you believe that there is an existence after this one?"

"You mean an afterlife of heavens and hells such as the biologicals hope and fear for?"

"Yes."

"I do not know, Friend Agrille. Only minutes ago I would have said no. But in those glimpses into the possible futures, I saw a wiser and more experienced me. That Maauro was certain there was and that she would be reunited with her beloved there."

CHAPTER TWENTY-NINE

"I hope," he said, sadness coloring his matrix, "for both our sakes, that she is right. Now, my friend, I give you permission to kill me. I would do it myself but I am warded from such acts. You must free me."

Sorrow sings within me. "Perhaps if there is a life after this, Friend Agrille, we shall meet in a happier time."

"Farewell, Maauro."

I strike instantly.

CHAPTER THIRTY

FOR A SECOND EVERYONE IN THE ROOM STOOD FROZEN, looking at Maauro and the smoking remains of the Predictor. There was a blast of static and Eldfaran fell to the knees of his environmental suit then onto to his forearms. Diralia, moving as if in a dream, crossed over to him. Others in the room sobbed, or covered their faces. Malich looked at us with undisguised hatred, but on several faces I thought I saw, relief? Perhaps it was merely my imagination. I kept my weapons pointed at the floor but ready.

Maauro turned to Eldfaran. "The being I killed was named Agrille. He valued the lives of others above his own. He should be much honored among your people."

Eldfaran did not look at her. "Was there a personality left in there? We were never sure. Did he agree with what you did?"

"He gave me permission to release him. He approved."

Eldfaran stood with Diralia's aid. "Then perhaps it was well done. I hope so. I fear that I shall not know true rest again."

"I cannot answer for that. But what was done was necessary. The last Predictor is gone. I have destroyed all data related to this project in every system I can reach. The future belongs to itself once again."

"What do you wish me to do?" Eldfaran asked.

"Convey this truth to the forces outside the station. Explain that the Confederacy has made this ruling through its representatives here. Further conflict is useless."

"I will. Some will bless you and others curse you for this. I do not know that they will let you leave with what you know."

"Leave that to me," Maauro said.

Eldfaran walked off. Shon rejoined us.

"All others," Maauro said. "Please seat yourselves on the floor. Dr. Malich, I will allow you sufficient access for you to have your security stand down. Additional conflict with us is unlawful and useless."

He nodded. "I'll do it. I don't want any more death on my watch."

Maauro indicated the speaker.

"All security forces, this is Malich. Stand down. Return to the security station and remain there. Do not seek to interfere with the intruders… with the Confed military who have landed and taken possession of the lab. Await further instructions there."

He looked at her. "I can't guarantee they will listen."

"Understood," she replied.

I upload all the information I have discovered to the Stardust's *computer AI, itself a clone of some of my more basic abilities. I set the autopilot and order it to break orbit and head for the warp point with all the information secured in its computers for Confed Intelligence to review. No crewed vessel can overtake her as she can exceed the limits of her AG field. If we are killed, our revenge will overtake the Ribisans. Pisces remains in orbit to provide our escape, if we can only reach it.*

Eldfaran returns. "I have reached a military officer commanding ships of the Commandant. He says he met you and conveyed you to the O2 portal after your meeting with the Pillar. Your reference for him would be Adjutant.

"Yeah, we remember him," Wrik responds.

"I have explained to him who you are, though I have said little about you, Maauro, lest I confuse him. I have told him that you and Lt Fels are equals in Confed Military Intelligence."

"I will speak with him," I say. While I could do so from inside the privacy of my own head, I use the labs equipment so Wrik and the others can hear me.

The screen in front of me lights up. I see the adjutant.

"The Predictor has been destroyed, along with the accompanying body of research. I have not injured any of the non-security civilian personnel to this point," I advise.

The Ribisan officer's sensory apparatus is fixed on me. "Your position is untenable. You must surrender into our custody immediately."

"My position is quite secure," I return calmly. "We are agents of the Confederacy with which your government is in alliance. We were sent to investigate the unlawful detention of oxygen-breathing, full member state sentients and irregular operations on board a Confed registered oxygen-breather station in low orbit of this gas giant. You may recall the station manager recognized our authority."

"On that station perhaps," the Ribisan returns.

"This is merely an auxiliary station to the main one in a lower orbit and also operated for O2 breathers," I continue. "Our jurisdiction applies here too."

"You have destroyed valuable Ribisan government property and injured personnel. You are under arrest."

"Unwise. The crews in our starships above have all of our reports to date, with particularity in regard to the Predictor. One ship has left orbit at high speed and I do not believe you will be able to intercept it. Should you make the ill-advised choice to interfere with our remaining ship, you will find it is more formidable then appearances suggest. Even if you succeed, you will merely have endangered your government with attacks on Confed personnel and ships in free navigation."

"You place me in a difficult situation," the Ribisan admits.

CHAPTER THIRTY

"Allow me to suggest means of extracting us both," I continue. "Your concerns with the dissidents and fundamentalists are an internal matter. The Confederacy has no desire to interfere in the internal affairs of even an associated member state.

"Our circumspect withdrawal from this world, with Diralia Shon, and to be followed by those O2 breathers wishing to return to Confed O2 territory, will end the matter as far as our employer is concerned. Our employer has a joint interest with your government in keeping information about the predictor technology under wraps."

"How can I trust that?"

"It is not in Confed interests to have member states find out that their losses of billions of lives and credits might have been avoided if your government has shared what it knew about the coming of the Conchirri and the Evolvers. One can only assume that the rest of the Confederacy would see such a betrayal as an act of war. Interstellar war is not in anyone's interest.

"This technology's further development is unlikely, but will be banned in any event. We therefore have the most secure of bases for trust: mutual interest and needs."

"I cannot agree to this on my own," the Ribisan replies. "I must consult those below. But I confess I am relieved by the rationality of your response. We will in the meanwhile keep dissidents and fundamentalists away from both stations, using deadly force if necessary."

"I urge speed," I return. "It would be unfortunate if in the midst of our rapprochement we are struck by an aircraft flown by vengeful fundamentalists, as our crews have instructions to make sure these matters are revealed to a wide variety of our superiors if we do not return. The more people in possession of a secret, the less likely it is to remain so."

"We concur in that. It may be...it may be that we are all best served that this Predictor no longer exists. Some among the dissidents have feared that it could undermine the fabric of existence."

Is the adjutant a dissident? Aloud I say, "Such fears seem most reasonable to me."

The Ribisan studies me, he either knew or suspected that I was more than the oxygen-breathing biological that I appeared to be. The Malich and the lab station personally will confirm it in any event. "I will be back to you as soon as I can, please maintain the status quo until then."

"Agreed, save that a shuttle will be landing on this base in twenty-minutes. If anything happens to it, the full sanctions that I mentioned before, will apply."

"It will be protected," the Adjutant assures.

The image flicks off the screen.

Wrik whistles. "Remind me never to play poker with you."

I nod. "It would not likely work out for you."

He grins for some reason.

I turn to Wrik. "I have signaled Jaelle. She will be here in the Guild craft soon."

"They may eventually get tired of us stealing their ships."

"I have a favor to ask, Wrik. I will tell Diralia what I want and she will not risk gainsaying me. But with you, dear...friend, Wrik, I can only ask."

His gaze at me is troubled. "I'd do anything for you. You know that."

If I had a heart it would skip a beat. "My emotional outburst before and what I said to you was the result of something that may or may not happen in the future. I wish it to remain only between us. It is something deeply personal to me, and it may never come to pass. Still, if she knew, I believe it might trouble Jaelle. I care for her. I would not be the cause of distress to her if it can be avoided." Honesty makes me add in the last caveat. I have seen a future and in it she was not immediately present. So I must acknowledge that it may not be avoidable.

He stares at me lips compressed. I am asking him to lie in a way, a lie of omission but a lie nonetheless. It will trouble him, yet I must have this. Finally he nods slowly. "Will you tell me more of what you saw?"

"Not now, dearest friend. Please do not be angry at me, but not now."

"Maauro, I trust you. I trusted you even when you were M-7. I will never be angry at you."

More than I want anything, I want that to be true. "Thank you, Wrik. Let us leave this place now."

CHAPTER THIRTY-ONE

MAAURO LOOKED BACK AT THE GAGGLE OF SCIENTISTS of both species, then at the destroyed Predictor. "We are leaving now. Please do not attempt any interference. I have no wish for any additional life to be lost today, for any reason, but I will defend my network...my people, with all force."

Malich looked at Maauro with undisguised hatred. "There's no point now. You've worked your madness and destroyed irreplaceable knowledge. There may never be another way to access this power."

"That, Doctor, may be the greatest hope that sentient life has," Maauro replied.

He blinked in surprise but his look at her remained grim and unforgiving.

We left them in Eldfaran's care and quickly made our way back through the deserted corridors to where we had landed only an hour before. From there we could watch the platforms outside. There was no place to bring the large shuttle into the loaded bay with all the damaged machinery lying about.

The heavy-lifter shuttle slid slowly over the surface of the platform, a welcome sight. We watched from the bay where we'd entered. "Dusko's piloting," I said.

Maauro looks at me. "True, but how did you know?"

"By the way he flies her – very, very cautiously. Jaelle has flair, but pain me as it does to admit it, Dusko is the better technical pilot. He's not using the ALS either."

"No, although I assured him the automatics are not compromised, he does not trust them as this is a hostile base."

"That's Dusko. Still, sometimes a little paranoia is a good thing."

"Then you will be pleased by my going out first. I will take up station where I can cover you all in case someone has changed their mind about our leaving."

Worry strikes immediately. "Out in that! Maauro you were frozen—"

"Do not worry. It will be the work of mere minutes and I am undamaged and at full power. There is no alternative. In those clumsy suits you could neither fight nor run effectively."

"True enough," Diralia adds.

The shuttle landed. The light on the lock began blinking red.

Maauro turned to the airlock. Her hands were empty; evidently she preferred her onboard weaponry for the gas-giant's atmosphere. I watched on the screen as she decompressed the lock and still had to fight a spasm of fear as the outer door opened. Ok, she was a deadly fighting machine from fifty millennia ago, but she still looked like a girl. Maauro took station on a beacon, easily climbing above the deck and taking no evident notice of the 1.8Gs and corrosive atmosphere.

"Let's go," I said, snapping my helmet closed and setting the servos to max for the gravity outside the AG field. I hustled Diralia into the airlock and with a last careful glance at the bay, closed the lock and hit the depressurization.

"Step carefully," I said as the door opened. We set ourselves as we passed through the AG gradient and the misery that was 1.8gs grabbed us. We made our best speed to the shuttle. Its overlarge airlock, made for people in environmental suits, opened, and I sent Diralia in first. I stood with my back to it, waiting for it to cycle, watching Maauro climb down and walk briskly over to me. She smiled and then took up station directly in front of me.

The light blinked red and the lock doors cycled. I stepped in. At the last second Maauro joined me. A green glow bathed us, indicating the atmosphere was safe, and I opened my faceplate. "So far so good."

The inner door opened and Jaelle stood there, wearing a more practical outfit then when I last saw her, a ship's jumpsuit. "Hey! No making out in the airlock."

I laughed out of sheer relief. Maauro merely gave me a small smile that somehow looked a little sad. I saw that Diralia was almost out of her environmental suit already. I moved in slowly, clumsy in my suit. There was time for a quick kiss with Jaelle, then she went back to helping Diralia. Maauro helped me out of my suit, easily handling the weight, without needing to use the onboard servers to walk the suit to a lockdown.

"Step it up people," Dusko cracked. "We are damned exposed out here."

"Take the second seat, Wrik." Jaelle urged.

I slid past her to find myself looking down at Dusko. The pupilless blue eyes stared back. I carefully put a hand on his shoulder. "Thanks for the ride."

The Dua-Denlenn looked surprised. "Yeah, okay. Buckle in."

Behind me, Maauro settled Diralia in the third row of seats. She and Jaelle then took the pair behind Dusko and me.

"All check," Jaelle said.

Dusko throttled up the shuttle, which lifted with agonizing slowness off the pad. He then pushed it into a long gentle slope upward as we sank into the special gel seats that distributed our weight to make the climb more bearable.

"Gods, by the time we get off this hellhole, my ass will be a mile wide and my tail will be crushed," Jaelle growled.

CHAPTER THIRTY-ONE

"Sorry, no special seats with cutouts," Dusko said, strain clear in his voice. "We got an hour to low orbit. You can bring the *Pisces* down? Right, Maauro?"

"The ship's AI is doing a braking orbit now. It will come as low as it can so we can use a boarding tube to abandon this shuttle. We will add the pinnace and Jaelle's shuttle to the bill for Candace."

"Well, that cheers me," Dusko replied.

On the screen in front of me, lettering and code appeared. "I have the course and speed for docking. Checking and putting on your board, Dusko."

"Altering course, increasing thrust," Dusko said.

We settled in for the long uncomfortable climb, I could see us being shadowed by Ribisan craft in the distance but there was nothing we could do if they elected to gun us. Nor could I tell if the occasional flashes in the distance were Cimer's horrible weather, or some engagement between the various forces that circled the base now disappearing into the murk behind us. Our safety lay in *Stardust's* high-speed run out of the system on autopilot. If the data onboard her could not be destroyed, then we could not be safely killed. Or so we so earnestly hoped.

There was nothing to do but think. Talking was far too much effort, which suited me just then. Whatever the others were thinking, about success, escape, or the scads of money to be collected from Confed Intelligence, my thoughts wandered down other avenues.

I flicked my eyes to the pilot-mirror overhead and the source of my deepest concern. Two women, for though one was of an alien species and the other was manufactured, they were unquestionably women to me. Two whose lives mattered to me far more than my own. They were so fundamentally different, some people might even argue that one wasn't alive in a true sense, but they'd better not do so with me.

Jaelle was light and heat, sensuality, sexuality and movement, as alive as any creature by whatever God you cared to imagine. Her yellow-gold eyes coveted the experiences of being in the universe.

And then there was Maauro, who was depth and stillness to Jaelle's dancing movement: a lifeform over 50,000 years old, but capable of a child's delight with a bit of yellow ribbon or a starry night. Gentle, yet deadly, sensitive, yet sometimes bound outside of the world of biological life.

Maauro had been the first person to see any value in Wrik Trigardt, even now she was the only one who knew my real name, knew the man who had destroyed himself in the skies over his homeworld. I didn't kid myself about it. When she first met me as M-7, I was merely useful to her, an unknown alien she threatened into cooperating. Soon the bond between us grew into something unbreakable. How could I become so close to something made when humans lived in caves? Yet there was no denying it.

At first I fought against it – told myself it was only my need for protection, but that period had ended quickly. All company besides hers seemed somehow incomplete. She became friend, sidekick, and little sister. That too passed into something deeper, an identity of souls. We were part of each other, prepared to live and die for each other. Maauro was my first real friend, a position that could never be occupied by any other being,

Still, she had occupied a different place than Jaelle, who I loved as a man loves a woman. With Maauro there was a great depth of feeling, but although it was somewhat possessive, it had never contained passion.

When Maauro broke free of the Predictor, she didn't even look like Maauro, there was fluidity to her movement, an animation to the grief-stricken face that I didn't believe she was aware of. Then there were the tears, real tears, in a body wracked by sobs that felt like a woman crying, not like a machine emulating it. Maauro had reached deep into the future and had seen my death. *Wrik don't die, don't leave me,* she'd begged. I hoped it was a long time in the future, but no matter how long it was, I would die before her. I sensed in her a new awareness of life, as well as a depth of emotion that had not been present before. The fact that she had sworn me to secrecy over something so deeply personal to her that she needed time to think it through, spoke volumes.

She looked at me differently since the Predictor and right now she wasn't looking at me at all, and yet I knew my glance at her was known. She was looking down and her long hair hung in her face. Maauro was hiding.

Maybe she wasn't alone in that. More than once on this voyage I had looked at her and what had stirred in my heart wasn't friendship, but something more. With that came guilt and confusion. My feelings for Jaelle had not dulled; they were as sharp and filled with wonder and delight as ever. How then could I have room for an entirely separate set of feelings for Maauro?

Could I love them both? Wasn't someone always coming out on the short end? Most of the time they were close, even playful, but I couldn't kid myself that at least on Jaelle's side there wasn't an edge to that playfulness.

My mind drifted back to the moment Maauro rose from my bed and let my shirt fall from her perfect, yet sexless body. Has she been trying to tell me something? Did she even know? Had her glimpse into the future changed that?

God, help me, I thought, *I'd rather die than hurt either of them.* I loved Jaelle with my body and my heart, but something in my soul was only satisfied by Maauro.

The truth now sat staring at me. Somehow I'd have to hold two different loves in my heart for as long as they would stay different and for as long as the three of us could dance our dance this way. I'd have to hope that the music would never stop, because I simply could not see past that point.

For now, it had to be enough that we were alive, and on our way home. There might be time enough ahead for me to learn what I needed to learn.

I looked at Jaelle, who as usual, sensed my regard. She gave me a wink then settled down a little in her seat and closed her eyes.

My eyes drifted to Maauro. I could speak to her head-to-head, but somehow it seemed an invasion and I could not catch even the ghost of a signal from her. Perhaps she had turned off the channel. Perhaps not. Finally her eyes rose to meet mine. Gem-bright, beautiful and deep as an ocean, again came the small, sad smile.

"It's all right," she sent as a whisper.

"Okay," I sent back, relieved.

Then as if imitating Jaelle, she too shut her eyes and the sense of her faded out of my mind, there was something final in it, at least for now.

Behind my closed eyes I consider time and the future possibilities for me and my network. In some, through estrangement, or other change, I go my own way. In others, death, alone or with the others, awaits me. In the one that commands my attention, something that I cannot presently fathom occurs between Wrik and me, changing me forever. I do not know how that came to be, nor do I know what transpired for Jaelle and her own love for Wrik. I am troubled by that, fearing a future dissonance in my network. Yet that future both compels, and I must admit, frightens me, who has never known fear for herself before.

I do not know what to hope for, what star to steer for. Yet, for now I am surrounded by my network and all parts are functional and in harmony. Considering the adventures and enemies we have faced, this is a remarkable achievement in itself. I am determined to savor both our victories and our continued existence. As for that mysterious future with Wrik that beckons, I will put aside for another day when the path becomes clearer.

I have time to hope, to become, and to learn to dream.

The End

ABOUT THE AUTHOR

EDWARD MCKEOWN is a writer and editor specializing in science fiction and fantasy with occasional forays into literary and nonfiction. Ed escaped from NY, but his old hometown supplies much of the background to his humorous "Lair of the Lesbian Love Goddess" shorts, as his new hometown in Charlotte, North Carolina does for his "Knight Templar" fantasy series. He enjoys a wide variety of interests from ballroom dance to the martial arts. He has also edited five Sha'Daa anthologies of wry tales of the apocalypse and a wide variety of short stories. Find him on Facebook and at edwardmckeown.weebly.com.

Ed is best known for his Robert Fenaday/Shasti Rainhell series of SF novels, set on the Privateer Sidhe, issued by Hellfire Publications.

MORE BOOKS BY EDWARD MCKEOWN

FROM

AN IMPRINT OF COPPER DOG PUBLISHING, LLC

MORE BOOKS BY EDWARD MCKEOWN

FROM AD ASTRA BOOKS

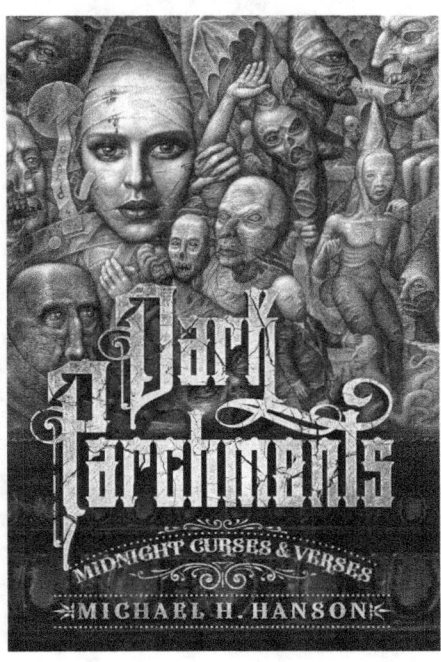

CHAPTER 1

ATTACK THE ENEMY BASE IN THE COMPANY OF TWO OLDER M4 COMBAT *androids. We are launched from a Daggerwing assault-ship and shed our mobility capsules as we land on the asteroid. The Infestation claim the base is a lifeboat station but Intel says it is equipped with heavy weapons and sensors.*

The weapons are there. A disrupter battery fires on us; another lashes out at the Daggerwing and the ships beyond. As we race across the surface of the iron asteroid, a disrupter hits the lead M4. It staggers and slows. Other weapons switch fire to the slowing android. It is destroyed.

I am an M7, the newest combat android, a prototype, faster and better armored. I duck into a crater and return fire from my armspac. Explosions bloom and the disrupter battery is wiped out. The remaining M4 and I crash through the base airlock. Infestor drone soldiers are inside, clad in vacuum suits. They open fire. There is no room to dodge, so we trade fire from our onboard weapons and armspacs. The Infestors' small-arms have little effect on the M4 and none on me. We destroy them and race through the rest of the facility, killing Infestors as we encounter them. I head for the command center. M4 will attack the long-range disruptors firing on our ships.

Explosion. The corridor I occupy shatters, killing those Infestors I have not already dispatched. A mine, or perhaps my weapon, has set off a secondary explosion. I pause for self-repair. I am made of hyper-alloyed metals, ceramics and polymers. My outer casing has ablative layers and sections made to absorb blast damage. I exchange damaged exterior parts for interior and extrude new material to replace vaporized sections. Fortunately, I have taken no core damage. I waste no time on the aesthetics that make me look like a member of my creator's race. I carry enough spare material inside to regenerate two legs and an arm so I can get my armspac and reengage the enemy. I am much smaller now, having used up my spare material.

M4 reaches the disrupter battery, sited atop an arsenal. The bulk of the Infestor forces are arrayed around it. We confer for a millisecond. The battery is firing at our ships in the asteroid belt. I am already damaged, as is M4, and additional resistance is possible at the command post.

By ourselves we may fail to take the station and suppress its weapons. We agree on a plan of action and M4 self-destructs, detonating its plasma generator. The blast destroys the disrupter battery and its supporting forces.

I continue my attack alone and resistance crumbles. M4 may have killed the unit queen with its explosion. I neutralize the command post and mop up the base. In the process, I take seven prisoners. These I drag to a lower level and interrogate. Little useful intel is gained from these low-level creatures. After the last Infestor expires, I cleanse myself of their fragments. Then I delete the memories of the actual interrogation while saving the intel. This procedure is technically against my programming, but the longer I operate, the more latitude I discover in my behavioral routines. I do not know why I feel the need to do this, save that of late I have found the process of interrogation disturbing. I was created to destroy the Infestation and have done so for the seven years of my existence, yet I find more reasons to delete such information as time passes. I function more efficiently without these memories.

I reach the surface of the asteroid and step out under the stars, triggering my recall signal. No answer. I repeat it several times, then extend my sensor net to maximum and pick up a cloud of ionized gas. M4 did not destroy the disruptors fast enough. The Daggerwing, along with the support and repair staff who care for me, are gone.

I detect flashes of nuclear fire beyond my ship's remains. Ambush. The base may have been bait in a trap. Our forces are destroyed or driven off.

Since I do not face imminent capture, I delay self-destruct and continue repairs. I am dismayed by my level of damage even though my exterior chassis is mostly restored. Much of the damage can only be repaired at home base, which now I doubt I shall ever see again.

I consider my course of action. If the system has fallen to the Infestation, they will likely return to this asteroid. I should lie in wait to ambush any rescue party.

I turn my scanners to the sky for a last long look at the stars, which now are my only companions, before turning to walk into the silent base. I switch to minimum power settings. My wait may be long.

CHAPTER 2

I HUNG AROUND IN BARS A LOT. NOT THAT I'M A DRUNK. I went through a short spell of drinking after I was cashiered from the service for cowardice. But the bottle is slow suicide and I'm too young and interested in living for that.

No, I hung out in bars because that's where a human can find work on Kandalor's Vanceport. The Spacewitch is one of the places expeditions launch from. Not the big government expeditions from the Confederacy or the Combines, which wouldn't use somebody like me, but the shoe-string expeditions from universities or organizations short on cash. I can fly interstellar. Not everyone can handle the hyperspace visualization. I can also fly atmo, which a lot of starjockeys can't.

So I staked out a small table in the back, away from the long bar with its brass and dark wood where the bad and dangerous hang out. My table sat under a hanging of red-fringed velvet, keeping me in comforting shadow. Square-D, the owner, knew me and would send over people looking for my type of skills. Square-D didn't care about me one way or another, but pilots brought trade to the Spacewitch and, he got a cut.

Luck was with me. Square-D was talking to a tall, dark-skinned woman in green fatigues. He nodded in my direction and she turned toward me. She was tall, with a pretty, symmetrical face and an overripe figure that strained the fatigues. I guessed her to be older than me, perhaps in her late twenties or early thirties. Her vest hung open and I saw a holster under it. She strode to my table.

"Wrik Trigardt?" The voice matched the body, round and pleasant.

I'd left my real name in the past, with my honor. "Just Wrik." I neither stood nor extended my hand; manners belonged to another time and place.

She slid into the booth and rested her breasts on the table as she leaned forward on her elbows. I got my eyes back up to her dark brown ones in time to catch the flash of white teeth against her dark skin. OK, she'd caught me looking, one for her.

"I hear you're a good pilot both on Kandalor and nearspace."

"Farspace too," I said. "I have an interstellar rating."

"Nearspace will meet my needs," she said. "You look kinda young to me."

I shrugged. "I've been flying since my early teens, military training as well. As they say: 'It's not the years, it's the light years.'"

I studied her. She had a slight accent I couldn't place. Something about her said Old Colonies or even Home World. "What needs are those, Miss...?

"Name's Candace Deveraux, out from Earth. Call me Candy and I'll shoot you in the knee. I'm looking for a private ship and pilot to take my colleagues to a certain riftoid."

"Treasure hunters."

She raised an eyebrow at me. "Prospectors and salvagers. You have a problem with that?"

I raised a hand. "No offense. I make a living hauling people around Kandalor and the near-rift looking for Old Empire relics and tech. Sometimes they even find stuff."

"But for every one who finds something, a thousand go broke," she quoted, leaning back. "True enough. Before we go much further, I'd like to know a little more about you. I gave you my name and world..."

"My name, you know. I'm out of a Confed colony world, former military pilot."

Her look said she knew this already. "Some people say you're out of Retief, a separatist colony. So why are you—?"

"Talking to a darkskin?" I finished for her.

She nodded. "Boers and Trekkers colonized Retief to get away from any contact with blacks. You regard us as inferior."

"I don't regard you as anything," I said, "assuming I was in fact born there. I take people as they are."

"Yet you fought in the Uprising?"

"As I said, you're assuming I was there. From what I heard, the Confederacy came in and told them to admit darkskins to Retief. Then they backed it up with force. Retief didn't last long after the Confederacy got serious.

"If that's enough 'get acquainted' for you," I said, and then, after sipping my drink, added, "I charge two hundred credits a day with fifty more if I go into vacuum. You pay for port fees and fuel. I get a hundred-credit advance now to reserve my time. You doubtless pulled my flight sheet at the port."

"Doubtless," she said, smiling. "I set the schedules and you learn where and when we fly when I decide."

"Deal." I tried to conceal my relief and surprise. She'd accepted my opening rates.

"Give me a number where I can reach you. You'll get twelve hours warning. Tell anybody where we are going and I'll shoot you in the other knee."

I passed my card to her and she inserted it into a portacomp. A few keypunches gave her my number and me one hundred credits.

She slid my card back to me. "You gonna buy me a drink with any of those credits, spaceman?"

"Uh, sure."

She laughed. "Just kidding. Next time come up with the idea on your own." She managed a nice sashay for a big woman as she walked away. I was tempted to whistle but afraid she might take target practice on my knees.

I finished my drink and slipped out the back of the Spacewitch after leaving a healthy tip with Square-D. Distracted a little by my good luck, I failed to do my customary check of the alley before I started down. I caught the heavy, earthy smell just before a thick, furred arm fastened over my throat and arm.

"So, Wrik, what are we up to?" I turned slowly in Truf's iron grip--there was no point in struggling with the bear-like Okaran--to face Dusko, the tall, Dua-Denlenn who ran a third of Vanceport's underworld. The Dua-Denlenn looked like a woodland elf gone to seed, with pale skin and blue pupilless eyes.

"Dusko," I nodded slowly. "I was just coming to see you."

"Of course, human," Dusko said, looking me over as if I were edible. "You owe me fifty credits."

Sweat trickled down my back. "I have it here."

"How fortunate for you, though perhaps disappointing to Truf here." The Okaran whiffed a breath in my ear. "There will be other opportunities."

"My cardcomp's in my inside pocket," I said.

"Let him go, Truf. This youngling's too prudent to be dangerous."

I pulled out the cardcomp and handed it to Dusko, who ran his own card- comp over it and made the transfer.

"Who was the offworlder you were talking to?" Dusko asked. "Anything I would be interested in?"

"A rift-haul for a prospector. She's cautious. No up front info from her."

"So no way to set her up," Dusko shrugged. "Doesn't sound worth my effort. You will let me know if there's a chance for mutual profit off her."

"I did last time," I said.

"True," Dusko said. "Their personal effects brought a nice sum. If it eases your conscience, they turned out to be druggers."

I tried not to remember the traders I'd led into Dusko's ambush. But it was either them or my ship and the ship was all I had.

"Good doing business with you," Dusko said. "As Truf said, there will be other opportunities. See you around, human." The languid Dua-Denlenn stepped back into the darkness, followed by his hulking guard. I leaned back against the wall, feeling the night air sift through my shirt and fighting the chill. Dusko was right. I was prudent. I had a knife in my boot and a slug-thrower in my back belt, but I wouldn't try an Okaran with the small caliber weapon at such close range. Throwing down on any of the established Guild was insane, anyway.

I decided to sleep in my ship, an old *Dauntless* class scout I'd named *Sinner*, a leftover from the Conchirri Wars long ago. Before heading out, I arranged for the port recorder to forward any message from Candace Deveraux to *Sinner*.

I hopped a native transport, which was the cheapest transport available. The open cart, towed by two oxen-like animals, was an odd contrast to ground cars or flitters but it was emblematic of Kandalor, which combined poverty and wealth as well as high and low tech. It had been a forgotten world until a Confed expedition stumbled across it and the races of the Old Concordiat. A few native Kandalorians, muffled in their robes, glanced at me with their bulbous black eyes but otherwise ignored me. I returned the favor and tried to breathe shallowly, the smell of the natives competed with that of the draft animals.

Sinner sat at the spaceport's edge under a metal overhang I'd rented to keep off the worst of the weather. She was about thirty meters long, a bulky ovoid with short stubby wings and lots of interior volume. I'd painted her anti-corrosive chrome yellow. Unlike military craft, we civvies want to be seen. I keyed in the secure code and locked myself in, letting my breath go in a rush. On Kandalor you live like a rabbit or a wolf. Maybe I'd have an extra big helping of carrots tonight.

One week later, I was doing some scut-work on a small Indie-freighter when my comp buzzed. I took off my gauntlets and sealed the engine port before answering. "Hello."

"It's Candace. Time to go prospecting. How soon can you launch?'

"I'm in good shape for a Rift run this side of the 38th in four hours. If we are going out farther, I'll need to add wing tanks."

"We aren't going farther. I've got the flight plan on file with the Port Authority. They'll download to you just ahead of launch."

"Cautious, aren't you?"

"Wouldn't want any problems with local interests."

I swallowed. "There won't be."

"Good, I'd hate to shoot such a pretty boy, at least until I was through with him." She laughed and clicked off.

Candace showed up at the *Sinner* early, as I expected. She liked to set the pace. Two men accompanied her. One was tall, with dark, suspicious eyes and a hooked nose over a beard, unusual in someone who expected to use a space helmet. The other was a dark-skinned like Candace, but whipcord thin and balding, with the look of a spacer.

"My associates," Candace said, gesturing to hook-nose. "Harung." She pointed at the other. "Maku Treska." Both nodded.

"We've got a cargo sled coming. My boys will do the loading," she said.

"Long as I check it after," I said.

Treska looked at me. "The kid doesn't trust us to load. I was flying when you were waiting to be delivered."

Candace looked at him with annoyance. "Quiet, Treska. I don't want to fly with anyone dumb enough not to check his own ship's load."

Treska grumbled but headed for *Sinner*'s capacious cargo bay. Harung gave me an unfriendly stare and followed.

I looked at her. "No weapons on my ship. Hope you left your knee-shooter in the port lockup. Explosive decompression can ruin your whole day."

Candace grinned at me. "Gonna pat me down, Wrik? I've got a lot of area to cover, many dangerous curves to hide things."

Her smile and manner had probably bent men to her wishes all her life. "Sounds like fun, but I don't think I want to pat down your buddies, though, so we'll use a scanner."

She gave a look of mock disappointment. I could feel my blood stirring. Human women were rare on Kandalor, and I had little to offer one. Truth was I didn't have much experience there, either. Candace's mocking smile told me that she suspected it.

Stick to business, I thought, *you're out of your depth with her.*

I checked the load and scanned my passenger for weapons. We boarded *Sinner* and settled in. Candace rode in the second seat on the flight deck. Her companions strapped in the far less comfortable cargo compartment, grumbling loudly enough to be heard. Candace smiled and shrugged.

Sinner kicked free of Kandalor's surface and started a slow ascent. Kandalor stretched out forever below us, seducing the eye and the imagination. Empires had come and gone on this world while humans lived in caves and waved stone axes.

"Beautiful," Candace said, looking out at the mountain and huge forests beyond the spaceport area. In the distance lay the ruins of one of the many lost civilizations. Haze made the wildly tilting towers appear blue.

"Yep," I said. "You've got spaceports and primitive tribes all on the same world, an archeologist's treasure trove."

"Here and in space," Candace said absently. "Those empires extended out for hundreds of light years. Lots of good stuff out there."

"Going to tell me what we're looking for?" I asked.

"Just drive the taxi, Honey."

"Yes, Ma'am."

Candace talked as we boosted toward the Rift, using my ion engine for a slow, steady thrust. I found myself liking her. I didn't want to; friends are an expensive luxury for a Rifter. I set the autopilot and we turned in early. I had trouble falling asleep, thinking of Candace's lush body in the bunk above me, wondering what it would be like.

We came up on the Rift in the next watch, not that there was anything to see. Even in as thick an asteroid belt as the Rift, it would be unusual for any two objects to be in visual range.

We set course for a large riftoid well in from the edge. One of a million such rocks unvisited by anyone since the planet blew to hell. Gradually the riftoid grew from a tiny point of light to a gray, pitted, roughly spherical rock about 2000 kilometers in diameter. Scanners showed it to be almost pure nickel-iron. A huge impact crater marred part of it.

"That's the one," Harung said. Everyone was crammed into my cockpit, staring hungrily at the pitted gray surface. "Just as I remember it."

"Probably part of the old world's core," Treska grunted. "That would account for all the metal. It'll give it a bit more gravity than you usually get in a rock this size."

We drifted down to the surface. Treska was right; gravity was strong enough that I didn't need to fix anchors. I did it anyway, space rewards the cautious.

"Suit up, everyone," Candace ordered.

I looked at her. "I'm just driving the taxi."

"Don't be like that, Honey. Now that we're here, don't you want to see what we came for?"

"Depends."

"What do we need him for?" Harung demanded.

I sighed. "She doesn't want to leave me behind in the ship so I can hold you up when you come back with whatever treasure you came for." I looked at Candace. "Ever get tired of working with people who aren't as smart as you?"

"No," she replied. "I only like smart men in bed."

Harung glared at me.

We suited up and walked out onto the surface of the riftoid. Treska unlimbered a large mining scanner. Evidently he got a fix on something, as he began moving in quick little hops, kicking up dust. Candace and Harung followed, lugging their equipment. I thought about waiting where I was, then decided it might be safer to stick with the herd. Five minutes later, we found ourselves in a small crater, looking at an oddly-shaped hatchway of yellow metal nearly three meters across.

"What the hell is it?" I asked, excitement getting the better of me. Dust indicated that the hatch hadn't been opened in a long, long time. The design didn't look like anything I'd ever seen.

"Maybe an Old Empire asteroid station," Treska said absently.

I looked around. "Over 50,000 years old."

"Or more," Treska said. "I spotted it when I was here with a freighter that came out of hyper too close to the Rift and had to dump delta-V to avoid a collision. I kept the readings on my scanner to myself. Those Combine bastards wouldn't have given me a percentage of any find."

"Why don't you tell him your life story?" Harung growled as he placed heavy jacks around the hatch.

Candace used a laser drill to place a monofilament probe through what looked like an inspection port. "As you suspected, Treska," she said, "hard vacuum on the other side. Start the jacks."

The power jacks took five minutes to crack the airlock. We used pry bars until we could squeeze through in space suits. A few more minutes on the inner door and we were shining our torches inside.

The interior of the station was familiar looking; form follows function. We saw a rack of odd-shaped spacesuits hung on the bulkheads. Whatever wore them had been much bigger than a human, multi-legged, with a large skull or a need for a lot of headroom. Boxes and tanks lay all over the floor. The metal of the floor worked with our magnetic boots.

"This is a military station," I said.

Candace looked at me. "Why's that?"

"A lot of compartmentation, thick hatches to deal with explosive decompression. Though I'm surprised a military station wouldn't have been dug deeper, for blast protection."

"Maybe it was converted from something?" Harung said.

"Who knows?" Treska shrugged.

Candace nodded. We played our flashlights around the gray and white metal halls, looking at unfamiliar inscriptions and dead light panels.

"It kind of reminds me of the old lifeboat stations they have in Sol's system from before the advent of hyperdrive." Candace said.

"We might find an Old Empire ship," Harung exclaimed.

We started down the sloping corridor and came to a partially opened doorway.

"Christ, look at that." Treska pointed.

At our feet lay a large pile of shredded fabric covered with white dust. Nearby lay boots, though not for any human foot, and a thing that could have either been a power rifle or some sort of heavy tool.

Candace bent down. "Crew. Must have died here in the doorway. Wonder what tore up the uniform?" Cautiously, she pushed open the doorway and looked in, a prybar in one hand and flashlight in the other.

Harung brayed a laugh. "Looking for something? That corpse has been there for fifty millennia in vacuum. The fibers degraded and fell apart. We'll bag what's left for the scientists. They'll pay plenty for material from the corpse of an unknown species."

"Look, a ship!" Candace exclaimed. Her light illuminated a small vessel beyond. It looked like it was made of some translucent, half-melted, dark-green glass. Yet it was recognizably a spacecraft.

"If you're right about this being a lifestation," I said, "there's your lifeboat."

Harung pushed past Candace and me with Treska on his heels. The smaller man accidentally kicked an alien boot. It spun silently away into the darkness beyond our lights. I shuddered.

Candace knelt by the fragments of fabric and the metal implement. "A weapon?"

"Maybe," I said. "It has that look, but I don't see any sights."

"Well, any charge it had must have gone before the pyramids were built."

The space beyond was wide and flat, big enough for several small craft. A hatchway that must have once opened outward formed the roof of the hangar; for all that we had seen no sign of the hatch on the surface. Harung and Treska clambered all over the small ship, peering into it with lights.

"Wrik," Candace called from the far side. I went over. She was standing over a pile of white dusty fabric and more boots, buckles and webbing. The fabric was shredded like the first one.

"What the hell?" I said.

"There's a passage up ahead. If this is like a Terran lifestation, it will lead to the medical and crew quarters."

"After you," I said.

She frowned at me. "You're a bring-up-the-rear kind of guy, aren't you, Wrik?"

"You weren't hiring at Hero's Hall."

We left the others to explore the ship. Our magnetic boots raised a thin film of dust, to hang and fall slowly in the low gravity. Colors here were more vibrant than in the more utilitarian areas. The combinations hurt my eyes.

We reached the crew quarters. Debris covered the area. All manner of odd-looking furniture lay scattered and broken.

"Decompression?" Candace asked.

I shrugged.

**IF YOU ENJOYED THIS EXCERPT, LOOK FOR
THE MAAURO CHRONICLES, BOOK 1,
MY OUTCAST STATE
AVAILABLE ON AMAZON.COM
AND
COPPERDOGPUBLISHING.COM.**

Copper Dog Publishing LLC

OUR IMPRINTS:

Pumpkin Hill Press

To find out more about our imprints
and our upcoming releases, visit our website:
www.CopperDogPublishing.com
or our Facebook page:
www.facebook.com/copperdogpublishing

www.ingramcontent.com/pod-product-compliance
Lightning Source LLC
Chambersburg PA
CBHW070639260626
47161CB00007B/2763